A Christmas Wedding

Fiona Ford

arrow books

1 3 5 7 9 10 8 6 4 2

Arrow Books
20 Vauxhall Bridge Road
London SW1V 2SA

Arrow Books is part of the Penguin Random House group
of companies whose addresses can be found at
global.penguinrandomhouse.com.

First published in Great Britain by Arrow Books in 2020

www.penguin.co.uk

A CIP catalogue record for this book is available from
the British Library.

ISBN 9781787464254

by

Printed a ... f S.p.A.

... to a
... ur readers
... m Forest

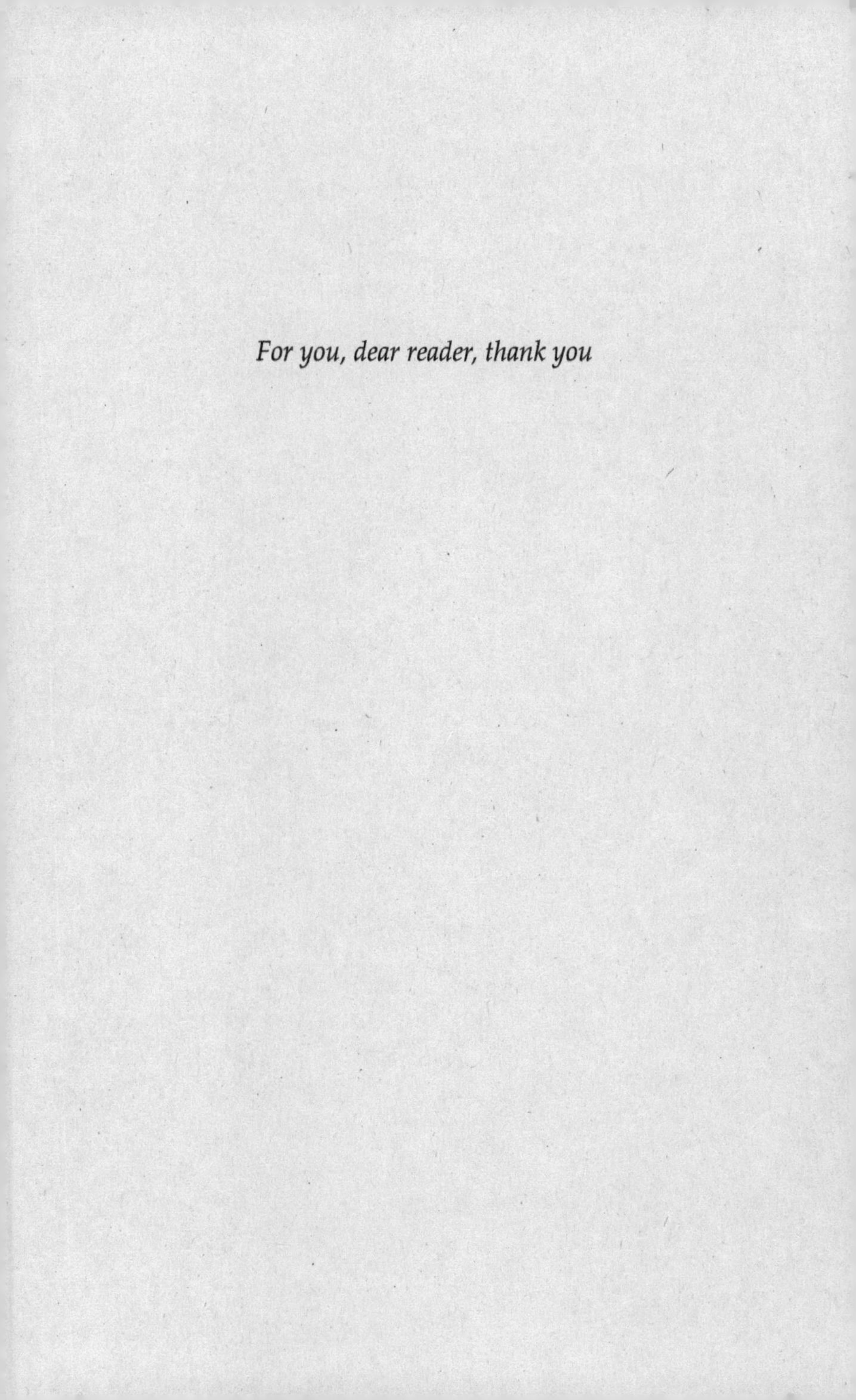

For you, dear reader, thank you

Acknowledgements

As always creating a book is a team effort and there are several rather lovely people I owe a large thank you to for helping bring the Liberty's series to life.

First of all a big thanks to the team at Liberty's for their support with this series. They have been stars from the beginning and I'm truly grateful for their suggestions and help. Thanks must also go to the staff at the City of Westminster Archives Centre who hold the keys to the Liberty's archives. Their patience as I spent weeks in the archive room diving through diaries, sales ledgers and guard books, along with all things Liberty's, has been so appreciated – thank you.

To my very dear family and friends – Mum, Dad, Chris, Becki, Karen, Bec, Craig, Kelly and saga-loving Claire, who have all listened patiently as I suggested plot ideas and started stories with 'during the war,' – thank you, I feel very lucky to have you all in my life.

Every author needs a writing posse and I would be lost without mine. Huge thanks to Kate Thompson, Jean Fullerton, Elaine Everest, Rosie Hendry, Dani Atkins, Faith Bleasdale and Sasha Wagstaff. Your support and friendship means the world.

A big thank you also goes to my fantastic agent, Kate Burke, who is always full of encouragement, help and sage wisdom. Frankly, I couldn't manage without her. Similarly I must also offer a large thank you to my wonderful editor, Emily Griffin, and all the fantastic staff at Arrow who have helped turn the kernel of an idea into a beautiful series.

I don't want this to turn into a long list of thank yous – that always gets a bit boring – but I would like to take this opportunity to explain a couple of the characters, names contained within this book. Brenda Higginson was in fact named after my great aunt, Brenda Williams, who very sadly passed away the day before her ninety-ninth birthday in August 2019. Brenda had been a huge supporter of my writing and was full of memories and help about all things wartime. Unlike her sister Elsie who worked in the munitions factory during the war, Brenda was 'called up to the Co-op' as she smilingly put it, and would think nothing of telling me tales of GIs, life in public shelters and rationing as war raged on in the Midlands. I wanted very much to honour this fantastic lady who led an exceptional life by naming a character after her, so thank you Brenda for all your support over the years.

Similarly, the name of Patricia Humm was a way of thanking all my fantastic readers who have been behind this series. As a thank you for all their support I invited readers to enter a competition a little while ago to have a character named after them. A rather lovely reader named Patricia Humm won and I sincerely hope, Patricia, that you are as happy with your character as I am.

With my fantastic readers in mind, I would like to say a huge thanks to all of them, along with the very special bloggers and Facebook groups who have supported this series. Your messages, glowing reviews and love for Liberty's and the cast of characters that make up these novels always make me smile, so thank you from the very bottom of my heart. If any of you would like to get in touch, share wartime memories or thoughts you can do so via facebook.com/fionafordauthor, where it is always a pleasure to hear from you.

Prologue

As the brightly lit window came into view it was all Dorothy Banwell could do not to run to it and press her face against the glass like a child. The Norwegian spruce that took centre stage was easily the largest and most beautiful tree she had ever seen. Craning her neck to drink it all in as it towered above her, Dorothy, or Dot as she was better known, felt alive with Christmas magic. She peered at the colourful glass ornaments, each one twinkling under the lights. In between the ornaments, small candles were perched as straight as soldiers and decorated with glittering aluminium strands instead of the usual silver – the only real sign in this spectacle that war had affected the country. Right at the top, with all the elegance you would expect from a window display at Liberty's department store, stood a large gold star, beaming all the way across Regent Street like a beacon and welcoming everyone inside from the bustling London streets.

'It's beautiful,' a voice beside her breathed.

At the sound of her old friend Ivy Penhaligon's voice, Dot turned around and smiled. 'I've always loved this shop. My mother used to bring me to look at the window displays when me and Olive were nippers.'

Ivy's eyes roamed greedily over the beautifully decorated tree before she looked down at her daughter. 'What do you think, Helen?'

The four-year-old said nothing for a moment, her hand pressed into Dot's now, seemingly as transfixed as she was by the display.

'Pretty,' she declared eventually.

Dot smiled down at her. 'It is pretty.'

Ivy nodded and turned her gaze to Dot. 'But not as pretty as you'll look on your wedding day.'

Dot laughed at the compliment. 'I hope you're not saying you're going to have me looking like a Christmas tree with this dress you're making me.'

Ivy giggled and Helen followed suit, finding the adults' laughter infectious.

'How long have you known me, Dorothy Banwell?' Ivy asked with a raised eyebrow.

Dot thought for a moment. 'A good five years now.'

'Precisely,' Ivy agreed. 'And in that time have I ever made you do anything that would make you look daft?'

Pretending to think again for a moment, Dot paused, before catching Ivy's twinkling eye. 'On reflection, no. Though there was that time I came to stay with you and Kenneth shortly before Helen's first birthday. You asked me if I wanted corporation pop. I thought it was something fancy, and then when I said yes you handed me a glass of water and both burst out laughing.'

Ivy grinned at the memory. 'I'd forgotten that. That's always been one of Kenneth's favourite jokes.'

Dot pursed her lips and gave Ivy a mock glare. 'And I've never forgotten it either.'

Ivy ran her tongue across her teeth. 'As I recall you told us how you felt at the time.'

'I've never been backwards in coming forwards,' Dot said, 'especially with old friends.'

'Best friends,' Ivy said softly, before looking back at the window. 'It is beautiful.'

'It is,' Dot confirmed.

'And don't they sell fabrics in there?' Ivy continued.

A gnawing feeling began to grow in Dot's stomach. 'They do.'

'Well, as I'm in charge of making your wedding dress, how about we go in and have a look at what they've got?'

Alarm pulsed through Dot. 'We can't go in there.'

'Why not?'

'Because it's not for the likes of us! My mother would have a fit.'

Ivy frowned. 'What's your mother got to do with it?'

'You know what Mother's like,' Dot said with a sigh. 'She'd start saying we weren't good enough for the likes of in there. That we weren't posh enough, that we had no business, that we should know our place. I mean, she used to bring me to look at the displays but she never took us inside.'

'So you've never actually been in this shop?' Ivy asked, the cool December wind whipping around her neck. She looked down at Helen, who was gazing up at Ivy. 'Helen, would you like to go inside?'

Wordlessly Helen nodded, the excitement in her eyes shining as brightly as the gold star on top of the tree.

'Looks like that's settled then,' Ivy said with a shrug. 'Let's go.'

As Dot looked into the little girl's copper eyes, which seemed almost as familiar to her as her own, she smiled. The last person she wanted to let down was this little girl. 'All right,' she said at last. 'But I'm warning you, if we get thrown out because we're not good enough, it's your fault not mine.'

With that Ivy shook her head in disbelief. 'When will you start believing in yourself, Dorothy Banwell? Honestly, it's a good job you've got me as your best friend. I dread to think how you'd cope without me.'

Chapter One

She had promised herself that she wouldn't cry. Not after she had used the last of her good mascara to make herself up for this very special occasion. Yet as Dot watched the newly married couple lock hands over the steel knife and slice through the cake she had saved her ration coupons to make, tears streamed down her face.

This day, and the union of this very happy couple, had been a long time coming – and what a beautiful day it was. Save for a few clouds first thing in the morning, the sun had broken through, giving an almost balmy feel to the celebrations. Daffodils peeped through the earth, the bright yellow of their blooms mirroring the spring sunshine and adding to the celebratory air. Now, as she watched her friends Mary Holmes-Fotherington and David Partridge look at one another with love in their eyes, Dot had never felt prouder.

So transfixed was she by the newlyweds that Dot barely noticed the crowd of well-wishers that had gathered around her in the small South London pub hosting the reception. Nor did she pay much attention to the newspaper decorations that had been made by her friends and colleagues from the fabric department of London's famous Liberty store. As for the small mark on the hem of her raspberry-coloured skirt, recently run up out of a pair of old curtains, Dot barely noticed that either. She didn't see the way her friend and lodger Alice Milwood smiled tenderly from across the room, nor did she see Alice whisper into the ears of her fellow Liberty girls, Rose Harper and Jean Rushmore, that the brash matriarch was crying.

In that wonderful moment, all Dot could think about was how sweet life could be, and how delighted she was that her precious Mary finally had the happy ending she deserved. As David, resplendent in his khaki army-doctor uniform, kissed his raven-haired bride on the lips, the crowd broke out into rapturous applause and Dot whooped and cheered loudest of all.

From the moment Mary had walked into Dot's life just over eighteen months ago, badly bruised, battered by life, and in desperate need of a helping hand, she had become like a daughter to her. Together with Alice, Dot had helped get Mary back on her feet, finding her a job with them at Liberty's, where she became a firm favourite with customers and staff alike. Now here Mary was, a married woman, a far cry from the girl that had arrived on her doorstep. As the new Mr and Mrs Partridge handed slices of cake to their guests, Dot locked eyes with her own sweetheart, Edwin Button, and smiled.

'Happy?' he asked her, reaching into his pocket for a handkerchief and discreetly handing it to Dot.

'Never been happier,' she sobbed, pressing the hankie to her eyes.

'Do you think we would have been as happy as Mary and David if we'd married all those years ago?' Edwin asked.

Turning to Edwin, Dot gazed into her sweetheart's copper eyes and gave him a tender smile. 'I think we'd have been happier, my love. I think it would have been perfect.'

It was the answer Edwin wanted to hear; Dot could tell that as he planted a gentle kiss on her head. 'Days like this are bittersweet for me, Dotty,' he whispered, using her old childhood nickname. 'I couldn't be more delighted for David and Mary, of course I couldn't, but it makes me wonder what might have been, if we hadn't parted when we were so very young. You know I always wanted to marry you, don't you? I always thought we would be Mary and David, with years of happy ever afters ahead of us.'

The wistfulness in Edwin's voice was unmistakeable. Dot and Edwin had met when Dot was just fifteen and he seventeen and had been drawn to one another like bees to roses. They had enjoyed an intense but brief courtship before Edwin moved away from South London and down to Kent because his mother was ill. Each had been broken-hearted to have lost the other, and promised to write every day, but their relationship, despite its intensity, quickly fizzled out. Both Dot and Edwin forged new lives, but never quite forgot what might have been,

When Edwin reappeared as Liberty's store manager in 1941 they couldn't believe they had found one another again and seized their second chance at happiness as they rekindled their love.

'You can't think like that, darlin',' Dot said. 'It wasn't our path. This time is our time, and I can promise you we've got the rest of our lives for happy ever afters.'

Edwin smiled and pressed another kiss on top of Dot's head. 'Does that mean one day you might do me the honour of becoming Mrs Button?'

A pang of something that felt like elation rushed through Dot's heart. They had talked about marriage before, but this was the closest Edwin had come to a proposal. Yet seeing Mary and David threading their way through the crowds towards them, a sense of decency came over Dot. This was Mary's day not hers.

'You'll have to ask me properly one day,' she teased, returning his kiss.

'One day I might just do that,' Edwin whispered as Mary and David reached them.

Dot turned to face the newlyweds and grinned with pleasure. Dressed in a navy fitted suit and matching hat, Mary looked breathtaking with a slash of bright Victory Red lipstick and a pair of heels borrowed from Alice.

Mary laughed as she took in Dot's expression. 'Don't tell me you're speechless!'

'For once, darlin', yes,' Dot said with a smile. 'Oh my days, you're a wonder. And David,' she said, turning to the equally delighted groom, 'congratulations to you both.'

'Yes, here's to a lifetime of happiness.' Edwin beamed, turning to shake David's hand and kiss Mary's cheek.

'Thank you,' Mary whispered, the smile on her face lighting up the entire room. 'And thank you, Mr B., for, well, for being my stand-in father today and giving me away. I don't know how I can ever thank you.'

'It was my very great privilege, Mary,' Edwin said gravely. 'There's no need at all to thank me.'

'Well, you did it perfectly!' Dot exclaimed. 'Mind, you've had enough practice after giving Flo away at her wedding last Christmas.'

'It's a shame Flo couldn't be here today,' Edwin said with a hint of wistfulness to his voice.

Dot smiled as he mentioned the former fabric manager of the eponymous Liberty department store and was just about to comment when they were joined by Alice, Rose and Jean, all delicately forking Dot's delicious wedding cake into their mouths.

'Flo's too busy flitting about the world serving her country,' Alice said through a mouthful of cake. 'ENSA needs her more than we do and I think it's good she followed her passion.' Their friend was singing for the troops with the Entertainments National Service Association.

'She's such a beautiful singer.' Mary sighed. 'It would have been wonderful if she could have sung for us on our wedding day.'

'I'm sure she's thinking of you though,' Rose said kindly as she tried to eat her cake whilst still holding on to her white cane. Seeing Rose was struggling, Jean immediately came to her rescue and discreetly helped the girl.

Dot felt a flash of affection for both of them. Since Rose had been left partially sighted thanks to an illegal hooch operation almost eighteen months ago, she did her best to live life as normally as possible. But the white stick and the fact she occasionally needed help from a friend meant it was impossible to forget the tragedy that had befallen the girl.

Mary nodded in agreement. 'She sent us a card for our wedding day and has insisted that she will return from foreign shores soon.'

'Of course she will,' David said. 'It's good that she's found some happiness. After her husband died, she must have been heartbroken.'

'I don't think she will ever get over Neil,' Alice admitted. 'But I think it tore at her more than she thought it would to leave her precious fabrics department and Liberty's behind.'

'And now look at it,' Dot sniffed. 'It's been in a right state without her at the helm.'

'No it hasn't!' Alice exclaimed. 'I've been doing my best with Mr Button.'

'She's right, Dot, we have been doing our best,' Edwin insisted.

'Well, if you ask me, your best ain't enough,' Dot said, turning to her sweetheart. 'So what are you going to do about it? We've got orders that haven't been filled, sales girls that don't know if they're coming or going and as for the state of that stockroom, well – don't get me started.'

'I didn't realise it was quite so bad,' Edwin said with a twinkle in his eye.

'No, I didn't either,' Jean replied, finishing her cake and setting her plate down.

'Well, it is,' Dot said firmly. 'And I don't like to see it that way and nor would Flo.'

'That's true,' Rose pointed out. 'Flo was very particular about things. I don't like to do anyone down but the paperwork has been a bit tricky for me to follow.'

'Quite right,' Edwin agreed. 'So why don't you take on the job, Dotty?'

At the suggestion Dot's jaw dropped with horror. 'Me? Fabric manager? Don't be so daft.'

'Why not?' Mary asked. 'You're the one that can see the problems. And you can see how to solve them.'

Fear coursed through Dot's veins. She wasn't remotely qualified to manage fabrics.

'I know nothing about running a department. Besides, I've only just gone full-time,' she protested. 'Who'll help Alice out with Arthur?'

'Doris down the road could take him more often,' Alice suggested.

'And what about Emma?' Dot asked, turning to Mary and enquiring about the thirteen-month-old daughter she and David had just adopted.

'Mary and I can share the post, and Doris can take them both.' Alice suggested. 'You know she won't mind doing a bit extra – look at how she took both Arthur and Emma back to hers today after the service.'

As Mary nodded in agreement, Edwin planted a tender kiss on her cheek. 'There you are, you see. Problem solved.

My dear, you've been running rings around all of us since the day you were born. It's high time you started believing in yourself. You were like this as a youngster and I never understood why when you were always so capable. Now, I spoke to the board last week about this very matter and they were in full agreement. You're perfect for the position.'

Looking across at the girls' smiling faces, Dot had a feeling she'd been had. Shaking her head, she downed her gimlet in one in an effort to calm her quaking nerves. Dot knew she talked the talk, and more often than not she believed it. But taking charge of an entire department, managing staff, dealing with customers: that wasn't something she was capable of. Her pulse quickened at the thought of all that lay ahead. How could she tell Edwin that despite her brash exterior she was still the same nervous fifteen-year-old he had courted all those years ago?

Chapter Two

Three days after Mary and David's wedding, Dot woke up in the middle of the night, sweat pouring down her forehead and her nightdress clammy and damp. Breathing heavily, she sat up, clutched the sheets to her chest and tried to calm her racing heart. It was the same dream, or rather nightmare, that had plagued her on and off since she was a girl. She was drowning in the sea whilst a group of people peered at her from the shore, all refusing to help apart from her best friend Ivy. But no matter how often Ivy called out to her, her baby daughter Helen perched on her hip, Ivy couldn't quite reach far enough into the sea to help her out of the water, and Dot was always left, arms flailing, fighting for survival.

Switching on the little lamp that stood on her bedside table, the room was bathed in an orange glow. Dot felt an immediate sense of relief that the sudden light offered her. Reaching for the glass of water she always kept by her bedside, she took a sip. The liquid trickled down her throat and she closed her eyes, telling herself, as she always did, that she was fine.

Within a couple of minutes her pulse was restored, her breathing less heavy and the sense of foolishness that she always felt after the nightmare swiftly followed. Wiping the sweat from her brow, she threw back the damp sheet and checked the time on her little gold wristwatch. Seeing it was half past three and knowing sleep would be a long time coming, she slid her feet into her heavily worn slippers and got up. The only thing that would get her back to the land of Nod at this time was a restorative cup of tea and a read of her latest Agatha Christie novel in the kitchen.

Keen not to wake Alice or sixteen-month-old Arthur, Dot padded quietly down the stairs. But when she reached the bottom step she saw a light coming from the kitchen. Pushing the door open, she saw Alice clutching Arthur in her arms, singing him a lullaby in the softest of tones.

At the sound, Alice swung around to face Dot, a guilty look in her eyes. 'Dot! Tell me we didn't wake you? I tried to get him to stay quiet.'

Dot shook her head. 'I was already wide awake. Thought a hot drink'd get me off.'

Spotting the teapot on the table, she reached for a cup from the dresser and poured herself a hot drink.

'So what's got you awake at this time?' Dot enquired, sinking back into the small armchair by the window, which was currently blacked out. The kitchen looked out on to a small courtyard garden, these days populated with a vegetable patch that Dot took great pride in cultivating, all with a little help from Edwin of course.

Alice sighed. 'Arthur's teething again.'

Turning to look at the little boy in Alice's arms, Dot smiled. He was sleeping soundly now, and with his eyes firmly closed he looked as if butter wouldn't melt.

'Poor lad,' Dot said fondly. 'Still, there can't be too many more to come through now. That trick of Jack's with the bread not working then?'

At the mention of Alice's sweetheart, American soldier Jack Capewell, her face lit up. He had been posted down to Bristol a few weeks ago and Alice saw less and less of him now. It was a shame, Dot mused, as the two were perfect for one another. Much more so than Alice's cheating rat-bag of a husband Luke Milwood. Luke had been a pilot for the RAF who had pretended to be missing in action for months, when in fact he had found a new love in a French Resistance fighter named Hélène.

'And what's your excuse?' Alice asked, interrupting Dot's thoughts. 'You should be firmly asleep.'

Dot shrugged. She had never told anyone about the nightmares she had endured for years on end, worried about the questions that would no doubt ensue as a result.

'Oh, you know me, always been a poor sleeper. I'm probably still recovering from all the excitement at the wedding the other day.'

'Thinking about your new position? Fabric manager eh?' Alice grinned as she cast a glance down at a now-sleeping Arthur.

At the mention of this Dot felt her pulse race. She closed her eyes for a moment and thought about Ivy, hoping the memory of her old childhood friend would calm her as it usually did. The two had met in 1908 when a fourteen-year-old Dot had enjoyed a family holiday to Torquay. But it wasn't until two years later, when Dot found herself on an extended holiday in the area, following her split with Edwin that her friendship with Ivy blossomed.

As the years had passed, Dot had returned to London and the two didn't see as much of each other as she would have liked, but their enduring friendship still meant the world to her.

'You still with us?' Alice barked, causing Dot to blink her eyes open.

'Sorry,' she said, 'nodding off.'

Alice looked at her for a second, her blue eyes twinkling with mirth. 'Don't tell me you're worried, Dot Hanson.'

'I most certainly am not.' Dot bristled, before softening slightly as she caught the concern behind Alice's teasing. 'Well, I will admit to being a bit anxious. Flo has left some rather large shoes to fill. I always thought we'd get someone in with a lot of experience.'

'Well, there's not a lot of choice, is there, with everyone at war? We need a new sales girl too but we can't afford to be choosy – I think at the moment Liberty's will take on anyone that applies,' Alice pointed out, not unkindly. 'But you'll do a fine job, Dot.'

'I dunno about that.' Dot sighed, reaching for her tea. 'I ain't so good with the airs and graces like Flo used to be. And I certainly ain't got the graces Mary has.'

Alice raised an eyebrow. 'I hope there's a compliment in there for me somewhere!'

'Oh, you don't need compliments,' Dot said, waving her concerns away. 'Edwin thinks the world of you. He'd never have kept you on as deputy manager if he didn't.'

'And he's made you manager,' Alice pointed out. 'That ought to tell you something.'

There was a silence then as Dot reflected on what her friend had said. It was true that despite the fact she and Edwin were a couple, he would never have entrusted her with the responsibility of running the department if he didn't think she was up to it. But then again, Edwin had always thought the best of her, even though she didn't always deserve it.

'Oh, while I remember, this came for you the other day,' Alice said.

Dot watched Alice reach up to the shelf above her and pull down a white envelope from behind her best crockery. She handed it over and Dot peered at the writing; she felt the usual pang of fondness and regret whenever she saw Ivy's familiar hand. Perhaps that was why she had dreamed of her? Perhaps subconsciously she had known that her friend had written.

'I meant to give it to you last week, but with the wedding and everything else that's been going on I forgot,' Alice admitted. 'I'm sorry.'

Dot ran her fingertips across the sloping writing. These were the letters she treasured. They arrived sporadically, sometimes every month, sometimes every six, but nevertheless they were letters she couldn't wait to read.

'It doesn't matter. I think I'll take it up now and read it.'

Alice frowned as she peered at Dot's almost full cup. 'But you haven't finished your tea.'

'Oh, if I finish that I'll only be outside freezing to death in the privy all night,' Dot said with a smile as she got to her feet. 'I'll see you in the morning.'

'Sleep well,' Alice called.

Almost racing up the stairs, clutching the letter tightly in her hand, Dot sank back on to the bed. Taking care not to rip the envelope, she pulled out the letter and settled herself against her pillows to read.

2nd April 1943

My dearest Dot,

It suddenly occurred to me the other day that it has been a good month since you were kind enough to write to me. I am so sorry it has taken me this long to send a reply, but it has been a very busy time for us here. I'm sure you remember the Easter festival from when you lived here all those years ago but I can say preparations for it have taken up a lot more of my time since I became leader of the local WI.

I was delighted to hear your friend Flo has found her calling with ENSA but I know how much you will miss her. Perhaps she will come our way – I'm sure you remember the theatre up the road from us at Babbacombe Downs? It has hosted ENSA a number of times and everyone in the area has always enjoyed them.

I know you must be anxious for news of Helen since she was so poorly when I last wrote to you. You will be glad to know that she is doing much better since her bout of pneumonia. She saw the doctor last week and he says that although she is still weak she is making good progress. He recommends good food and exercise. The sea air, of course, is a great help, but the food, well, with fresh meat so hard to come by these days, it's been difficult to give her what she needs. She is doing much better, though, and she is now well enough to get out and about. She has a new job up at Barton Motor Company, though it's a munitions factory now. Helen's just helping out in the office part-time but she enjoys it. She's become involved in the church as well, flower arranging for the services and crocheting in her spare time – you remember how fond she always was of knitting and the like.

Occasionally she comes to one of my Sunday-school mornings and helps out with the little ones. Last time one of the younger children there started poking fun at her because of her deafness. She said she wasn't upset by it but I heard her crying in the privy later. I must admit I am worried about her. Lots of the children have now started to taunt her because she's deaf. I had hoped that the church community would be more tolerant but it seems that people are afraid of difference. Her confidence has taken a bit of a battering I'm afraid, but I'm sure that with time and love she will find a way through this.

I hope that everything continues to flourish for you and that things are going well between you and Edwin. You should bring him down with you the next time you visit, though I can't help noting it's been several years since you last came this way. It would be lovely to see you though Dot, and wonderful to meet Edwin after all this time.

Your friend,
Ivy

As Dot finished reading the letter she sighed. She was sorry Helen was struggling. It had been the story of the poor girl's life. It had to be hard on Helen and Ivy, Dot knew that and she wished, not for the first time, that there was something she could do. Yet Dot also knew that Ivy was more than capable of sorting out Helen's problems, it was something she had been doing for years.

Putting the letter down on her bedside table, Dot snapped out the light, rested her head against the pillows and fell into a dreamless sleep.

Chapter Three

Just four short hours later Dot found herself feeling refreshed and standing in what she would privately describe as a dream world. The nerves she had felt at taking the job as fabric manager were still very much with her, yet as she had got off the trolley bus and strolled determinedly down Argyll Street towards Liberty's she had reminded herself that the best thing to do was take this new job a day at a time.

She kept this mantra in the forefront of her mind as she stood in the heart of fabrics, behind the long oak cutting table, and surveyed the department. Although the store didn't open for another hour and a half, she had wanted to get in early to check the stock, assess the order books and drink in the fact that she was now in charge of one of the most important departments of Liberty's.

Greedily her pale grey eyes roamed the store. The mock Tudor building was made of two nineteenth-century warships and Dot wasn't sure she would ever grow tired of the beauty that surrounded her. Everywhere you looked there was something new to discover, whether it was a stained-glass window panel, or a unique wooden frog or flower carved into one of the balustrades. The wonder of Liberty's was everywhere and Dot shivered with nerves and pleasure as she walked across to one of the display cases and ran her fingers across the rolls of brightly coloured utility print.

The sudden sound of footsteps behind her made her jump. Whirling around, Dot saw Henry Masters, the deputy store manager, stalking across the floor towards her with a sheaf of papers in his arms.

'Mrs Hanson, a pleasure,' he said in his deep northern brogue.

'Dot, please,' she replied with a tight smile. 'I thought I could rely on you not to start standing on ceremony with me.'

Henry laughed, revealing a mouthful of white teeth. 'Fair enough. Just thought, you know, I ought to pay you a bit more respect now you're in charge.'

'Why change the habit of a lifetime?' Dot quipped as she pointed to the papers. 'They for me?'

As Henry set the papers down with a thud, Dot could see that amongst the order slips, invoices and usual Counting House reports there were some new employee forms to look through as well.

'What's all this?' she said, pulling out the sheets.

'New starter for you,' Henry said.

'Well, we could do with the help, that's for sure, darlin',' Dot said, drumming her slender fingers against the wooden cutting table. 'Spring's our busiest time with the warmer weather around the corner.'

'Then you're in luck.' Henry beamed. 'Our newest employee, Brenda Higginson, will start with you tomorrow.'

Dot read through the form and raised an eyebrow. 'It says here that she's never worked in a shop!'

'That's right.'

'And she's only twenty!'

That heady nervous feeling Dot had been doing her best to quell rose once more. Taking on the challenge of running the department was one thing, training a new starter barely out of nappies was something else entirely. She pinched the bridge of her nose and took a deep breath.

'We were all young once, Dot,' Henry pointed out. 'Try casting your mind back to those happy days – that's assuming it'll travel that far, of course.'

Dot deftly slapped him with the papers across his arm and chuckled. 'Cheek!'

Giggling, Henry rubbed his arm, pretending to have been wounded. 'Trust me, you'll like her.'

'Hmmm,' Dot replied, deliberately non-committal. 'And if I don't?'

'Then I'll send Stan in instead.'

At the mention of Henry's eleven-year-old brother, Dot smiled a genuine grin that reached her eyes.

'How is the little so-and-so? Still up to no good?'

'I'll have you know he's a very well-behaved lad,' Henry replied, a twinkle in his eye.

'Then you've got it all to come,' Dot snorted. 'I've never met a boy yet that could behave himself. More importantly, how's he getting on at that new school?'

For a moment Dot and Henry's faces were grave. Neither one had forgotten the terrible tragedy at Sandhurst Road School just three months earlier, when a lone German bomber had dropped a bomb on a school full of children, killing teachers and children in one devastating attack. Tragically, the school had been destroyed and many of the children had relocated to other schools out of the borough.

'He's getting on all right,' Henry said finally. 'He misses his teachers and friends . . .'

As his voice trailed off, Dot rested a hand on his shoulder. 'It gets easier,' she said quietly. 'When I lost my husband during the last war I thought I'd never get over it, and I suppose I haven't.'

Henry looked at her in surprise. 'You do a fine impression of someone that has.'

'I've just learned to live with it,' she said simply. 'I find happiness where I can, and I suggest you try and do the same, Henry. If anyone knows how precious life can be it's me.'

'And what about Edwin?' Henry asked. 'Did you get over him when you went your separate ways all those years ago?'

At the mention of her childhood sweetheart Dot found herself giving him her second genuine smile of the morning. Edwin had always made her happy. She had known it from the first time she had clapped eyes on him and she knew it now.

'No, I don't think I ever did,' she admitted. 'Losing Edwin felt like losing a bit of me. I was changed when we parted. But now, well, now I feel lucky we've got this second chance to find our happy ending – so you listen to me, Henry, when I tell you to treasure the moments of happiness wherever you find them.'

Henry was about to reply when the clatter of more footsteps across the wooden floor made them both jump. Looking up, Dot was thrilled to see Mary, Alice, Rose and Jean walking towards her with big smiles on their faces.

'We thought we'd pop in early to help you on your first day,' Alice offered.

'We don't want you letting the side down,' Mary teased. 'Imagine what Flo would say if she thought you didn't have a grip on fabrics.'

Dot folded her arms and glared at the girls as she did her best to dampen the nerves that were never far away. 'I can assure you the store will be in very good hands. And while we're in this department, you can start showing me a bit more respect.'

From the corner of her eye she could see Henry looking slightly alarmed. She wondered if he was beginning to worry they had created some sort of monster. She was about to continue with her speech when Henry coughed.

'Actually, there is something else. I was just going to talk to Dot about it, but as you're all here, and it affects you too, you might as well know. The fact of the matter is that our accounts are not in a good way at the moment.'

'Well, we know that,' Alice barked. 'Things were already hard enough without the blackmailing and pattern-stealing from our rivals at Botheringtons.'

'Quite,' Henry replied. Dot glanced at him; she could see his right temple throbbing. 'The point is we have to change the fortunes of the fabrics department. You all know this department better than I do. Fabrics is in your blood. You'll know how to get through to the customers, and have them walking out of the door singing our praises.

'Your new sales assistant, Brenda, will be here tomorrow, your department is still busy and the board sees fabrics as one of Liberty's most important departments. So I'm asking you all for ideas on how we can get our customers singing our praises outside the shop. They are our best hope.'

As Henry finished his speech silence descended across the room. While the girls looked as if they were in deep thought, Dot felt the nerves she had temporarily been keeping at bay return with a vengeance. Taking on fabrics when things were going well was one thing; this was another challenge altogether.

The words her father used to lay at her door echoed in her mind. *You're useless, Dorothy, a chocolate fireguard's got more about it than you.* Years of being thought of as no use had taken their toll and in spite of the life Dot had built for herself in adulthood she still had very little faith in her abilities. There were days when she could tell herself that she was a highly capable woman, but then memories of the biggest mistake of her life would flood into her mind, and she would realise just how right her parents had been.

Surveying the girls and Henry, Dot knew that she adored this department, but quite whether she was the woman to save it from the brink was another matter.

'Well, it's certainly a lot to think about,' Alice said finally. 'And it won't be easy. But us girls will get this sorted, won't we?'

''Course we will,' Jean replied, lifting her chin in defiance. 'When I think of everything this department has gone through in the last few years, we sure as eggs are eggs are going to survive this – and emerge all the stronger.'

'Quite right,' Mary said, her cheeks still flushed pink. 'Leave it with us, Henry, we'll have some ideas for you by the end of the week – won't we, Dot?'

'Yes of course,' Dot replied, doing her best to offer their deputy store manager a comforting smile.

As the girls nodded and beamed with genuine confidence, Dot wanted nothing more than to go home and pull the covers over her head. Sorting this would require nothing short of a miracle.

Chapter Four

After a long day, which had left Dot feeling shell-shocked, she was relieved to find herself in the French Pub enjoying a gimlet. Ever since Flo had introduced her to the tipple before she left to sing with ENSA, she had to admit she had become rather partial to the gin-based drink.

'Here's to you, Dot!' Mary smiled, raising her glass of port and lemon in a toast. 'A triumphant first day.'

Alice grinned. 'You were wonderful!'

'To Dot,' Jean said, holding her own drink aloft and touching it against the others.

As the girls clinked their glasses together and wished her well, Dot found her shoulders start to loosen and the knot in her stomach unfurl. Despite her concerns, everything had run like clockwork. Orders had been filled, customers had been served in a timely fashion and there had been no unexpected problems to deal with. Well, apart from the challenge Henry Masters had set them to turn around the fortunes of the store.

'So have any of you got any bright ideas about how we're going to get more customers through the doors?' Dot asked.

Jean sighed as she fiddled with the hem of her teal dress. 'I've been thinking about this all day. I can't see what else we can do apart from be extra lovely to the customers.'

'We're already extra lovely to the customers. We need to make them see we're far better than Botheringtons, that's all,' Alice said firmly.

'We could always slate them,' Rose growled.

'No, that won't work.' Dot sighed. 'We need to be positive. If we fight fire with fire that makes us no better than them.'

'Dot's right,' Mary agreed. 'We have to get one step ahead.'

With that the girls fell silent, each contemplating how best to save the department. But after several minutes it was clear nobody had anything to say and so Dot changed the subject.

'Has David gone back to the army now, Mary?' she asked.

At the mention of her husband, Mary nodded sadly. 'Yes, he went back two days ago. No honeymoon for us. We barely got the chance to spend the night together.'

'But you must be so happy now you're married and living in a home of your own,' Rose breathed. 'You, Emma and David are a proper family.'

Mary nodded. 'It was lucky he kept his flat in town on, but I miss you and Malcolm. I adored living with you both. Are you managing without me?'

Rose smiled. 'We're fine. Dad might be an injured war hero with a bad leg but he can cope better than he lets on, and so can I. Besides, there isn't room for you and Emma with us. You should be living as a proper married woman, Mrs Partridge.'

At the mention of her new married name Mary flushed red with pride. 'It still takes some getting used to: Mrs Partridge.'

'Suits you though,' Dot mused. 'Better than that mouthful Holmes-Fotherington.'

Mary made a face. 'It's not that difficult. And I must say, having just the one surname does feel a bit common.'

Alice rolled her eyes at Mary's legendary haughtiness as Jean looked on in amusement and changed the subject.

'It really was a wonderful day,' Jean breathed. 'Emma was the perfect bridesmaid.'

Mary grinned with pleasure at the mention of her adopted daughter. Emma was in fact David's niece. But as Mabel Matravers, who was Emma's birth mother as well as David's sister, was serving time in prison for her part in a hooch ring that had damaged the sight of many, including their very own Rose, Mary and David had been delighted to adopt Emma.

'She did, didn't she?'

'And you looked gorgeous,' Jean continued before turning to Alice. 'Have you heard any more from Jack? Will you see him soon?'

Alice shook her head. 'No idea when he'll next be back up on leave. He's so busy training new recruits I don't want to burden him anymore.'

'You must miss him,' Rose said quietly.

'I do, more than I thought I would,' she admitted. 'And I think Arthur does as well.'

'He'll be back soon,' Dot consoled her. 'First chance he gets.'

'I hope so,' Alice sighed.

'So does anyone have anything else to share?' Mary asked, taking a sip of her port and looking around the assembled group expectantly.

'Bess has gone back to work,' Jean said triumphantly.

At the news there was a collective gasp of delight. Up until last year Bess, who lived covertly with Jean in a lesbian relationship, had worked as a canary girl in a munitions factory in Hayes. But an accident with one of the grenades had caused her to lose her right hand and it had taken her a long time to come to terms with her ordeal.

'That's wonderful news, darlin',' Dot said with a large grin on her face. 'I take it she ain't working with the explosives again?'

Jean shook her head. 'She's just going into the offices a couple of days a week. It'll be a treat for her to get out of the house though.'

'She going to be staying with you all week at Flo's or is she going to live back up in Hayes when she's working?' Alice asked.

'We'll both be at Flo's. Bess won't be doing full days so she'll be able to come back easily enough.'

'Well, I think that's marvellous news!' Mary cheered. 'Good old Bess.'

Holding her glass aloft for another toast, Dot caught Rose's eye and saw the girl looked as if she had something she wanted to say.

'You all right, darlin'?' she asked.

Dot could see a combination of excitement and fear pass across Rose's delicate features and wondered if something had happened about her eyes. Was it possible the girl they were all so fond of was getting more of her sight back?

'I've actually got a bit of news myself,' she said quietly.

'What is it?' Mary asked. 'Are you going to make the first-aid nights more frequent? Because, if you are, I would love to help.'

Rose shook her head. 'It's not that. Though I do want to make sure we keep them up, even when I'm not here for a bit.'

'Why wouldn't you be here for a bit? Where are you going?' Dot asked.

Excitement shone from Rose's face. 'The thing is, I found out last week, well, I'm expecting. I'm having a baby.'

At the news, everyone was up on their feet, gathering the auburn-haired girl in for a hug. Dot squeezed her so tight, she could feel the rim of Rose's glasses pushing against her shoulder.

'This is wonderful news,' Dot cried, tears pooling in her eyes. 'When are you due?'

'September,' she said shyly. 'It happened when Tommy was here at Christmas.'

'Congratulations,' Mary said, her eyes shining with joy. 'A new baby for Emma and Arthur to play with.'

'Have you told Tommy?' Alice demanded, her arm still firmly clamped around her friend's shoulders.

Rose nodded. 'I got a letter from him this morning. He couldn't be more pleased. All he's ever wanted is to be a father. He can't wait to get home now and it's all I want too. When will this wretched war end?'

At that question the Liberty girls fell silent. Everyone was sick of the war that had been raging for three and a half years now. There were days when people wondered if it wasn't so much a case of when the war would end but if.

'Let's not think about all that now, darlin',' Dot said. 'We've a new life to celebrate, and that's what's important.'

'Couldn't have put it better myself!' Alice beamed. 'Come on, Rose, let's get a milk stout down you, none of this port rubbish. You need to keep your strength up.'

With that Alice and Mary disappeared to the bar and Dot sank back in her chair and surveyed Rose and Jean, who were chattering excitedly about babies. She smiled. This was where she was at her best, amongst the friends she thought of as family, who all appeared to be on their way to finding their very own happy endings.

Chapter Five

The following morning, Dot felt drained. She had slept well but she reasoned that the previous night's interruptions, not to mention the fact she was still anxious about her new job, meant her mind wasn't quite where it should be. The one saving grace had been Ivy's letter. It had been a treat to hear from her old friend and even though Dot was worried about Helen, it did appear that it wasn't all bad news if she had a new job at the factory.

She held on to that thought as she began her duties at work that morning. Plastering a smile on her face despite her exhaustion, she threw herself determinedly into the mound of paperwork that Henry had left her. Not only were there the usual invoices to file, but she needed to sort certain forms out ready for Brenda, who would be joining them for her first shift that day.

At the thought of the new starter, Dot shook her head in despair. Rereading through the brief résumé Henry had provided, Dot learned that Brenda had spent the last three years in service and, unless part of that job had been running up clothes for the lady of the house, Dot doubted the girl knew one end of a reel of thread from the other.

With a flash Dot wondered if this was how Flo had felt when Mary had started. The girl couldn't have known less about fabrics but Flo had taken her under her wing and given her a chance. Dot knew that despite her own insecurities it was down to her to do the same. Taking a deep breath, she stood up straight and steeled herself for the day ahead. As she did so her eye fell on the dust across the cash register. She reached under the desk for a cloth and ran it quickly over the surfaces, then walked over to the cutting table to give that a once-over as well.

As she did so she caught the eye of Beatrice Claremont from the beauty department. Dot usually managed to avoid the woman. Though all had been forgiven since Beatrice had been sacked from fabrics Dot still bore a grudge for her appauling behaviour. She had been reinstated in gifts as a sales assistant before proving her worth and moving to beauty, but Dot still tried to keep the woman at arm's length.

'Morning, Beatrice,' Dot said as she saw the woman stalking her way across the floor, dark hair piled on top of her head.

'Dot, glad I caught you. I wanted a word,' Beatrice replied, getting straight to the point.

Dot raised an eyebrow. 'Oh?'

'I wanted to congratulate you on your new post. Very well deserved.'

'Thank you,' Dot replied, unsure whether or not the woman was having a dig or being sincere.

'And I've heard about the pressures on the fabrics department.'

Dot sighed. 'I'm sure it will all blow over.'

'I'm sure it will too,' Beatrice agreed. 'But in case it doesn't I wondered if I could help in some way?'

At the mention of help, Dot snorted. 'You! Want to help us?'

Beatrice's face flushed as red as the crimson skirt she was wearing. 'I appreciate it might sound a bit rich coming from me, but I owe the department and I want to help you put this right. Fabrics has suffered enough.'

Cocking her head to one side, Dot regarded Beatrice carefully. She seemed to be sincere, and even though every instinct was telling her not to trust a word that came out of the woman's mouth, she wondered if it might be time for a new approach.

'Did you have something in mind?' she asked at last.

Beatrice shook her head. 'Not yet, but I thought we could all put our heads together – I do know the department after all.'

'That's true,' Dot conceded, privately realising that it might be a blessing if there was another pair of experienced managerial hands for her to rely on. 'I'm sure the girls will be glad to have someone else onside; they're very worried.'

Beatrice nodded. 'I can appreciate that.'

There was a pause then as Dot gathered her thoughts. 'You'll have to understand if they're a bit suspicious though. I mean, after everything that happened when you were in charge.'

'I've said I'm sorry for that, and I've been allowed to come back.'

'True,' Dot replied, patting a stray lock of grey hair into place. 'But you've a lot to make up for. I don't want you thinking you can come in here and ride roughshod over us all. I've a long memory, lady, and whilst I don't want to trample on your offer if it's a genuine one, I'm just letting you know that I'm marking your card.'

Beatrice held Dot's gaze, and for a moment the new head of fabrics thought she saw a flash of anger before the older woman composed herself and looked contrite.

'I understand, Dorothy, truly I do. I behaved terribly and I'm grateful that Alice was able to help me get my job back. I want the chance to make up for everything I did and to say thank you.'

Dot gave a brief nod of her head, 'All right. I'll let the girls know.'

It wasn't until midday that Dot, Mary and Jean met the latest member of fabrics, Brenda Higginson. Hearing the familiar sound of Henry's gruff northern tones, Dot looked up from the cutting table where she was marking out a pattern for a regular customer and saw a tall, timid-looking girl with bobbed blonde hair walking alongside him. Dressed in a dowdy navy skirt and blouse that Dot had a feeling she had saved for best, she appeared to be hanging on to his every word.

As Brenda approached the department, Dot watched, grateful for the chance to examine the new recruit unobserved. At first glance she appeared young and green-looking, but as Brenda drew closer Dot saw a defiance, as well as something she recognised only too well in herself – fear. She was clearly doing her best to hide it as she strode alongside Henry, her tall, willowy figure keeping pace with him as she held her shoulders back and nodded along. But there was something in her brown eyes that gave her away, something that told Dot she was scared.

Instinctively Dot found herself warming to the girl. As she bade goodbye to the customer she had been serving, she saw Henry and Brenda loitering by the Tana Lawn prints, clearly waiting for her to finish.

'Mrs Hanson,' Henry said with a smile, 'please allow me to introduce Brenda Higginson.'

Dot locked eyes with the girl and flashed what she hoped was a welcoming smile. 'Welcome to Liberty's, Brenda. I hope you'll be very happy here.'

'I'm sure I will,' Brenda replied. 'I'm very grateful to you for taking me on, like, especially when I've got no experience.'

Lifting her right arm, Dot made a waving gesture with her hand. 'Don't worry about that. We'll have you trained up in no time. Now, as I understand it, you've spent your working life in service?'

Brenda nodded, and Dot saw that flash of fear in her eyes again.

'That's right. For a family over near Guildford.'

'Well, I've never been to Guildford but I'm sure it's very nice,' Dot replied. Then she looked at Henry. 'Shall I take over now then? Show Brenda the ropes?'

'Good idea,' Henry agreed. 'Brenda, any problems talk to Mrs Hanson. As head of the department, she will address any concerns you have.'

With that Henry left Brenda in the capable hands of Dot. She had barely walked a step across the floor when Jean, Mary and even Rose appeared from heaven knew where to meet Brenda.

'Hello, I'm Mary Holmes-Fotherington. Sorry, Mary Partridge! I just got married at the weekend and I'm forgetting myself. A pleasure,' Mary gushed, holding out her right hand and pumping Brenda's enthusiastically.

'And I'm Jean Rushmore,' Jean said, shoving her way past Mary.

'I'm Rose Harper,' Rose said. 'I work upstairs in the office but am often in fabrics. I love it here.'

The girls made their introductions and Dot rolled her eyes heavenwards as she caught Brenda's face. The look of moderate fear that she had worn in her eyes had now been replaced by abject terror.

'Yes, that's enough. We'll come and find you later, girls. Let me show Brenda the fabrics first before you scare the girl half to death.'

'We're only trying to make her feel welcome,' Mary said with a hint of petulance.

'Well, you're making me feel on edge with all your enthusiasm, never mind poor Brenda,' she admonished, turning to Brenda. 'Come with me, darlin'.'

Quickly, she ushered Brenda down the steps and into the coolness of the stone stockroom. There, where it was just the two of them surrounded by boxes, files and rolls of Liberty print, Brenda seemed to relax.

'Are you all right, darlin'?' Dot asked kindly, taking the girl's arm and leading her to an upturned box.

Brenda nodded. 'Yes. Just a bit overwhelmed, I think. It's so grand here, and them girls upstairs are so well spoken. I think I'm just more used to life below stairs.'

Dot smiled again. She could understand that. Before she had joined Liberty's she had spent most of her working life as a dishwasher or stallholder down the Elephant and Castle's Lane. 'It can seem a bit overwhelming. The shop's beautiful, but it is just a shop, darlin',' she said. 'We sell things and people buy 'em, just like any other shop. Now, I'm not being funny or anything, but you must have had an idea what Liberty's was before you applied. If you don't mind me asking, what made you want to work here?'

Brenda stared down at her newly polished black shoes before she looked again at Dot, the expression of fear in her eyes replaced by desperation. 'I saw an advert in the paper and I needed a job,' she whispered. ' I know places like this are finding it hard to come by staff these days, what with the war and shortage of people. I'm sorry, I know that probably ain't what you want to hear but it's the truth.'

With a sigh, Dot leaned over to squeeze the girl's hand. Brenda was right. It wasn't what she wanted to hear, but over the years Liberty's had become a second home for those in need, and in that moment Dot had a feeling a second home was something Brenda needed very much indeed.

Chapter Six

'She's a bit flamin' shy,' Alice remarked over a port and lemon in the French Pub later that night.

'And she looked like she was going to run a country mile when she saw a customer,' Mary added, sipping her gin and orange. 'Are you sure she's right for the department, Dot?'

Dot raised an eyebrow as she took a gulp of her gimlet. 'Oh, and of course you two arrived at Liberty's fully formed, didn't you, eh? You', she said, turning to Alice, a glint in her grey eyes, 'knew all there was to know about the shop when you were a stores girl barely out of nappies, and as for you,' Dot continued, her eyes now glowering as she turned to Mary, 'I expected more from you. I mean it was common bloody knowledge you could barely tell one end of a roll of Tana Lawn from the other. So may I suggest you both shut your cake holes and remember what you were like when you started.'

As Dot finished, Alice and Mary looked suitably apologetic; they stared down at the round wooden table and mumbled a quiet sorry.

'Well, I think Brenda will be good for the department,' Jean said matter-of-factly, setting down her milk stout.

'Come on, darlin',' Dot reasoned. 'I know we said we should give her a chance, but that don't mean we've got to go singing her praises just yet.'

'We know that,' Rose agreed, her round glasses slipping down her nose. 'That's why I invited her down for a drink with us so she can get to know us better. She's going to come down with Henry when they've finished going over the Liberty Rules.'

'Oh my days,' Alice muttered, earning herself a glare from Dot.

'Very neighbourly of you, darlin',' Dot said. 'Now look, change your faces, they're here.'

With that the girls got to their feet as Henry and Brenda approached the small table in the snug.

'Fancy seeing you here,' Henry joked, pulling out a chair next to Alice for Brenda to sit down on.

'Fancy!' Dot chuckled. 'You buying us all a drink then or what?'

Everyone laughed apart from Brenda who let out a slight gasp at what she guessed incorrectly to be insubordination from Dot.

'Just this once,' Henry said, his grin reaching his brown eyes. 'What's it to be?'

As the girls rattled off their requests only Brenda remained silent.

'You not having a drink, sweetheart?' Alice enquired. 'Henry's buying and – trust me – you want to make the most of it.'

'All right, all right,' Henry groaned in mock despair as the girls laughed again.

'I'm fine, thank you,' Brenda replied, her eyes still locked on to the floor.

'Oh come on, Brenda, we want to toast your success,' Henry said encouragingly.

'Thank you, sir, it's very kind of you, but I don't drink,' Brenda said.

Dot looked at her in astonishment. 'Don't drink? Christ alive, you'll never survive Liberty's if you don't have a glass of something every now and again. Henry,' she said authoritatively, turning to her superior and raising her own glass, 'get her a gimlet.'

'Oh now, Dot,' Alice put in with a frown. 'She'll want something a bit gentler than that.'

'Yes, get the girl a port and lemon,' Mary said in a tone that brooked no argument.

Once Henry was on his way to the bar, the girls smiled kindly at Brenda.

'How was your first day?' Rose asked gently. 'It can be ever such a lot to take in.'

'It was,' Brenda agreed, tugging the cuffs of her long-sleeved blouse over her wrists. 'I think my head's doing somersaults taking in all them rules.'

'You'll get used to it,' Dot promised. 'Anything seems like a lot to take on when you first start; then it gets easier.'

The fear in Brenda's eyes told Dot the girl remained unconvinced.

'Look,' Mary said, 'it does get easier. I mean, you must know that from your life in service.'

'True,' Brenda replied. 'But that was so very different.'

'Tell us about it,' Rose said, encouragingly. 'What did you do?'

Brenda lifted her chin and smiled. Dot caught a hint of pride in her eyes at the question.

'I worked as a housemaid, and had just worked my way up to lady's maid,' Brenda said. 'I dressed the two youngest daughters.'

Mary clapped her hands together in delight. 'How wonderful. I remember my first lady's maid, Hilperton, she was called. An absolute delight.'

Alice rounded on her and shook her head in disbelief. 'You had a lady's maid?'

'Of course.' Mary shrugged before a cloud passed across her face. 'But that was a long time ago. A past life.'

Gently Alice leaned over and squeezed Mary's hand in sympathy. Once again Dot felt a flash of anger at the way her precious girl had been treated by her nearest and dearest. She was just about to say as much when Henry arrived carrying a tray overladen with drinks.

'Ah, there's a sight for sore eyes.' Mary smiled, indicating the subject was closed. Standing up to help Henry unload the tray, she passed a port and lemon to Brenda.

'There you go, drink that all up, you've earned it.'

Looking doubtfully at the glass, Brenda sniffed it and recoiled. 'No offence, but if that's what I've earned, I'll definitely work harder tomorrow.'

At the joke the girls laughed.

'It's not so bad.' Rose grinned. 'Trust me: after a few sips you'll get a taste for it.'

Dot looked at Brenda and saw she still looked doubtful, so she decided to change the subject. 'Where are you living, darlin'? You got lodgings somewhere?'

Brenda nodded. 'Yes, over in Silvertown. I'm living with a lovely lady named Mrs Rogers. She's got three children and I help out with them sometimes; her husband's away with the navy, see.'

'And how long have you been there?' Henry quizzed.

'Just a few days. She's been very kind to me.'

'Good.' Dot nodded approvingly. 'Get her to pop into the store sometime, it'll be nice to meet her.'

'I will, Mrs Hanson,' Brenda replied, giving the matriarch a shy smile.

Dot laid a hand on the girl's arm. 'It's Dot, darlin'. Mrs Hanson was my mother-in-law and a right old battleaxe she was. We don't bother with all that in our department, but keep it under your hat.'

At that Dot could see Brenda's shoulders start to relax just a little.

'So have you got brothers and sisters?' Alice asked. 'Or any family that live close by?'

Brenda shook her head. 'No. It was just me mum and me, but Mum died shortly after I went into service.'

'And what made you leave service?' Mary asked, getting to the point.

At the question, Brenda coloured. 'They had to let some people go. You know how it is. Big houses like that are less busy these days with fewer people in 'em.'

Mary nodded authoritatively. 'It's true for everyone. Since the last war houses like ours have been winding down for years. You were lucky to have been taken on when you were.'

'Yes, it was lovely for a while,' Brenda admitted, tucking a lock of hair behind her ear. 'But anyway, I needed a job and saw Liberty's were after more staff so thought I'd apply.'

'Had you been to London before?' Henry asked.

Brenda shook her head. 'I thought it wouldn't be that much different from Guildford. I mean, the family I worked for always said London was like a lot of villages strung together. I thought that sounded nice, but now I'm here it's a bit daunting.'

'It can be,' Rose agreed. 'But we can show you around, can't we, girls?'

Dot nodded her head enthusiastically. 'Oh yes. You ain't really seen London until you've seen the farriers mucking out the horses down the back of the Lane.'

Henry chuckled. 'Or the resident drunk at the Elephant and Castle get thrown out on his ear by Charlie the landlord.'

The girls laughed again, but Brenda's pretty young face looked terrified.

'We're teasing,' Alice said gently. 'There's a lot of very nice things about London – once you get past the bombed-out buildings – and we'll show you them.'

'We could start with one of them lunchtime recitals at the National Gallery Myra Hess does,' Rose suggested.

'That sounds lovely – if you've got time.' Brenda smiled. 'I don't know much about music though.'

'That doesn't matter,' Alice countered. 'You know what you like and that's all that matters.'

Mary's eyes lit up at the prospect. 'Oh yes, that would be wonderful. I could bring Emma along – she would love it.'

'Stan might too,' Henry said thoughtfully.

Dot rolled her eyes. What was wrong with going to the pictures? 'I think they'd love it as much as a trip up the dentist.'

Mary narrowed her eyes as she fixed her gaze on Dot. 'What was that?'

'Nothing, darlin', but count me out, will you? I've got Liberty's to sort out. The last thing we want is competitors like Botheringtons getting one over on us,' Dot said gloomily.

'Well, we'll help any way we can,' Mary said kindly. 'Is that what you were talking to Beatrice Claremont about earlier today?'

Dot raised an eyebrow in surprise. 'Where did you hear that?'

Mary shrugged. 'I've got my ears to the ground.'

'I'd have said they were more like an African elephant myself if you picked that up. But yes, it's true. Beatrice did want a word. She wants to help us get fabrics back on its feet.'

'She'll have it back on its arse if she gets involved,' Rose growled.

Choking back a bark of laughter, Dot looked at Rose in surprise. 'You all right, darlin'? Not like you to use that sort of language.'

'I'm fine.' Rose sighed. 'It's just the thought of that woman getting her paws stuck into fabrics again.'

'She's all right,' Alice replied. 'She's paid her dues and she's said she's sorry. I say we let her help us.'

'Me too,' Mary agreed. 'Life's too short for grudges.'

Brenda coughed suddenly and looked up at Dot. 'Is the department in trouble?'

'Nothing serious,' Dot replied. 'We just need to think of a way to get customers singing our praises when they walk out the doors. Botheringtons has been taking a lot of our business lately.'

'I see.' Brenda looked thoughtful. 'Then perhaps we could offer customers something extra when they leave, so they remember how special Liberty's is.'

'What, like five bob to tell their pals about us?' Alice teased.

'No, an incentive. Something like a discount off your next fabric purchase over a certain amount,' Brenda suggested.

Dot's jaw dropped open in surprise. The girl might actually have hit upon a good idea. Glancing around the table, she took in Henry's surprised expression. Could she have underestimated this shy, inexperienced new starter?

Chapter Seven

Over the next few days the weather was up and down with bursts of bright sunshine one day, and thick dark clouds the next. Sitting at home on Sunday morning, staring out into the sunshine-filled allotment, Dot couldn't help thinking how often the weather seemed to reflect her own emotions. One day she felt as though she had a zest for life, capable of taking on the world and saving the fortunes of Liberty's. The next she felt as if she were ground down and ready for nothing but the knacker's yard.

Sipping her tea, she gazed across at Edwin, who always spent his Sunday mornings at her table, lost in the papers. Dot tried to read his expression but his face seemed filled with despair and she couldn't blame him. Since Monday's annual government budget, the papers had been full of reports that the war had cost a grand total of thirteen billion pounds so far and continued to cost fifteen million per day. The figures were staggering and Dot struggled to digest them. They seemed like fantasy numbers and, like a lot of the customers who had called into the store that week, she wondered if the country would ever get back in the black. Would this mean a lifetime of rationing to help repay the country's deficit if they ever did see an end to this war?

Dot drank her tea and tried to concentrate on the vegetables that were beginning to grow through the soil outside.

She had never imagined she would become so green-fingered, but the war had forced them all into doing new things.

Her eyes strayed to the letter from Ivy she had received the other day. It stood in the middle of the table, a gentle reminder that she hadn't yet replied. Dot had been savouring the chance to write back, but there was so much on her mind, so many questions she wanted to ask, and the task seemed a large one.

'Penny for 'em?' Edwin said, the rustle of the pages alerting Dot to the fact he had put his paper down.

'Oh, nothing,' Dot replied with a faraway smile. 'Just thinking about this budget.'

Edwin raised an eyebrow. 'That all?'

Dot shrugged. 'And my never-ending list of jobs.'

'Is replying to that letter on there?'

Looking at him in surprise, she smiled. Even when they were young he had known just what she was thinking. It was an extraordinary gift.

'Amongst other things,' she replied in a non-committal tone.

'Who is it from anyway?' Edwin asked, reaching for the brown teapot to refill his cup.

'Ivy, old friend. Lives in Torquay,' Dot replied, already feeling a flash of panic at giving away more than she intended.

'Do I know her?'

'No,' Dot said.

'So tell me more about her.'

'She was a nurse. I met her very briefly during a family holiday to Torquay when I was fourteen. Then I went back for a longer summer holiday a couple of years later and we became good friends.'

Edwin offered her a rueful smile, his copper eyes containing a hint of sadness. 'The year you and I parted company.'

'1910 was the year you went to Kent and left me broken-hearted,' Dot replied heatedly.

'1910 was the year I moved to Kent to be with my dying mother who believed the sea air would help her tuberculosis,' Edwin said, arching an eyebrow.

Dot shook her head. She was in no mood to go down this part of memory lane again and so she veered the conversation back to safer ground. 'Ivy was a bit older than me and lived near to where I was staying. We got on like a house on fire.'

'You've never mentioned her.'

Dot frowned. 'Haven't I? She's my oldest friend.'

Edwin shook his head in confirmation. 'I would have remembered. So what's all the mystery?'

'Mystery?' Dot bristled at the word. 'No mystery. There was a period of thirty-odd years where we didn't see each other, Edwin, we can't possibly hope to know everything about each other.'

'Well, you know everything about me. I haven't got any mystery friends tucked away across the country,' Edwin teased with the hint of a smile.

'That's 'cos you haven't got any friends,' Dot said, not meaning to be unkind. 'Men don't – they rely on their wives to keep up friendships.'

Stroking his chin, Edwin looked at her thoughtfully. 'I suppose that's true. Ethel always made sure we did things with her pals, and my old muckers in the army sort of fell by the wayside. Though I will say that when Ethel died they were quick to offer their condolences. Henry in particular was a marvel.'

'You see,' Dot said, jabbing her finger against the table now her point had been proved.

Edwin laughed. 'Yes, I see. So does that mean then that Ivy is now my friend? I mean, we are as good as married these days, Dotty.'

A look of alarm passed Dot's face. 'We are *not* as good as married, Edwin Button. We may have made promises to each other as youngsters but those don't carry over thirty years. You'll have to ask me properly if you want to inherit my pals.'

'Dotty, I can ask you now,' he said, a look of seriousness passing across his face as he leaned forwards in his chair.

Dot laughed. 'With me in my old housecoat?' She chuckled, pulling at the old floral cloth that covered her clothes. 'I don't think so.'

Sitting back in his chair, Edwin smiled. 'So I'll have to find a time when you're not in your housecoat.'

There was a pause then and Dot felt a thrill of delight at the idea of being Mrs Edwin Button, a name she had secretly practised in her old jotter as a child. How funny to think dreams could come true. Her old mum, Mary Banwell, had always said that things work out for a reason, and Dot reckoned that on this occasion she was right. Though Mrs Banwell had always thought Edwin a cut above with his well-to-do accent and a mother who believed she was as posh as the landed gentry her father had worked for, her mum had always had a soft spot for Edwin. Now she would no doubt think it right that he and Dot had found their way to one another again.

'Why don't you take some time to see her?' Edwin suggested, breaking her train of thought. 'I'll come with you.'

'No!' Dot snapped; then, seeing the look of alarm on Edwin's face, she rearranged her face. 'I mean, you're busy running the shop and I'm busy with the department now and of course Ivy is rushed off her feet.'

'Is she still nursing?' Edwin asked.

'Yes, part-time, and she's got the WI to run as well as her daughter Helen to think about.'

'She sounds even busier than we are.'

Dot nodded and set her now-empty cup down. 'It's the way Ivy likes it. And with no husband any more, it's all on her shoulders.'

Edwin looked solemn. 'This war's been tough on everyone, but women especially. The hardships they face now . . .'

'I've got news for you, sunshine. It's always women what have faced the hardships,' Dot said bluntly. 'You fellas have just never realised it. Speaking of hard-done-by women, did I tell you Beatrice Claremont came to me the other day offering to help me sort out fabrics?'

At the mention of the woman's name a cloud briefly passed across Edwin's features. Alice had persuaded him to give the woman another chance last year, but it hadn't come easily to him. She had betrayed the store and the employees in a way he had found intolerable and whilst he didn't bear grudges, he was a great believer in fairness. His ability to always try to see the good in others, even if he didn't want to, was one of the things Dot most valued in him.

'What did you say?' he asked eventually.

Dot sighed. 'My first instinct was to tell her to shove it, but maybe it's time to forgive and forget. She seemed genuine enough.'

'Might be a nice way to build some bridges. And if you and the rest of the girls can't face talking to her perhaps let Brenda be your referee. After all, she doesn't know the history.'

Pausing for a moment, Dot thought Edwin could well be right. Brenda knew very little about the troubles of the past and she had in fact come up with some good ideas herself about how to rekindle the department's fortunes. Perhaps she was the best woman for the job.

'I'll think about it,' she said. 'And what about you?'

Edwin looked blank. 'What about me?'

'Well, now you've stopped consulting for the Board of Trade, what are you doing to do with all that extra time? Haven't you got any bright ideas of your own to help fabrics out?'

With a chuckle, he leaned over and kissed Dot's cheek. 'You're never backwards in coming forwards, are you, Dotty?'

'Never have been in the past and not about to start now,' she said fondly, reciprocating his kiss.

'Not about to start what now?' a voice boomed behind them.

Spinning around, Dot saw Alice standing in the kitchen doorway with Arthur in her arms, Bess and Jean beside her.

'Never you mind.' Dot smiled, holding out her arms to take baby Arthur.

Alice immediately handed him to Dot, helped herself to a cup of tea and then poured out two more cups for Bess and Jean.

'What are you two doing here?' Dot said, gesturing for the girls to take a seat at the table.

'We were just passing and thought we'd pop in.'

Dot raised an eyebrow. 'Nobody in London just passes anywhere.'

Bess laughed. 'Not a lot gets by you, does it?'

'I just say it as I see it,' Dot said, not unkindly. 'Anyway, you haven't said what you're here for, or taken your coats off.'

'We've had an idea,' Bess said, resting her one hand on the table.

Dot couldn't help wincing at the sight. It had been a tragedy the way that Bess had lost her hand in the munitions factory at such a young age. She had coped with it admirably and Dot thought there were plenty of people who could take a leaf out of her book.

'Famous last words,' Alice joked, interrupting Dot's train of thought.

Jean shook her head at Alice, used to her teasing by now. 'I'll have you know we've come to invite you to a party but any more of your cheek and we'll change our minds.'

At the mention of a party, Alice's eyes lit up. 'Ooh, what's the occasion?'

'We want to thank you for all you did for us last year,' Bess replied.

Edwin waved his hand away. 'What rot. We didn't do anything.'

'You did more than you know,' Jean said softly, an earnest expression in her eyes.

'You were all towers of strength when Bess had her accident and when the truth came out about our relationship, well, you were so supportive. You made us feel as though we were worth something, rather than two people with a filthy horrible secret.'

At that Dot felt a pang of emotion in her heart and reached across to squeeze Jean's hand. 'Your secret will always be safe with us, darlin'. It's not ours to tell, and it's certainly not our place to judge.'

'Quite right,' Mr Button said brusquely, feeling wrong-footed by all this emotion. 'There's nothing to thank us for.'

Bess's mouth was set in a firm line. 'Well, it's nice of you to say that, sir, but we will be throwing a little get-together at Flo's and we would be thrilled if you could all come.'

'We should be delighted.' Dot said, a smile a mile wide on her face. 'When were you thinking?'

'On Saturday in three weeks' time,' Jean put in. 'We thought it would be a nice spring do.'

'What a wonderful idea,' Alice agreed. 'I'll write to Jack, see if there's a possibility he might be able to come.'

'That would be lovely.' Jean smiled. 'You must miss him.'

'I do,' Alice said. 'But there's no point crying over spilt milk. Not now there's a party to look forward to.'

'Absolutely,' Bess agreed. 'A party is just what we all need.'

At that Dot couldn't disagree. A party could be just the thing to lift their spirits and help them all feel brighter about the days ahead.

Chapter Eight

'A party?' Brenda echoed, her eyes widening in terror.

'Yes that's right,' Dot replied patiently as they stood in fabrics the following Tuesday. 'You know, darlin', usual thing, bit of chatter, bit of grub, possibly some dancing if anyone gets in the mood.'

Brenda looked doubtful and started tugging the long-sleeved rayon blouse awkwardly over her wrists.

Dot felt a flash of irritation. She and Brenda had been going over the guard books during a quiet spell that morning and Dot had been pleased at how quickly Brenda seemed to have picked things up. She thought it was a sign that Brenda was getting the hang of it all and coming out of her shell but the look on her face at the mention of a party told a different story.

'Darlin', it's a do you've been invited to, not an execution.' Dot sighed. 'What's the matter?'

'Nothing,' Brenda replied in a tone that left Dot certain that something was very much the matter. 'I won't really know anyone ...'

'You'll know me and the rest of the Liberty girls, and that's enough, ain't it?' Dot said carefully. Closing the latest guard book full of prints and design, she shoved them under the till and leaned against the wooden desk. 'You know, if there's ever a problem you can always talk to me,' she offered. 'That's what we do, us Liberty girls, we share our problems.'

Brenda looked up at Dot in earnestness. 'I don't have a problem. I'm very happy at Liberty's.'

Dot raised an eyebrow. She wasn't convinced and tried again. 'I know it ain't easy starting again, trust me, I know—'

'What do you know?' Brenda asked, cutting Dot off mid-flow.

If Dot was surprised at the interruption she didn't show it. Pausing for a moment, she surveyed Brenda for a second and then looked around the department. It was just after opening time and the store so far was empty. Alice and Mary were out of earshot sorting through the racks of Tana Lawn and Jean was giving the tops of the cupboards a much-needed dust.

Turning back to Brenda, she gave a smile. 'Let's just say that when I was a bit younger than you I had to start again. I was faced with a difficult situation and I got through it as best I could.'

Brenda narrowed her eyes. 'You mean when you split up with Mr Button?'

Dot paused. The way gossip flew around Liberty's was incredible. For some reason the girl in front of her reminded her very much of herself when she was younger. Brenda was keen but cautious and appeared to wear her emotions for all to see. In that moment Dot was tempted to tell her the truth about her childhood, something she had never told anyone else. She had a feeling Brenda might find it helpful to know that things usually worked out in the end – or that at least you learned to live with the endings you gave yourself, even if they weren't always happy ones. But as Dot saw resident floorwalker Dreary Deirdre begin her usual mid-morning security checks, the temptation left her.

'No, I don't mean that,' she said, 'although that was part of it. No, I found myself in a situation where I had to make a new life for myself. If it hadn't been for the help of some very loyal friends then I don't know how I would have managed.'

Looking at Brenda now and seeing that she still hadn't reached her, Dot frowned. 'What I'm saying to you, and I'm not doing it very well, is that I know a little of what it's like to find yourself in a new place feeling lost and a bit overwhelmed.'

Brenda nodded slowly and Dot could see the girl's eyes shining with tears.

'I thought that when I started my career in service I had a job for life,' Brenda began, her shoulders starting to tremble at the memory. 'But a couple of years in, when I was being trained up as lady's maid, things started to change at the house.'

'What sort of things, darlin'?' Dot's voice was gentle now.

'The family was different with me. I never had much to do with them before but as I started spending time upstairs they were more familiar, I suppose.'

'Was that difficult?'

'Not at first. The girls were lovely to me and let me try on all their clothes.' Brenda grinned at the memory. 'We were a similar age and sometimes it felt like we were just three friends having a nice time. But her ladyship, the girls' mother, well – she didn't like it. Said it was inappropriate for me, a girl from below stairs, to become friends with her girls; she said I was a bad influence, that the fact my father ran off when I was a baby and my mother had died when I was fourteen meant I was a savage ...'

Brenda's voice trailed off and Dot felt a stab of anger on behalf of the girl. Whoever her ladyship was, she sounded to Dot as if she was a rather stupid, stuck-up cow. How could she let Brenda think that what happened to her parents was her fault?

Resisting the urge to tell Brenda what she thought of her ladyship, Dot squeezed the girl's arm. 'Go on.'

Dot's touch seemed to bring Brenda back to the present. Lifting her chin, she offered the department manager a weak smile and wiped the tears that had pooled in her eyes with the back of her hand. 'Things changed. It became obvious over time that I couldn't stay, that I was no longer welcome. It broke my heart, having to leave the place I'd grown up in.'

Dot nodded, sensing she had got as much as she could from the girl that morning and it was a good idea not to push. 'I can imagine, darlin', but anyone can make a success of a new start. I'm living proof, and all of us here, we want to help you.'

Brenda smiled for the first time since she and Dot had started talking. 'So you're saying I ought to go to the party?'

'I'm saying that I think it would be a nice place to start, to help you integrate into your new life.'

Nodding, Brenda smiled weakly once more, as if doing her best to convince herself that her fate was sealed.

'Well, that's settled then.'

Just then the sound of footsteps combined with a stick tapping on the ground told Dot that Rose had joined them.

'Hello, darlin', how's tricks upstairs?'

Rose, her tortoiseshell glasses perched on her forehead, sighed. 'Busy. More files to sort through, more to pass on to Mr B. that aren't in braille and of course the phone hasn't stopped ringing.'

'It's tough at the top, but you want to take it easy in your condition,' Dot warned.

Rose waved Dot's concerns away. 'You sound like Mr Button. He says I should remember what's really important.'

'For once I can't say I disagree with him, but I don't think that's why you've come, is it, darlin?' Dot replied, noticing the stack of Manila files under Rose's arm.

'No, I've got a pile of invoices for you to sign,' Rose said hurriedly, the glasses that were perched on her head now falling on to her nose.

Dot straightened them on her face. 'Give 'em 'ere and I'll make a start.'

'Thanks.' Rose sighed gratefully as she went to turn away, clutching her tell-tale white cane.

'You go steady, mind,' Dot replied, only for Rose to collide directly with a customer.

'Will you watch where you're going?' the woman spat.

Rose's cheeks flushed with embarrassment and Dot felt angry on Rose's behalf at this woman's unfortunate choice of words. Could she not see from Rose's cane she had problems with her sight?

As the woman glared at Rose, Dot took a moment to observe her: tall, with greying raven hair cut short, narrowing emerald eyes, and angular, almost haughty-looking features. Dot got the feeling that she had seen this woman somewhere before but for the life of her couldn't think where.

'I'm so sorry,' Rose replied, holding her hands out to try and help the woman and failing to locate her as she banged her stick on the ground. Dot's heart went out to her friend. This woman ought to be apologising, not Rose, but it was typical of the girl to take the blame for something that wasn't her fault. Dot rushed to help, only to find the woman drawing herself up to her full height to straighten her coat and ignoring Rose's apologies.

'Rose, darlin', are you all right?' Dot asked as she helped Rose find her feet.

'I'm fine. I just feel bad for this lady, I'm so sorry, ma'am.'

'Quite all right,' the woman replied but Dot couldn't help glowering at the woman.

'She's fine,' Dot said, shooting the woman a look of annoyance. 'I think you came off worst. The white stick you carry ought to be a dead giveaway that you can't see as well as the rest of us.'

'Well, I never!' the woman cried. 'Such insolence. I am a customer and that girl walked straight into me.'

Dot looked pointedly at the woman's empty gloved hands. 'Forgive me for saying so but you don't appear to have bought nothing yet so you're not strictly speaking a customer, are you? What you are, in fact, is being downright rude to a girl who can't flamin' well see.'

'Dot, please,' Rose begged, her pale cheeks flushed with embarrassment. 'Calm down. There's no harm done. I'm fine and so is the lady by the sounds of things.'

The woman sniffed as she examined her bag. Dot could tell it was good quality: Italian leather if she wasn't mistaken.

'My bag's a little scuffed, but nothing that won't polish out, I'm sure,' she sighed.

'That's a relief,' Dot said sarcastically as she turned back to Rose. 'You all right getting back up to the office, love, or do you need some help?'

Rose shook her head. 'No, I'm fine. Nothing a nice cup of tea back at my desk won't cure. Good day to you, madam, and apologies again.'

With that Rose made her way back up the stairs and Dot turned her attention to the woman in front of her, feeling a surge of fury. What sort of person blames the partially sighted for knocking into them? In that moment Dot could have cheerfully swung for the woman, but given she wasn't down the Lane and was instead representing Liberty's, she decided to try behaving with a little more decorum.

'What brings you to Liberty's today?' she asked as politely as she could. 'Spring fabrics perhaps?'

'I'm not here to buy anything,' the woman said briskly. 'I'm looking for someone.'

Dot tried hard not to grimace. She should have known that this battleaxe wasn't a customer, Liberty customers were usually very nice indeed, unlike the woman standing in front of her.

'Who?' Dot asked, not bothering now to hide her irritation.

'Mary Holmes-Fotherington.'

'We've nobody of that name here,' Dot said, being deliberately difficult.

'Oh, what rot. I know my own daughter's name, thank you very much.'

Dot let out a gasp as the penny dropped. Of course. It all made sense now. This dreadful woman was Mary's mother; she remembered the last time she had visited the store, telling Mary in no uncertain terms that she was dead to the family and should never show her face in their home again. Dot had torn the woman to shreds at the time and, feeling the hackles on the back of her neck begin to rise, she realised she was more than ready to do it again – on the Liberty shop floor if need be.

'You clearly don't,' Dot bristled, 'as if you did, you would know she is now Mrs Mary Partridge.'

Mrs Holmes-Fotherington's jaw dropped as she took in Dot's words. 'She's married?'

'She is,' Dot confirmed. 'But given you told her never to darken your door again I'm sure you can understand why she hasn't told you. Now, what is it you want with her?'

'I, well, I wish to see her,' the woman said. Her voice was soft now; the news of her daughter's marriage had clearly distressed her.

'Why?' Dot asked bluntly.

'That's my business not yours.'

'As her friend and boss, who has been here for her when you haven't, I think you'll find it's very much my business. She's happy now, she's got a new life for herself and she don't want you coming in here upsetting her with your cheap insults, thank you very much.'

'That is not why I am here,' Mrs Holmes-Fotherington protested, only to be ignored by Dot.

'I think you'll also find that she told you to sling your hook last time she saw you,' Dot hissed, 'and so, to save Mary the bother of doing it again, I'll do it for her. I don't know what you want with that girl but I can imagine you only want to cause trouble, so if you don't leave now I shall have no choice but to have you forcibly removed.'

Leaning over the desk, Mrs Holmes-Fotherington jabbed Dot in the chest. 'You wouldn't dare.'

Not to be outdone, Dot leaned forwards, their faces so close now Dot could see the lines around the older woman's eyes that she had unsuccessfully tried to cover with make-up. 'Try me, lady. I don't know how many times you have to be told, but you ain't wanted here.'

Chapter Nine

'What on earth is going on?'

At the sound of Mary's voice the women sprang apart. Casting a glance at Mary, Dot felt a mix of concern and anxiety come over her. The sight of the woman who had told Mary she no longer wanted anything to do with her must be torture.

'Everything's fine, Mary, darlin',' Dot offered, stepping away from Mrs Holmes-Fotherington and keen to try and defuse the situation. 'We were just having a little chat.'

At that Mary turned to her mother and stared, disbelief in her eyes. Dot couldn't miss the look of despair in Mary's eyes. The girl should be on cloud nine following her marriage and the adoption of baby Emma. It wasn't right that this woman was here ruining all of that for her.

'Mrs Holmes-Fotherington,' Dot said in her politest tone of voice. 'Given that this is a place of business, can I suggest that you perhaps write to Mary if you wish to see her rather than just dropping in?'

Mrs Holmes-Fotherington made no move to leave and instead stood gawping at her daughter. There was disbelief in her eyes, Dot noted, but still she could feel no sympathy for the woman after everything that had happened. When Mary had arrived at Dot's door needing help in September 1941 she'd been battered and bruised after suffering a terrible betrayal and loss. To make matters worse, her family had turned their backs on Mary, wrongly accusing her of destroying the family name and reputation.

Dot had been furious when she'd found out, and still was to this day. Together with the rest of the Liberty girls, she had helped Mary find her feet as well as a new home and new family.

'What are you doing here, Mother?' Mary asked.

Mrs Holmes-Fotherington turned away from Dot and took a step towards her daughter. 'I've just heard you have married. Congratulations. I assume it's to the doctor you were courting?'

'The one who asked for your permission to marry me and you chose to ignore?' Mary said coldly. 'Yes.'

Mrs Holmes-Fotherington gave a smile, but it didn't reach her eyes. 'I'm thrilled for you, darling. I'm just sorry we couldn't be there to witness your special day. I'm sure you looked beautiful.'

'She did,' Dot snapped. 'Any mother in her right mind would have been proud as Punch.'

'As would I, had I been present,' Mrs Holmes-Fotherington replied, seemingly ignoring Dot's outburst. 'I wish you a lifetime of happiness, my dear, and it only makes me so sorry that things are the way they are between us.'

At that Mrs Holmes-Fotherington looked Mary in the eyes and Dot saw a flicker of emotion, and an almost pleading look pass across her features.

The slight gesture was, however, lost on Mary, who remained rooted to the spot, hands by her sides. 'What is it you want, Mother?' she asked again.

'I'm here to see you. I think we should talk.'

Mary's face remained impassive. 'What about? I think we've said everything that needs to be said.'

Mary's mother was wrong-footed. 'There's no need for that, darling. I understand why you would be a bit upset but surely you didn't think we would be estranged forever?'

'Ha!' Mary let out a bark of laughter. 'You mean when you told me that I was dead to you and the rest of the family I shouldn't have regarded that as permanent? How bally silly of me.'

Dot watched agog, eyes fixed on Mary's mother. As Mary delivered her final line, the woman's mouth remained in a firm line.

'It was bally silly of you, darling. Your father has been so incredibly ill, it was all a shock, a period of adjustment, surely you can see that?'

Mary said nothing; instead she folded her arms as she glanced at Dot and then back to her mother. 'Do you see that woman over there beside the cash register, Mother? That's Mrs Dorothy Hanson, and she has been twice the mother to me in the short time I have known her than you have ever been.'

Dot saw another flash of emotion pass across the older woman's face. It was only momentary, but Dot caught the look of pain that touched her eyes and she knew that Mary had hit her mother where it hurt.

'I know that I perhaps haven't been the most supportive of mothers, Mary, but you must understand why we behaved the way that we did. We were devastated by your news.'

'*You* were devastated by my news,' Mary spat, clearly flabbergasted at what she had just heard her mother say. 'There are times, Mother, when you render me speechless and this is one of them. May I suggest you do as Mrs Hanson has asked and leave?'

This time the pain on Mrs Holmes-Fotherington's features was obvious. 'You can't mean that. We've barely spoken. You don't know why I'm here.'

Mary shook her head, her cheeks now puce with rage, Dot noted. 'I don't need to know. I've heard everything I will ever need to from you. Now go, please.'

There was a pause then, as if Mrs Holmes-Fotherington wasn't sure whether Mary meant what she said. Eventually, sensing her daughter wasn't going to change her mind, she began to walk towards the door. As she passed her daughter she stopped for a second and reached into her good leather bag. Fishing out an envelope she pressed it into Mary's hand.

'It's from your father,' she said sombrely. 'I hope you will read this letter and come to your senses. You'll know where to find us when you're ready.'

With that Mrs Holmes-Fotherington marched through the department doors and didn't look back. Once she was safely out of earshot, Dot turned to Mary, who was rooted to the spot, her right hand clutching the letter her mother had given her.

Dot walked to Mary's side and gently wrapped an arm around her. 'You all right, darlin'?'

Mary said nothing, and alarm flooded through Dot.

'Mary, darlin',' she tried again. 'Can you hear me?'

There was silence for a moment and then, just as Dot was thinking about slapping Mary to bring her back to reality, the raven-haired newlywed came to.

'Sorry, Dot,' she said. 'I was miles away.'

'I suspect you'd like to be as well,' Dot murmured, steering her around to the chair behind the till as if she were no more than a toddler. 'Now you just sit there and I'll ask one of the girls to fetch you a cup of nice sweet tea for the shock.'

Mary laid a hand on Dot's arm. 'No, don't do that – there's no need to make a fuss. I'll be fine in a moment. I just need a second to compose myself.'

'You take all the time you need, darlin',' Dot replied, leaning back against the desk and observing her friend. The sudden encounter appeared to have drained her.

'Did you know she was coming?' Dot blurted.

Mary shook her head. 'I had no idea. David suggested that I write to them again before we married, invite them to our wedding as a peace offering, explain to them about Emma.'

'I take it you didn't?'

'No. They had made it quite clear how they felt about me, and I had already tried in the past to make things right with them. They shunned me last time; I wasn't going to set myself up for hurt or ridicule again.'

'Quite right,' Dot said as her eyes strayed to the envelope. 'You going to open that, then, or what?'

It was as if Mary had forgotten the envelope existed, so surprised was she to see the white Basildon Bond stationery in her hand.

Wordlessly she tore it open, her eyes expressionless as she read the short note.

'Well?' Dot asked, unable to bear the suspense any longer.

'See for yourself,' Mary said morosely as she shoved the letter in Dot's direction.

18th April 1943

Dear Mary,

I can imagine that if you are reading this note then you have refused your mother's overtures to make amends. If I am honest I cannot say that I blame you. I warned your mother no good would come from visiting you and that we had burnt our bridges. I told her that I had taught you as a child to be determined and never give in; I never imagined how those words would come back to haunt me in years to come.

My dear, I am a man of few words and even fewer emotions so I shall make this letter brief. Firstly, allow me to apologise most sincerely for the terrible way your mother, sister and I have treated you. It was unforgivable and after the ordeal you endured I feel wretched. It is something I shall never forgive myself for and I shall go to my grave forever in your debt for the way we treated you.

Which leads me on to the second reason for this note. By the time you read this, Mary, I will be possibly days from death. I had hoped you and I might have resolved our affairs in person but I fear this is not to be. The cancer has spread, my darling, and the fight I have been losing for the past eighteen months is almost at an end.

This letter is in no way meant to make you feel angry or ashamed at what has gone before. The purpose of this letter is to say goodbye. Whist I am preparing to meet my maker, I could not go without first letting you know that I love you and that I am sorry.

Yours in sorrow,
Your ever-loving father

As Dot finished the letter there were tears in her eyes. She hadn't expected to be so moved by the words Mary's father had written, but there it was, as plain as day: he was filled with remorse.

'What do you think I should do?' Mary asked.

Dot looked at her in surprise. 'Do?'

'Do you think I should go up there? Try and see him, say goodbye in person before he goes?'

Dot thought for a moment, conscious there was only one answer that was right. 'Yes, darlin'. Forgiveness goes a long way in this world and I've half a mind it'll carry you through to the next as well. Go and see him, make things right.'

With that Mary stood up and pulled Dot into her arms for a cuddle. As Dot felt the familiar weight of the woman she had come to love as if she were her own child, she hoped that she too would be able to persuade others to forgive her past mistakes.

Chapter Ten

It was later that night and all Dot wanted to do was sink into a chair with her latest Agatha Christie and drink a cup of tea. Now they were almost at the end of April the days were longer and with the sun shining all day she had planned to get out into her vegetable patch and check on the progress of her carrots. But when Arthur began crying just as she finished making up a bottle for a screaming baby Emma, she realised the world and his wife had other ideas.

Following her mother's visit and the letter from her father, Mary had quickly decided that she wanted to go straight up to her family home in Cheshire. Dot had sent her home to make arrangements and promised she would look after baby Emma for a few days. But with Emma's screams now reaching ear-piercing levels mere hours after Mary had departed, Dot wondered if perhaps for once she had bitten off more than she could chew.

'I'm not sure about this,' Alice said for the umpteenth time.

Dot sighed as she lifted Emma out of the hastily made cot she had cobbled together out of a kitchen drawer and turned to Alice with gritted teeth. 'I don't know how many times you want me to go through this with you. The decision was made and I think it was the right one.'

'I know you do,' Alice fired, doing her best to soothe a still-wailing Arthur. 'But the way Mary's family treated her was unforgivable. If it had been my dad I'd have told him where to shove it.'

'You did tell him where to shove it, if I remember rightly,' Dot said, casting her mind back to the funeral of Alice's sister, Joy, and the letter Alice had sent her father telling him he would always be dead to her. 'And it was different with your father: he's a wrong 'un, through and through. All this with the Holmes-Fotheringtons, well, it's not the same, darlin'.'

'Why, because they're posh and we're working class?'

Dot raised an eyebrow. She had no time for politics and class wars in her house. As far as she was concerned you dealt with your lot in the world no matter whether you were Queen Mary or Charlie Chaplin.

'No, because they made a mistake. The father in his letter at least seemed genuine. The mother, well, she still strikes me as a stuck-up old cow,' Dot said tartly.

'I must say I agree with you,' Edwin piped up for the first time from his position in the corner of the kitchen. Nursing a cup of tea with the paper on his lap, he looked very much at home as he waited for his supper, and not for the first time Dot found herself cursing the fact this was very much a man's world. Looking down at Emma, who was now happily sucking on her bottle, Dot had a feeling the only time she would get to put her own feet up was when she was six feet under and some man had thrown half a ton of sod on top of her.

'Really, Mr Button,' Alice gasped. 'I never thought you had it in you to say or think such things about people.'

'You'd be surprised,' Dot replied with a laugh. 'It takes a bit of a push, but he's never suffered fools. Remember that time we went down the Elephant one Saturday night after we'd been courting a while? Some silly sod was going on about how good he was at cards and there wasn't a man in South London that could take a hand off him. Well, that was like a red rag to a bull for Edwin, who challenged him and whipped the smile off his face.'

'Did you win?' Alice gasped.

'Not only did I win but I won me and Dot here drinks for free for the next month. It turned out the landlord was as sick of him bragging as the punters!'

Dot chuckled. 'That and he didn't know a thing about cards.'

'Well, how did you win then?' Alice asked incredulously.

'Because I could see he was cheating,' Edwin explained. 'I've never liked a cheater, and I wasted no time in pulling up his sleeves and showing the pub how he was playing with two decks and not one.'

Alice's jaw dropped in shock. 'You didn't.'

'Oh, he did!' Dot laughed. 'Not only was your store manager not a sufferer of fools but he weren't afraid of anyone, or afraid to stand up and say when something wasn't right.'

'I like to think I'm still that person,' Edwin said with a smile, 'but I might be a bit less brazen about it. I mean it was lucky for us there weren't any bobbies on the beat that night or they'd have had us up for underage drinking and gambling too!'

Dot laughed at the innocent memory and Alice shook her head in disbelief.

'You're a dark horse, Mr Button, sir,' Alice said admiringly.

Edwin looked embarrassed and gave Dot a small smile. 'Anyway, to get back to what we were saying, I do think you're right about the father. It must be a difficult thing to face your own death and know you're estranged from your child. I expect he wants to set his house in order and I imagine it's also put rather a lot of things into perspective. Surely family rows pale into insignificance at a time like this. Making things right is all that matters now and I imagine that's what Mr Holmes-Fotherington has in his mind.'

'Not sure the mother thought it was the right thing,' Dot muttered. 'She couldn't believe Mary didn't go running straight into her arms.'

'Well, I suspect, despite everything she says, that she must want her family in her life,' Edwin mused.

'True,' Alice agreed as she planted a kiss on sleeping Arthur's forehead. 'It must have been awful for her getting married without her family there, and obviously she couldn't take Emma. The bedside of a dying man is no place for a child.'

'This child's got us.' Dot smiled at Emma, who was happy now she had finished her bottle. Taking it from her warm tiny hands, Dot winded the child and then placed her down in the makeshift cot.

'Well, Dorothy, I must say you are a marvel,' Mr Button said admiringly. 'For a woman with no children of her own it's as though you were born to be a mother.'

Dot shrugged as she set about reheating last night's Woolton Pie leftovers. 'What can I say? Nothing I can't turn my hand to.'

'She's right.' Alice laughed as she set about peeling the potatoes Dot had pulled from the garden at the weekend. 'A very talented woman is your other half.'

'Well, I don't know how you do it,' Mr Button said, taking another sip of his tea. 'Much as I love children I wouldn't know one end of a baby from the other.'

'Didn't you and Ethel want a family?' Alice asked, peering over her shoulder.

'Alice! That's a bit personal,' Dot remonstrated, before turning back to Edwin, not missing a beat. 'Was that what it was, darlin'?'

'No, it was simply that the fates didn't smile down favourably on us having children. It was a great sadness to us both. We learned to live with it, and we have some wonderful nephews and nieces who are a comfort to me. But, Dorothy, it's a shame you and George weren't able to have children.'

'Weren't meant to be for neither of us, was it?' Dot shrugged. 'George was killed so soon into our marriage we never got the chance.'

'Was there never anybody after that?' Alice enquired.

Dot glared at Alice and shook her tea towel at her. 'You're getting a bit sodding personal with these questions, lady.'

Alice giggled. 'I think you mean impertinent.'

'Don't you tell me what I think!'

Edwin stood up. 'Ladies, please. You'll wake these very beautiful sleeping children. How long do you have Emma for, Dorothy?'

'I said we would keep her here as long as Mary needed us to, but she seems to think that she won't be gone more than a couple of days,' Dot replied, looking at Emma and smiling.

'No doubt Mary will send a telegram if there's a problem,' Mr Button said, 'and of course she should take all the time she needs.'

'It won't be an easy path she's on.' Dot sighed. 'But making up with her family is surely the right thing to do.'

With that Dot's mind strayed to Ivy and Helen. Ivy had been her friend for so long she was like family. Perhaps now was the time to take Edwin up on his offer and take a couple of days off work and go and visit them.

'You know, when Mary gets back, I think I might like to go down to Devon and see Ivy after all,' Dot said.

'Well, about time,' Alice said, rolling her eyes. 'That woman's been writing to you for years pleading for a visit.'

'I've never had the time before,' Dot said, 'but all this with Mary's family has got me thinking. I should like to see them again.'

'Splendid.' Edwin beamed. 'How about I come with you? We could take the train, make a little holiday out of it and find a bed and breakfast somewhere.'

Alarm flashed across Dot's face. 'No! I mean, no thank you, darlin',' she said, trying to soften the blow as she saw Edwin's jaw drop. 'I think it might be better on my own. I haven't seen them both for such a long time now, there will be a lot for us to catch up on.'

'All right,' Edwin said, his face still crestfallen. 'I just thought it would be nice. There's so much we've missed out on after so many years apart. I suppose I want to make up for it all.'

Dot's face softened. 'I know, darlin', I feel the same and we will. But I wouldn't mind a bit of time to myself with them first. You can come with me another time.'

'All right,' Edwin replied, seemingly mollified.

With that Dot turned back to the kitchen sink and smiled. Soon they would all be reunited.

Chapter Eleven

The sun was out in full force the following Saturday morning and in turn the customers had come out in their droves to admire the new spring prints. It was all hands on deck as without Mary the store was woefully short-staffed. Jean and Alice had been run off their feet serving customers and answering queries and poor Brenda had been thrown in the deep end, learning how to measure and choose fabrics that best suited a pattern. Dot felt proud of the way the fabrics girls were all holding down the fort. It was just one of the many things that made working together at this very special store such a pleasure. Yet after lunch she had to admit defeat and call in reinforcements. She found herself picking up the phone and asking Henry Masters to come down and assist.

'I must say I'm quite enjoying myself,' Henry said after measuring and cutting a rayon fabric for a customer keen to make a tea dress.

Dot raised an eyebrow. 'I'll bet you are. I saw the way you were flirting with Mrs Hawthorn earlier. Sex ain't the only way to get a sale!'

Henry threw his head back and laughed so loudly you could hear him upstairs in carpets. 'Oh, Dot, you're a tonic. They should bottle you and sell you. You'd make a fortune.'

'I'll just settle for a department run without immoral behaviour,' she said pointedly.

At that Brenda looked up from the pile of zips she was sorting through. 'I've been thinking about the department and how to get our customers back from Botheringtons. I've got another idea.'

Henry raised an eyebrow and Dot had to admit she felt a surge of affection for the new recruit. 'Go on, darlin'.'

'Well, I was thinking that beauty is doing all right at the moment, isn't it?'

Dot rolled her eyes. 'And don't we bloody know it. Beatrice Claremont isn't shy in telling us about it – it's a miracle given they're selling very old, sparse stock.'

'Language,' Henry cautioned before turning to Brenda. 'Did you have something specific in mind?'

As Dot and Henry's eyes fixed on her, Brenda's cheeks flamed red with embarrassment at being the centre of attention. 'I was just thinking of something a bit like Rose does with the first-aid nights. I thought perhaps we could encourage customers to come in and learn how to make do and how to make things last. Whilst they are here they could learn about utility prints and if they buy an item here they could get a discount coupon.'

'That's not a bad idea,' Dot said, drumming her fingers on the table. 'But the board don't want us having any more events out of hours.'

'What about a lunchtime event?' Henry suggested.

'Yes, that could work,' Dot said, eyes flashing with excitement. 'Do you think Beatrice will be keen?'

'I'm sure she'll do whatever we think is best,' Henry said with a wry smile. 'And actually I'm having a drink today with an old friend of mine, Peter. He used to do a lot of the advertising artwork for Liberty's and might be able to help with this. Shall we go for a drink and you can meet him?'

Brenda and Dot exchanged anxious glances.

'Can I just have a lemonade?'

Dot laughed. ''Course you can. But I can't stay long, Henry. Doris down the road has got both Arthur and Emma today and I don't like to take the proverbial.'

'Fair enough.' Henry nodded. 'We can make it quick.'

Dot rubbed her hands together with glee. 'Well, it sounds to me like we are halfway there. Want me to talk to Edwin?'

Henry smiled. 'I'm sure if you're happy he will be.'

With the prospect of something to help set the fortunes of fabrics back on an even keel Dot felt as if a rather large weight had been taken from her shoulders. She was sure that if she could just start to ease one of her troubles then the rest would surely follow. Life had ground her down with its drudgery and misery of late, and so this new venture could be the promise of a lift for them all.

By the time the bell for closing time sounded Dot was filled with excitement at the thought of meeting Henry's friend. In her mind he had gone from a chap who could help them out with a bit of promotional artwork to the saviour of the fabric department – something she wasted no time telling Beatrice Claremont.

'Are you sure nobody will mind me coming for a drink?' Beatrice asked for the third time since the doors had been locked shut.

Dot glared at her as she buttoned up her tweed overcoat. Even though May was just around the corner and the sun had been shining all day there was still a cool breeze whipping around her neck. 'If you keep on like that, I will mind. Now shut your cake hole and let's get off. I haven't got long.'

With that the two women, together with Brenda scurrying along behind, made their way through the streets of Soho to the French Pub. Spotting Henry at a table in the saloon Dot made a beeline straight for him.

'Where's your friend?' she asked, getting to the point.

Henry jerked his head towards the bar. 'Getting the drinks in. You girls sit down and tell me what you want and I'll go and get them.'

As the ladies rattled off their drinks order, Dot had a look at Henry's friend. Average height with broad shoulders, pale skin and sparkling blue eyes. He looked younger than Henry, she thought, placing him in his early thirties, but he was wearing an army uniform and there was something about military dress that shaved a few years off most fellas. She'd had half a mind on occasion to ask Edwin to slip his old fatigues on, but he didn't always share her sense of humour.

When the boys returned with the drinks Dot reached for her port and lemon and raised it in gratitude.

'So what tears you away from the army tonight?' she asked.

At the question Peter's face broke into a wide grin. 'Evening off. Thought I'd look up my old chum Henry.'

'Did you two serve together?' Dot asked.

Peter shook his head. 'No, I'm an artist.'

'An artist,' Brenda echoed in wonder. 'I ain't never met an artist before.'

'Me neither,' Dot added. 'Mind, we don't have a lot of call for 'em down the Elephant.'

'Is that what you did before you joined the army then?' Brenda asked.

'Yes, though I still do a bit now. That's how Henry and I met,' Peter explained, taking a sip of his pint.

'He used to do some work for me at Bourne and Hollingsworth. Designed all our advertisements,' Henry explained.

'Oh, did you do them ones with the matches?' Dot asked. 'I used to love them.'

Peter blushed at the praise. 'Well, I didn't come up with the concept, just the art. That was all down to Henry.'

'Still, that was ever so clever of you,' Brenda said, giving him a shy glance from under her lashes.

'Now come on, don't go giving the lad a big head,' Henry teased, giving his old pal a friendly nudge with his shoulder.

'So would you have time to come up with a bit of artwork for our new lunchtime events then?' Dot asked bluntly. 'I imagine the army keep you pretty busy.'

'They do,' Peter nodded. 'But as I'm in the NCC we don't do quite the same work or hours as everyone else.'

At the use of the acronym Dot's face fell like a stone. 'You're in the NCC?'

Peter lifted his chin and shot Dot a defiant look. 'I am. And don't go thinking I don't take my life in my hands every day like soldiers out there on the front line. I dismantle bombs amongst many other things.'

Dot said nothing as Brenda sent a curious glance Peter's way. 'What's the NCC then? I thought the army was the army?'

'It is except when it ain't,' Dot snapped. 'The NCC, Brenda, darlin', is the Non-Combatant Corps, or, as I like to call 'em. National Cowardly C—'

'Thank you, Dorothy!' Henry said quickly, cutting Dot off before she had chance to cause real offence.

'What's that then?' Brenda asked again.

'It means it's a strand of the army for conscientious objectors,' Henry pointed out.

'You're a conchie?' Brenda gasped, the penny clearly dropping. 'So you don't love our country?'

'That's not what it means at all,' Peter said through gritted teeth.

'Must do,' Dot said glibly, taking a sip of her port and lemon. 'I mean, otherwise you'd be putting your life on the line like all our other brave boys. You lot should be in bloody yellow not green.'

Peter's face was puce now. 'I adore my country, I just happen to think that there are better ways to fight for it than to engage in warfare. I don't agree with killing innocent people and I'm not prepared to raise my hands against another in combat.'

'But we're at war!' Dot said, feeling anger course within her. 'It's the only language the Jerries understand. You've heard Mr Churchill's speeches. How can you sit on your hands like this? An artist, my eye. It's not art we need, it's all hands on bloody deck. You should be ashamed of yourself!'

'That's enough, Dot,' Henry said, a note of warning in his voice. 'Peter is serving his country in his own way.'

Dot thought her heart might explode with rage. 'How can you say that? You were in the army yourself!'

'Which is why I understand what it's like to love your country and not want to fight. I've seen too much, as has Edwin. Peter is doing his bit, Dot.'

'I don't think it's right and most right-minded people don't think it's right either,' Dot said, gulping her port and lemon down in one. 'Brenda certainly don't, do you, darlin'?'

As all eyes fell on her Brenda shifted uncomfortably on her seat. 'I understand what you're saying Dot but I think Peter's right,' she said nervously. 'I don't really agree with all this fighting neither and I think there must be a better way. I agree with Henry too: I think it sounds as if Peter's serving his country in the best way he can.'

Staring at Brenda in disbelief, Dot shook her head at the girl. What was wrong with her? What was wrong with all of them? Had they all been working in bohemian Liberty's for too long? Didn't they think like everyday folks any longer? Couldn't they see how wrong it was to be a conscientious objector when their brave boys were fighting day and night for freedom, risking their lives every day? Being a conchie was tantamount to saying you hated Britain and all it stood for. No, there were people that might be all right with it but they were in the minority and Dot wasn't prepared to give in.

Chapter Twelve

A week after Dot had met Peter she still couldn't shake her anger. The rage she felt about him letting his country down in this way consumed her. Sometimes you simply had to do the right thing, however hard or bitter a pill it might be to swallow.

'Don't you think you're being a little harsh?' Alice said as she warmed her hands over a cup of tea in the staffroom that morning. It might have been the first day of May but it was still chilly and Dot felt the cold in her bones as she cradled her own china cup during her afternoon tea break.

'I didn't think you would see it that way.' Dot exclaimed, glancing at her friend in surprise. 'I thought you'd hate conchies as much as the rest of us.'

Alice pursed her lipsticked mouth and held Dot's gaze. 'You and I are similar in many ways, Dot, but you've got to try and think about what it's like for people that genuinely believe war is wrong.'

'Whoever thinks war is right?' Dot thundered, her hands shaking so much with fury that she sent droplets of tea all over her paisley skirt. 'It's about doing the right thing – and what's right about not serving your country? What do you think your Jack would say if he could hear you talking? The Yanks love their country – don't they pledge allegiance to the flag every time they step out the front door?'

Alice leaned back in the hard wooden chair and gazed out through the little window and across the rooftops. Dot followed her gaze and felt her mood become even darker. Everywhere you looked there was devastation and evidence of lives snuffed out in a heartbeat. Bombed-out houses, with abandoned washing still on the line, wallpaper torn and shredded and even pictures hanging crookedly on half-destroyed walls. It was devastating what they were living through. If she were able to she would go and fight for king and country herself.

'I think you're going to have to get on with it,' Alice said finally. 'Despite what you said about Peter, Henry still wants him to do the artwork for the new event. His work is very good. Those adverts he did for Bourne and Hollingsworth were wonderful.'

'Well, I agree with you, Dorothy,' Beatrice Claremont piped up from across the other side of the room. 'I don't think conchies deserve a place here at all and it's terrible Liberty's is encouraging them. I know we're more free and easy in this store with the way we support artists and designers who are – shall we say – a bit more liberal with the way they view the world, but I don't think it's right.'

Alice frowned. 'I don't think they're encouraging anyone. Peter is a very good artist.'

Beatrice got to her feet, bringing her own cup of tea with her and sat down at the table in between Alice and Dot. 'But we have to have standards. This war means we're all doing things we don't like. We don't pick and choose.'

'Too right.' Dot jabbed her finger on the table in agreement. 'If we start saying anything goes, where will we be? We have duties to king and country. What if all our boys said they didn't want to fight? Where would we be then?'

'These conchies are a disgrace!' Beatrice thundered. 'There's a woman down my road been going with one

– well, the looks she gets, not to mention the insults that are flung her way.'

'Can't say as I'm surprised,' Dot said. 'In my view conchie sympathisers are as bad as conchies themselves. It's a sin.'

'The two of you are in cloud cuckoo land.' Alice sighed, gazing at one and then the other. 'Why not let people be who they need to be?'

'Because life ain't like that,' Dot snapped. 'You should know that better than anyone. I can't believe you don't feel the same, Alice. Most people out there think like me and Beatrice, and if word gets out amongst our more traditional customers that a conchie has designed the artwork for our promotions then there'll be hell to pay. Anyway, Beatrice,' Dot said, turning to face her old enemy and feeling strangely benevolent towards her, 'perhaps you and I ought to have a cuppa later this week and go over some ideas for this new lunchtime event.'

'Wonderful idea, Dot,' Beatrice said, getting to her feet – almost regally, Dot noticed. 'I'll be in touch.'

With that the former fabric manager swept away, leaving Dot and Alice alone once more.

'Didn't realise you two were becoming such good pals,' Alice said, a hint of bitterness in her voice.

'She's not so bad.' Dot shrugged. 'Maybe I misjudged her.'

'And maybe you've misjudged Peter,' Alice said wryly, setting her cup down and checking her watch. 'Time for me to get back to the floor. What time is Mary coming?'

'I'll come with you,' Dot replied, draining her own cup and getting to her feet. 'Mary sent a telegram yesterday saying she would be back before the store closed. I think she's going to come back to the Elephant and get Emma from Doris.'

Alice gave Dot a sympathetic smile as they walked back through the labyrinth of corridors and back down the wooden staircase towards the shop floor.

'I hope it hasn't been too awful being at home with her family again,' Dot said.

'I hope she managed to make peace with her father before he passed away,' Alice replied.

'It sounds as though she did if she made it to the funeral.' Dot said, giving Henry a smile as he passed them on the stairs.

Alice shrugged her shoulders as they walked across the atrium. 'Funerals are funny things, though, aren't they? They bring up all sorts of emotions. I just hope that sister of hers didn't give her any trouble – or her mother.'

For the rest of the afternoon Dot found herself fervently hoping the same. As she countersigned orders, prepared invoices, dealt with customer queries and measured fabric, her mind was full of Mary and how she must be getting on. Over the last eleven days little Emma had helped keep Dot's mind occupied in Mary's absence. But she had been desperately worried about her friend and longed to see her to find out how she really was. Mary had been through a terrific ordeal over the past year and a half and although she had now found happiness with David, Dot fretted over how much more she could cope with.

Sure enough, as Dreary Deirdre the floorwalker completed the last of her evening checks, Dot heard the familiar sound of Mary's steps across the wooden floorboards and felt her heart bang against her chest in anticipation.

The glare from the overhead electric lighting gave Dot a good insight into her friend's health. There were large grey shadows under her eyes, and her skin looked wan and pale, but there was something else too, Dot thought as the girl walked towards her. Dot wasn't sure if it was in the way she carried herself, or if it was in her smile, yet as Dot embraced her, enjoying the comforting feel of Mary's arms around her, she knew that something had changed.

'How did you get on?' she asked, stepping back to examine Mary.

'Fine,' Mary replied, loosening the silk scarf she had tied around her neck. 'Or at least as fine as you can expect under the circumstances.'

Dot nodded as she saw Alice and Rose approaching them.

'Mary!' Alice exclaimed delightedly, half running as she neared the cash register to wrap her arms around her friend. 'Am I glad to see you! Are you all right?'

'It's wonderful to have you back,' Rose added warmly as she stood behind Alice waiting for her turn to hug Mary.

'And it's wonderful to see you too,' Mary replied, 'all of you in fact,' she added, turning to Dot. 'How has Emma been?'

At the mention of the little girl, Dot's face broke out into a wide smile. 'She's wonderful. She's been ever so good, though she's missed you, mind.'

Alice nodded in agreement. 'She has; she's been a treasure. Arthur adores her, of course.'

Mary laughed. 'She's already got him wrapped around her little finger then?'

'Just like her mother,' Rose teased, before asking more gently, 'So how are things with your family?'

Letting out a large sigh before she spoke, Mary looked at the girls. 'It was all right. It was awkward at first, of course. Mummy was dreadfully stiff with me and Clarissa my sister radiated not quite hatred but certainly a strong sense of dislike. But then Daddy was asking for me and so I went straight up to find him and, oh heavens, girls, I wasn't prepared.'

'How d'you mean?' Dot asked getting to the point.

'He didn't look like Daddy any more. He was so thin and grey, he barely looked human. I almost wanted to leave, I couldn't stand to see him like that and hear the noises he was making.'

'Was he crying out in pain?' Alice asked gently.

Mary shook her head. 'No, but his breathing was so laboured. I got the sense that he had been waiting for me, hoping he would see me before he passed ...'

Mary's words hung in the air and her eyes filled with tears at the memory. Dot's heart went out to her.

'What did you say, darlin'?'

'I walked over to his bedside, I held his hand and I told him how sorry I was, that I never meant to bring shame on the family.'

'You never did, Mary,' Alice pointed out. 'You were attacked by a man in a position of power what ought to have known better. None of what happened was your fault.'

Mary nodded. 'I know that, and so do my parents now. Daddy told me how sorry he was. Then he told me how he, Mummy and Clarissa had let me down and how he would go to his death feeling racked with guilt at what he had done and the way he had treated me. Oh, girls, it was awful the way he just kept saying how sorry he was.'

The thought of Mr Holmes-Fotherington lying on his death bed begging forgiveness was too much for Dot to bear and she found her own eyes became damp with emotion as she listened to Mary's story.

'I forgave him, of course,' Mary continued. 'I said how we had to put all of that in the past, that we had to concentrate on loving one another and being a family. That I understood why they had done what they had done and whilst it had been hurtful at the time it has made me the woman I am today. It was then Daddy told me how very proud of me he was, how much he loved me and how he knew that it was these very qualities of strength that would make me the very best mother in the world to Emma. Then he closed his eyes again, let out one final breath and died.'

'Oh, Mary,' Rose gasped, clutching her hands to her heart as Mary finished her story. 'You are a wonderful mother and I am so pleased you made up with your family before it was too late.'

'So am I, darlin',' Dot added, clamping a hand around Mary's. 'You've had a hell of a time.'

'It has been rather hellish.' Mary sighed. 'Clarissa went straight back to Ceylon but Mummy and I talked. It was why I stayed so long and took some holiday. I found that after the funeral things changed with Mummy. She's softened and she's ever so alone.'

'I can imagine she is,' Dot sympathised. 'It won't be easy for her now.'

'Quite,' Mary agreed, before she looked at the girls hesitantly. 'That's why she's moving to London. We're going to live together and make up for lost time.'

Chapter Thirteen

After Mary had dropped her bombshell, a deathly silence had passed around the department as nobody knew quite what to say.

'Your mother is going to live here?' Alice gasped, her mouth falling open so wide a lock of blonde hair fell from her chignon. 'In London?'

'Yes.' Mary nodded.

'But where will she stay?' Rose asked.

'Daddy left me the house in Mayfair and Mummy and I will move in there together.'

'So when are you moving out into this fancy palace then?' Dot asked brightly, determined not to spoil Mary's moment.

'Tuesday,' Mary replied. 'Mummy will be there on Monday and will get everything organised, then I can move in with her. David can come and stay with us when he comes back and I'm sure someone who's been bombed out of their home can make use of David's flat in the meantime.'

'And you're sure this is what you want?' Dot asked, a hint of doubt in her tone.

'It is,' Mary insisted. 'You're the one who told me I should reconcile with my family if I could and you were right, Dot. I don't know if this will last forever, or if Mummy and I will even get along, but she's all alone now. Clarissa has returned to Ceylon, and that old manor in Cheshire is far too big for Mummy to rattle around in alone. It's time, Dot.'

Dot had known Mary was right, much as she thought it was a terrible idea. But she had also known that sometimes people need to work things out for themselves.

And that's why, three days later, on a bright spring Tuesday evening, Dot was standing outside a very posh-looking house in the heart of Mayfair surrounded by boxes, with baby Emma in her arms.

'Is this really all yours?' she said, standing back to admire the white townhouse and elegant tree-lined street. 'It's like this road's done a deal with Hitler – it's untouched.'

Mary smiled as she fiddled in her attaché case for the keys. 'It's all mine and, yes, I know what you mean. Though of course we've made our own contribution to the war effort – you can see how the metal railings have all gone now.'

At the sight of the stumps that once housed the elegant black railings which Dot always privately thought looked like spears she hid a smile. Oh, how the rich'd had it bad the last four years.

'Come on, you can take that working-class chip off your shoulder,' Mary said brusquely as she unlocked the wide, heavy wooden door. 'We're all in this together.'

As Mary led Dot inside, Dot couldn't help thinking that was very far from true as she took in the rich green hallway, the thick pile carpet on the floor and the stuccoed ceiling.

'I should say we're all in this together,' she murmured into Emma's ear as she clung to the baby and expertly shucked off her coat before hanging it on the end of the bannister.

'Rose and Jean said they would be along soon to help with the boxes, though it looks as if Mummy's done most of the organising already,' Mary murmured, walking through the long hallway and out towards the kitchen at the back.

Dot walked into the room and gazed at the beautifully carved wooden cabinets, and the long pine table beside the French doors. Just beyond lay a small but beautifully manicured courtyard garden. Dot noted in the dusk how it didn't look as if the ground had been given over to the 'Dig for Victory' campaign.

'You going to do some planting then?' she asked, jerking her head towards the garden. 'Your Emma will love getting her hands grubby in the soil.'

'I hope so.' Mary nodded as the bell rang. 'That will be Rose and Jean.'

As she hurried out to answer it, Dot found herself clinging even tighter to a sleepy Emma, resting her head against the soft downy hair of Emma's head. Dot hated to admit it but she felt very uncomfortable here and longed to return to the safety of Bell Street. It also unnerved her how much Mary seemed at home, almost as if she had reverted to her roots in a heartbeat without thinking of all she had worked towards and achieved since she had arrived in London all that time ago.

But as Emma jerked noisily in her arms, she mentally kicked herself. Mary had just lost her father and was renewing her relationship with her mother. Of course she would be doing her best to fit in and make sure everything worked out. If Dot were any sort of friend she would be encouraging her rather than trying to find fault.

Just then the sounds of Rose and Jean walking along the hallway echoed into the room and Dot found their excited chatter soothing as they commented on everything from the art on the walls to the thick carpet underfoot.

'We're down here,' Dot called, settling Emma down into the white voile-covered cot that stood next to the window.

'Isn't it beautiful?' Jean called excitedly. 'I don't think I've ever been in a house like this.'

'I haven't myself.' Dot sighed, looking around her once more and feeling distinctly out of place.

'Come on, Dot, it's just a house,' Mary reasoned.

A thought suddenly struck Dot. 'What does your David think about all this? You have spoken to him?'

Mary regarded Dot carefully. 'He understands. I sent him a telegram from Chester and he replied straightaway. He knows this wasn't about me moving out of a home I was perfectly happy in, it was about my mother.'

Feeling suitably chastised, Dot turned her attentions to the garden and saw Mary's mother standing outside, looking up at the sky.

'What's she doing out there?' Jean asked. 'It's almost dark.'

Mary walked over to the little kettle that stood on the range, picked it up and filled it with water.

'I imagine she's looking up at Daddy. It's something she's been doing since he died.'

In that moment Dot's heart went out to Mary's mother. She remembered only too well how bereft she had felt when George died. Much as she disliked Mary's mother, she had to remember the woman was a widow now and no doubt enduring the darkest hours of her life. It wouldn't kill her to offer the woman some human kindness. Rapping lightly on the door, Dot waved to catch her attention.

A brief flicker of annoyance coursed across Mary's mother's face before she walked briskly inside.

'Hello, Mary dear,' she said coolly. 'I didn't realise you had visitors.'

Mary pressed a cup of tea into her hands and gave her mother a comforting smile. 'I told you, didn't I, that the girls were coming over to help me unpack?'

Mary's mother wrinkled her nose as if she had a bad smell under it as she took a sip of tea. 'I didn't know you meant these girls.'

At the use of the word 'these' Dot felt herself bristle but she refused to rise to the bait. Instead she stepped forward and held out her hand to Mary's mother. 'I'm sorry, I don't think we've got off on the right foot in the past. How about we start afresh?' she said pleasantly. 'I'm Dorothy Hanson, but most people call me Dot.'

Mary's mother ignored the hand that was offered. 'I am Geraldine Holmes-Fotherington. I am usually known as Geraldine, unless of course I'm addressing the help, when I am known as Mrs Holmes-Fotherington, and I suggest that's how you and your associates address me.'

'Mother!' Mary cried, her face wincing with distaste. 'Please don't talk to my friends like that.'

Dot glanced at Mary and saw to her surprise that her head was hung in deference and despite the request, she appeared fearful.

Mrs Holmes-Fotherington glared at Mary. 'My dear, now that you and I are reunited I trust you will be giving up your unfortunate position at Liberty's and stopping your association with women of this ilk.'

There was a pause then as Dot felt the blood boiling in her veins. She looked once more at Mary but unusually the girl remained silent.

'Women of this ilk? That right is it? And what precisely do you mean by *this ilk*?' Dot said, taking a step towards Geraldine.

'Dot,' Mary protested weakly. 'Let me handle this.'

But Dot had heard enough. She might not have much confidence in her abilities as department manager but gone were the days when she'd let people like this walk all over her. This high-and-mighty cow wasn't above feeling her wrath.

'No, Mary, darlin', I said when I came in here that I'd try with your mother but it's clear she hasn't the manners or sense she was born with. Your daughter', she continued, turning to face Mrs Holmes-Fotherington, 'was in pieces when we found her. You lot turned your backs; we were the ones that picked her up, fed her, gave her a home, love and a job. Whether you like it or not, she's not just our friend, she's family, and so, *Geraldine,* I suggest you get used to me, my associates and women of this *ilk,* because we've more kindness and compassion in our little fingers than you and the women of your ilk will ever know.'

With that Dot turned to Mary and gave her a sympathetic smile. 'I'm sorry, darlin', I said what needed to be said. I didn't want it to turn out like this but I won't be spoken to like that, not for you nor nobody.'

Mary said nothing. She looked awkwardly at her mother, who was steely-faced; then she turned back to Dot before whispering, 'I'm sorry.'

Dot leaned in and kissed her cheek. 'Nothing for you to be sorry for. I wish you well with this path you've chosen. I understand why you've chosen it and I think you've done the right thing, but with a mother like that I think you've got your work cut out.'

With that Dot swept out of the room, walked down the long corridor, grabbed her coat from the bannister and left the house, slamming the door shut behind her. Her days of being ashamed of who she was had passed a long time ago.

Chapter Fourteen

The following morning Dot found herself in the unusual position of sitting on the cold hard floor of the fabric stockroom between Brenda and Beatrice Claremont. Together they had been tasked with drawing up plans for the beauty and fabrics event they'd decided to call Beauty is Your Duty. Whilst Dot was keen to do all she could to improve the fortunes of the fabric department, at that moment she was feeling positively murderous, the altercation with Mary's mother having rattled her more than she cared to admit.

Whilst she was glad she had held her ground and told the stuck-up old bag where to go, there was part of her that deeply regretted the way things had turned out. For Mary's sake more than anyone else's she'd hoped that they could be civil to one another and perhaps even get along. The landscape had changed such a lot with the passing of Mary's father and yet it seemed that even the death of her husband hadn't softened Geraldine yet.

The last thing Dot wanted was to be responsible for any disagreement between Mary and Geraldine. While Dot might think the woman deserved a slap around the face with a wet kipper, if Mary wanted to reconcile with her own mother then Dot needed to support that. But there was something else that troubled her too. Around her mother, Mary seemed to regress to the shy young girl that had first arrived in London. Dot found the change in her friend troubling and as a result she had gone to bed with a heavy heart, tossing and turning until the small hours.

At four in the morning, she had finally admitted defeat and gone downstairs. In the kitchen she'd sat in the battered old wooden rocking chair she and George had bought when they first married and contemplated her lot in life.

Before long her eyes had strayed to Ivy's still unanswered letter, which now stood on the fireplace mantel next to George's old carriage clock. Instinctively she reached for it and pulled the well-worn notepaper from the even more worn envelope; she knew the time had come to reply. She had sat down many times over the past few weeks to scribble a response to Ivy, but each time she had tried she simply hadn't known what to say until now. What her old friend needed was love, understanding and support.

5th May 1943

Dear Ivy,

How lovely it was to hear from you after all this time. Things are still the same up here. Liberty's is thriving – well what passes for thriving anyway. I've been made up to fabric manager! I think they'd run out of people to ask, to be honest, but I'm enjoying it.

I was sorry to hear of Helen's troubles, and I'm even more sorry I haven't written to you before now. I don't think it will come as any surprise to you to know that I found it difficult to keep my temper under control when I read your letter. However, I know what you both need is something to take your mind off it all rather than me spouting forth.

That's why I've been thinking about coming to see you both. I'm owed a couple of days off and it would be wonderful to see you after so long. I wonder if the end of May would suit if it's not too short notice?

I'll look forward to hearing from you soon.

With love as always,
Dorothy

Reading back through her scrawl, Dot had smiled and shoved the letter in an envelope, writing the Devon address in a thick, clear hand. Popping a stamp in the top right-hand corner she'd felt a sense of peace wash over her. She was pleased she had made a decision finally and taken some small element of control back over her life. Returning to bed, Dot slept soundly until the alarm woke her but the same sense of peace remained. Or at least it had until she had arrived at work and had to listen to Beatrice prattling on to Brenda about how to run an event successfully. After an hour, Dot found she hadn't the patience to listen to any more.

'Right, well, I think we've done enough this morning,' she said, getting to her feet.

Beatrice looked surprised at the sudden halt to the proceedings and shot Dot a curious glance. 'We've hardly started,' she said, looking at her watch. 'It's only quarter past ten. We've got masses to go through yet.'

Brenda nodded in agreement. 'We've only settled on a date, Dot. We need to organise what we're going to do, where we're going to host it and the sort of artwork we need Peter to produce.'

At the mention of Peter's name Dot's mood darkened further. 'We've got a date, we're going to tell women how to make the best of the very little they've got and the even less they can buy, we're going to host it in the crypt and as for that Peter, I think it's best, Brenda, if you deal with him rather than me getting involved. Right then, I've got to sort out the rotas for next month. Excuse me.'

Without a backward glance Dot made her way back up to the shop floor where, to her surprise, she found Edwin behind the till, a guilty look on his face as he held on to a cup of tea with both hands.

'What are you doing?' she gasped as Edwin held out the tea.

'Peace offering.' He sighed. 'I feel as if I pushed you into that meeting with Beatrice before you were ready.'

Dot shrugged as she took the tea. 'Well, I can't say as it made my morning.'

'Alice told me about your run-in with Mary's mother,' he said in hushed tones. 'I'm sorry to hear it didn't go well.'

'Oh, it doesn't matter, darlin', water off a duck's back.' She shrugged. 'As long as Mary's happy, that's the main thing.'

'Well, it looks very much as if we're about to find out,' he said, nodding towards the figure making her way across the atrium floor towards the department.

At the sight of Mary, Dot's heart went out to the girl. She looked flat, as if the life had somehow been sucked out of her.

'Morning, Mary,' Edwin said, greeting her somewhat formally, Dot noticed.

'Morning Mr B.,' she replied before turning to Dot. 'Dot, I just want to say how sorry I am again about my mother. She should never ever have spoken to you like that.'

Dot gave her a sympathetic smile. 'It's not you that should apologise, darlin'. In fact I think it's down to me.'

'You?' Mary and Edwin echoed.

'Yes, me.' Dot sighed, setting her tea down on the desk. 'I shouldn't have risen to her like I did.'

'Dot, you did nothing of the sort,' Mary exclaimed. 'It was all down to her, and I've told her she has to apologise.'

'There's no need,' Dot said, waving away the idea.

Mary remained stony-faced. 'There is every need and I've asked her to say she's sorry.'

There was a pause then as Dot considered what Mary had said.

'Mary, darlin', she began softly. 'I'm touched, really I am, but this is a very difficult time for your mum.'

'It's a bally difficult time for me as well.'

Dot exchanged an awkward glance with Edwin and took a deep breath before she addressed Mary again. 'I know that, and you've been through a terrible ordeal. But, darlin', your mother's lost her husband. I know how devastating that is.'

'And I've lost my father,' Mary replied matter-of-factly.

'I know that too,' Dot soothed. 'But you have to look at this from your mother's point of view. She's lost her husband, her role in life, she's moved down to London when we're in the midst of war and I imagine the scenery isn't quite as comforting as the rolling hills of Cheshire. Then there's the fact that she's made up with her estranged daughter and she's doing her best to get to know her again as well as her granddaughter. All that whilst knowing at the back of her mind how shabbily she treated you. I bet she feels like a proper fish out of water.'

Mary sighed. 'Perhaps, but it all feels so different with her here now. I don't feel myself, I don't recognise or agree with anything she says. She's already talking to poor Emma about finishing school, for heaven's sakes! The child has only just turned one! It's as though she's living in a different age.'

'You need to be patient with her,' Dot said firmly. 'I imagine you both feel overwhelmed.'

Mary said nothing for a moment and then gave Dot a sheepish smile. 'Perhaps.'

Dot smiled at her. 'Just give it time, darlin'.'

'Oh Dot,' she whispered, tears pooling in her eyes. 'Whatever would I do without you?'

Dot smiled and slid the cup of tea Edwin had made her across the desk towards Mary. 'Lucky for you, you'll never have to find out. Now go and drink this down in the stockroom and get yourself together before you face the customers.'

Wordlessly Mary dried her eyes with the back of her hand and took the tea. As Dot watched her go downstairs she felt a tug of emotion. One of her own was struggling and she would do all she could to help her.

Suddenly aware of a sniffing sound beside her, Dot turned and was astonished to see Edwin dabbing at his eyes with a handkerchief.

'What on earth's got into you?' she gasped.

'I just think you're such a natural with people, Dorothy,' Edwin said, his voice catching in his throat. 'You always know the right thing to say and the right time to dispense that advice. It's a real skill.'

Dot smiled and leaned her head on Edwin's shoulder. 'You soft old so-and-so.'

'I mean it, Dorothy,' Edwin whispered into her hair. 'I'm so grateful I found you again, I'd have waited another thirty years if it meant we could be together again. I love you.'

For a moment Dot said nothing; then she lifted her head, turned to look up at Edwin and smiled. 'Then let's just be grateful for what we have got. It's all we can ever do.'

Chapter Fifteen

After work that Saturday, the last thing Dot felt like doing was going to a party. But she knew Jean and Bess had gone to a lot of trouble and she hated to disappoint anyone. The last few days had been so difficult, what with Mary's mother and the work around the new store event they were holding in a week's time.

Reaching the staffroom, she pulled on her navy jacket and matching hat and walked down the old stone staircase, nodding her goodbyes to her colleagues. She was all set to step out into the cool spring air when she felt a gentle hand on her shoulder.

Jumping right out of her skin, she whirled around to come face-to-face with a beaming Edwin. 'Christ alive! You didn't half scare me, Edwin Button. Whatever are you doing hiding around corners?'

Edwin chuckled at the sight of Dot clutching her chest. 'Sorry, my dear. Wanted to surprise you.'

'Well, you did that all right, and added a few years on to my life, not to mention a few grey hairs.'

Edwin squeezed her hand and pulled her towards him. 'I'm sorry, but I was hoping to catch you. I had a sneaking suspicion you might be looking to duck out of the party this evening.'

Guilt flashed across Dot's features. How well Edwin knew her. 'Well, I wouldn't say that exactly. More that I thought I would go home, freshen up and pop back up to town.'

Edwin raised an eyebrow. 'I think we all know how likely that is. In fact,' he said, offering her his arm and leading her down the stairs towards the crypt, 'Jean and Bess came to me earlier in the week and expressed concern about this very issue.'

'What issue?' Dot asked, feeling confused and by now very tired.

'That people wouldn't fancy traipsing across the city for a party.'

'Well, it's a long way after you've been on your dogs all day,' Dot agreed. 'I don't understand why they came to you though.'

Reaching the store's crypt, Edwin laid his hand on the brass handle of the door, turned to Dot and smiled. 'I think they were rather hoping that I could do this.'

He pushed open the door with such force that Dot thought she might fall straight through it. She stepped inside the crypt and gasped in delight. Gone was the staid brown-and-white-tiled tea room that hosted refreshments for those on fire-watch duty. In its place stood a decadently decked out replica dance hall straight out of the roaring twenties.

Everywhere Dot looked, she could see red and green fabric artfully woven around the pillars and up into the ceiling vaults. Candles stood all over, giving the room a rich golden hue, while the slightly battered wooden tables had been transformed with stylish white tablecloths, complete with wine and what Dot thought looked like very fancy goblets. At the other end of the room stood a gramophone player and a small square had been formed in the centre of the room to create an informal dance floor.

The party already appeared to be in full swing, with guests from across the different Liberty's departments in full attendance. There were a couple of girls Dot recognised from the munitions factory Bess worked for as well and Dot felt pleased that Bess and Jean had seen fit to extend the Liberty's welcome far and wide.

It didn't take long to spot the girls. At the end of the room stood Bess and Jean, looking elegant in green and teal evening dresses that Dot was sure had been borrowed from kindly Betty Crawford in the ready-to-wear department.

'What is all this?' she asked, turning to Edwin.

'We thought we would bring the party to Liberty's as Bess and Jean wanted to thank everyone who works here for being so supportive.'

Dot walked inside and gazed around in awe. 'Who got it all ready?'

'Bess came down earlier,' Edwin explained. 'And Rose and I helped.'

'You soppy old so-and-so.' Dot smiled, standing on her tiptoes to give Edwin a kiss on the cheek. 'You are a soft touch, aren't you?'

'I am not!' Edwin exclaimed, a twinkle in his eyes. 'I just thought it would be nice for the girls to have their party here.'

At that moment, the girls arrived at Dot's side.

'What do you think?' Jean asked, excitement shining in her eyes.

'I think I feel very underdressed.' Dot chuckled, casting her eyes over Jean's teal off-the-shoulder floor-length silk gown.

'Nonsense,' Bess admonished, looking lovely in her rich green silk with high neck and cap sleeves. 'You look perfect.'

Dot gazed down at the red and blue tea dress she had donned that morning. It was at the very least a dress, and she knew her purse contained the last of her Victory Red lipstick she had been eking out for months.

'Well, I don't know about that, but I do know you've done a lovely job here. Are we the first from fabrics to arrive?'

Bess shook her head. 'No, everyone's examining the records we've got.'

'And bickering over what to play next,' Jean grumbled. 'Alice wants Max Monroe; Mary wants some jazz band we've never heard of.'

'Leave 'em to me,' Dot said with a roll of her eyes. 'You can't have that pair running your do, not after you've worked so hard and everything looks so beautiful.'

With that Dot walked around the corner to find the two girls arguing just as Jean had said, heads bent low, while Rose looked across at them. Dot found herself shaking her head in despair.

'For heaven's sakes, you're like a pair of kids,' Dot said, elbowing her way between the two of them and picking up a record by Betty Driver. 'Here,' she said, handing it to Alice. 'That's settled. We'll have that.'

The girls looked at the record and nodded their heads.

'Good choice, Dot,' Mary exclaimed.

'I'm known for my bright ideas and common sense.'

'That's not what I'd heard.'

Dot recognised the voice as belonging to Mary's mother. At the sound, her heart sank but the last thing she would do was give Geraldine the satisfaction of knowing she was rattled.

'Gerry,' she said heartily, plastering a smile on her face and simultaneously catching the warning signal Mary was giving her mother with her eyes. 'How lovely to see you here. Though I must admit I didn't think this sort of occasion would be quite your thing.'

'Dorothy, dear, a pleasure,' Mary's mother replied, her voice dripping with sarcasm. 'Yes, I admit I didn't think this would be quite my cup of tea at all but so far it has been quite pleasant. Though in the last few moments the most unpleasant smell has reached my nostrils.'

Dot bit back the urge to slap the smile off Mrs Holmes-Fotherington's face and instead continued to smile sweetly. 'I think you'll find that's 'cos you're standing within a hair's breadth of the lavvies, darlin'.'

'Well, really,' Geraldine gasped, 'I have never heard anything quite so disgusting. Mary, come with me.'

'Can you give me a minute, Mother?' Mary asked in a small voice. 'I need to talk to Dot.'

Recognising she wasn't about to be invited to join the conversation, Geraldine huffed her way across the room, leaving Dot with her girls.

'You old bugger, Dorothy Hanson.' Alice chuckled. She was dressed in a simple utility raspberry tunic dress and looked stunning, her blonde hair taking on even more of a golden glow in the candlelight. 'You shouldn't have teased her like that.'

'She got off lightly,' Dot growled. 'Anyway, I didn't start anything.'

'No, you didn't,' Mary sighed.

'How is everything going with her now?' Rose asked gently.

'It's fine,' Mary said, grinning with a smile that didn't reach her eyes, which reflected the glorious emerald green of the tea dress she was wearing. 'It's lovely to have a mother again.'

''Course it is,' Alice said, nodding her head a little too vigorously.

'It's a lovely opportunity for you both,' Rose added.

'It is,' Mary agreed. 'She's doing so many wonderful things. She loves being a grandmother and has even hired a nanny to help out with Emma.'

Alice looked at Mary aghast. 'Why?'

'She thinks it's better if Emma has more hands-on care,' Mary said quickly as she took a sip of her gin and tonic. 'I must say I agree with her and perhaps it is inappropriate for Doris to look after her. I mean, Mummy's right, she doesn't have any particular childcare skills.'

'Skills? That woman's been looking after kids up and down the road all her life. Hundreds of 'em,' Dot gasped.

'I know.' Mary nodded. 'I think Doris has been wonderful. But it's about what's best for Emma.'

Alice opened her mouth, but Dot laid a warning hand on her forearm. 'Of course it is, Mary, darlin'. Whatever you think is best will be the right thing to do, as long as you and your mother are getting on all right.'

Mary shot her a grateful smile while Alice's jaw dropped open in surprise as she gaped from Dot to Mary.

'Oh, we are,' Mary said happily. 'I never thought this day would come, when I would have my mother back in my life, and she seems to want to settle down here. Look at the way she's laughing with Mr B. over there.'

At that all heads swivelled towards Edwin. Dot, to her amazement, saw that he was engrossed in a conversation with Mary's mother, who appeared to be eating out of the palm of his hand.

'Well I never,' Alice marvelled.

'He's always had a charm about him.' Dot grinned. 'Even when we were nippers. Always knew the right thing to say.'

'What was he like when you were young? Rose pressed suddenly.'

Alice gave her a gentle nudge. 'Yes. You've never told us much about what you two were like when you were younger.'

Dot shrugged. 'What's to tell? We were kids.'

'Yes, but you were obviously sweet on each other. How long were you courting for?' Rose asked.

'About a year.' Dot smiled. 'Everyone loved him. Even my old man, and he didn't like anyone. I remember how Edwin came for his tea for the first time. He knew my father was into fly fishing so he brought him a fishing rod, of all things, for him to use up the River Lea. Mum wasn't forgotten neither – she got a fresh pair of leather gloves. Gawd knows where he got the money from, I've never asked, and I have a feeling they were knock-offs from down the Lane, but of course Mum didn't care.'

'He had it all worked out, didn't he?' Mary marvelled. 'A real charmer.'

Rose smiled. 'And now he's charming your mother, Mary.'

'Perhaps we ought to rescue him.' Mary sighed. 'She'll monopolise him if he's not careful.'

Dot agreed. 'Come on then. Let's get a drink on the way, me throat feels as dry as the Sahara.'

With that the girls helped themselves to drinks from the table and then made their way towards Edwin. Only, as they did so, Dot found herself knocking back hers in one. Despite all her assurances that Mary was doing the right thing, Dot could see what was happening. Mary was returning to her old self – becoming more timid and eager to please others. Dot could see why Mary was behaving the way she was – she wanted to make things right with her mother – but for Mary's sake Dot found herself hoping that her friend wouldn't stray too far from the confident and gung-ho young woman she knew and loved. She herself knew what it was like to lose a sense of yourself and how miserable it could make you feel.

Chapter Sixteen

As the party got into its stride, Dot's anxiety started to ease. However, as she looked at her half-empty third glass of port, she realised that it could have something to do with the alcohol she had been enjoying.

Glancing around the room at all her friends she felt a sense of gratitude. Her family life had never been easy, and getting older it had only become harder. Her relationship with her sister Olive was very up and down, and she had never quite seen eye to eye with her parents. Dot had always found them a little inward-looking, happy to settle for their lot in life, whereas she had always wanted to reach for the stars. As a child she had dreamed of a life away from London in the country-side where she would run a bakery and take care of her husband and large brood of children. Sadly life hadn't worked out like that, especially after George had been killed. Yet over the years Dot had found that friends had become her family which was why they all meant so much to her.

At that moment Dot felt a smooth warm hand reach for hers. She knew instinctively from the size and feel of his fingers to the callus on his palm just who it was. As Edwin wrapped his hand around hers, she felt grounded, calmer somehow. What mattered was this night, and Jean and Bess celebrating their love for one another and the friends that had brought them here.

Watching Bess stand on one of the larger tables and then extend her one remaining hand out to Jean to help her up, Dot felt a flash of affection for the pair. Love took many forms, that was something she had discovered over the years, and being in the presence of these two at this moment in their lives was a privilege.

'Good evening, ladies and gentleman,' Bess began, a broad smile on her face. 'We want to say a very big thank you to you all for coming this evening.'

'A *very* big thank you,' Jean interrupted.

'We know that we owe you all a debt of gratitude for everything that you have done for us, for the love and support you have shown and continue to show us. That is the purpose of this evening,' Bess continued.

As Bess paused Jean flashed a hesitant smile before she turned to address the small crowd.

'We know our way of life isn't easy for many of you to understand. And yet you have shown us nothing but kindness and acceptance, and for that we couldn't be more proud or more grateful,' Jean said.

'And so, without any more interruption from us, please enjoy the party, and eat, drink and be merry,' Bess finished, a triumphant grin on her face as she held Jean's hand and raised it aloft.

With that everyone in the room erupted into a round of applause. Everyone, Dot noted, apart from Geraldine, who was gaping in wide-eyed astonishment while Mary whispered something in her ear. As Mary finished, she watched Geraldine let out a gasp, her cheeks pink with anger, and then heard her mutter something about disgusting behaviour.

Dot raised her eyebrows at Edwin and he gave a helpless shrug.

'I thought it was strange that she wanted to come,' Dot remarked, sipping her port.

'I must admit it felt like a gamble on Mary's part,' Edwin admitted. 'Although I imagine she wants her mother to feel included.'

'I imagine she does. Especially as the woman expects her daughter to leave her job at Liberty's. I think this is Mary's way of getting her mother to understand just how much this place means to her.'

At Dot's words, Edwin's mouth gaped open in astonishment. 'Mary's leaving Liberty's?'

Dot rolled her eyes. 'That's not what I said. I said that Mary's mother *wants* her to leave. She doesn't think it appropriate that her daughter works in a shop.'

Edwin bristled. 'We are not just a shop.'

'I know that and so does Mary.' Dot sighed. 'This will blow over.'

Edwin was just about to open his mouth and say something else when Bess tapped him on the shoulder.

'Mr Button, sir,' she began. 'I wondered if now might be a good time for you to play your fiddle?'

'Ooh goodness me, is it that time already?' he gasped, checking the oversized silver wristwatch Dot knew had been handed down to him by his father.

'Time for what?' Dot frowned.

He beamed. 'Time for me to give the girls a song and dance.' Leaning down to kiss her cheek, he disappeared into the crowd.

Within minutes Edwin had struck up a merry ditty on his violin and Dot couldn't help smiling. He had always loved music, and when they were young he had already been a gifted violinist. Now, though, it was clear to see that he had really honed his craft and had the ability to stir deep feelings when he played his violin. Looking around the crowd, Dot could see she wasn't alone in her appreciation and the crowd whooped and cheered as he played the old-fashioned melodies.

Suddenly, she felt an arm link through hers. Turning around, she saw Alice with a ready smile on her face.

'Thought you might like a dance,' she said before tugging Dot on to the makeshift dance floor.

All too soon, Dot found herself swept up in a fizzing, energetic hoedown that left her breathless.

Glancing at Edwin, she wondered if he was feeling the strain as much as she was, but, rather than looking tired, he looked thoroughly immersed in the music. His fevered brow and glassy eyes lost in the energetic folk tune.

'Easy, Alice, darlin',' she panted. 'I'm not as young as I was.'

'Give over.' Alice chuckled as she skipped her way around the matriarch. 'You're fitter than the rest of us put together.'

'I dunno about that,' Dot shouted over the frenzy of Edwin's ditty. 'He'd better play a slow one next or the only dance he'll be doing is that of the merry widow.'

As if reading her mind, Edwin didn't just move on to a slower dance, he stopped altogether and looked at the crowd.

With silence as the only accompaniment Edwin put down his violin and stepped on to the table from which Bess and Jean had made their speech.

'Whatever is he doing?' Alice asked, her eyes narrowing in confusion at the unexpected interruption.

'Giving us a bloody breather, I hope,' Dot panted, clinging on to Alice for support with one hand and using her other to take a sip of port and quench her thirst.

'Ladies and gentlemen, do forgive the interruption,' Edwin began. 'I won't keep you long and all being well I shall get you back up on your feet within moments. But whilst I have you here I would very much like to echo Bess and Jean's sentiments and say that I have come to think of all of you wonderful Liberty colleagues as family. And of course, as all of you know, it's in this glorious store where we are all so privileged to work that I was reunited with my first love, my childhood sweetheart, my Dorothy.'

As his eyes found hers in the crowd, he gestured to her and smiled. At that everyone turned to stare and clapped and cheered, and Dot found her cheeks now flushed not with exertion but embarrassment at being the centre of attention.

'And that's why,' he continued as the applause died away, 'I rather felt this special night amongst you all, where we are gathered to celebrate love, was the perfect time to ask Dorothy something I first wanted to ask her when we were young and I have wanted to ask her ever since we rekindled our love.'

There was a pause as Edwin looked hesitant. Then, with love shining in his eyes, he addressed Dot directly.

'My love, my Dorothy, in front of all our friends and loved ones, may I ask you this question: would you do me the very great honour of becoming my wife?'

There was a collective gasp amongst the crowd and Dot's jaw fell open in shock. Looking at him now, down on one knee with what looked like his grandmother's old diamond ring resting on his palm as he waited for her answer, she felt as if she couldn't breathe. Although they had often talked about marriage, she had never truly believed, deep in her heart, that he would actually ask her. But here he was, more than thirty years after their first meeting, asking her the question she had always hoped he would ask.

Could the happiness she had waited so long to find finally be within her grasp? Looking into Edwin's eyes the years seemed to melt away and she felt as if she were that youngster once again.

'Yes, my darlin', oh yes please.'

Chapter Seventeen

The moment the words were out of her mouth, everyone whooped and cheered and Edwin got to his feet and rushed through the crowd towards her. Slipping on the ring, which fitted perfectly on ther finger, he scooped her up in his arms and whirled her around just as he used to when they were young with the world at their feet.

'Oh, Dotty, you won't regret this, I promise. I'll make you the happiest woman on earth,' he cried.

'I know you will,' she replied, her voice thick with emotion. 'And I will spend the rest of my life loving you as you deserve to be loved. My boy, my Edwin. We've found each other again.'

As Edwin set her down on the ground and kissed her, the familiar touch of his lips against hers felt more intense somehow. It was as if she had finally found her home. But as they broke apart, the sound of a woman shouting caught their attention.

Whirling around, Dot was surprised to see Geraldine with a face like thunder, furiously dabbing at her dress with a handkerchief, trying to mop up something that had spilled all over her. Beside her was a distraught-looking Brenda, who was bending down and trying her best to help. But judging from the look of anger Geraldine was directing at Brenda, Dot imagined that fabrics' latest recruit was the guilty party.

'How many times, just leave it, girl!' Geraldine hissed.

'I'm sorry, madam, I'm really sorry,' Brenda said, stumbling over her words.

Unsure what was going on, Dot was about to go over and find out when she saw Geraldine push Brenda roughly out of the way.

'You've made more than enough of a mess as it is,' she snapped.

With that, Geraldine raised her hand, and Brenda squealed.

'I'm sorry. Please don't hit me.'

Brenda fled from the room and clattered up the stairs.

Wide-eyed with shock, Dot turned to Edwin and he simply nodded. There was no need to say anything. Dot turned and ran past Geraldine and out of the room; she was determined to find Brenda. Something was wrong, and no matter how it distracted from her own happiness, if one of her Liberty family was in trouble, Dot was determined to find why.

It didn't take long to find Brenda. There were only so many places in Liberty's to flee and have a good cry. Brenda would no doubt have preferred to go out into the street and find her way home, but Dot also knew that Brenda had her pride and would no doubt try to compose herself before going anywhere.

With that in mind, Dot made her way to the ladies' bathrooms and, finding the cubicle at the end locked, knocked gingerly on the door.

'Brenda, darlin', it's me, Dot. Are you all right?'

No answer. Just the sound of muffled sobs.

'Brenda, darlin', please talk to me,' Dot tried again. 'I want to help. I saw what happened with that old cow outside. You mustn't let her get to you.'

The sounds of sobbing subsided. 'It's not her,' came a strangled voice. 'It was me. I got upset, carried away in the moment. I don't know what people must think of me. I made such a fool of myself.'

'You haven't made a fool of yourself at all,' Dot said kindly. 'We're just worried. Now please, open the door and come out and talk to me. I ain't cut out for shouting through doors, contrary to popular belief.'

There was a pause then, but within a few seconds Dot could hear the sound of the latch being pulled back and the door opened. Then Dot was face-to-face with Brenda, and she pulled her straight into her arms.

As she felt Brenda's weight against her chest, Dot found herself soothing the girl, rubbing her back and stroking her hair as the tears continued to fall.

Eventually, once they had subsided, Dot led Brenda to the pair of red brocade chairs that stood next to the wash-basins in the corner of the room and encouraged the girl to talk.

'Mrs Holmes-Fotherington reminded me of the lady of the house where I used to work, the Countess of Guildford,' Brenda began.

Dot frowned. 'Your old employer. Why?'

With a sigh Brenda rubbed her face. 'She was posh like her, full of silly ideas, but at least she was always kind to me. It was down to her I was made up to lady's maid and was allowed to dress the two daughters. My ma had worked for the family years before I was born and when she died I think the countess wanted to do right by me.'

'Well, that doesn't sound like Mary's mother at all,' Dot teased, before sensing now was not the time for jokes. 'What happened, darlin'?'

'She sort of changed overnight. It happened when one of her daughters ran off with a farmer's boy and married him. The countess said it was my fault! That I had been filling Lady Anna's head with ideas, but I knew different.

Those two had been in love with each other since they were babies, the whole village knew it, but the countess wouldn't accept it. She said that the girls had changed since I had become their lady's maid and she would make me pay.'

'How?' Dot asked gently.

'Just little things at first.' Brenda sniffed. 'She would make me work extra hours, ask me to prepare things that never needed preparing then find fault with whatever I'd done. At first she'd just tell me off in front of the butler and all the servants. Then she started hitting me.'

'Hitting you?' Dot echoed, aghast. 'Surely not.'

Brenda nodded, a fresh tear rolling down her face. 'It was just a slap on the hand at first, when I went to take the tea tray before she had finished with it. It was as though she hated me for not standing up to her, speaking my mind. But I couldn't. Mother had always told me to respect my elders and employers so I said nothing, hoping it was just a one-off.'

'But it wasn't?' Dot asked in confirmation.

'It wasn't.' Brenda shook her head sadly. 'She saw it as an opportunity to take out all her frustrations on me. From that moment on she hit me every chance she got. Little slaps around the back of the legs or the arm, but then it became worse.'

Dot's eyes widened and she felt a sickening sense of dread rise within her as she took in the enormity of what Brenda was saying.

'How much worse?' Dot demanded.

Brenda looked away from Dot and down at her lap before her gaze rose back up to meet the matriarch's. Slowly, her eyes never leaving Dot's, she pushed up the sleeve that hung over her wrist and showed Dot a large mark on the underside of her forearm. Dot's hands flew to her mouth.

The raised triangular-shaped scar clearly showed the girl had been struck with an iron, and the coward behind the act had clearly left it there for some time too.

'Did the countess do this as well?'

Brenda nodded.

'Oh, darlin', that's awful,' Dot gasped. She thought the rich knew how to behave, but clearly not. 'Is that why you left?'

'Yes. Mr Carrington, the butler, was appalled. He knew I had to get out of the house as quickly as possible and so he said a friend of a friend was on the board at Liberty's and if I wanted he could find me a job at the store straightaway. I hadn't ever worked in a shop before but I didn't have many options. Mr Carrington arranged the job and lodgings for me and I left that day without looking back.'

'Have you heard from the family since?'

'No,' Brenda whispered. 'But I dream about the countess every night. I'm so frightened of her, Dot. I know it's silly, she doesn't know where I am, but she terrified me so much. I think Mary's mother took me right back to that time with the family. When I spilled that drink all over her she went mad, and when I tried to make amends and she raised her hand to me it was like I was back in that house and about to get beaten again.'

At that Brenda collapsed into a fresh round of tears and Dot pulled the girl towards her again, and held her tight.

'It's all right, darlin', you're safe,' she murmured soothingly into the girl's ear as if she were no more than a baby. 'I'll make sure nobody ever hurts you again. You can rely on me.'

Chapter Eighteen

Over the next few days Dot found that instead of allowing herself to become swept up in wedding plans she was in fact preoccupied with keeping an eye on Brenda. The truth of why the girl had been forced to look for employment had left the matriarch reeling. Over the years, Dot thought she had seen the very best and the very worst of human behaviour, but hearing how a countess had inflicted violence on such a young girl had upset her.

It had taken bravery for Brenda to tell her story, Dot understood that. She also respected the girl enough not to break her confidence. This was Brenda's tale and one Dot hoped the youngster would share when she felt comfortable enough with everyone else. In the meantime Dot was worried. Brenda reminded her of herself when she was a girl. Dot might have only got a few whacks around the back of the legs from her mum and dad when she was younger but they had left deep scars and Dot didn't want Brenda to suffer a lifetime of emotional torment as she had.

Looking at Brenda now, in the store, smiling intently as Alice showed her how to cut a pattern for a customer with no waste, Dot felt a flash of affection. She knew the girl could soar if she wanted to. She was bright, capable, and stronger than she realised if she could move miles away from Guildford and start again in a new city. That's why

Dot wanted Brenda to take centre stage at the Beauty is Your Duty event later that day. She thought she would get her handing out the refreshments, and then ask her to do a little introductory talk, as Rose usually did before one of her first-aid nights. She hadn't actually asked the girl yet, thinking it would no doubt send her into a blind panic, but Dot was sure it would be the making of her.

'What are you plotting?' Edwin asked, interrupting her stream of thought.

Turning around to see her intended by her side, Dot smiled affectionately. 'Our wedding.'

Edwin raised an eyebrow. 'You looked like you were worrying over something, Dorothy. And you've looked that way ever since Jean and Bess's party.'

'How well you know me,' Dot said. 'I'm sorry, my darlin', lot on my mind.'

'Like your latest charge, you mean? You're known for taking in any waif or stray,' Edwin continued as if reading her mind. 'Brenda I'm sure falls into that category, and you were with her for heaven knows how long in the ladies' toilets after she fled from Mary's mother.'

A flash of affection passed through Dot. How lucky she was to find this man again, who was so perceptive. 'Let's just say I'm keeping an eye on her. She's fragile; I want to see her do well here.'

'She will with you to guide her.' Edwin smiled. 'Don't let her take up all your time though, Dorothy. You and I deserve our happiness too.'

Dot patted his hand. They hadn't waited all these years for her to let the wedding she had always dreamed of fall by the wayside. 'You know you're top of my priorities, Edwin Button. Our wedding will be everything we've ever wanted.'

A wave of relief swept across Edwin's features. 'That's all I needed to hear you say, Dotty. I'm sorry I doubted you even for a second.'

'How much I love you is something you'll never have to doubt,' Dot whispered, 'but I do feel I have to look after the younger members of staff.'

Edwin squeezed her hand. 'I know that. You've always been so giving, Dotty; it's just one of the many things I love about you.'

Dot was just about to reply when Brenda bounded up alongside Alice, having said goodbye to the customer.

'That went very well,' Alice said warmly. 'You're getting ever so much better at cutting fabric.'

Brenda blushed. 'Thank you, but I find I still get ever so much waste.'

'Not any more you won't.' Dot beamed. 'Alice is a good teacher. She'll take care of you when I'm away at the end of the month.'

'Of course, you're going to Torquay, aren't you? I'd forgotten that,' Alice said.

Dot nodded, a warm feeling seeping through her body at the thought of spending a few days with Ivy and Helen. 'Yes. I haven't seen Ivy and Helen for about ten years now.'

Alice raised an eyebrow. 'Well, it's about time. What took you so long?'

Dot shrugged, feeling uncomfortable at the question. 'You know, life gets in the way. Particularly with a war on.'

'Which is all the more reason you and I ought to set a date, Dorothy,' Edwin put in.

Alice clapped her hands in delight and Brenda beamed at the happy couple.

'Yes, come on, you two. I would have thought you would have already booked the church,' Alice said with a grin.

Dot shot a shy look at Edwin before she addressed the girls. 'We want to but I just don't know when. There's so much to organise.'

Edwin waved away her concerns. 'Stuff and nonsense. I'd marry you tomorrow in my old suit with a plate of anchovy sandwiches. I just want you, Dotty. Always have, always will.'

'There you are then, Dot,' Alice said. 'I mean, it's not like you're getting any younger, and as you just pointed out, there is a war on so why not get on with it?'

Dot shook her head at the girl. 'Thank you, mouth almighty. We can always rely on you for your discretion, can't we?' Turning to Edwin, she smiled and linked her hand through his arm. 'I suppose I just want to enjoy our engagement a bit. It's not every day I get asked to be someone's wife. I want to take my time with that part, enjoy the planning.'

At that Edwin beamed, and squeezed Dot's hand. 'Whatever you want, my love.'

'Anyway,' Dot said, changing the subject and turning to Brenda. 'Perhaps we ought to get set up. We're due to start the Beauty is Your Duty event in ten minutes.'

'We're all ready.' Brenda smiled. 'We're just waiting for Peter.'

At the mention of the conchie, Dot's face coloured. 'Whatever is he coming for?'

'He's just got some leaflets for us with discount coupons attached.' Edwin pointed out. 'I don't know why you're being so hard on him.'

'And I don't know why you lot insist on sticking up for a man who doesn't serve his country as he should,' Dot countered. 'I'm surprised at you, Edwin. You're an army man; you fought in the last war.'

'Yes, and it was fighting in that war that made me see how awful it can be. I may not agree with conchies, as you call them, but I can certainly see why they disagree with combat.'

Dot looked at him in astonishment. 'But you love your country. What's changed?'

'Nothing has changed.' Edwin sighed. 'I just got older, saw more of the world. Peter is a perfectly decent sort of chap.'

Dot bristled. She knew she was being uncharacteristically unreasonable but there was something about Peter she just didn't like. Duty was duty; you did what you had to do whether you wanted to or not. This man wasn't doing his duty and it didn't sit right with Dot at all.

'If you say so.'

'I do say so,' Edwin insisted. 'Now, Henry will be along presently to take over the department so let's head downstairs. This event could be the thing that starts turning the fortunes of fabrics around.'

Minutes later Dot found herself amongst a throng of women in the crypt eager to hear how they could make the most of the make-up they owned, along with their clothes and accessories. As she weaved her way through the group she wasn't surprised to hear so many saying how they were fed up of using beetroot to stain their lips and gravy browning to replicate stockings on their legs.

'I swear if I'm told to draw another line up my legs with an eyebrow pencil I'll go raving mad,' one woman fumed.

Dot couldn't help smiling; she too had heard it all before and could only hope Beatrice had something new to offer. The idea, after all, was to encourage the women to use all departments in Liberty's and the hope was that by talking about beauty, clothes and accessories, the women would realise the beautiful fabrics Liberty's had to offer could give them as much of a boost as a new lipstick.

Reaching Brenda, she was about to greet her when she saw Peter threading his way through the crowd. 'Haven't you got work to do?' she said as he joined them.

'I'm just delivering these promotional leaflets and I'm also in London on army business,' Peter replied, his eyes never leaving Dot's. 'As I was here I thought the least I could do would be to wish Brenda well for the event.'

At the mention of her name Brenda flushed red and offered Peter a shy smile. 'You didn't need to do that.'

'I wanted to,' Peter said, his tone gentle now.

Dot felt a flash of fury as she witnessed the exchange. She could see that Peter was interested in Brenda and clearly the young girl felt the same way. But Brenda needed guidance; she was too young to see that Peter wasn't right for her.

'Well, as kind as that is I don't want you to put Brenda off her work, Peter, particularly as I would like her to give the talk about fabrics,' Dot said, looking at Brenda encouragingly.

Brenda looked at her, fear in her eyes. 'I can't do that. I don't know enough.'

'Nonsense,' Dot insisted. 'You can just welcome people to the event. Then I can talk about anything you're not sure about, such as how to use muslin around butter to make knickers.'

Brenda looked down at the floor, her bottom lip trembling. 'I'm sorry, Dot, I don't think I can.'

'Well, I do,' Dot said, her tone firm now. 'Come on, Brenda, darlin', it'll be the making of you.'

Peter furrowed his brow. 'Now look, Mrs Hanson, I don't want to get in the way of anything but if Brenda says she doesn't feel as if she can do it, then I don't think she should.'

At the interruption Dot felt a flash of irritation. 'What business is it of yours how I run my department? Now, I've given Brenda an order and I expect her to follow it.'

'And she's already told you she's not comfortable,' Peter said, drawing himself up to his full height.

About to open her mouth and let rip, Dot was short-changed from unleashing the full extent of her fury by Beatrice, who had taken centre stage on the makeshift podium at the front of the crypt.

'Hello, ladies,' the former fabric manager said with a smile. 'Let me welcome you all here today. I know this is a beauty event but really it's about how to make the best of every aspect of ourselves. I'll be covering beauty, and Mrs Hanson from the fabric department and Mrs Johnson from jewellery will also be on hand to tell you how to make the best out of very little. Without further ado, allow me to welcome Mrs Hanson to the floor.'

As the applause rang out, Dot turned to Brenda and gave her a nod of encouragement.

'Go on, just say a few words,' she coaxed.

But Brenda stood mute, and then to her dismay Dot saw Peter reach for her hand in solidarity.

'She said no,' he said firmly.

Fury passed through her bones but Dot knew there was nothing she could do as she addressed Peter. 'You and I will be having words.'

As she took her place beside Beatrice, Dot beamed at the crowds but the last thing she was doing inside was smiling. Instead she found herself looking at Brenda and Peter, silently praying that Cupid didn't strike the pair with his arrows.

Chapter Nineteen

The late spring sunshine streamed through the windows of the fabric department and Dot found herself peering through them admiring her handiwork. In the fortnight since the Beauty is Your Duty event footfall had increased in fabrics, resulting in an increase in sales and mucky handprints all over her glass and wooden banisters. Now, however, the glass was sparkling and Dot knew her hard work had been worth it.

'You finished?' Alice enquired as she gathered the last of her belongings. 'Or are you going out the front to whiten the step as well?'

Dot flicked Alice with her wet cloth. 'Cheek! I'm just making sure everything's in order before I catch the train.'

'It's only a weekend, Dot,' Alice teased. 'I'm sure we'll manage.'

'Of course we will,' Mary added. 'Alice is a wonderful deputy.'

'I'm sure you will 'n' all, but I like to leave my house in order.' Dot sighed, untying the pinny she had worn around her middle to protect her clothes from the dirty water. 'Besides, now you've given in your notice, Mary, there will be more for us to do so it's as well to get ahead now while you're still here.'

At the mention of her impending departure from the store Mary's cheeks flushed with colour. 'I'm sorry. I just think it's better I'm at home with Emma.'

'And that's the right way to think,' Alice agreed. 'We'll just miss you, that's all.'

'We will all miss you,' Rose said insistently as she handed Dot some files from upstairs. 'But we'll still see you.'

''Course we will.' Dot flushed, feeling guilty. When Mary had handed in her notice Dot hadn't taken it very well and had gone out of her way to let Mary know how she felt. Despite Mary being open about the fact that her mother wanted her to leave the store, Dot hadn't thought that she would ever do it – after all, Mary adored fabrics and Liberty's itself. But then last week Mary had handed over a letter with Dot's name inscribed in her neat hand and Dot knew there was only one thing it could be. Sadness had coursed through her, but there was no point in trying to get Mary to change her mind. And so Dot had merely accepted the note and promised the girl a good send-off.

'It's just a good time for me to get to know Mother again, and as she has reinstated my trust fund, well, it means that I don't need to work any longer,' Mary added.

'Which is the way it should be,' Dot said, without a trace of irony. 'Now, you know Mrs Pennington will be in to collect her order tomorrow and Lady Weir will be in as well to talk about some new utility prints. She wants to put her name down for the first lot of new designs.'

Alice frowned. 'But we don't do that.'

'We do now.' Dot shrugged as she reached for the tightly packed suitcase she had stored behind the cash desk. 'It's been that way ever since that Beauty is Your Duty event. It was popular and Edwin wants to make sure we capitalise on that by keeping our regular customers happy.'

'So all outside attempts to destroy our reputation have failed,' Mary remarked with a smile.

'Seems so,' Dot confirmed. 'Our customers are happy, and they keep coming back.'

'And the department's figures are up,' Rose said, stifling a yawn. 'Oh sorry, girls, I've been ever so tired lately.'

Dot glanced at Rose's growing belly and smiled. 'I'm not surprised; you're five months pregnant, you'll be exhausted.'

'Oh, I remember only too well how tired I was at that stage.' Alice beamed with fondness as she leaned forward to stroke Rose's stomach. 'It'll all be worth it when he or she arrives.'

Rose smiled. 'As long as he or she doesn't put in an appearance on the shop floor like Arthur did, I'll be happy.'

At the memory of Mary and Mr Button delivering her baby on the shop floor, Alice grimaced. 'Don't remind me.'

'He was worth it though,' Mary added.

'Every baby's worth it,' Dot said, 'and any labour is proof of the fact you've no more control of that little life growing inside of you than you have over what they do when they grow up.'

Surprise was writ large across Mary's delicate features as she glanced at Dot. 'That's very cynical.'

'That's what nearly half a century on this planet does for you, it makes you cynical,' Dot said sagely.

'She's right.' Alice sighed. 'I mean, how do I know what sort of mischief Arthur's going to get himself into when he's grown up?'

'All we can do is our best for them,' Rose offered, removing her glasses and rubbing her tired eyes.

Dot nodded, brushing a piece of lint from her A-line skirt. 'Which is why I want you to keep an eye on Brenda while I'm away.'

Alice looked at her in surprise. 'Why? She's not a child.'

'No, but she's one of us and I'm worried about her.'

'Me too,' Mary agreed. 'She was very stroppy at the Beauty is Your Duty event. And all that after she cowered away from Mother. I mean, she had thrown a drink all over her, what did she think Mother was going to say?'

'I noticed that,' Jean added, emerging from the stock-room with a pile of guard books. 'I had hoped that the event would have given her a bit more confidence – after all, the discount leaflets were her idea – but she seems to have gone further into her shell. I suggested we run her up a short-sleeved dress for the summer months at a sewing evening, thinking it would be a nice way of getting to know her, but she positively blanched at the idea.'

'Really?' Mary looked surprised as she reached for a guard book and flicked through it. 'Perhaps I'll talk to her. She can't keep going around in those long-sleeved dresses; she'll be boiling in here come mid-summer.'

'Leave that to me.' Dot said, looking kindly at the girls. 'I know you all mean well, but I'm in charge and it should be down to me to sort out things like dress wear. What I'm more worried about is her hanging about with that conchie.'

Jean rolled her eyes. 'He has a belief system, Dot, it's just not the same as yours.'

'Too right it's not, and it's not good enough for Brenda neither. I don't want her head turned by that fella, I want her concentrating on her work.'

'You're not her mother, Dot,' Alice said stiffly.

'I know that, but I am her boss and as such I'm looking out for her welfare. All I'm asking is you keep an eye out while I'm away.'

'And then what?' Mary asked. 'How do you propose bringing her out of her shell and further into the Liberty fold when you're back?'

Stuffing her hands in her skirt pockets Dot looked at the group expectantly. 'I thought what might be a nice idea would be a fabric girls' night out when I get back from Torquay. What do you think?'

'What a lovely idea,' Jean exclaimed. 'Could we go for a Chinese?'

'Why not!' Mary beamed. 'Mother can babysit, I'm sure.'

'And can I bring Bess?' Jean asked shyly.

''Course you can.' Dot smiled. 'She's as much a Liberty girl as we are.'

At the praise Jean coloured, and Dot could see how much her statement of inclusion meant to the girl.

'So that's settled then. Weekend after next all right for everyone?'

As the girls nodded only Mary looked disheartened. 'I'll have left by then. I won't be a Liberty girl anymore.'

'You'll always be a Liberty girl,' Alice exclaimed, clamping her arm around Mary's shoulders.

'And you'll always have a job here too,' Dot said gently. 'If anything ever changes.'

The words hung in the air and Dot said nothing more as Mary looked at her with tears pooling in her eyes.

'What have you got in there?' Alice asked, breaking the silence. 'You look like you're packing for a year's holiday.'

'I wish.' Dot chuckled. 'I've just got a couple of dresses I've run up for Helen – you know, Ivy's daughter – and a little something for Ivy too.'

'Well, I'm sure she'll appreciate it.' Alice smiled. 'Now, do you want some help with that bag? You'll never get to Paddington on the Tube with that.'

'Oh, I'll be all right,' Dot reasoned.

'Nonsense!' Mary replied. 'I'm taking a cab home tonight. We'll go via Paddington and drop you off. Mother can pay.'

'Well, if you put it like that' – Dot chuckled – 'who am I to argue?'

Within minutes Dot found herself in the back of a hackney carriage, her beloved Mary beside her. 'It's very good of you to drop me like this,' she said, feeling very grand as the taxi pulled away.

'Don't be daft. You can't manage that case all by yourself, though I half thought Mr B. would have given you a lift.'

'He's got a meeting with the Board of Trade and his motor spirit coupons have all but run out. The only lift Edwin would have given me is one aboard Shanks's pony.'

Mary laughed and Dot felt a pang of longing at the sound. She would miss that burst of mirth.

'Are you sure leaving is what you want to do?' she asked before she could stop herself.

'It is.' Mary sighed, throwing her head back against the cab seat. 'But to be honest, much as I love working at Liberty's I adore Emma more, and if I can spend more time with her and give her the stability and security that she deserves after such a dreadful start in life, who am I to turn that down? It's Emma that's the priority now, not me, Dot.'

Patting Mary's hand, Dot nodded. 'You'll always matter, Mary, d'you hear me?'

'I know,' Mary said, squeezing Dot's hand. 'And I'll never be more grateful to you for all you've done for me. But this is what I have to do.'

As the cab pulled into Paddington, Dot nodded. She stepped out and waved Mary goodbye. 'We do what we have to do, darlin'.'

Just half an hour later Dot found herself on board the seven o'clock train, westward bound. As ever it was standing room only with servicemen jockeying for seats amongst civilians. Boarding the crowded carriage Dot had half expected to have to join them in the luggage rack, but thankfully some kind GI had tipped his hat and offered Dot his seat.

Now, as she got herself settled and looked out of the window at the outline of the buildings still visible in the evening haze, her thoughts turned to Ivy and Helen and she felt a pang of excitement. It had been too long since she had seen them, and she was looking forward to spending time with her old pal.

Watching the London skyline give way to the countryside beyond she allowed herself to think about what Mary had said. More often than not life was about putting others before yourself, especially when it came to family.

Chapter Twenty

It was dark by the time the train pulled into the little station in the Devonshire town, and Dot was longing to disembark. It had been a long, noisy and crowded journey with many stops as they pulled into sidings to allow military trains to pass. By the time she reached Exeter to change Dot felt done-in but was delighted to find her train to Torquay already waiting on the platform.

Now, as Dot reached for her case from the luggage vestibule, she was so tired she could barely smile her thanks to the young man who helped her with her things.

Stepping out of the carriage, she took a moment amongst the hustle and bustle to stop and breathe. The first thing she noticed was the air: it was so much cleaner than London – purer and fresher, despite the grubbiness of the steam train that still stood beside her and she was soon breathing in great lungfuls of the stuff.

Feeling calmer, she looked around. The trees that she knew surrounded the grey limestone station were nothing more than dark shadows now, but just knowing they were there gave her comfort. She found herself thinking about the time she had come to the town on holiday when she was just fourteen. It had been here she had played on the golden sands and enjoyed long walks along Meadfoot Beach with her sister Olive. It hadn't been until a few days later that she had met Ivy while she was out walking. The two had struck up a friendship almost on the spot, which they had rekindled two years later.

As if the mere thought of Ivy had somehow conjured her up, Dot was delighted to see her friend strolling casually along the platform towards her now, a thick black cape covering what Dot was sure would be her nursing uniform. Dot recognised her friend in a heartbeat and found herself running towards her.

'Well, you're a sight for sore eyes!' Dot cried, falling into her old friend's arms for a hug.

'And you,' Ivy exclaimed, a lock of grey hair falling from her neatly wound bun brushing Dot's cheek. 'How long has it been?'

'Too long,' Dot sighed as she pulled away from Ivy and looked at her. The hair was greyer, she could see that, and there were more laughter lines around her eyes. But the essence of her, the smile that reached her eyes and the welcoming air, that hadn't changed a bit.

'Where's Helen?' Dot asked, realising Ivy was alone.

'She's helping out with the Sunday school group.'

'Despite them little sods calling her all sorts?' Dot gasped.

Ivy smiled in answer as she linked her arm through Dot's and guided her down the path towards the town. 'Despite all that. You know I think the best way round a problem is through it so I encouraged her to face her fears. I also thought that would give us time for a little glass of port before we go home. What d'you say?'

Dot grinned. 'I say you're a bleedin' angel. Let's go.'

Ten minutes later and the old friends found themselves in a pub not far from the harbour. In the dark it was impossible to see much of the old town that she had become fond of as a girl. However, it was just about possible to make out the dark expanse of sea along with the eerie black clouds she knew to be the barrage balloons that lined the harbour.

Inside the pub, Ivy wasted no time in ordering the drinks and Dot smiled as Ivy placed a port and lemon in front of her. Taking a sip Dot felt restored as the liquid trickled down her throat. She reflected that, even though the presence of war was everywhere, there was at least space to think and breathe.

The warmth of the pub seeped through her bones and she took a moment to look at her friend properly in the light. She was still the same, Dot was pleased to find. Still tall, beautiful and full of confidence. Her long golden hair, of which Dot had once been so jealous, was now a silvery grey, but the blue eyes that sparkled as bright as the Devon sea were still sharp.

'So what have you been doing with yourself the last ten years, Dorothy?' Ivy asked, leaning back in the wooden chair.

'You know!' Dot cried. 'There's been a war on, I've taken in more lodgers, I've a job up Liberty's, I'm a manager now.'

'Yes, you mentioned it in your letter,' Ivy said. 'Well done you.'

Dot made a face. 'I'm not much good at it. Terrible with numbers.'

'Don't do that, Dot,' Ivy said firmly. 'You've never believed in yourself and it's high time you did. They wouldn't have promoted you up to manager if they didn't think you were up to the job.'

'I think they'd just run out of people to ask,' Dot said with a shrug.

Ivy said nothing, choosing to let the comment go.

'And Edwin?' she asked after a pause.

Dot coloured at the mention of his name. 'We're getting wed. He asked me a few weeks ago.'

A flash of delight passed across Ivy's face and she clapped her hands together in joy. 'Congratulations! You must be over the moon.'

'I am,' Dot said, a shy smile creeping across her face. 'I never thought I'd find love again after losing George, and certainly not with Edwin.'

'Life's a funny thing.' Ivy smiled. 'I couldn't be more delighted for you both. Have you set a date?'

'We're working on it,' Dot replied. 'Edwin would marry me immediately, but I want us to enjoy this bit. We'll never be engaged again.'

'Were you ever engaged when you were kids?' Ivy asked, leaning back in her chair and observing her friend.

Dot shook her head. 'We talked about it. And I told Mum and Dad we wanted to wed when I was twenty-one.'

Ivy raised an eyebrow. 'I only met your mum and dad briefly but I seem to remember they were very scathing when it came to you and Edwin.'

'That they were.' Dot laughed. 'Thought Edwin was too good for me.'

'Shouldn't it have been the other way around?' Ivy asked.

'You would think so, wouldn't you?' Dot mused. 'I remember that spring, when Edwin left for Kent, me mum said I would never hear from him again, that it was only a matter of time before he took up with someone else. She said he'd get tired of my common accent and my lack of confidence. A man like that, she said, was set to be a leader and he would need someone more educated, more worldly than me on his arm.'

'What a load of old codswallop!' Ivy said, reaching for a cigarette in her bag and lighting it. 'You seem as if you've become more confident over the years.'

Dot shrugged. 'Over some things. Mud sticks though, doesn't it? I still get those little flashes of fear where I think I can't do something, that I'm not capable.'

'I think you've proved you're more than capable of a lot of things,' Ivy said, taking a drag of her cigarette. 'Look at you now, running Liberty's fabric department.'

'And a right mess I'm making of it too,' Dot said with a groan.

'I bet that's codswallop 'n' all,' Ivy said. 'You've always been your own worst enemy, Dot. You're more capable than you realise – and you've a heart of gold to boot.'

Dot laughed at the compliment and took another sip of her drink. 'That's you, darlin', all you do for the community.'

'Well, that's Kenneth's influence.' Ivy smiled. 'As a schoolteacher he was always the heart and soul of the community. When he died I wanted to continue his work so I got involved with the WI, the Red Cross and the church, and I've encouraged Helen to do the same.'

'Is that why you've been pushing her to work in the Sunday school then?' Dot asked. 'Because of Kenneth?'

'Helen was the apple of Kenneth's eye,' Ivy said with a hint of wistfulness. 'As you know, it was such a struggle for us to have children that when Helen came along Kenneth all but worshipped the ground she walked on.'

Dot smiled at the memory. She hadn't known Kenneth very well, but he'd certainly loved the bones of Helen. Her disability hadn't been an issue for either of her parents, and over the years she had seen them both encourage Helen to reach for the stars. It had worked. The girl had a job, some friends and a loving family. Their attitude had been very different to that of Dot's own parents, who had always told Dot what she couldn't do rather than what she could.

'She was lucky', Dot remarked, 'to have the both of you.'

A flash of colour crept up Ivy's neck. 'It's been us that's been lucky to have a daughter like Helen. My only regret is Kenneth was killed when she was just five years old and she never got to know her father as an adult.'

Dot sighed; there was nothing she could say. She knew herself how devastating it was to lose a husband in wartime. Like her George, Kenneth had died in the last war. He had been in one of the units that left Plymouth for Gallipoli and of course Ivy had been heartbroken when he, like the rest of his unit, had been killed. A dark silence fell across the pair then as they each reflected on the losses they had suffered. It was all too much for Dot, who hated to feel maudlin at the best of times.

'Enough of all this talk of the past,' Dot said, breaking the silence. 'You still up Torbay Hospital?'

'I am.' Ivy nodded. 'Though it's been hard after what happened at the Palace Hotel.'

Dot said nothing; she remembered how Ivy had written to her and told her how she had been asked to nurse in the government-requisitioned hotel. The hotel had served as a convalescent hospital for RAF officers until it had been bombed last October. Ivy thankfully hadn't been working that day but the aftermath had been traumatic as she had had to say goodbye to many friends.

''Course the place will all look very different since the last time you were here,' Ivy pointed out. 'So many of the town's hotels have been taken over by the RAF, there are troops everywhere doing their training. If we hang about here long enough you'll probably see them practicing their square bashing by the harbour. And then there's the fact that we've been bombed ourselves plenty of times. Nothing like you've had in London, but what we have endured has hit the town hard.'

Loosening the Liberty scarf from around her neck, Dot sighed. 'I heard about that one last August bank holiday causing devastation at Babbacombe.'

Ivy winced. 'There were so many casualties, but we keep on going. What else can you do? Look around: we're a community that thrives.'

Dot observed the townsfolk around her and was pleased to see that they were all in good spirits, laughing and joking their way through a typical Friday evening as though nothing untoward was happening. People had finished work, sweethearts were courting, and friends were exchanging gossip after a long week.

It was the way of things, Dot thought, to carry on regardless. The country was united, whether in the north, the south or the capital; nothing mattered apart from putting an end to the cowardice and violence of Hitler.

'Penny for 'em,' Ivy said, observing her friend.

'Just taking it all in. Torquay's been a good friend to me over the years.'

Ivy raised an eyebrow. 'I'm glad to hear you say that. I'm never sure how you really feel about the place.'

Dot drummed her fingers against the wooden table as she considered the question. 'It's a difficult place for me to return to.'

Ivy smiled. 'Which is why I appreciate you coming back all the more. You're a good friend to me and to Helen, Dorothy.'

'How is Helen?' Dot asked gently.

'She's all right.' Ivy sighed. 'Good days and bad days.'

'How bad is the teasing?'

Ivy made a face. 'It's bad. It's just one lot of kids, but you know how relentless children can be.'

'They can be vicious little sods!' Dot remarked. 'That's why their parents should be giving them a clip round the ear and Helen shouldn't be taking any notice.'

'The trouble is I rather think that some of the parents encourage it,' Ivy said wearily. 'I've heard some of the unkind comments from the parents about how she belongs in an institution and the like. No doubt that's where the kids have got it from.'

'And haven't you said anything to these parents?' Dot gasped. 'I mean it's hardly poor Helen's fault she was born deaf, is it? Talk about pig ignorant.'

''Course I've said something,' Ivy growled. 'But the fight has to come from Helen. It's no good me sticking up for her all the time. One day I won't be here to fight her battles for her. She's got to stand up for herself.'

'I take it she doesn't fight back then?' Dot asked.

Taking a sip of her drink, Ivy shook her head. 'No, she doesn't. I've tried to tell her, you know, every time someone slaps you, give 'em a bigger slap back, but Helen's too timid.'

Dot said nothing and merely observed Ivy.

'I wonder if I've spoiled her. Wonder if the fact she was only five when Kenneth died made a difference. Perhaps she'd have been more confident if she'd had him around.'

Dot could remain silent no longer. 'That's enough. You're a terrific mother, always have been. You can't do it all for her, even though as her mother you might want to – you said so yourself.'

Reaching forward to pat Dot's hand, Ivy smiled. 'You're right, and besides, mostly, people have taken her to their hearts.'

'No reason why they shouldn't.' Dot bristled. 'Deafness shouldn't be belittled the way it is.'

'No, but you and I both know that's just how it is.'

'Times ought to be changing,' Dot remarked. 'I mean with so many coming back from the war injured now it's commonplace to see disability on every street corner.'

Ivy laughed. 'I've missed your bluntness, Dorothy, and you're right, you would have thought two wars in recent history would have made people see things differently but we've a long way to go. I go out into the community and do what I can to explain that disability is not a weakness, that underneath any difference we are all human, but I'm preaching to the wrong crowd half the time.'

'Your words fall on deaf ears, is that it?'

Ivy smiled at the joke. 'Something like that. But at least Helen has found some kind souls around here. Our neighbour Connie, she's a widow like me and she's very good, always keeps an eye on her.'

'Do you think Helen will ever leave Torquay?' Dot asked carefully. 'I mean she's thirty-three at the end of the year, surely she doesn't want to be a spinster forever?'

'No, but marriage is not something she's ever expressed an interest in,' Ivy said. 'We've worked hard to create as normal a life as possible for her. She has a job, she helps at the WVS and contributes to the war effort. I'm proud of her.'

Dot smiled. Ivy had every reason to be proud; Helen might be facing some difficult times but, with Ivy to support her, Dot knew Helen would come out the other side.

Chapter Twenty-One

It was the scent of sea air that filled the room and the screech of seagulls that woke Dot the next morning. Sitting upright in bed, she realised this was the first good night's sleep she had enjoyed in months.

Peeling back the bedclothes of the narrow single bed she'd slept in at the top of Ivy's modest terrace, she washed her hands and face. Then she got dressed in a heavily darned Liberty blouse and rayon skirt and made her way down the stairs.

Ivy had lived in this narrow house in St Marychurch ever since Dot had known her. It had been handed down to her by her father when he died and Ivy had been grateful for the welcoming marital home it had provided and later, the refuge it afforded her to raise her daughter as a widow.

Now Ivy and Helen lived in it alone but, judging by the sound of voices coming from the kitchen at the back of the house, it didn't appear as if either one of them was lonely.

'My word, what on earth's all this?' Dot cried, pushing open the door to find Ivy standing over a pan of what looked and smelled suspiciously like bacon and eggs.

'Morning, love!' Ivy called, turning round and smiling at Dot. 'We saved our rations up so we could eat like kings, didn't we, Helen? Take a seat, Dot. Helen, pour Dot a cup of tea.'

From her position at the head of the small square table that stood next to the window Helen nodded and smiled shyly up at Dot before looking down again as she reached for a cup and the teapot. Unable to help herself, Dot immediately walked over to the woman and planted a kiss on her chestnut hair. The sudden gesture made Helen jump and she spilled hot tea all over the table, much to her and Dot's horror.

'I'm so sorry,' Helen said, in a slow voice, whilst jumping to her feet with all the speed of a cat on hot coals.

A pang of guilt flashed through Dot as she exchanged an awkward glance with Ivy. She had tried to be too affectionate too soon. How many times had she been told to treat Helen with care?

'It was my fault,' Dot said calmly, laying one hand on Helen's forearm in what she hoped was a reassuring manner. Deftly reaching for a tea towel that stood on the dresser she cleared up the mess and offered Helen a reassuring smile. Then she poured herself another cup of tea and promptly topped up Helen and Ivy's cups at the same time. 'No harm done.'

'And all sorted just in time for breakfast,' Ivy said smoothly as she set down three plates in front of them all.

Pulling out her chair, Dot looked at Helen, who still seemed forlorn. 'It doesn't matter, darlin,' she said quietly, hoping to soothe the girl.

But Helen didn't respond and instead limply lifted her wrist to pick up her fork.

Anxiously Dot looked at Ivy for help, who merely rolled her eyes. 'Dorothy, Helen is deaf,' she said in a loud voice. 'We don't go in for soft tones in this house, do we, Helen?' she said, this time shaking the girl's wrist and looking at her directly in the eye. 'Dot was saying you don't need to worry; it was an accident.'

Dot could have kicked herself. In her excitement at seeing the girl, she had quite forgotten. No wonder she had made her jump by kissing her straight on the head like that. Watching the way Ivy mouthed her words carefully she felt an even bigger fool. The girl might be deaf but she was an adept lip-reader.

With an encouraging glance from Ivy, Dot reached out and gingerly touched Helen's other arm. The girl turned to Dot and smiled, her face open, as beautiful now as the day she was born, Dot thought. Unable to help herself, Dot drank in the girl's features saw just how like her father she looked.

'I'm sorry, darlin',' she now said carefully. 'It was all my fault. Don't take on.'

'If you're sure,' Helen replied, an edge of doubt to her voice. 'Mum's always telling me how clumsy I am.'

At that Ivy cackled with laughter. 'Only because it's true,' she said as Helen turned back to face her. 'You sent that shelf of Bibles flying at Sunday school last week because you didn't see them.'

Helen looked indignant. 'Only because you moved them and didn't tell me!'

At that the two women both burst into more raucous laughter and Dot felt a flash of affection for mother and daughter. They clearly had a warm, open bond and Dot was delighted to be a part of it that weekend.

'So what would you like to do while you're here, Dot?' Ivy asked once the laughter had settled.

Dot shrugged. 'I'm here to see you girls so whatever you want. I won't get in the way.'

Ivy and Helen exchanged glances before Helen spoke in a quiet monotone.

'We thought we might have a walk up to Babbacombe Downs, it's not too far. Then we could stop for tea in the café near the cliff railway. If they've got any in, they do lovely cakes in there.'

Dot nodded her approval. 'What a nice idea. Let me treat you.'

'You don't have to do that,' Ivy said sharply. 'It's our pleasure to have you here.'

'And it's my pleasure to be here,' Dot said firmly. 'Shall we go after breakfast? The sunshine looks as if it's set to hold.'

'Yes, it seems so,' Ivy agreed. 'That's settled then.'

Just over two hours later and Dot found herself striding across the downs, enjoying the view across the sea, the sunshine warming her bones. They had walked via the little church as Helen and Ivy had a couple of things to drop off ready for the service and Sunday school the following morning. After that they had carried on down the road, Dot enjoying the crisp, fresh air filled with the salty sea tang and the easy chatter.

It hadn't taken long for them to reach the cafe. The waitress, who knew Ivy and Helen, quickly found them their best table, with a view of the sea. Within minutes they had ordered a pot of tea for three and a slice of carrot cake each, all at Dot's insistence.

'I feel like I'm on holiday!' Dot beamed as she sat back in her chair and gazed out at the view beyond. 'You two are lucky to live in a place like this. All I've got for my view is soot, grime and shells of bombed-out buildings.'

Ivy smiled as she pushed a slice of cake towards Helen. 'We feel lucky, don't we?'

Helen nodded. 'Thank you Dot, for the cakes.'

At the almost childlike statement, Dot smiled at the girl. She seemed so much younger than her thirty-two years.

'You're more than welcome, I bet you come here a lot with your friends,' Dot said, taking care to make sure she faced Helen and spoke slowly so she could lip-read.

'Sometimes,' Helen said shyly. 'Usually it's just me and Mother.'

'Your mum tells me you're very busy with the church these days?' Dot said, remembering Ivy's reminder from years ago that you were best not saying too much to Helen at once.

At the mention of the church Helen nodded. 'Yes, I get to help out Mother with the little ones.'

Dot smiled encouragingly. Helen was such a pretty woman, she thought, worthy of just as much love and affection as anyone else her age. It was a shame that society judged her so harshly because of her lack of hearing. It wasn't Helen's fault, and it wasn't as if she didn't have a lot to offer.

Dot was just about to open her mouth and ask more, when she suddenly noticed that Helen was now staring in horror at two women her mother's age. They were dressed in heavily mended macs and worn shoes, gossiping and pointing towards the girl.

'What's that all about?' Dot asked, hackles immediately rising.

Ivy laid a hand on Helen's forearm whilst simultaneously answering Dot. 'They're nobodies. Couple of people from Helen's new job at the factory.'

'Well, why are they laughing and pointing over here?' Dot asked, narrowing her eyes as the women continued with their churlish behaviour.

'Why d'you think?' Ivy said in a low voice, her face carefully turned away from Helen.

Dot glanced at Helen and saw that the smile from moments earlier was gone and now she looked ashen, her gaze firmly on the floor trying to block out the taunts. From nowhere a flash of protection rose within Dot, and before she knew what she was doing she was on her feet and charging towards the women with all the energy and grace of one of Hitler's raids.

'Is there something I can help you with?' she asked, nearing the women who had taken a seat at the back of the café.

'No,' the older of the two replied, clearly taken aback at Dot's interruption.

'Then perhaps you could tell me why you're pointing and laughing at my friend?' Dot thundered.

The women exchanged glances with one another. 'Well, it's Deaf as a Post Helen, isn't it? She makes the whole town laugh, what with the way she looks at you so intently and that funny way of speaking she has.'

'She ought to be kept away from upstanding members of society,' the other woman piped up, clearly warming to her theme.

Dot was filled with fury; her heart was racing so hard she could hear the roar in her ears. Leaning forward, her face just inches from the two women, she banged so violently on the table that she upended their cups of tea, sending floods of brown liquid on to their laps.

'That woman is a very dear friend of mine with a heart and soul twice as big and decent as yours. If anyone wants putting in an institution, it's you two for your nasty mouths and narrow-minded ideas. If I hear any more of that filth from you, I'll be on you two harder than a pound of stale rock cakes. Do you hear me?'

As the two women stared open-mouthed in silent shock, Dot banged the table for emphasis once more. 'I said, do you hear me?'

'Yes,' the women chorused, their eyes wide open with alarm.

'Good,' Dot said as she straightened up and regarded the two women once more. 'Then we will say no more about it.'

With that Dot turned her back on the women and walked back towards Ivy and Helen, ignoring the fact everyone was staring at her in shocked silence.

'I think that's sorted that,' she replied, pouring them all another cup of tea as the café began to flood with chatter once more.

Chapter Twenty-Two

Sitting down at Ivy's pine kitchen table nursing a cup of tea, Dot watched her old friend scurry about as if her feet were on fire. It was only seven in the morning but she was sure the world wouldn't collapse if Ivy sat down for just a minute.

'What are you doing?' Dot said. 'You're making me feel tired just looking at you.'

'I've got to get Helen's things ready this morning. She's got a bit of a head cold so she's sleeping in for a bit. That means I need to sort her things as well as my own for our Sunday school session this afternoon,' Ivy explained.

Dot set her cup down and thought for a moment. 'If Helen's not well, why not let her stay here this morning? She might feel better by the afternoon.'

Ivy made a face. 'I think it's more a case of she feels a bit embarrassed after yesterday. Those two old crones are regulars at the church.'

Not for the first time Dot felt a flash of guilt at how she had handled the situation in the café yesterday.

'Well, how about after church this morning I help you instead? Let Helen stay here if she wants, lick her wounds.'

Ivy raised an eyebrow as she set a stack of Bibles down. 'Didn't realise you were up on your Christian teachings, Dorothy.'

'And I didn't have you down as looking a gift horse in the mouth when you were offered it,' Dot said bluntly. 'Besides, it'll do Helen good if she can have a rest and perhaps it'll allow me to make amends.'

'If you don't mind, then thank you, that would be a big help.' Ivy grinned. 'I'll let Helen know her services are not required today.'

With that Ivy bustled upstairs to break the good news to Helen and Dot cleared away the breakfast things. An hour later and the two women were ready to make their way to the church nearby.

'I don't remember a day when you didn't worship at this church,' Dot said as she stood for a moment and gazed up at the church tower surrounded by white clouds.

'It's very special to me,' Ivy replied as she followed Dot's gaze. 'It's where I was christened, it's where Helen was christened, it's where me and Kenneth were wed, it's where my mum and dad were wed, never mind his mum and dad. It means a lot to me, to all of us in the community.'

'I can see that,' Dot murmured, noticing the large cluster of people that had gathered to worship and tip their heads at Ivy as she made her way inside.

Stepping inside, she took her seat next to Ivy on a pew in the middle of the church. Shifting her hymn book out of the way, her eyes came to rest on the font next to the altar. All too vividly she remembered the day Helen had been born, a fortnight early. She had been a tiny scrap of a thing with a healthy set of lungs, and the way Ivy had looked at her as if she were her whole world had filled Dot's heart with wonder. She knew from that moment on that Ivy was destined to be a wonderful mother.

That said, neither Ivy nor her husband Kenneth could have predicted the challenges that lay ahead. Helen had been around three when they noticed she was having problems with her hearing but it had taken many more doctors' examinations to confirm that she had none whatsoever.

Ivy had been devastated. Dot had never forgotten her face when she broke the news. She had taken the unusual step of coming up to London to see her shortly after Helen's diagnosis, and Dot had been the supportive shoulder her old friend had needed.

'It's not as if I mind for me,' Ivy had wept as Helen slept beside her on Dot's worn settee. 'But what sort of life will she have? Subject to ridicule, unable to work, go to school, never mind make friends.'

Dot had cast her eyes over Helen and taken in the gentle slope of her mouth and the pretty curl of chestnut hair against her cheek, and simply smiled. She knew in her heart Helen and Ivy would cope, no matter what life threw at them. 'You two are strong, you always have been. You'll be all right.'

The church service was a good one, Dot thought, having not being a regular churchgoer for some time. The sermon was all about love, forgiveness and finding your feet and Dot found herself identifying with the words more than she could ever have expected. Stepping outside afterwards, she was pleased to see the day was continuing to be a glorious one.

Finding Ivy chatting with some of the locals she waved and smiled, and her friend broke off and joined her.

'Don't worry about helping me out this afternoon, Dot,' Ivy said. 'You're here on your holidays. Lily over there's bringing her kids down. She often lends a hand so it'll be easier if she does it.'

Dot chuckled. 'I've always admired your forthrightness, Ivy.'

'I say it as I see it,' Ivy said with a smile. 'Tell you what, why not pop over to the downs, enjoy the sunshine and the view. Helen might join you later this afternoon.'

'I had wondered what was best to do about Helen,' Dot admitted.

A flash of understanding passed across Ivy's face. 'She'll be all right. She's embarrassed, I expect. Why not go back to the house after lunch and then the two of you could meet me when I've finished this afternoon? Perhaps we could walk down to the harbour if either one of us has the energy. I'm not sure we'd find a bus.'

'Lovely, darlin',' Dot breathed, already enjoying the thought of the clean fresh air in her lungs as she tucked into a sandwich.

Saying her goodbyes to Ivy, Dot found herself ambling along the road and back towards the downs. With the sun beating down she had to take off the basket-stitch cardigan she had knitted herself earlier that year. With the sun warming her arms, Dot felt as if she were a million miles away from London and the war. Taking Ivy's advice she sat on a bench in the sunshine and contented herself by gazing at the magnificent view and watching the world go by.

Carried away in thought, Dot was astonished when she saw it had gone two. What had she been doing all this time? She would have to hurry if she were going to make it back in time to make herself some lunch, before collecting Helen and meeting Ivy back at the church.

She jumped to her feet and quickly set off, making her way back, keeping an even pace, the cardigan wrapped carefully around her shoulders and the matching lemon hat in her hands. The sun was strong now, and she found herself panting with effort as the warm rays scorched the back of her neck.

By the time she let herself into the house she was pleased to see Helen sitting at the kitchen table reading a book.

'There you are.' Dot beamed as she laid a hand gently on Helen's forearm to attract her attention. 'Feeling better?'

Lifting her head and catching Dot's easy smile, Helen nodded. 'Yes. Sorry about this morning. Did Mum mind?'

'She understood,' Dot said, spotting the pot of tea on the table and dumping her bright yellow cardigan on the chair. Helen's eyes roamed over it.

'That's beautiful, did you knit that yourself?'

'I did.' Dot nodded proudly. 'I got the wool in Liberty's sale some time ago and knitted it up last winter.'

Helen ran her fingers across the garment and admired the stitching. 'I was thinking of doing something similar myself but I haven't got enough wool.'

'I'll get you some from Liberty's if you like,' Dot said eagerly. 'I'll use my discount.'

Looking at her in surprise, Helen's face broke into a delighted smile. 'You would do that?'

''Course.' Dot shrugged. 'I'll get it organised next week. Now how about that tea?'

Lifting the pot, Helen began to pour when suddenly the sound of something Dot didn't expect to hear in Devon rang out. Eyes widening in alarm, Dot knew only too well what it was: the tell-tale low wail of Moaning Minnie that terrified anyone that heard it.

Looking across at Helen, who clearly had no idea of the danger they were in and was now setting the pot down, Dot sprang into action. Without explanation, she reached for Helen and pulled her under the table which also doubled as a Morrison shelter.

Crouched in what Dot hoped was safety, she turned to look at Helen and saw fear and confusion in her eyes.

'What's going on?' Helen asked. 'Why are we here?'

'Everything's fine, darlin',' Dot said, wrapping an arm around her shoulders and taking care to speak slowly. 'Everything's fine. The air-raid siren's gone off. It's probably just a drill.'

At the mention of the word 'fine', Helen seemed to relax and Dot cursed herself for lying to the deaf girl. Because judging by the rapid sound of machine-gun fire and the tell-tale blasts of bombs dropping, everything was far from fine.

Chapter Twenty-Three

It felt like hours had passed since the air-raid siren sounded but by the time the all-clear signal went off Dot was surprised to find it had only been just over forty-five minutes. Her arm hadn't moved from Helen's shoulder and now as she heard the whine that signalled they were free to move she began to pull away, earning herself a look of reproach from Helen.

'Is it over now?' she asked, her voice trembling slightly at the question.

Dot nodded. 'It is. I'm just going to see what's what. Will you stay here a bit longer for me?'

Helen's face was determined. 'I want to come with you.'

Pausing for a moment, Dot met Helen's gaze and felt for her. She knew how scared Helen must be at something like this happening in what felt like a safe community. But Dot had survived the Blitz. She had experienced the bombs falling like rain and the devastation that followed. She also knew that on occasion the all-clear had sounded when that was the last thing it was. Whilst Dot knew that Helen would want to check if her mother was all right, equally Dot felt a stronger pull of protection. She had to make sure Helen stayed safe. Life after a bomb raid was tough enough if you had all your five senses; for Helen there could be untold danger out there, and she was better off under the kitchen table.

Dot turned to her, and took Helen by her shoulders, looking directly into her eyes. 'Let me go up the church, darlin'. You stay here.'

Helen opened her mouth ready to argue, but something in Dot's demeanour must have told the younger woman the matriarch was serious. And so, Helen nodded in agreement. 'Promise you'll come back soon as you can?'

'I promise, darlin'.'

Giving Helen's shoulder a squeeze of assurance, Dot crawled out from under the makeshift Morrison shelter and got unsteadily to her feet. Gingerly she padded across to the window and looked outside to check how much damage had been caused. Usually in this instance the air would be thick with dust: debris and soot from the carnage flying through the air making it difficult to breathe. But strangely Dot couldn't see much of that. There had been too much noise, though, for the town to have got away scot free, and so she pulled the curtain back and gazed towards the centre of town. Alarm tore at her heart as she caught sight of the thick clouds of black smoke coming from the direction of the church.

Without waiting to tell Helen where she was going, Dot flew out of the front door, barely bothering to close it in her haste.

The streets were filled with people scampering at breakneck speed towards the church to see what had happened. Cries of 'Johnny! Johnny! Where are you?' coupled with sobs of terror and fear echoed through the streets. For once Dot was speechless. Usually she would have wanted to do nothing more than offer comfort, help and above all hope as she had so many times after a raid, but not this time. Now her mind was full of only one thing: Ivy.

Reaching the top of the road, Dot paused to take in the devastation. A line of houses had been destroyed, snuffing out the lives within. Photos of loved ones were smashed on the floor, faces ripped from frames and glass destroyed in the raid. Washing was torn but still clutching on for dear life to the line, waiting to be claimed by owners who were never coming back. Paintings of otherwise happy scenes still hung on bombed-out walls, a sign of better times from the past. As Dot sniffed the air, the scent of burning filled her nostrils. After all the bombs she had seen in London she'd thought she would be used to this, but in Devon, a raid like this seemed even more devastating.

Her gaze strayed to the church that stood just yards away from her now. Tears pooled in her eyes as she saw the devastation up close. The once welcoming place of worship appeared to be reduced to nothing but a pile of rock and rubble. She tried to move, but something had happened to her legs. They felt as if they were filled with lead.

The sound of children crying caught her attention and Dot saw youngsters of all ages emerging from the devastation covered in dust, screaming and crying over what they had witnessed. Anxious parents clutched the hands of those lucky enough to have survived, tears of relief coursing down their faces that at least their child had not been killed.

'What happened?' Dot demanded, catching the eye of one of the women who was clinging on to her son as though he were a precious jewel.

'A Jerry's bombed the church,' she explained, her voice thick with emotion. 'One of the teachers told the kids to get down behind the pews just in time. But it's awful in there. They're bringing out bodies ...'

As her voice trailed off, she wiped the tears away with the back of her hand and Dot offered her a smile of consolation as the woman walked away, tightly gripping the hand of her boy.

Finding the strength in her legs, Dot moved quickly towards the church and it was now that she could see just how bad the damage was. It looked like the chaos of any other raid but Dot knew that the volunteers who had quickly assembled immediately after the blast would be sticking to a tight drill.

Scores of people were working together to clear the rubble and free those trapped at the front of the church, which had taken most of the damage. Without waiting to be asked, Dot pushed up her sleeves and joined what looked like most of the community to help clear the bricks and beams from where the pews had once stood. It was backbreaking work, and the cries of anguish from children stuck underneath the devastation tore at her heart.

Dot could tell that those around her felt the same; their faces were set in grim determination as they worked. It was worth it when, after an hour, she found one little boy, who couldn't have been much more than eight, lying with a comic in his hands beneath the rubble. He was covered in so much grey soot and lying so still that for a moment she thought he was dead. Yet, as tenderly as if he were her own, she wiped the dust from his face and cleared his airway. Dot was just preparing to ask one of the men to help her carry him outside when he gave a little cough. It was the sweetest sound she had ever heard.

'Oh my darlin',' she cried as the little boy blinked his eyes open.

'What's happened?' he whispered.

'Don't try to talk,' she said, placing a finger to her lips. 'There was a bomb, darlin', but you're going to be all right. Your mum and dad are waiting for you. Now, no sudden movements mind, but can you just wiggle your fingers and toes?'

The boy did as he was instructed and Dot felt a flood of relief as she watched him move first one foot and then the other, and finally both his hands.

'You're going to be just fine,' she promised as she caught sight of a first-aid volunteer and beckoned her over to help. Once the little boy was in the care of a professional, Dot smiled at him, squeezed his hand and said goodbye. There was still so much more to do, and other children who weren't so lucky, she thought as she caught sight of one badly injured child being carried out crying in pain, a bone in his leg sticking out at a right angle and blood oozing from the wound.

Turning away from the scene, Dot knew she had to steel herself. Getting upset would help nobody, not when there was a job to do. And so with a renewed vigour she carried on the search to find her missing friend.

Chapter Twenty-Four

As the sun began to set, Dot felt increasingly frantic. She was still no closer to finding Ivy. Surveying the wreckage before her, she could see that despite the volunteer teams' best efforts, there was still a long way to go, yet she wouldn't give up.

Spotting one of the women she remembered seeing chatting to Ivy that morning, Dot picked her way through the rubble to reach her side.

'Ivy, have you seen her?' Dot begged.

The woman shook her head sadly. 'She was right at the front, sorting through the Bibles, when we heard the sirens. She suddenly shouted "Duck!" and the children and us teachers dived under the wooden pews.'

'Then what?' Dot demanded.

The woman looked ashen; her clothes were torn and her face was streaked with soot and dirt.

'And then I saw a flash of light at one of the stained-glass windows and suddenly the whole church seemed to fall on top of us.'

At that the woman cast her eye across the scene and Dot followed her gaze. It was devastating. There were no other words to describe it. Dot had lost count of the lifeless bodies that had been pulled from the wreckage. Then there had been those who had survived. The wailing and the screaming as the first-aiders had tried to help them was a sound that would stay with her long after this day. Yet so too would the gritty determination of the volunteers who had worked tirelessly to save the lives of those caught up in this senseless attack.

A flash of fear coursed through Dot. She knew that the longer Ivy stayed buried under the rubble the less chance she would have of surviving. Gazing at the remnants of the pews and the smashed font, it wasn't lost on Dot how just hours earlier she and Ivy had been sitting on one of these benches, listening to a church service. How had it come to this? That she was now trying to find her friend, hoping against hope that she was still alive?

Just then she felt a tap on her shoulder. Turning around, Dot saw Lily, the kind-looking lady who had agreed to help cover Helen's work at the Sunday school.

'You're Ivy's friend, aren't you?' Lily said, her voice low.

Dot nodded, the knot of fear in her heart growing as she took in the woman's grave expression.

'I'm so sorry, love, but she's gone. We found her body about an hour ago.'

At the news Dot felt her legs give way. Nausea rose within her as she slumped to the floor, and she feared she might vomit on the spot. Ivy dead? Surely there'd been a mistake. She struggled to take it in. Her wonderful, beautiful friend had been wiped out by a single act of evil. Yet the biggest question on Dot's mind now was: How on earth was she going to tell Helen?

It was pitch black by the time Dot left the church and began the long walk back up the hill to Ivy and Helen's house. It seemed cruel that the sunshine from earlier that day gave the air a warm, balmy, holiday-like feel. Dot's mind was whirring, and she found herself wishing Edwin was by her side. Calm, worldly, safe. Edwin would know what to do and what to say. Now it was down to her and her alone to break the news of Ivy's death to Helen.

By the time Dot reached the little terrace and let herself in, she was feeling more prepared. Walking down the passageway and into the little kitchen at the back she found Helen sitting at the old pine table, her fingers steepled together.

'I already heard,' Helen said, lifting her chin to face Dot as she walked through the door. 'Connie came straight round and told me the church had been hit, before she rushed off to help the WVS.'

Dot steeled herself as she took in the girl's eyes red raw from tears and her cheeks pinched with grief. It was now Dot needed to be strong for her. What she said in this moment would help Helen deal with whatever came next. She did her best to rearrange her expression into one that wasn't quite so ashen-faced and took a seat opposite.

'Helen, darlin', there's something I have to tell you,' Dot began, reaching out to hold her hand.

Helen glanced down briefly. 'Mum's dead, isn't she?'

At the bluntness of speech, Dot raised an eyebrow in surprise. 'Yes, darlin'. I'm so sorry. She didn't suffer. She was killed outright, so I'm told.'

It was funny how the untruths tripped off her tongue, Dot thought as she gazed at Helen and willed her to believe these lies. Dot knew there was nothing she could do or say to make this moment any easier but if she could give Helen some form of comfort in this very dark hour, then God forgive her she would do it.

'Were many killed?' Helen asked finally.

'We don't know yet. There were a lot of casualties,' Dot said slowly. 'Many were taken to hospital.'

'Those poor children.' Helen began to weep. 'Mum would have been devastated she couldn't save them.'

Dot nodded in agreement. Ivy would have felt no fear at the time, she would have merely felt concern for the young lives in her care, and would have done anything she could to protect them. The responsibility now fell to Dot to do the same. Gazing into Helen's eyes she couldn't help but hope that she could do her old friend justice.

Chapter Twenty-Five

Just over three weeks later and Dot found herself staring into the vanity mirror she kept on the dressing table in her Bell Street bedroom. She wasn't a vain woman, never had been, but this morning she was fascinated with how she looked. She felt as if she had become an old woman since that dreadful bomb that killed twenty-one children and three teachers. Her cheeks sported burst blood vessels while her eyes had lost their old sparkle. Her hair was dry and brittle and her face, which always appeared healthy, now looked long and thin, her complexion grey. It didn't help that she wasn't sleeping again. She was suffering from a new recurring nightmare that had plagued her since returning from Devon.

In this new dream Ivy and Helen were buried under the rubble of that blessed church, both begging her to bring them out safely. Dot always promised faithfully that she would but every time she went to help them, they disappeared from view, their cries for help ringing in her ears.

She would wake, her sheets damp with sweat and her pillow wet with tears, in the middle of the night. Then she would either get up and make herself a good strong cup of tea to drink until it was time to get ready for work, or lie in bed tossing and turning.

Now, as she tried to pinch a little colour back into her cheeks, her eyes strayed to her bedside table and the letter that lay next to her alarm clock. It was only a white envelope with her name scrawled in the centre, but it was a note Dot couldn't bear to open as it contained Ivy's last words to her. After the funeral Helen had pressed the envelope into her hands and said her mother had instructed her some time ago to give it to Dot should she die unexpectedly. Dot had looked at her curiously, anticipating questions, but Helen had shrugged and said Ivy had left letters for all their friends. Dot had taken the letter gratefully, but been unable to open it. Although a part of her wanted nothing more than to spend some time in the company of her friend, Dot also knew that reading the contents would mean that she would never hear anything else from her friend. These would be the last words Dot would ever hear from her. And whilst Dot knew that Ivy had gone, she couldn't quite face dealing with the reality of that fact, at least not yet.

A knock at the door interrupted her thoughts.

'Dot love, can I come in? I've brought you a cuppa,' came Alice's voice, strong and clear.

'Yes, darlin',' Dot replied.

Immediately, Alice's face appeared through the door, a cup of tea in one hand and a plate of toast in the other.

'You looked like you needed a treat.' Alice set the plate on the bedside table and handed the cup to Dot.

'What am I, the Queen of Sheba or something?' Dot said, doing her best to raise a smile as she took the tea gratefully.

Alice shrugged and perched on the end of the bed, the pink eiderdown creasing underneath her. 'Heard you pacing up and down again. Thought you might need a bit of help getting ready this morning, what with it being stocktake day.'

Dot pinched the bridge of her nose. How could she have forgotten? It had been in the diary for weeks, but with everything that had happened, it had slipped her mind. But then of course she hadn't exactly had her mind on the job since getting back from Torquay.

Edwin had been incredibly understanding. He had been sympathetic, and had even offered to join Dot in Torquay for the funeral, sending an urgent telegram expressing his desire to do so the moment he heard what had happened. But Dot had said no, that the last thing Ivy would want would be a fuss. So he had left her to get on with it, reminding her that he was there for her any time she needed.

Yet even though she was now back in London, Liberty's couldn't have been further from Dot's mind. She was constantly arriving late, leaving early and, if it hadn't been for Alice picking up the slack, the paperwork would have been all over the place. At any other time in her life Dot would have felt guilty about letting things slide, taking it as a sign that she wasn't up to the job, but at the moment she couldn't help it.

'Mr Button called me into the office last night,' Alice said, her gentle tone breaking into Dot's thoughts. 'After you'd gone home.'

'Oh?'

'He said that I could take over the stock-take if you weren't feeling up to it. In fact he insisted upon it.'

Dot nodded. She and Edwin had discussed the idea when she'd returned home a week earlier. Even though she'd sent him a telegram to tell him that she could manage on her own, he had been waiting for her the moment her train crawled back into Paddington. When she'd spotted him waiting for her on the platform, her heart weary and broken, she had gasped, 'You came,' sinking into his arms.

'Of course I came,' Edwin had whispered into her ear, wrapping his arms around her. 'I'm so very sorry for your loss, Dotty my love.'

Dot had felt love pure and true course through her at the selfless gesture. 'Thank you, darlin'. It's all been such a shock.'

'I know.' Edwin had patted her hand as he guided her outside towards his car. Wordlessly he had taken her case and put it in the boot before carefully driving her home.

'I'm thrilled to have you back, Dotty. I've missed you.'

Dot had turned to look at him, and felt her heart sing just as it had when she young. 'I've missed you, Edwin. It's been ... awful.'

Edwin had glanced across at her and taken his hand from the steering wheel to squeeze her fingers. 'I bet it has. You've dealt with a lot. Let me look after you now, Dotty.'

As Dot allowed herself to relax back into the passenger seat she had smiled across at Edwin. 'I can think of nothing I'd like more.'

He had been her salve, her saviour that night, and he had continued to be her protector at work and home. He frequently escorted her to the Tube if he couldn't drive her, and overlooked her disinterest in Liberty's. He hadn't once brought up the wedding or suggested they think about something nice like their honeymoon. He had instead just been there for her, as she knew he always would be. The fact that Edwin had spoken to Alice and suggested that she take on some of Dot's workload came as no surprise. In fact she was touched he was being so thoughtful.

A rush of pleasure shot through her – the first she had felt since that dreadful day her friend had died. There were still some things in life to be grateful for, some things to cherish, and Edwin was one of them. Perhaps she ought to start planning their wedding now. She and Edwin belonged together and she didn't want to wait any longer to become his wife.

Turning back to Alice, Dot gave her a smile. 'It's probably for the best, darlin', my mind ain't really been on the job the last few days.'

'And it's understandable. Nobody minds, Dot; we want to help you. But you're the one that's always said work will help you heal. You drummed that into me when Luke went missing,' Alice said in a gentle tone.

Had she? Dot was so tired at the moment, she could barely remember what had happened yesterday, never mind years earlier.

Alice sighed. 'You need to be kinder to yourself, Dot. It's not your fault you're still here and Ivy isn't.'

Dot winced at Alice's bluntness but knew she was right. 'I know that, darlin', but I feel all sorts of things just now. I can't bear the thought of Helen alone down there in Torquay with her grief to deal with.'

'But she's at home,' Alice counselled. 'And you asked her if she wanted to come here to stay with you and she refused.'

'I should have tried harder to persuade her,' Dot protested. 'I didn't do enough.'

Alice laid a hand on Dot's arm. 'It sounds like you've done more than enough. You've written to her almost every day and sent a telegram asking her if she's all right since you got back.'

'A few words on a page!' Dot sighed. 'It's not enough, is it?'

There was a silence then as Dot gazed into Alice's face. She had asked Helen to move in with her, at least for a time. But Helen had been adamant. If it hadn't been for Connie next door promising to call in on her every day then Dot wasn't sure she would have returned to London at all.

It had been difficult, of course. Ivy's funeral had been one of the hardest days of Dot's life. And she couldn't bear to think of Helen left on her own. How could she, Dot, have abandoned her like that? It was no good saying it was Helen's choice to stay in the home she had lived in for over thirty years. Helen needed her now, of that Dot was sure. It felt like a betrayal to leave her down there to her own devices.

As if sensing where Dot's mind was wandering, Alice offered her a sympathetic smile. 'That's quite enough of that. You're needed here just as much as down there. As well as the stock-take there's something else you need to know about today.'

Alice had now got to her feet and had her arms crossed over her chest. Dot looked up at her blankly. 'What do you mean?'

'I mean that Mr B. is having lunch with Mary and her mother and a friend of her mother's. Her mother's friend is something big in fabrics in Paris, or used to be back in the thirties before the war. Mary's mother thinks she and Liberty's could be useful to one another.'

At the thought of Mary's mother Dot let out a groan. Geraldine was the last person she could do with seeing and she could quite understand why Edwin hadn't mentioned it.

'And how does this affect me?'

'She wants a tour of fabrics and Mary said you and I would be best placed to show her – and she's right, of course. I can put them off if you like, which is why I didn't tell you until now. I thought it might be better if it was just left to me, but Mr B. was insistent, and if we're all involved in the stock-take then perhaps it's best if you take on Mary's mother.'

'Anything else?' Dot asked, resigned to the difficult day that lay ahead.

With the question out in the open Alice grimaced. 'There is one more thing. It's Brenda.'

'Brenda?' Dot looked blank.

'I was thinking that perhaps we ought to promote her now Mary's gone.'

Dot's jaw dropped open. 'But she's only just started. Do you think she's ready?'

Alice nodded, just as the sound of Arthur's cries started to fill the hall. 'I think it's just what she needs. Let's make her up to a proper sales assistant rather than junior. She's come on a long way in the couple of months she's been with us.'

'And how often has she been seeing that conchie?'

Alice sighed. 'Does it matter? A couple of times, I think.'

''Course it matters,' Dot replied. 'How do we know she'll have her mind on the job?'

'Well, if anyone knows about that it's you, but we aren't running around tearing strips off you, instead we're rallying round to help,' Alice pointed out, not unkindly.

'I asked for that, didn't I?' Dot sighed. 'All right then, if that's what you think's best then we'll make her up to be sales assistant. I'll sort the paperwork when I get in.'

'Make sure you do,' Alice replied over the rising sound of Arthur's cries. 'The department's going to pieces, Dot. Fabrics might not be front of your mind at the moment, and that's fine, but don't forget that some of us do care, and some of us want Liberty's to shine – Brenda included.'

Chapter Twenty-Six

Even the clear blue skies and the musical sound of the birdsong that accompanied Dot on her way to work that morning hadn't managed to lift her spirits. As always her mind was filled with woe about Ivy and Helen, and how best to take care of the girl who meant so much to them both.

Yet, when she arrived at work, Dot made sure she kept her promise to Alice, and busied herself filling out the forms for Brenda's promotion. She was just signing the declaration of approval when she noticed, out of the corner of her eye, Beatrice Claremont smiling at her. She was just about to mouth something in reply when she spotted Edwin, closely followed by Mary, her mother and another, regal-looking woman gliding down the stairs.

At the sight of the little party, Dot's heart sank. How was she supposed to feign interest in fabrics for some former Parisian bigwig and, even worse, be polite to Mary's mother? She shook her head in irritation and then caught Edwin's gaze. He had a stern but almost pleading expression in his eyes. The look took her back to when they were children – Edwin had always been able to make her heart melt when he wanted something and she had always been unable to resist. It had been the same look that had persuaded her to rekindle their romance thirty years after they split up.

Now, seeing that look in his eyes again, she didn't want to let him down. And so she plastered on her best smile and gazed warmly at the little group as they made their way into the department.

'Mrs Hanson,' Edwin called, walking right up to the cash desk. 'How are you?'

Dot did her best to hide a smirk at the formality of her name. 'Very well, thank you, sir.' She beamed, turning to Mary. 'And lovely to see you here. Missing us already?'

Mary laughed, her eyes sparkling as she flashed Dot her pearly white teeth. 'I can't keep away; it's my second home.'

'Was,' Mrs Holmes-Fotherington said. 'I imagine your second home is David's flat now your father has given you the Mayfair property.'

Dot bit back a reply and instead carried on smiling. 'Well, we all miss her.'

'Allow me to present Lady Patricia Humm,' Edwin said smoothly. 'She's working on a top-secret project for a collective of furniture designers, isn't that right?'

Lady Humm nodded, her face lit up with pleasure. 'Edwin is being far too kind. It's not so much a secret project, more a hope that a group of us can come together with our love of design and prepare for a much happier life once the war is over.'

Dot raised an eyebrow. 'You think the war will be over soon?'

'That's the hope,' Lady Humm said, looking slightly crestfallen. 'Isn't that everyone's expectation? I mean, look at what the RAF did a couple of weeks ago, staging that huge raid on Düsseldorf.'

'Virtually decimating it, if reports are to be believed,' Edwin added. 'We're winning the war. The Jerries are on their uppers: everyone can see that.'

'Of course they are,' Mary agreed. 'Our marvellous boys are making our country very proud.'

Noting the positive tone in the air, Dot quickly realised this wasn't the time for barbed comments.

'Well, yes, when you put it like that, I see what you mean,' she said smoothly. 'How about I run through the fabrics with you then, Lady Humm. I appreciate they aren't furnishing fabrics but they'll give you an idea of just how extensive and wonderful the Liberty range truly is.'

Lady Humm's eyes lit up at the prospect. 'I would like that very much. I came back to Britain ten years ago, and I told all my designer friends it was because I missed the grandeur of the original Liberty's stores. Tell me, Mrs Hanson, how long have you been at Liberty's?'

'Oh, Mrs Hanson's an old hand, Lady Humm.' Mrs Holmes-Fotherington's eyes narrowed with dislike as she gazed at Dot. 'Can't you tell by her worn appearance just how long she's been here? She's part of the furniture.'

'Mother, don't talk about Dot like that,' Mary said in a plaintive tone.

But Dot, whilst she knew Mary's mother was being unkind, didn't have it in her to argue. Turning to Lady Humm, she flashed her a cheery grin. 'Mrs Holmes-Fotherington is right, although I have only been here a couple of years. I've always loved fabrics, and have taken a keen interest in sewing – well you have to these days, don't you, when everything's so scarce? Nobody can afford to rest on their laurels anymore.'

'Not even when they're the size of Dorothy's!' Mrs Holmes-Fotherington added, with a raucous cackle.

At the last remark, everyone turned to glare at Mary's mother, while Mary stared at the floor looking for all the world as if she wished she was anywhere but beside Geraldine. Whilst Dot was grateful for the support she knew bad feeling was the last thing the department or

Edwin needed. Not when everyone was working so hard to ensure fabrics flourished. This meeting would be a sign to their customers Liberty's was the place to be, particularly if designers were returning to their fabrics.

'Mrs Holmes-Fotherington's right. My laurels might be as large as my backside, but so is my love for fabrics. So shall we get going?'

As Lady Humm flashed her a warm smile, Dot felt herself relax; she liked this friend of Geraldine's. And although Dot was finding it hard to care about fabrics at the moment, she did care about Edwin and the rest of the girls. And so for the next couple of hours she took great pleasure in showing her ladyship everything on offer. Lady Humm seemed suitably impressed and looked as lovingly at the fabrics as Dot always did. It wasn't lost on Dot how enamoured Mary appeared to be as well as she cooed and clucked over the Sungleams and rayons and seemed almost moved by the new utility prints that had recently come into stock.

'I can see the love shining in your eyes just as it does in Dorothy's when you talk about the store, my dear,' Lady Humm said to Mary. 'You ought to continue with your love of fabrics somehow, even if you don't choose to work here any longer.'

At the remark Mrs Holmes-Fotherington let out a large sigh. 'Well, of course Mary is too busy being a wife and mother to continue with her shop work, but nobody can say she didn't pull her weight at the time.'

'She did more than pull her weight,' Dot said loyally. 'She was the backbone of the department. Nobody knew more about fabrics than Mary, and she had a real way with the customers too.'

'Quite right,' Edwin added. 'She was a very valuable member of staff.'

Mary shot Dot and Edwin a grateful look before turning to Lady Humm. 'It's true that I'm busy with Emma now but I still adore Liberty's and would love to help out when I can. I've already offered to help out with any events at the store and of course I do love to share my love of fabrics with anyone who'll listen!'

Lady Humm smiled at Mary, her wide face lighting up with pleasure. 'Well, in that case I wonder if you're the girl to help me with another little idea I've had.'

'Oh?' Mary replied, a flash of confusion passing across her features.

Edwin slipped Lady Humm a conspiratorial glance. 'There's something else we've been discussing. As you know, since the outbreak of war our staff outings have been somewhat limited.'

'But we want to change that.' Lady Humm beamed. 'You may not know this but I have a rather large home near Newton Abbot and Mr Button and I have been talking about the possibility of running a training weekend away from the grandeurs of London. We thought we could have it in my home instead and perhaps invite some of the Liberty's staff and some of my designer friends that are dotted about the country as well.'

'What a wonderful idea,' Mary gasped. 'When would it take place?'

'Well, we were thinking August, and that it should involve something about pattern-cutting, versatility of fabric, customer-service skills, and of course something about the history of fabrics too. Mary, would you be interested in attending as a guest speaker?'

Mary clamped her hands to her chest and smiled. 'Do you really think I could?'

Edwin nodded. 'You would be a natural. I was intending to invite staff from some of our nearby agents too, to help them understand the beauty of Liberty fabrics and appreciate how best to showcase them.'

'How bally marvellous, a staff beano to Devon,' Mary breathed. 'I can see it now. Drinks on the lawn in the splendour of the Devonshire countryside, the perfect setting to appreciate the wonder of Liberty fabrics. Magnificent.'

As Mary finished her speech, Dot felt a tinge of happiness. This was the first time she had seen a hint of the old Mary since her mother had returned. Mary's mother was the only one that looked concerned at this.

'Have you lost your mind, Patricia?' she hissed. 'Whatever do you want a whole load of shop staff trampling through your beautiful home for?'

Dot couldn't help herself and sighed. She knew she ought to find the fight from somewhere to argue with this ridiculously rude woman but somehow she just couldn't summon the strength. Thankfully, Lady Humm seemed to have no such problem. She drew herself up to her full height and somehow seemed to tower over Mary's mother, which, given that she couldn't have been more than five foot, was rather impressive.

'I think you'll find that the Liberty staff are some of the very best in the world. They are talented, loyal, and their attention to detail is exemplary. Your daughter is an utter credit to them, Geraldine, and quite why you find the need to run down anyone who isn't of your perceived social standing at every opportunity is beyond me. There's a war on, in case you hadn't noticed, and it's down to us all to muck in together. Not only will we be working on fabrics at this weekend, we will also be honing our first-aid skills. I have asked our local WI to come in and showcase their knowledge. It's down to us, the landed gentry, to do all we can to support the war effort. It's a shame you've seen fit to flee your large Cheshire pile to interfere in your daughter's life rather than bucking up your ideas and doing what you can to help your own community.'

As Lady Humm's speech came to a close, Mary's mother was left opening and closing her mouth like a goldfish, and Dot had to work hard to suppress the first burst of laughter that she felt rising inside her since the death of her friend.

Desperately thinking of some way to redeem the situation, Dot started to turn to Edwin, only to feel Lady Humm lay a hand on her forearm. 'Mrs Hanson, would you be able to come along a few days early and help us prepare for the weekend? There would be quite a bit to do. You could stay with me, of course.'

At the offer Dot's mouth dropped open with shock as she swung round to look at Edwin. 'How do you feel about this?'

Edwin rested a hand on Dot's shoulder, and she felt him give her a gentle squeeze, his support for her flowing through his touch. 'I think we can more than manage without you and this is a wonderful opportunity for Liberty's.'

The love Edwin continually showed her made Dot's heart sing. 'In that case, I would be thrilled, your ladyship. Your kindness means the world to me.'

Lady Humm's eyes crinkled with delight. 'It's my pleasure, Mrs Hanson. I have a feeling you and I will get along famously.'

With that the little group turned away, and as Dot watched Lady Humm's retreating back she felt a flash of happiness. Not only would a few days in Devon help her lick her wounds but it would also give her a chance to see how Helen was getting on.

Chapter Twenty-Seven

Since the invitation from Lady Humm and the announcement of the staff beano to Devon, Dot had found a renewed enthusiasm for her work. She was beyond delighted at the thought of spending precious time with Helen. Her excitement was infectious and the rest of the team found themselves swept up in Dot's excitement at the prospect of a week away from the grime of the London streets out in the countryside surrounded by their precious fabrics.

The only slight concern was Rose. As Dot watched her now, waddling down the stairs, clearly in pain with her large bump, Dot wondered if she would be up to the task of running a first-aid event in Devon.

'You all right, darlin'?' she asked sympathetically as Rose approached the cash desk, her arms full of papers.

'Fine,' Rose puffed, her round glasses slipping down her nose thanks to the sheer effort of moving.

'You look as though you ought to be sitting down, not carrying all that about,' Dot remarked, taking the piles from her hands and setting them down on the cash register with a thud. 'I'll have a word with Edwin, making you work like this.'

At the suggestion Rose looked alarmed. 'No, please don't. I'll go mad at home. Dad's bad enough, trying to get me to sit down all the time and then burning the tea or shrinking the clothes he washes. He does his best but he can't manage.'

'Have you nobody who can help you?' Dot fumed. 'You should let me look in on your dad a bit more.'

'You've enough on your plate.'

'Even so, you need a rest. You're not up to running the first-aid talk in Devon. It'll see you off. Lady Humm should never have asked you.'

'She didn't, I volunteered,' Rose said firmly.

'I've said as much myself,' Jean said, addressing the group once she had said goodbye to her customer. 'You know Bess has offered to take over the event, don't you? She can take time off from the munitions factory so you can put your feet up.'

'Has she?' Dot exclaimed. 'Well, that's kind. What do you say, Rose?'

'I say I want my holiday in Devon and I don't see why I should miss out just because I'm expecting!' Rose fumed. 'I've never been to Devon and Dad swears blind he can manage, in fact he's offered to go up to his sister Lottie's in Berkshire for a few days.'

'Well, maybe he could do that more often,' Dot suggested. 'Or could she come to you?'

'I've already said I'll come and help you out, Rose,' Alice added as she finished scribbling in her sales book. 'I don't know why you won't let me?'

Rose folded her arms and gazed at the group, her face a picture of frustration. 'If I want to bring this baby up right I've got to manage by myself – or at least try to. I might be partially sighted now and Dad a cripple but we don't want charity.'

'And that's not what anyone's offering,' Dot blasted. 'How long have you known us all now, Rose, darlin'? Have any of us ever talked of charity? It's called helping each other out, being there for each other, and it's what our community is founded on.'

'I suppose.' Rose sighed, taking a seat on the chair behind the desk. 'It's just seems such a liberty.'

'Well, it's not, darlin',' Dot said tenderly. 'There's no need for you to suffer. In fact, I've an idea. How would you feel about coming down to Devon early with me?'

Rose looked at her blankly. 'What do you mean?'

'Well, Lady Humm suggested I go a bit early – before the weekend – to help with getting it all set up. Mary'll be there too. Why don't you come along with us?'

'I don't know about that.' Rose looked doubtful. 'I don't want to put anyone out.'

'You wouldn't be,' Dot insisted. 'You'd be helping me and getting your own section of the event ready all while taking in a bit of rest and fresh air.'

'It's a brilliant idea,' Alice chimed in. 'If anyone had offered me anything like that when I was pregnant I'd have bitten their hand off.'

'Well, I don't want to do anything that would put anyone out,' Rose repeated.

Dot rolled her eyes heavenwards. 'How many times! You're not putting anyone out; in fact you'll be doing me a favour, you'll have me feeing less like a spare part in Lady Humm's beautiful home.'

'Mary's going to be there?' Alice countered.

'Yes, but you know Mary's different,' Rose put in.

'No she's not, she's a Liberty girl through and through,' Alice protested. 'I do miss her.'

'We all do. I'm sure she'd come back if it weren't for her mother,' Jean said, leaning on the counter, earning herself a sharp tap on the arm and a disapproving frown from Dot.

'Don't you think she's changed since her mother's come back?' Alice said.

'How do you mean?' Jean asked.

Alice ran a hand over her victory roll as if thinking of the right way to say what she wanted to. 'I mean she's all timid and mousy around her.'

'What was she like before?' Brenda asked.

'The very opposite.' Jean laughed. 'Kind, thoughtful—'

'Though she is still all of those things,' Alice pointed out.

'True, but she wouldn't take any nonsense off anyone. She'd put them in their place,' Jean continued.

'I think she still would now,' Rose put in. 'I think she's only a bit different with her mother. It's as though the confidence has been knocked out of her.'

Dot didn't know whether to feel pleased or upset that others had noticed. She had half hoped that she was wrong, that her friend hadn't changed and it was all in her head.

'Look, she's bound to behave differently around her mother,' Dot said eventually. 'She's lost her family once, and now her father's dead and her mother wants her in her life, her perspective has changed. Plus she's a mother herself; she needs to give Emma a solid foundation, and better that she does that with a family around her.'

'So you're not worried about her?' Alice asked with a hint of incredulity to her voice.

'I didn't say that, darlin',' Dot replied. 'But she has to realise for herself that she's changed and if she's going to regain her confidence then she has to be the one to find it.'

As she finished speaking she remembered the conversation she had had with Ivy when she had stepped in to defend Helen against the two old crones who had taunted her. A pang of sadness washed over Dot as she realised just how much she missed Ivy, her friendship and her wisdom.

'But don't you think we should say something?' Rose suggested. 'We're her friends.'

'Which is precisely why Mary has to find out for herself. All we can do is be there for her when she realises her relationship with her mother's not healthy.'

'I hope she realises soon.' Alice sighed. 'What with Flo gone and now Mary, fabrics just don't feel the same no more.'

'Then all the more reason for this event in Devon to get us back on track,' Dot said firmly. 'I'm also hoping I might be able to see Helen as well.'

'I wondered if you would,' Jean said. 'Have you written and told her?'

Dot nodded. She had exchanged a few letters with Helen since Ivy's death but Dot had been careful not to push her. Dot knew that she herself was still struggling with grief over the loss of her friend; how much worse must Helen be feeling? All Dot could do was take it one day at a time, it was what she had done when George had died and what she was doing now. There were days where she thought she was coping with her loss quite well, but then there were others when she wanted to stay in bed and do nothing but weep all day. She still hadn't managed to open the note Ivy had left. She had picked it up countless times and run her fingers over the letters that made up her name but she couldn't quite bring herself to read it; she still wasn't strong enough to face the utter finality of Ivy's last words to her, at least not yet.

'Yes, and she's written back and suggested we have a cup of tea,' Dot said. 'Though she didn't sound all that excited about it. I don't want to make her do something she doesn't want to.'

'It's been a difficult time for her, Dot. She's lost her mother, her world in fact, and here you are suddenly wanting to become her best friend. You need to give her time,' Alice reasoned.

'You're right, I'll stop reading so much into it.'

With that, Dot turned around ready to go back to work but Jean spoke. 'I have got one question though, Dot,' she began. 'I can't help wondering why she's so important to you? Helen I mean.'

Dot felt her cheeks flame red at the question. Stalling for time, she turned slowly to allow her face to adjust and smiled at Jean. 'She's my best friend's girl and she's in need.'

'You have to remember, Jean,' Alice put in, 'Dot's famous for having a soft spot for those that need a helping hand.'

'Well, I certainly tried to help you when your old man buggered off and I gave you a roof over your head.' Dot laughed. 'Now can we get back to work, please? Last time I checked Liberty's was a shop that employed people.'

With that the little group disbanded and went back to their work. Watching them walk away Dot breathed a sigh of relief. Much as she hated secrets she knew she could never tell anyone why Ivy and Helen had always meant so much to her.

Chapter Twenty-Eight

Over the last couple of weeks, Dot found that things at work had been running a lot more smoothly, which boosted her confidence in her own abilities as department manager. Summer was in full swing now and the scent of roses in bloom on the daily commute helped lift her spirits.

Now, this morning, there was just the paperwork from the recent stock-take to go through. Sorting through the numbers, she was pleased to see that everything had tallied up as it should. It had been tough for the girls, and Alice, as always, had done a fine job taking charge of everything when Dot was feeling less able. Stock-taking was never an easy task: it was a dirty, time-consuming job even when they had all hands on deck. The fact that they had been two pairs of hands down, with no Mary or herself to help with the task, must have made things very difficult indeed.

Signing off the tallies with a flourish, Dot pushed the paperwork to one side, resolving to deliver it to the Counting House later, and took a moment to survey the department.

Alice was explaining patiently to a new customer how Sungleam would give her a much better cut to the pattern she had in mind, and would be cheaper too. Jean was running a duster over the windowsills in between serving customers and Brenda was studying the customer books, still placing names to faces now she had been promoted.

She felt proud that the girls were all so self-sufficient and capable. Checking that there were no customers in the department, she beckoned them over to the cash desk.

'I owe you all an apology,' she said, looking at their worried faces. 'I have been a terrible department head, so how about I take you all for a drink tonight, to say sorry.'

The girls exchanged doubtful glances, leaving Dot feeling perturbed. What was so wrong with going out for a drink? Had she been that unbearable to work for?

'We'd love to, Dot, but you don't owe us an apology,' Alice said eventually.

'I think I do, and I'd like to make it up to you.'

Exchanging yet more worried glances, Brenda spoke up. 'The thing is, the girls are coming out with me and Peter tonight, to celebrate my promotion, and well, with the way things are between you and him …'

Her voice trailed off but Dot was under no illusion as to what Brenda meant. She had given the poor girl such a difficult time about going out with a conchie it was no wonder she hadn't been invited.

'Well, that's all right,' she said brightly, willing herself to believe it. 'I'll bring Edwin – we can all celebrate your promotion and toast your success. You deserve it.'

At the gesture, Brenda's face lit up with relief. 'Are you sure, Dot? It would be lovely to have you but I don't want to put you in an awkward position.'

'You're not,' Dot said firmly. 'Trust me, we'll all have a lovely time and the drinks are on me.'

Just after half past six, Dot found herself at the bar of the French Pub beside Edwin, giving her drinks order to the barman.

'You should have let me do that,' Edwin grumbled, straightening his tie as he looked helplessly at Dot fishing a handful of coins from her purse. 'I have always said the bar is no place for a lady.'

Dot gave him a playful nudge in the ribs. 'Well, lucky for you I ain't no lady. When are you going to get it into your head, times are changing, Edwin, darlin'.'

'And not necessarily for the better.' He sighed, the awkwardness he felt at not paying for the drinks evident on his face. 'In my day a lady didn't even enter a public house alone, never mind approach the bar.'

'The war's changed us all, you know that,' she said briskly as the barman placed six port and lemons on a tray. 'I'll take these and leave the pints to you.'

Carefully she carried the drinks back to the table, taking care not to spill a drop, and was delighted when her efforts were rewarded by cries of jubilation from her friends.

'Never thought I'd see the day when I'd find you at the bar.' Alice chuckled as she reached for Rose's drink as well as her own.

'Me neither,' Mary exclaimed with a wink, seizing her own glass, happy her mother had offered to babysit for the night so she could join them.

'Cheek!' Dot said with a mock scowl. 'Here am I trying to do a nice thing and here are you, ruining it for me.'

'No, she'd only be ruining it for you if she took advantage by asking for a double,' Jean quipped.

At that the girls laughed harder, just as Edwin followed with three pints. Setting them down, his face went blank.

'Where are Henry and Peter?'

'They're just on their way,' Brenda explained with a smile. 'Henry wanted to give Peter a brief for the Devon beano. He's doing the artwork for the welcome leaflet as well.'

Dot felt her hackles rise, but said nothing. She had promised to give Peter a chance, and although it went against every fibre of her being, she was determined to try. 'How lovely, darlin'. He did an excellent job with those vouchers for the Beauty is Your Duty event.'

It was true, she thought, taking a sip of her drink. He might be a conchie but he did have a lovely way with a paintbrush.

'I'm glad you think so.' Edwin beamed. 'I rather thought we would ask Peter to do us some artwork for our wedding. Perhaps a table display.'

It was to Dot's credit, she thought, that she didn't balk at the idea straightaway. Fortunately she was saved from answering by the arrival of the two men walking through the door.

'Ooh, speak of the devil,' she said, getting up and waving them over.

'Drink already on the table,' Henry exclaimed, a look of pleasure crossing his face as he took a seat next to Edwin. 'I'll come again when you're in the chair, Dot.'

'Don't get too comfortable,' she teased. 'Next round's on you and mine's a double.'

There was a peal of laughter from the table at the remark and Mary thumped the table. As Peter sat down next to Brenda, Dot couldn't miss the look of wariness in his eyes and resolved to remain friendly.

'I'll drink to that,' he said eventually. 'Many thanks, Dot. Very nice of you.'

'You're welcome,' she said a little stiffly.

She would do her best to welcome Peter into the fold, for Brenda's sake; the girl was obviously sweet on him. However, Dot found it difficult, to say the least.

'I've just been hearing about you doing the artwork for our Devon beano,' Dot said in what she hoped was a friendly tone.

'That's right.' Peter nodded. 'Though I won't be able to make it to Devon itself; my unit needs me here.'

'I think it's jolly good what you're doing,' Rose said, pushing a lock of auburn hair behind her ear. 'It must be difficult to do something like defuse bombs when you don't believe in war.'

Peter sighed, a faraway look forming across his features. 'It is. It doesn't mean I don't love my country. We all want to keep our boys safe, whatever that means to us all.'

Dot glanced at him. He looked tired, she thought. His features seemed grey somehow, but there was a certain fire in his eyes as he glanced across at Brenda. He was easily ten years older than the girl, and naturally he had more life experience. But he did seem genuinely taken with her. Even so, Dot wanted to be sure of his moral standards. Brenda had been through enough; the last thing she needed was a man of no moral fibre taking advantage of her.

'That may be true,' Dot said, doing her best to keep her tone even. 'But what would we do if all our boys felt that way? Jerry'd be over here sooner than you can say pass the sauerkraut.'

Peter set his pint down and leaned back in his chair, surveying the table. 'I appreciate my way isn't everyone's way. But I would never ask someone to do something they don't believe in, and for me that's fighting.'

'Well said,' Alice put in, shooting Dot a glowering stare. 'And now we've sorted that out, how about we change the subject?'

'Good idea,' Edwin said. 'I've actually got something I would like to discuss.'

'Oh, it's not about the stock-take, is it?' Jean asked, looking fearfully at her boss. 'I'm still scrubbing grime from my fingernails after all that time I spent scrabbling about on the floor checking we hadn't mislaid stock.'

Dot patted her knee and smiled. 'All part of the job, darlin'. I'll be doing it next time to make up for my lack of attention this time around.'

There were murmurs of appreciation at that and Edwin had to clear his throat to make himself heard above the noise.

'Actually, I wanted to talk to Dorothy. I would have done it in a more private setting but she's so busy at the moment, and, well' – a sheepish look passed across his face at this point – 'you are all like family to us and so I thought Dorothy wouldn't object to me mentioning this in front of you.'

'Mention what?' Dot asked, feeling blindsided. Whatever he had to say, she wished he would get on with it. She hated surprises.

'Well, a date for our wedding, Dorothy. I hope you don't mind but I've had a word with the vicar at the church in Elephant and Castle and he says the earliest date he has is October the eighth. It's a Friday so we might have to do a bit of jigging about with the staffing levels but it's nothing we can't manage for one day I'm sure.'

'This year?' Dot gasped in amazement. 'Can we really get married so quickly?'

'We can if you'll have me,' Edwin said, his face sombre. 'I know I've done it without talking to you but you've had ever so much on your plate, Dotty, I wanted to give you something to look forward to. I wanted us to share the load, just as we will when we're married. I hope I haven't offended you.'

Looking into the face she knew almost as well as her own, Dot shook her head in wonder. How could this boy, this man, her Edwin, ever think that by organising a date for their wedding she would be offended? She leaned across and tenderly kissed him on the lips, leaving him in no doubt that the sooner she became Mrs Edwin Button the better.

Chapter Twenty-Nine

An hour later, and with the news of Dot and Edwin's upcoming wedding date creating much excitement, the evening was in full swing. The girls were on their third port and lemon, all paid for by Dot as she kept pointing out, and the atmosphere was jubilant.

So far they had discussed what Dot should wear (talk of customising her old wedding dress had scored very highly), where they should hold the reception and whether Emma, Arthur and Rose's new-born should act as pageboys and bridesmaids for the special day. Whilst Dot was thrilled that she and Edwin now had a date to look forward to, she couldn't help wanting to talk about something else; after all, she had never been comfortable in the spotlight.

'Does anyone have any ideas about how much fabric we ought to take down to Devon?' she asked, exchanging a knowing glance with Edwin to urge him to help her change the subject.

'Oh yes, good thought, Dorothy. I would have said as much as you can send down there without leaving stocks short for the Saturday rush. We'll be relying on skeleton staff from other departments like carpets to man the fort while you're away.'

'We could leave the rayons.' Alice frowned, drumming her short fingernails on the beer-soaked table. 'They're not very inspirational.'

'Neither's the cotton,' Jean chimed in.

'What rot!' Mary exclaimed. 'The Tana Lawn is pretty and functional – perfect for a designer.'

'What about a selection of each?' Brenda suggested above the din. 'That way we can talk about everything and there will still be enough left for our customers to look at while we're away.'

Dot shot her a winning smile and held her glass aloft in Brenda's direction. 'And that's why this girl deserves her promotion. Look at that, up there for dancing,' she said, tapping the side of her head with her glass and sloshing port on to her hand in the process, 'and down there for thinking, as the expression goes.'

'I think it's the other way around, Dot,' said Rose, laughing, 'but we take your point. Yes, good idea, Brenda. I'll organise it.'

'And have you thought any more about whether you'll join me early?' Dot asked.

Rose's cheeks flushed red. 'If you're sure it's not an inconvenience and Lady Humm doesn't mind?'

'Of course Lady Patty doesn't mind!' Mary exclaimed. 'I'll be there as well with Emma. We'll have a little party – it'll be such fun!'

'Speaking of fun,' Edwin put in, 'I've had an idea.'

'Not another one!' Dot exclaimed. 'You'll run out if you keep this up.'

Rolling his eyes at Dot's droll remark, he leaned under the table and rooted about in his leather case. Pulling out what looked like a sheaf of papers, he fanned them out on the desk.

'Here!' he said proudly, pointing to a series of familiar-looking periodicals.

'The *Liberty Lamp*,' Jean gasped, leaning across the table for a better look. 'I've heard of that – isn't that the old staff magazine?'

'That's right,' Edwin replied, looking pleased with himself. 'I came across them the other day and thought we should have a go at reinstating it.'

'But with paper rationed do you really think we can?' Alice asked doubtfully as she picked one up.

'Not as a regular thing, no,' Edwin replied carefully, 'but Henry and I have been talking and we thought we could perhaps produce two issues. One to commemorate this rather wonderful beano in Devon and another at Christmas. The staff party will have to be cancelled due to a lack of funds and I thought this might drum up a bit of cheer instead.'

Dot raised an eyebrow as she helped herself to an issue. 'You thought a magazine would be a good substitute for an evening out at the company's expense? I wonder about you, Edwin Button, sometimes, I really do.'

'Birth announcements, marriage announcements and department announcements,' Mary mused, flicking through the magazine, 'jokes and – my word – the Liberty Belles!'

She held the page aloft for everyone to see; Dot craned her neck and soon saw what Mary was talking about: a picture of a young girl who worked for the store along with some scant biographical facts and of course her thoughts on Liberty's.

She rolled her eyes. 'Don't you think this is all a bit frivolous for wartime?'

'Absolutely not,' Edwin exclaimed. 'They kept it up during the last war. Where's the harm in doing it as a one-off now? Look, we can add Rose's baby for the Christmas issue—'

'And details of your wedding,' Jean breathed, cutting Edwin off midway through. 'Imagine what a lovely keepsake it would be. Oh come on, Dot, don't be a killjoy.'

Shaking her head, Dot had to smile. The group around her looked so earnest and, really, where was the harm? 'Who am I to stand in the way?' She sighed. 'I'll warn you though, I'm no Liberty Belle.'

'No, but we rather thought Brenda might be,' Henry said with a smile.

'Me?' Brenda looked aghast. 'But I'm nobody.'

'Don't talk about yourself like that,' Peter said quickly, rushing to her defence. 'You're bright, clever, funny and talented – you should be a Liberty Belle.'

At the compliment Brenda said nothing but grinned from ear to ear like a Cheshire cat. Dot felt a swell of pride to see the girl so overjoyed.

'Anyway, I'm glad you all support the idea,' Henry said, his gruff northern brogue interrupting Dot's train of thought. 'As that's something else Peter will be doing for us, during his spare time away from the army of course.'

'You'll be knocking up the *Liberty Lamp*?' Rose asked incredulously. 'My word, I wouldn't know where to start.'

'It won't be that hard, and a lot of the old team who used to work on it are still at Liberty's,' Peter added, slipping Brenda a shy smile.

'Yes, I have a feeling Beatrice Claremont used to head up one or two of the sections when she first started working for us,' Edwin said, scratching his head. 'I wonder if she'd think about doing it again.'

'I'll ask her,' Alice offered. 'I could do something for fabrics if you like.'

'Would you?' Edwin brightened at her offer. 'And, Rose, perhaps you could take on the social committees? Obviously there aren't that many anymore, but a brief round-up would be wonderful. You could dictate to Mrs Marks as you usually do with any reports for her to type up.'

'All right,' Rose agreed, looking thrilled to be given some responsibility.

'Then that's settled,' Edwin said firmly. 'Goodness, I feel as if we've got an awful lot sorted out tonight.'

'There is one final thing,' Mary said, looking doubtful. 'My mother's asked if she can come to the training event next month.'

'What?' Dot asked, aghast.

'She doesn't want to miss meeting the designers Lady Humm hobnobs with.'

'And I will also be bringing Stan. I can't find anyone to look after him,' Henry added. 'We can stay in the town though. I don't want to put anyone to any trouble.'

'Nonsense,' Mary said authoritatively. 'Lady Patty's pile is huge. More than enough room for everyone, which is why Mummy wants to come.'

'Just as long as she don't cause no upsets. Look at how she was the night of Jean and Bess's party.'

At the memory Mary winced. 'I know, but she's promised to be no trouble.'

Dot couldn't help herself; she snorted into her port and lemon as she swallowed the last of the dregs. 'Famous last words, darlin'.'

'Trust me, she will. Lady Patty won't stand for any nonsense from Mummy.'

'Well, I suppose we've got no choice, have we?' Henry sighed. 'It's that or no beano as she did introduce us to Lady Humm.'

As Dot glanced in Brenda's direction she couldn't miss the look of fear on the young girl's face. Dot disliked Mary's mother as much as anyone could, but she knew it would be good for Brenda to face the old bat again: it would help her realise she was more than capable of dealing with her. Besides, she would make sure nothing happened to her and was about to say as much when Peter got to his feet.

'My round, I think,' he said, squeezing Brenda's shoulder. 'And perhaps, if you don't mind, you could give me a hand?'

Dot saw Edwin about to open his mouth, no doubt about to protest again about a lady going to the bar, and shook her head. Peter had clearly seen the effect that the idea of Mary's mother joining the Devon beano had had on Brenda and was giving her a distraction.

'I'll have a gimlet if you're buying,' Dot said quickly. 'I've had enough of the port and lemons. Time for a bit of class.'

At that the table broke into another round of laughter and Peter, his face a picture of bemusement, and went to the bar with Brenda following quickly behind.

'Oh Dot,' Alice said, tears of laughter running down her face. 'What would we do without you?'

Dot leaned forward and patted her friend's hand. 'Let's hope you'll never have to find out. Besides, I don't know what's so funny. It's Mary here you want to blame for my love of gimlets. If she hadn't served 'em at her wedding then I wouldn't have developed a taste for 'em.'

Mary held her hands up in defence. 'It's nothing to do with me and I don't think you drinking gimlets is what the girls find funny, more the way you ask for them.'

Dot's eyes swivelled towards Mary. She gave the younger woman one of her customary glares, so menacing that even Edwin grimaced. 'And what's wrong with the way I ask?'

But Mary never got the chance to answer as, just before she opened her mouth to speak, the sound of raised voices coming from the bar caught their attention.

Craning her neck to see what the fuss was all about, Dot was horrified to see Brenda standing behind Peter as he remonstrated with two angry-looking men at the bar. In their fifties, red-faced with fury and drink, the men were shouting now, prodding Peter in the chest. Dot wasn't close enough to hear what was being said but, by the look on the men's faces and the fear that appeared to course through Brenda's body as she moved closer to Peter, her fingernails digging into his arm, she could tell it wasn't anything good.

Exchanging worried glances with Edwin, she was relieved when he and Henry wordlessly got to their feet. They reached the group within seconds and Dot felt a flash of pride as she heard Edwin address the men in a calm voice.

'Now then, chaps, what seems to be the problem?'

'Yes, there's no need for this,' Henry added, his tone serious.

But the men weren't to be placated. 'There's every need,' the one nearest Peter growled.

Dot felt a stab of concern. Looking at the rest of the girls, she could see they were as worried as she was.

'What's happening?' Rose asked, hampered by her partial sight.

'I'm not sure,' Alice replied. 'It looks as though a couple of men at the bar have a problem with Peter, and Mr Button and Henry have gone to try and calm things down.'

'But why would anyone have a problem with Peter?' Rose asked.

No sooner had the words left her mouth than the reason became clear. As Dot craned further forward to get a better view she saw to her horror one of the men reach into his bag for what looked like a large packet.

'Here, you bloody coward,' the man shouted, ripping off the top with fury and raising his arm towards Peter.

'And this is for you as well, love, you should know better than to hang about with a bleedin' conchie.'

With that the man threw the packet towards Peter and Brenda. Dot gasped as she realised what it was. A packet of white flour now covered them both from head to toe, making them look like a pair of ghosts.

The other man leaned forward, his whole face alight with anger as he looked at Brenda and Peter and sneered, 'Now the whole world'll know what a pair of bloody cowards you both are. You're a disgrace.'

Chapter Thirty

It was one of those sunny warm days where it felt too claustrophobic to remain inside no matter how many windows you threw open. Dot had done her best to take advantage of the good weather that Sunday morning and so she had got up early, done all the laundry and even washed the windows. But by eleven, Dot declared the house too hot to get anything else done and so she suggested to Alice that they take Arthur for a walk in nearby Brockwell Park.

'It'll do the lad good to get some fresh air,' Dot insisted. 'He's getting big now, he shouldn't be cooped up with us all day.'

Alice smiled as Arthur's face lit up at the mention of the word park. 'Go on then. The place feels more like an oven than a house. Can't say I fancy getting on the Tube though, even if it is a couple of stops.'

'It'll be cool underground,' Dot protested before seeing Alice's horrified face. 'Oh all right, we'll take the bus.'

Just half an hour later and the two women were perched on the top deck with Arthur nestled between them. The familiar sights of South London whizzed past them: the old bombed-out Electric Pavilion and of course the skyline of the partially built Battersea Power Station. The sight of it never failed to make Dot wince. It was supposed to have been a state-of-the-art power facility, set to change the way power was supplied to the city and beyond, yet with work on the second plant stalling because of the conflict with Germany, the half-built shell was yet another reminder of the way lives felt half-lived because of war.

It wasn't long before the bus arrived at the park, and an eager Arthur cooed excitedly as they got off the bus.

'Pigs,' he cried, showing off one of the few words he had mastered while gesturing wildly in the direction of the park. 'Pigs.'

Dot rolled her eyes. Every time they came to the park the pigs were the first thing Arthur wanted to see. She couldn't blame him; three sites in the park had been given over to pig clubs for food production and the pigs, housed in bits of rubble and brick from bombed-out local buildings, made quite a sight.

Alice beamed at her son. 'Go on then.'

Picking their way through the park, the sun warming their skin, Dot sniffed the air. The pigs were getting closer.

'You heard anything from Brenda?' Alice asked, the pigs coming into view.

Dot sighed. 'Not since she ran off with Peter covered in flour.'

'And she's still definitely sick?' Alice asked.

'Apparently,' Dot replied. ' She's got some bug.'

'But that was over two weeks ago. She can't stay away from work forever,' Alice pointed out. 'I'm guessing she's embarrassed at what happened' – she put Arthur down as they neared the pigs – 'but it's gone on for too long now. What happened in the pub wasn't her fault.'

'No, but if she didn't hang about with conchies then it wouldn't have happened,' Dot said, a little more fiercely than she intended.

'Come off it, Dot,' Alice scoffed. 'That could have happened to any one of us. Men like that just want to have a fight, they don't care who it is, they just want to let off a bit of steam – probably because they're too old or injured to fight themselves. Peter seems like a nice lad – don't you think it's time you eased up on him a little?'

Dot said nothing as they stood and surveyed the pigs. Alice had a point, but equally Dot couldn't help feeling that if Brenda had agreed to have nothing more to do with Peter then she wouldn't be in the mess she was in now. Dot had to admit Peter wasn't a bad lad. He clearly cared for Brenda and appeared as worried about the girl as the rest of them, if the way he had gone chasing after her when she fled into the night was anything to go by. But still Dot couldn't shake her dislike at him being a conchie. She had been brought up to believe, like many of her generation, that you served your country no matter what.

'Maybe,' she said in reply, tearing herself from her train of thought to face Alice. 'I mean, he's not a bad lad.'

'No. Look at the way he came into the store the day after the flour incident before he was due to return to his unit,' Alice reasoned. 'He went straight up to the offices to talk to Henry and Peter to see if they had heard anything and if he could do anything.'

'I hope she's all right.' Dot sighed. 'Peter said she was inconsolable after she left the pub and fled back to her lodgings in Silvertown. Do you think I should go and see her?'

'See her?' Alice echoed, glancing between her and Arthur who was doing his best to pull a pig's tail.

'I'm away in Devon from Monday week and I don't want to leave it until after I get back. She might never return at this rate. The longer she leaves it the harder it will be for her to come back.'

'What does Mr Button say?' Alice asked. 'And speaking of him, where is he? I haven't seen him for a couple of days.'

'He's gone down to Devon to go through things with Lady Humm before the beano. He'll be back before I go. He thinks I ought to leave things with Brenda – that as her manager I shouldn't interfere.'

'Well, he's right,' Alice said. 'But when has that ever stopped you?'

Dot made a face. 'I'm worried about her. She's made such good progress with her promotion and after everything that happened at her last job I'd hate to see her go backwards.'

'What happened at her last job?'

At the question Dot shook her head. 'I might be an interfering old bag but I'm also not a gossip. That's her secret to tell you, darlin', not mine.'

'Fair enough.' Alice shrugged. 'But the thing is, Dot, Mr B. isn't here, and you've always interfered in my life.'

'Charming!' Dot snapped.

'If you'll let me finish,' Alice groaned. 'You have always interfered in my life and I know you've done it because you care. I wouldn't be where I am today without your interference and I'm grateful for it. Now, I don't know what was said when you and Brenda had that heart-to-heart at Bess and Jean's party and you're quite right not to tell me. But what I do know is a few words from you made all the difference to her that night and they could do the same again.'

Dot thought for a moment. Only the noise of the pigs grunting interrupted the silence. What if Alice was right? What if she could get through to Brenda somehow and convince her that all was not lost?

'Would you mind if I nipped off, Alice?'

A wry smile played on Alice's lips. ''Course not. Me and Arthur can find our own way home.'

Later on, Dot found herself standing outside a house that looked very similar to her own home. A two-up, two-down, grey London brick terrace with a smartly scrubbed step and black front door. The only thing that marred the house's appearance was the brown tape gummed to the windows to stop bomb damage, but as Dot surveyed the street and saw about half the homes in the Silvertown road had been hit she could understand why.

She knocked sharply on the door and it all but flew open. Dot found herself face-to-face with a woman a few years younger than herself. Dot smiled expectantly at the woman.

'Hello. You must be Mrs Rogers, Brenda's landlady. Is she in? I'm a friend of hers from Liberty's.'

At the mention of her lodger, Mrs Rogers's face darkened. 'Don't mention that girl to me. She's nothing but trouble.'

'Really?' Dot said with a frown. 'She's ever such a good girl at work.'

'That might be the case,' Mrs Rogers said with a grimace, 'but she's a bad lot, you mark my words. This latest stunt, hanging about with a conchie no less, I won't have it. Turning up at my home covered in white powder like that. I'm a respectable woman and I won't have conchie sympathisers in my house.'

'What do you mean?' Dot asked in as polite a tone as she could manage even though she was beginning to lose her patience.

'I mean, I've told her to sling her hook,' the landlady shouted. 'I mean, she don't live here no more.'

Alarm pulsed through Dot. 'Since when?'

'Since she came back that night looking like a bleedin' bomb victim. I told her when she took the room on that I wouldn't have no trouble and she assured me she was a good girl. I've three kiddies to think about.'

'So where is she now?' Dot asked, gritting her teeth as her patience rapidly disappeared.

Mrs Rogers looked at Dot as if she were something nasty stuck to the bottom of her shoe. 'How the bleedin' hell should I know? I told her to get out that night and that's as far as my duty went. Showing me up – girls like that, you can't teach 'em.'

It was in that moment that the patience Dot had been holding on to so valiantly suddenly evaporated.

'You mean to tell me you sent a young girl out on to the streets in the state she was in?' Dot asked, her voice perilously low.

'So what if I did?' The landlady shrugged. 'Ain't no skin off my nose. She ain't bleedin' family or nothin'.'

By now Dot's blood was on fire and she longed to lean forward and give the woman a good old-fashioned South London crack around the back of the legs. But she knew that no matter how much she wanted to, violence wouldn't help her or Brenda.

'You should be bleedin' well ashamed of yourself,' Dot snarled, looking around at the neighbours' net curtains twitching at the sound of the row. 'Throwing a young girl out on her ear in the dead of night. Handy the way you're worried about your reputation when you've a tea stain on your tabard and there's a filthy footprint on your step.'

'Where?' the woman demanded, peering down at the freshly whitened step.

'Right there.' Dot smirked, wiping the shoe that was still covered in pig's muck from her earlier trip to the park deftly on the woman's step. 'I should get that cleaned up quickly if I were you – you don't want a filthy step blackening your reputation.'

With that Dot withdrew and marched back down the road, her mind full of Brenda and where the hell she might have gone.

Chapter Thirty-One

'What does he mean, he doesn't know where Brenda is? If *he* doesn't know then who the hell will?' Dot thundered, jabbing Peter's telegram as if he were standing in front of her. It had been two days since Dot had learned of Brenda's disappearance and she was still no closer to finding out where she had gone. 'I bet he's hiding her somewhere nearby, all so he can have his wicked way with her.'

'Dorothy, please.' Edwin sighed, taking off his glasses and rubbing his eyes. He had only recently returned from Devon and was feeling very tired. 'You're being ridiculous. Peter was very good to have got in touch with us and let us know Brenda wasn't with him as quickly as he did and where on earth do you think he would hide her? Under his bed before lights out? No army barracks in the land would tolerate such abuses. Now please, stop pacing up and down my office and calm down. You'll wear the floorboards out and I can assure you Liberty's does not have the funds to replace them.'

Sensing Edwin was about to lose his patience, Dot did as he asked and sat in the chair opposite him. Letting out a deep sigh, she did her best to try and calm down and get a sense of perspective. Since learning of Brenda's disappearance Dot had sent herself into a frenzy of worry. Resisting the temptation to batter Mrs Rogers with her handbag, she had instead stalked off down the road, racking her brains to try and think about where Brenda could have gone.

The first place she had tried was the WVS in nearby Shoreditch but they hadn't heard a thing. They had offered to keep an eye out and let Dot know if Brenda turned up, but other than that they hadn't been much help.

She had returned home, confused and afraid, to sit in the kitchen lost in her worries. In that moment she had longed to pen a letter to Ivy and tell her all about it. She could of course write to Helen, but Dot knew it wasn't fair to burden the girl any further.

Instead she had waited until Alice had finished bathing Arthur and then, when the girl was ready, Dot revealed everything. The disbelief in Alice's eyes had been hard to miss, as she too tried to make sense of the fact that Brenda was missing. The two of them had racked their brains to think where she might have gone, calling in not only all of the Liberty girls for help but Edwin and Henry too. Together, they had agreed to send telegrams to Peter along with Brenda's old employer, but other than that they had been at a loss. Dot knew that Brenda's mother had passed away and she had never mentioned the father who had run off. She wasn't sure who else was in the girl's life.

She had clung to the hope that Brenda had travelled down to be with Peter and that together they had come up with some hare-brained scheme that would see Brenda installed in a love nest. Even Dot had to admit it was a bit far-fetched but it was all she had to go on at the time.

But Peter's reply had reached the store that morning and Edwin had called Dot straight up to read it. Racing up the wooden stairs, the echo of her heels ringing through the store as she threw her feet down furiously, she hoped that it was good news.

Sadly, the scant words on the telegram had made her realise that good news was the last thing it was.

Brenda not with me. Not heard or seen from her for days. No idea where she is. Coming up to London as soon as I can. Peter

She had read through the message on the slip of paper at least ten times, hoping she might have missed something, but of course there was nothing. She had pinned all her hopes on Peter having the answer and knowing that he didn't had left her reeling in despair.

Now, as she sat in the office, Dot was struggling to recover her equilibrium when she heard the clatter of feet and a sharp rap on the door.

'Come in,' Edwin called clearly.

At that, Henry, Rose, Jean, Mary and Alice all burst through the door.

'What are you all doing here? Who's minding the department?' Dot asked, aghast.

'Mr Button asked us to come up,' Alice explained. 'And Mrs Kearns from gifts is keeping an eye on fabrics.'

'That's good of her. And what about you, madam?' she asked, her gaze turning to Mary. 'Why aren't you with your baby?'

'Mr B. telephoned me. I said I was coming into the store later anyway to go over plans for the beano so I came in early to talk about the Brenda situation. Mother's taking care of Emma.'

'So the cavalry's all here,' Henry said with a wry smile.

Dot turned to look at him. Perched on the edge of Edwin's desk, he looked so relaxed it was as if they were discussing a bit of missing paperwork, rather than a valued employee.

'Brenda is a young girl. She can't be on the streets. It's not safe.'

'It's not safe for the thousands bombed out of their homes who rely on the charity of shelters and the WVS every night, but they manage and Brenda will too. She's a resourceful girl,' Henry countered.

'Who's been through a lot,' Dot said firmly.

'I take it her old employers haven't heard anything from her either?' Edwin asked.

'No.' Alice sighed. 'We received a telegram from them at home yesterday and they've not seen her since she left.'

There was a silence then for a moment as everyone racked their brains for an idea of where she might have gone.

'She must be all right though,' Mary said, piercing the silence with her clipped tones. 'Otherwise she wouldn't keep ringing in to say she's not fit for work.'

It was as if a light bulb had gone off. 'Of course,' Dot shrieked, jumping to her feet in excitement. 'Of course she's fit and well, otherwise she wouldn't be able to call. She must still have some money then, or the ability to get to a telephone at the very least.'

'That's true.' Rose sighed. 'Or she's asked someone to call for her.'

'But why doesn't she just come back?' Alice protested. 'It make no sense. It wasn't her fault those clowns threw flour over her. It's their ignorance not hers.'

Dot bit her lip. She knew it wasn't Brenda's fault and no doubt Brenda knew it too, but it was an extra humiliation to bear. Dot knew that after what had happened with her old employer this could very well have had a damaging effect on the girl. She looked around at the group. Was now the time to share Brenda's story? With a heavy heart she believed that it was.

'I don't like telling tales but in this instance I think you should know that the reason Brenda left her previous post was because someone was hurting her.'

'Who?' Rose demanded.

'I'll bet I can make an educated guess,' Henry said, his eyes full of menace. 'Bound to have been the master of the house. It's a story as old as time.'

Dot shifted in her chair, feeling uncomfortable. 'Not quite, Henry, no, but that's not what's important here. Brenda swore me to secrecy and I don't feel as if I should tell all and sundry.'

Alice snorted. 'Charming.'

'As I was saying,' Dot said, ignoring Alice's outburst, 'the reason I mention it is because I'm worried about what's going on in her mind. She's fragile, yet she's really perked up the last few weeks, since she had that promotion.'

'And she obviously still cares about that,' Mary interjected. 'Otherwise she wouldn't be ringing up each day and asking to speak to the superintendent's office to say she can't come in.'

'Or someone's ringing up for her,' Rose repeated.

'She must realise this isn't right though, surely,' Jean said, looking exasperated as she leaned against the door. 'I don't mean to sound unsympathetic but not coming into work isn't the best way to keep your job.'

'But if she's homeless then her clothes won't be washed and cleaned for work and she won't feel capable of coming in. I bet she feels like a failure at the moment.' Alice sighed. 'She's been humiliated in her last job, humiliated at her second and now she's been thrown out on her ear by a landlady in a city she barely knows.'

'Which is all well and good, but none of that helps us work out where she is,' Rose put in. 'I mean, what's she doing for food? Sleep?'

'Same as the rest of London what's been bombed out, relying on scraps and hand-outs from the council,' Dot fired. 'No, she deserves better than this. Whilst I don't agree with her choice to form a friendship with Peter, none of this is her fault. We need to get through to her somehow.'

'Which we could do if we could find her.' Henry ran a hand through his hair. 'There must be someone who knows where she is.'

'Or someone helping her at the very least,' Mary offered.

At that the room fell silent again. Dot did her best to think. Brenda was friends with nobody in the city. Where she had gone was a mystery.

Just then the telephone rang and Edwin leaned forward to answer it. Dot knew she shouldn't eavesdrop but she couldn't help herself and quickly realised it was Peter on the phone.

'Very good,' Edwin replied. 'We shall see you tomorrow.'

With that he put the receiver down and looked at the group. 'As you probably gathered,' he said, looking pointedly at Dot, 'Peter is coming up tomorrow evening. He has been granted leave and has said he will help us look for Brenda. But he makes the point that now might be the time to call in the police.'

'The police?' Rose gasped. 'Surely not.'

'The girl has been missing for nearly three weeks with nobody apart from the superintendent's office hearing anything from her at all.' Mr Button sighed. 'Either we hope to goodness she turns up soon or we ring the authorities. I think the time has come.'

Dot thought for a moment. Contacting the police was a good idea but it was possible that men in uniform might scare Brenda off, or make her think there was something wrong. There had to be another way, something they could do that wouldn't put the frighteners on her. Not only that but with the beano fast on the approach Dot wanted this sorted soon. She couldn't bear to go away and leave the girl stranded.

'Let's just give it a couple more days,' she said. 'If Peter's coming up tomorrow we may well have another idea to consider and I think that involving the police, if that is what we decide, could very well frighten Brenda – which is the last thing we want.'

'I agree,' Henry said. 'Brenda, while fragile, is sensible. She won't do anything stupid. Let's give it a bit more time, see if she comes to her senses.'

As Edwin glanced around the room he saw nods of assent and Dot felt pleased.

'All right.' He sighed. 'Put your thinking caps on and see if you can come up with anything else, but if we've no new leads by Thursday I shall be handing this matter over to the police.'

He stood up to dismiss them all and Dot got to her feet too. She flashed Edwin a grateful smile. She had made a promise to Brenda that she would look out for her and she wasn't about to let her down now. Come hell or high water she would find that girl, and she wouldn't rest until it was done.

Chapter Thirty-Two

It had been two days since Mr Button had threatened to call the police and the Liberty girls were still no closer to finding Brenda. Peter had come up to London as promised, his face a picture of concern as Dot was pleased to note. But he had only been able to stay for an hour before he had to return to his unit and really there was nothing he could do and so it had all been a little bit pointless, though of course that was something Dot had kept to herself.

And yet despite Brenda's disappearance life still carried on. There was the beano coming up next week and many of their usual customers wanted to know when the autumn range of utility prints would be out and when they could start ordering them.

There was also the little matter of a wedding to organise. It was something Edwin had started to remind her about, and on top of that, Lady Humm and Mary's mother were due in the store later that morning for a final meeting with the rest of the team travelling to Devon to discuss final arrangements.

It was enough to make a grown woman weep, Dot thought as she slumped on the cash desk for a moment, head in hands.

'Don't let the customers catch you like that,' Rose quipped as she placed a large file in front of her.

Opening her eyes, Dot surveyed the file and then Rose. 'You look tired, darlin'.'

Rose grimaced as she rubbed the arch of her back. 'Yes, I suppose I am a bit. Struggling to sleep now I'm almost eight months gone but I am looking forward to going away next week.'

As she finished speaking she clamped her hands over her mouth in horror at what she had just said. 'Oh my days! I can't believe I just said such a thing and with Brenda missing and all.'

Dot smiled; it felt good to see someone acting normally for once. 'Life goes on, darlin'. There's no reason you shouldn't say something like that.'

'Even so,' Rose sighed, taking a seat behind the counter for a moment, 'I shouldn't have been so selfish.'

Dot let out a bark of laughter. 'I should think selfish is the last thing you are.'

'I have to say I agree entirely,' said a familiar voice.

Looking up, Dot saw a radiant-looking Bess and smiled. 'I didn't know you were coming in today.'

'Rose asked me yesterday if I could make it to the meeting. I'm on the executive first-aid committee,' Bess said authoritatively, removing her ruby-red felt hat to show she was serious.

'Well, I had no idea.' Dot smiled. 'Does that mean you're coming to Devon?'

'Yes.' Rose beamed, linking her arm through Bess's. 'I've said I'll need a trusty assistant if I'm to give a proper first-aid talk to the masses and so Mr B. said he was sure we could find a place for Bess.'

'Well, that's wonderful,' Dot said, her eye catching the stump where Bess's right hand used to be.

Bess shrugged. 'I don't know about that, but I do know that it will be nice to support Rose.'

'Jean tells me you've been doing a bit more first-aid work in the community when you can,' Dot said.

'That's right. I've been trying to reach as many people as possible. Rose really drummed into me the importance of first aid,' Bess replied.

'So where have you been going?' Dot asked.

Bess extricated herself from Rose for a moment, reached into her bag for a pamphlet entitled 'YOUR FIRST AID, YOUR LIFE' and passed it across the desk towards Dot. 'I've been sharing this with everyone. So they've got something to remember with the demonstration. I've gone all over London delivering these. 'Course it was hard to get the paper but the powers that be reckoned it was worth it.'

'Good on you, darlin',' Dot breathed, casting her eye across the paper. 'I suppose you meet all sorts.'

'Oh yes.' Bess smiled, a knowing grin on her face. 'Which reminds me, I wanted to let you know I think I saw your Brenda the other night.'

Dot dropped the pamphlet like a hand grenade and looked at Bess in surprise. 'You saw Brenda? Where? What did she say? Was she all right? Where is she staying? When is she coming back?'

Bess shrank back slightly. 'Calm down! I only said I saw her and that was it. I'm afraid I didn't get a chance to talk to her. It was at an event I was doing in the Quakers' hall round the corner, in the function room.'

'The Quakers' hall?' Dot frowned. 'What on earth was she doing there?'

'Search me. The WVS were there before I was, dishing out meals to the homeless, and she looked as if she had just finished eating, but she was all right, or at least she appeared to be.'

It was the news Dot had been hoping for but it still didn't explain what she was doing or where she was living.

'Did she look homeless, do you think?' Dot demanded.

'What does homeless look like?' Rose asked.

Dot sighed. 'You know what I mean. So, did she?'

'I don't know,' Bess said. 'She looked tired more than anything, but trust me, Dot, she's going to be closer than you think if she's turning up to events within these few streets.'

'You think she's somewhere near Liberty's?' Dot asked, her heart full of hope.

Bess nodded. 'I would expect so. I'll keep an eye out for her; there's a chance she'll come back to another meeting, especially if the WVS are giving out free meals.'

With that Bess and Rose slipped Dot a smile, and then walked upstairs to the office for the meeting. Watching them go, Dot felt a thud of pleasure: Brenda was all right, and really that was the only thing that mattered.

Bess's news had put Dot in such a good mood that she didn't mind one bit that she had to sit in a room with Mary's mother on such a beautiful morning. She took her place in between Lady Humm and Edwin, letting the barbed comments about her terrible dress sense and the many laughter lines on her face slide. None of it mattered as long as there was a possibility Brenda was all right.

'So where are we with final arrangements?' Edwin asked once pleasantries had been made and the meeting had got started.

'I think we're full steam ahead.' Lady Humm beamed, her ash-blonde hair glinting in the sunshine that streamed through the glass windows of the conference room. 'The designers are set to arrive first thing on Saturday the fourteenth. Some will be staying with us, some in the village nearby.'

'Blimey, and you've room for all of us as well,' Bess marvelled.

Geraldine smiled sarcastically. 'Dear, I can assure you that you will be well catered for. It's good of Lady Humm to let your sort stay in her home at all. One can only imagine what you will get up to.'

Dot felt irritated at the woman's rudeness but before she could say anything, Bess spoke up.

'My sort?' she said, smiling sweetly. 'What do you mean by that?'

'I mean, everyone knows what the working classes are like.' Geraldine sighed. 'If Lady Humm still has her silverware intact by the end of your stay it will be a miracle.'

Dot turned to Mary, sure the girl would say something at such abject rudeness, but she just blushed and stared at the table.

'Oh, come on now, Geraldine, you're joking, I'm sure!' Edwin chuckled.

'I'm sure she isn't,' Dot muttered under her breath, before addressing Lady Humm. 'Just how many bedrooms have you got, if you don't mind me asking. Have you enough?'

At the question Lady Humm frowned. 'Gosh, do you know, I have no idea. I've never counted.'

Dot patted her arm. 'If you don't have to count, darlin', I'm fairly sure you've got enough. Now, Mrs Kearns in gifts has kindly offered to take over fabrics for us while we're all away.'

'That's nice of her,' said Rose. 'And everyone knows that Dot and I will be away from next Monday?'

'We do.' Edwin nodded, and then turned to Henry. 'Henry will accompany you on the way down as well.'

'With Stan?' Rose begged, her eyes shining with delight.

'With Stan,' Henry confirmed with a smile. 'It's the kids' school holidays, isn't it, and Lady Humm kindly offered to have him come down for a little holiday.'

'It's no trouble.' Lady Humm smiled. 'It'll be a pleasure to have some little ones running about the place.'

'You won't be saying that when he's knocked off your best china,' Henry said. 'Stan can be a bit ... boisterous, shall we say.'

'So we are looking forward to welcoming Liberty's and friends to Haldale Hall next week,' Lady Humm finished. Getting to her feet, she signified that the meeting was over; as everyone else followed suit, she turned to Dot. 'I hope you don't mind but I've rather a treat in store for you.'

'Oh?'

'Yes. Dear Edwin told me you and he are getting married very soon, and, well, one of the designers that will be coming is a wedding-dress designer. I rather thought he might help you with a design to customise your old dress, and of course it would make a wonderful talk for our other designers. Perhaps you could bring it with you?'

Dot's jaw dropped in astonishment at the gesture and she turned to look at Edwin. She was surprised to see that he looked as delighted as Dot felt. About to open her mouth and say yes she was confronted with a stab of guilt. She didn't deserve such generosity and she didn't want to waste anyone's time, not least someone of Lady Humm's standing.

'What a lovely idea,' Mary gasped, before Dot could say anything. 'We had a fashion show last year and the winner was a lady that customised Alice's old wedding dress, wasn't it, Dot?'

Nodding, Dot smiled at the memory. It had been a lovely occasion. 'It's very kind of you, Lady Humm, but I don't want to put nobody to no bother.'

'Don't be silly – it's wonderful to even think about something as happy as a wedding rather than this blasted war and all the things we can't have,' Lady Humm replied.

'I think it's a wonderful idea,' Edwin exclaimed.

'It's certainly generous of you,' Dot added, taking care not to appear ungrateful.

'Well, that's sorted then.' Lady Humm smiled. 'I shall see you on Monday.'

With that she turned to go and Dot found tears pooling in her eyes at the kindness everyone was showing her. Looking at Edwin, she could see he felt the same, and she knew they could marry in a tin hut and their wedding would still be special so long as they were surrounded by so much love.

Chapter Thirty-Three

The little terrace in Bell Street was a flurry of activity that Sunday as Alice, Dot and even Arthur joined in to help Dot pack for Devon. There were clothes strewn across her bedroom, files and paperwork scattered along the landing in what Dot was sure was an orderly fashion, and in the middle of it all her good tan leather suitcase containing, so far, just three sets of underwear.

'You know you could probably take just those and get them washed down there,' Alice suggested.

'What, and use Lady Humm's mangle?'

Alice let out a bark of laughter. 'Don't be daft. I'll bet she's got one of them electric washing machines and staff to do the laundry for her.'

'Don't be ridiculous.' Dot sniffed. 'I shall not be giving my smalls to someone else to launder, thank you very much!'

Turning back to face the few clothes she deemed suitable for her stay, she sighed. There didn't seem enough here for a weekend never mind an entire week. She had picked out her most suitable garments – largely her Liberty's wardrobe – but she wasn't sure if they would be expected to change for what Lady Humm called dinner and Mary had been no help at all when she had asked her, simply saying wear whatever you feel like.

Dot frowned again. She didn't feel like doing any of this, not when Brenda was still no closer to being found. And then of course there was Helen to consider. She was looking forward to getting to know the girl better over the coming week but since the telegram Dot had sent suggesting tea on Thursday at three in the café in the department store, Dot had heard nothing. Should she still go to Torquay? And how would she get there?

Sinking on to the bed, Dot felt done in with worry.

'Why don't you borrow a couple of things from ready-to-wear? Mrs Crawford said you would be more than welcome to, didn't she?' Alice suggested.

Dot sighed. 'She did, but I don't want to be a bother.'

'She wouldn't have offered if she thought that,' Alice pointed out. 'Why don't you go and pick a couple of things up? You probably won't even need them but it might give you peace of mind. You've got a key to get into the store, haven't you?'

Dot nodded again and got to her feet, feeling decisive for the first time all day. 'You're right. And it will do me good to get out of here, I think. Edwin's popping over at six, but I'll be back well before then.'

An hour later and Dot was letting herself into the staff entrance of the store feeling like a cat burglar rather than an employee. It felt as if she were breaking some sort of cardinal rule by entering the store on a Sunday and she half expected a policeman to tap her on the shoulder at any moment to ask her what on earth she thought she was doing.

Locking the heavy wooden door carefully behind her, she padded up the stairs towards the staffroom. Out of habit more than out of need, she put her belongings into the staffroom and made her way towards the shop floor.

Walking down the central wooden staircase Dot felt a sudden thrill to see the store laid out before her. It felt like her own personal playground and she gasped in delight as she took in all the little details that she never usually had time to appreciate. The beautiful blue and white tiles that made up the sitting room near gifts; the ornate display cabinet stained a dark mahogany and lined with a rich red velvet to showcase the latest jewellery department treasures; even the beautiful stained glass that filled the window panes by the stairs, each depicting a different moment of Tudor life.

By the time Dot reached ready-to-wear she felt a little blindsided at all the beauty she had just witnessed and so she wasn't sure what to choose to take down to Devon. Thankfully Betty Crawford had taken the sting out of the choice: Dot saw to her delight that the department manager had selected two floor-length dresses, one in a delicate shade of pink and another in a navy, that were both her size and left them hanging up behind the cash register.

For you, Dot! Don't get your dinner down them or you'll be footing the bill! Enjoy, Betty Crawford

Reading the note, Dot chuckled. Betty was a woman after her own heart and didn't mince her words. She doubted that she would ever wear the dresses, but Alice was right, just holding them in her hands made her feel better, more prepared somehow for the week ahead. Dot wasn't sure what a week in a country house was going to involve but the last thing she wanted to do was look like the hired help.

As Dot walked away from the dresses and towards fabrics she realised her stomach was doing cartwheels at the thought of all that lay ahead. It was laughable that she had been asked to mix with designers and landed gentry. But as she made her way across the floor towards her department, Edwin's face came to mind and the words he had said when he offered her the job, *I believe in you Dotty.* Just seeing his handsome face in her mind's eye gave her comfort and her heart burst with love at the thought of this perfect, wonderful man who would be by her side for the rest of her life. This wedding of theirs would be such a celebration, she thought to herself with a smile, a testament to the love that they had rediscovered.

Passing by beauty she was amazed to see Beatrice Claremont working away on some filing. Walking across the floor, the heels of her heavily worn low navy court shoes making a click-clack sound across the parquet, Dot stood before the desk and greeted Beatrice warmly.

'I thought I was the only one daft enough to come in here on a Sunday! What's your excuse?'

Beatrice looked up, and whilst she mirrored Dot's warm smile the matriarch saw something else in those eyes – something that resembled panic or fear.

'I was just catching up on some paperwork after the stock-take. We found some deficits and I volunteered to go over them this weekend,' Beatrice replied, her cheeks pinking with colour.

'Sorry if I startled you,' Dot tried again, sensing she had somehow rattled Beatrice.

Beatrice's hands flew to her throat. 'Oh, not at all. I'm sorry. These figures make for depressing reading; I was a bit engrossed.'

'Bad, is it?'

Beatrice grimaced. 'Let's just say something's not quite right. Either we've made a terrible mess of recording all the stock in the last stock-take we did or someone's made a terrible error when selling items on the shop floor. We're almost a hundred pounds down.'

Dot's eyes widened with horror. A mistake like that could really cost the company, especially when times were so hard. It was down to all of them to ensure that there was no waste and every single item of stock was sold at the right price and accounted for.

'I've said it once and I'll say it again, it's a flaming good job the leather goods department over-bought all those handbags before the war otherwise we'd have nothing to sell. I swear they're the only things keeping us afloat.'

'You're not wrong, Dot.' Beatrice sighed as she pushed a pen behind her ear, messing up the grey chignon that was tied neatly away from her face. 'To tell the truth, it's nice to see a friendly face – I've felt a bit alone up here.'

'You must have been here a while,' Dot remarked as she gestured to the string of empty teacups that stood on the counter. 'Make sure you clear them away before Dreary Deirdre turns up tomorrow or you'll be for it.'

'Yes, of course,' Beatrice said with a smile that didn't meet her eyes. 'Sorry, Dot, tell me about you. It would be nice to have something else to think about besides all these missing items. Are you ready for tomorrow?'

'I am now Mrs Crawford's lent me these,' Dot said, patting the bag that contained her dresses. 'Though of course there's so much going on here that I feel guilty for going away. You might have missing stock; I've got a missing sales girl.'

'I heard about Brenda,' Beatrice said, her tone soft. 'You must be out of your mind with worry. What a wicked cow that landlady is, kicking a young girl into the street like that.'

Dot smiled. She found Beatrice's sympathy a comfort. 'Yes, hard to believe anyone would be so pig ignorant. I know none of us like a conchie—'

'Quite,' Beatrice agreed, cutting Dot off mid-sentence. 'But is that really a reason to throw someone out? The poor girl must be beside herself and so embarrassed.'

'Yes, but there's no need for her to be. We all just want to see her home safe and well.'

'And of course no family either,' Beatrice continued. 'She must feel very low. Have you had any news at all?'

'Bess thinks she saw her in the function room at the Quakers' hall nearby when the WVS were handing out hot dinners the other day. However, she fled once she realised Bess had clocked her so it's possible she's still nearby.' Dot sighed. 'I'm just so worried about her. I wish we could help her, because I'm sure we can. Running off isn't the answer – there's all sorts out there.'

'Well, you go off to Devon and try and forget about all this for now. I'll keep an eye out for her,' Beatrice promised. 'I'll even pop down to the Quakers' hall again on WVS night and see if she's there. If she is I'll talk to her.'

Relief flooded through Dot. 'Would you really, darlin'? That would be a weight off, thank you.'

'My pleasure,' Beatrice replied with a grin that, this time, met her eyes. 'Now, haven't you got better things to do than waste your time talking to me? You've got an early start, I'm sure, tomorrow.'

'You're right.' Dot beamed. 'I'll be off, and thanks again, Beatrice.'

'Anytime.'

Feeling a lot more cheerful than she had when she arrived, Dot made her way to the staff entrance and let herself out. As she stepped into the gleaming sunshine she reached into her bag to lock the door behind her when she stopped and realised something. She was sure she had locked that door when she came in. In fact she would swear to it. She always checked the handle to make sure it was in place and she had done that very thing before she raced up the stairs. As she took a step back and observed the scruffy door from afar she realised one of two things had happened. Either she was losing her marbles, and on some days she might well agree that was the case, or an intruder had done a very strange thing and broken out of the store.

Chapter Thirty-Four

'I have said I will look into it and I will,' Edwin replied for what he was sure was the twelfth time that morning.

'I know you think I'm losing my mind, and perhaps I am,' Dot said as she stood on the busy platform of Paddington Station waiting for her train. 'But there are young girls working in that store, and if there is some sort of intruder up to Gawd knows what then we should call the police.'

Edwin scratched his head and pushed the glasses he found he was reliant upon more and more these days back up his nose and sighed. 'Dorothy, I am not prepared to keep repeating myself. I will look into this issue. Now, please, will you board the train and let me worry about what's happening with store security.'

Sensing she had made her point, Dot nodded and reached down for her suitcase, only for Edwin to lay a hand on hers. 'Excuse me,' he said gently, 'but whilst ladies may be at the bar these days, I think you'll find they don't carry their own suitcases. Now let's get you to your seat.'

She smiled with affection as Edwin took her case and walked through the carriages until he found her seat right next to the window. Securing her case in the luggage rack, he helped her settle in her seat and, whilst she knew it wasn't very modern of her to admit it, Dot did rather enjoy being fussed over.

'I'll see you on Friday,' she said warmly.

'You will,' he replied, tipping his hat as another lady entered the carriage. 'Would you like me to wait until the others get here or will you be all right?'

Dot rolled her eyes; she might like the occasional fuss but that didn't mean she needed mollycoddling. 'Get away with you, will you? You've a store to run and an intruder to find.'

Edwin lifted his eyebrows. 'How many times, Dorothy?'

'And how long is it before you realise I'm pulling your leg?' she said softly, leaning forward to give him a kiss. Pulling back she saw the love radiating from his eyes and knew she had reached him just as she had when he was a boy and she was nothing more than a shy teenager.

'I'll miss you,' he whispered.

'And I you,' she replied. 'Now go.'

Edwin smiled and as she watched him walk away she knew that she would miss him more than she realised. He had fast become her world, and after so many years on her own after George's passing, it was a very odd sensation indeed to feel so reliant upon one other person to make you feel whole.

Peering through the grimy window she saw Edwin disappear into the crowds and felt a sudden sadness wash over her. This was supposed to be an opportunity to see Helen and to get to know her better, but everything felt as if it was spiralling into chaos.

It also felt odd, she realised, to be sitting on an Exeter-bound train knowing that her friend wouldn't be at the other end of the line to welcome her. Devon without Ivy in it made very little sense to Dot and if she was honest with herself she was frightened that she wouldn't manage, that the pain of losing her friend and seeing Helen without her would be the undoing of her.

A lone tear trickled down Dot's cheek and she gave in to the feelings of sadness that had been threatening to overwhelm her. Turning her face back towards the window, she saw Mary, her arm linked through Rose's as they walked along the platform looking for their carriage. Not far behind them were Henry, Stan and Emma. Henry was clearly carrying everyone's bags while Emma had been entrusted to the care of Stan, who was very proudly pushing her pram along the platform.

Wiping the tear from her eye, Dot stood up and waved. Mary was the first to catch sight of the matriarch and wave back, excitement plastered all over her face. As the others joined in Dot felt those feelings of sadness begin to leave her and she smiled at the little group she was proud to call her friends and helped them all on board.

'Blimey! It's a few days away, not a year-long holiday,' Dot said as she took in the sight of all the luggage. There weren't just suitcases, but boxes, attaché cases, bags and hat boxes.

Mary shrugged as she settled Emma on her lap. 'Who knows what we'll need. There was talk of shooting at one point?'

'Shooting?' Henry raised an eyebrow.

'Oh, don't worry.' Mary grinned, waving his concerns away. 'Anything we bagged would of course be given to the food-supply chain.'

Dot shook her head. It was another world. 'Never mind all that, are you all right, Rose love? You do look a bit tired.'

'I'm always tired.' Rose smiled as she sat in her chair opposite Dot. 'I think that's the way every pregnant woman feels.'

'I imagine it is,' Henry said. 'But you must say if you're not feeling up to anything, Rose. You look almost grey.'

'Thank you, Prince Charming,' she teased, earning herself a round of laughter.

'Anyway, more excitingly, what's all this about an intruder?' Mary asked. 'I bumped into Alice this morning on my way here. She gave me a few scant details and promised you would fill me in on the rest.'

'It's nothing.' Henry sighed. 'Crossed wires, I think.'

Dot felt a swell of fury. 'It was not crossed wires. There was an intruder.'

Quickly, she told the group what had happened, earning herself glances of incredulity and horror.

'So was it a big monster?' Stan asked when Dot had finished. 'Did you see him?'

Dot shook her head. She had been aware when she was recounting her story that Stan was only little and she didn't want to scare him.

'It wasn't anything, Stan,' Henry added. 'I'm sure it was just a misunderstanding.'

'Are you definitely sure you locked the door?' Mary asked.

Dot felt a stab of frustration; this was just what Edwin had repeatedly asked her. 'Of course I'm sure. I always lock the door behind me if I go in after hours, just as we all do.'

'Well, someone didn't then,' Rose said. 'It's not likely to be a burglar though really, is it? I mean, it was broad daylight and, let's face it, everyone knows the shops these days have nothing to sell.'

Rose's comment earned her another peal of laughter and even Dot managed a smile.

'You make a good point, darlin', but if it's not an intruder then who was it?'

A brief silence fell across the group as they racked their brains for alternative ideas as to who could have broken into the store but nobody seemed able to come up with anything.

Eventually the little group gave up thinking about the incident and instead turned their attention to the lush countryside that passed before them as the hours of travel went by. Dot had always loved this particular train journey down to Devon, enjoying the coastal track between Starcross and Teignmouth where the train travelled so close to the sea it almost felt as if you were riding the waves on a boat rather than being powered through the county by steam train.

As they passed Coryton Cove, Dot felt a flash of pleasure seeing Stan press his face right up to the window. The combination of rich red rocky cliff next to bright blue sea, interwoven with the emerald-green countryside that perched on top of the cliff edge, made for a magnificent view.

Stan's excitement was almost enough to take Dot's mind off the nervousness she was feeling at returning to the county that had filled her with so much heartache. But as she took in the familiar sights of the journey ahead, she steeled herself and thought of Ivy. Whatever lay in store over the next few days, she owed it to her friend to find the confidence Ivy knew she had and face whatever was coming her way.

Chapter Thirty-Five

The mansion was nothing short of beautiful. In fact, Dot couldn't help but think that to call Lady Humm's stately pile a mansion was doing it a disservice. It was more of a castle – after all, it did boast six turrets! And with its sweeping gravel drive surrounded by landscaped colourful gardens filled with exquisite topiary and privet hedges, not to mention beautifully manicured gardens that Capability Brown would have been proud of, it definitely deserved castle status in its own right.

The gardens were nothing compared to the house that Dot would call home for the next few days. She had never seen anything like it. Set in a U shape, the castle (as she called it) was three storeys high, lined with beautiful sash windows that gleamed to within an inch of their lives. Large double oak-panelled doors that reminded Dot of Liberty's formed the entrance. There was also a liveried butler, old enough to be her father, whose age was perhaps the only sign that war had touched Lady Humm's home – that and the outline of the blackout blinds which hung ominously from the windows overhead.

Once they had been shown inside, Dot had done her best not to stare at the beauty that lay before her. It was hard not to feel out of place and Dot had instantly found herself looking down at her worn shoes (though they were her best) and skirt, which she knew had a slight hole in it, and felt ashamed. What was she doing in a place like this?

Yet the moment Lady Humm greeted them all with a big smile, wearing a pair of muddy wellies and heavily patched tweed skirt, Dot had felt herself relax. As their first evening wore on Dot had found herself feeling more comfortable. There had been no need to dress for dinner as she'd feared, and when she'd asked Lady Humm what she would be wearing, the woman had looked confused and simply said, 'What I've got on, I expect. Life's too short to change for dinner.'

And so Dot had found she settled into life at the castle remarkably quickly. She had been here three nights now and had become used to sitting at the grand dining table for her meals. She was also getting used to Jenkins, the butler-come-handyman-come-do-anything-Lady- Humm-needed-chap, pouring her a cup of tea just when she wanted.

But most of all she was grateful for the chance to relax. She and Mary had thrown themselves into their Liberty's duties in readiness for the event at the weekend. Together they had organised the shipment of fabrics that had arrived on the Tuesday by train; they had put together thoughtful presentations to discuss the nature and use of the fabrics, and had helped Rose with her first-aid event so she could rest as much as possible.

Despite the fact there had been a huge amount of work to get through and she still struggled with those old nagging doubts that she simply wasn't capable of anything but the mundane, Dot had felt the weight on her shoulders lessen and the knot in her stomach grow smaller. She had also slept soundly since she had arrived and could only put it down to the fact there seemed less to worry about here.

This morning, however, that familiar knot of worry had re-emerged as she knew later that day she would be seeing Helen. Thankfully the girl had sent a note to Lady Humm's home after Dot had written to her letting her know where she would be if she needed her. It had arrived yesterday, confirming the time and the meeting place Dot had suggested in her telegram, along with a few brief words saying she was looking forward to it.

Now, as Dot sat at the breakfast table with a freshly poured cup of tea courtesy of Jenkins, she found she was too keyed up to drink it. She had worried how she would get to Torquay but Lady Humm had told her it was no problem. Jenkins was an ARP warden for the area and as such had received a fresh supply of motor spirit coupons; consequently he would be able to take her and Mary into Torquay, naturally ensuring he performed ARP duties while there. Mary was delighted at the prospect of being able to stroll along the harbour front, as Lady Humm had kindly offered to take care of Emma.

And so, just after lunchtime, Dot found herself nestled in the back seat of a car, Mary by her side and Jenkins at the wheel.

'You must be nervous,' Mary remarked as the car sped through the country lanes.

Dot jumped a little. Was it really so obvious how she felt? 'What makes you say that?'

Mary turned to face her, incredulity spread across her pretty, angular features. 'Well, I would be nervous going to see the daughter of my best friend who had just died. I'd be worrying about what to expect.'

'And what would you expect?' Dot asked. This conversation was making her feel awkward.

Turning to look out of the window, Mary thought for a moment. 'I think I would expect nothing. Grief is a terrible thing; none of us knows how it's going to impact on us, or how we'll feel.'

Dot clamped a hand over her friend's and allowed the warmth of her skin to seep into her soul. 'Your father,' she said softly. 'I think we all keep forgetting to ask how you're doing. What with you sorting everything out with your mother, we all expect you to be right as rain.'

There was a silence before Mary spoke and Dot wondered if the girl had heard her.

'I miss my father dreadfully, Dot. I think about him all the time and I so wish things could have been different between us. It's something I shall regret every day for the rest of my life.'

'But it wasn't your fault,' Dot said fiercely. 'You know that. This is on your parents, not you.'

'I know,' Mary said. 'But now I've a chance to make up for lost time with Mother and I'm grateful for that. It's what Daddy wanted before he died.'

Dot thought for a moment. 'Didn't you say how proud he was of you for all you had achieved on your own?'

Mary nodded and gazed down at her hands resting in her lap. 'He was. He said I reminded him of himself and how he had worked for everything he had.'

'Then why are you allowing yourself to change who you are?' Dot asked gently.

The younger woman looked up, a flash of outrage crossing her face. 'I'm not. What makes you say that?'

Dot paused for a moment. She had vowed to keep her mouth shut but the subject seemed to have crept up quite naturally and she wanted to be honest with her friend.

'You're not being yourself around your mother. That strong, confident and capable girl we have all come to love: she's nowhere to be seen when your mother is there. You let her get away with murder. The old Mary wouldn't have stood for half the things she says.'

'That's not true,' Mary said with a hint of defiance in her voice.

'Isn't it?' Dot whispered.

At that Mary turned away and gazed out of the window. For one awful moment Dot agonised over what she had just said. She shouldn't have spoken to Mary like that; she should have kept her mouth shut. What happened to letting Mary come to the realisation herself? She was about to apologise when Mary broke the silence.

'You're right,' she admitted. 'I know I've been different. I'm starting to despise myself for it.'

'That's silly, darlin',' Dot admonished. 'This has been a very difficult time for you; we all do what we can to survive.'

Mary nodded, tears still spilling down her cheeks. 'I know that – it's just that I already lost my mother once, I don't want to lose her again. I'm scared if I'm not agreeable she'll disappear, that she won't love me anymore. I just don't think I could go through all that again.'

At that Mary started truly weeping, great sobs racking through her body as she heaved backwards and forwards with the sheer effort of sobbing for the family she had lost.

Dot rubbed her back as if she were no more than a child. Glancing at Jenkins, she saw he was looking straight ahead, taking great care to ignore the scene playing out in the back.

'Darlin', you've suffered a terrible ordeal and thankfully you made up with your father before he passed on. You are a wonderful young woman, you are bright, clever, funny, strong and bursting with confidence. Your mother should know the real you, warts 'n' all, because that, Mary, is very much worth knowing.'

Mary lifted her chin and wiped her tears with the back of her hand. 'Do you think so?'

'I know so.'

'And what if she turns her back on me again?'

Dot took a deep breath and thought for a moment. She knew what it was to risk losing your family over one decision. 'Darlin', if she doesn't want to be around you because you're being true to who you are then she's not worth having in your life. You've got David, Emma and all your friends who love you for who you really are. You deserve better, my darlin'.'

Silence fell between the two of them as the car pulled into Torquay, and they took in the sights of the little seaside town. Dot could see already how the town seemed different somehow since the bombing. It had more of a subdued air; the people seemed joyless. Dot was saddened. The war had changed the spirit of so many towns and cities; nowhere was untouched.

Once Jenkins had brought the car to a stop near the harbour he opened the door for the two women and the pair stepped out. Thanking him, Dot turned to Mary, about to make an arrangement to see her later when the girl laid a hand on her arm.

'You're right, Dot. I can't give in to Mother any more. I've come too far; I've got to be who I really am. If I'm not, what sort of message am I sending to Emma? I want her to be a strong and capable woman. If she sees me lying about who I am and pretending to be something I'm not then I've no business raising a woman in this world. What do you think, Dot?'

At the question Dot smiled. This was the Mary she knew and loved. 'You don't need my approval, darlin', but for what it's worth I think you're right. We owe it to each other to be who we are, and we should never apologise for it. Be true to yourself, darlin'; it's all we can ever do.'

Chapter Thirty-Six

After Dot bade Mary goodbye with promises to meet her at six o'clock by the hotel on the harbour front, she made her way towards the café. It had just gone half past two and so she knew she had plenty of time before she was due to meet Helen, though she didn't want to be late. Dot wanted to get a good table and some decent food into the girl.

Following her conversation with Mary in the car, Dot felt buoyed with enthusiasm. She had always hoped that Mary would find her feet again given time and encouragement. Dot had never wanted to push her friend – she knew that approach would only send her in the other direction. The girl had needed time and now it seemed as though she would be making inroads towards living the life she deserved.

Walking up to the top floor and into the café, she realised with a start that she too could do with taking a leaf out of Mary's book. When was she going to start being true to herself and living the life she deserved? Spotting a waitress approaching her, Dot gave her best smile and was pleased when the older woman led her towards a table that overlooked the sea.

As her gaze drifted towards the water she allowed herself to relax and put all her worries aside. She was about to see Helen again, and she wanted to make sure she gave the girl her undivided attention.

At five minutes to three, Dot caught sight of Helen walking through the café door. She stood up to wave but her welcoming smile slipped as she took in Helen's appearance. There was no other way to describe it: the girl looked dreadful. Her clothes were falling from her painfully thin frame, her hair was dirty and unkempt, while the pleated skirt she was wearing had so many holes in it, it could have passed for a string bag.

'Hello, darlin',' Dot said, doing her best to smile as Helen drew near, leaning across to give her a kiss on the cheek. 'How are you?'

Helen took a seat and nodded at Dot. 'I'm fine.'

Dot said nothing. Just as she had with Mary, Dot realised that she would have to pick her moment to talk to Helen about how true that statement really was and now, when they had just met, wasn't the best time.

'You been keeping well?' she asked, signalling the waitress that they were ready to order.

Nodding, Helen remained mute.

'And you still been working up the factory?' Dot asked again after giving their order to the waitress.

Now Helen shook her head. 'They sacked me.'

'Sacked you?' Dot asked in alarm. 'Why?'

'Said I was always late. They told me to set an alarm clock, but I told them I can't hear an alarm clock and so Mum was always the one that woke me, but she's not here anymore ...'

As Helen's voice trailed off Dot felt a flash of sadness. Her heart went out to Helen; she hadn't just lost a mother, she had lost the woman who had been her compass through life. It was heartbreaking.

Looking around at the other café-goers, Dot could see – though they were trying to hide it – from their hushed tones and the way they were all casually glancing over their shoulders when they thought Dot and Helen weren't looking, that they were gossiping about them. Dot felt furious. How dare these people judge an innocent girl like this? They ought to be helping Helen in her hour of need not gawping at her as though she were a side show. Where was their community spirit?

She wanted nothing more than to go over there and have a go at them all, but having done that once before she knew that wasn't what was required. Instead what she needed to do was focus on Helen.

'You look like you need something to eat,' Dot said eventually, pushing across the table towards her a tongue sandwich that the waitress had helpfully just delivered.

Helen shrugged. 'I'm not hungry.'

'Well, I am,' Dot said, helping herself to a sandwich and then pouring them each a cup of tea. 'And I hate eating alone – people think you're a right greedy guts and you won't make me look like that, will you? Not in public?'

Dot wasn't sure if she had said too much for Helen to be able to lip-read but the girl seemed to have got the gist and raised a smile. Helen picked up the sandwich and Dot felt a flood of relief as she saw her take a bite.

'So have you seen much of your friends?' she asked after a moment.

Helen nodded.

'That's good,' Dot said encouragingly. 'And your neighbour Connie? Has she been around?'

'Yes,' Helen replied, her tone listless as she picked at her sandwich. 'But she has her own family and can't stay long. She helps me clean the house though.'

Dot said nothing. She could well imagine the state Helen was living in if her clothes were anything to go by.

'So how are you coping?' she asked gingerly. 'For money, like, darlin'?'

Helen shrugged. 'I've got a bit put by. Mum left me some, and there's the house that was hers.'

Not for the first time in her life Dot found herself thanking her lucky stars she and Ivy had been blessed with husbands who had left them their own bricks and mortar to live in. Heaven only knew what would have happened to Helen by now otherwise.

'And are you eating? Getting to the shops and getting your rations?'

'Connie does that for me but it doesn't change anything.'

'Change anything?' Dot echoed. 'How do you mean?'

Helen pushed her plate away from her and folded her arms. 'I mean Mum's gone, Dot, and there doesn't seem any point to life any more. She was my world; we did everything together. Nothing matters now she's not here to share anything with. I miss her. I miss my mum.'

With that silent tears streamed down Helen's face and Dot wrapped an arm around her shoulder and let the girl sob for the woman who had been her world. As Helen continued to weep Dot very much felt like joining her. She too missed Ivy more than she could bear. There were times she thought her heart would break with the pain of it all – especially when she thought about her wedding. Whilst she wanted nothing more than Edwin to be by her side, there was something very cruel about planning something so wonderful without her childhood friend by her side to share in the magic. Now, however, wasn't the time to join in with Helen's tears. This was a moment when she had to be strong for Ivy's girl. A few minutes later, when she stopped crying,

Helen lifted her chin from Dot's shoulder and managed a watery smile.

'Sorry, I've made your shoulder all wet.'

Dot smiled. 'Don't be daft, darlin', my shoulders are broad enough for all your tears.'

'Thank you,' Helen whispered.

Taking that as her cue to return to her seat, Dot regarded Helen carefully. The cry seemed to have done her good. She was breathing more easily and seemed to have found a little appetite, judging by the more enthusiastic bite she was now taking out of her sandwich. Dot took a sip of tea and thought for a moment. It was very clear to her that Helen wasn't coping but she wasn't sure how best to handle it. Dot would do anything to see the girl smile again; perhaps the time had come for Dot to be brave.

'Listen, Helen, darlin',' she began, 'I don't know if I've told you but I'm getting married in October.'

At the word 'married' Helen did indeed manage another smile. 'That's lovely. Congratulations, Dot. Is it to that Edwin who you were courting when you were younger?'

'Yes. Did your mum mention him?' she asked.

'Occasionally,' Helen replied. 'Not often. She did say that even though you adored your husband George you had always had a soft spot in your heart for your first love Edwin.'

Dot shook her head in wonder. How well her friend had known her. Of course she had always loved Edwin. They had shared a very special bond and yes, whilst she had always adored George, her heart had never forgotten Edwin.

'The thing is, I would have asked your mum to help me organise things,' Dot began, 'but, well, with her not being here, I wondered if you might like to help instead?'

Helen glanced at her, curiosity in her eyes. 'You mean take on some of Mum's role?'

'That's it,' Dot said encouragingly. 'I mean, you're ever such a good knitter, would you mind knitting me a shawl perhaps? Or helping out with some decorations?'

'How would I get everything to you?' Doubt was sweeping across Helen's face now.

'You could come and stay with me for a bit,' Dot offered carefully. 'In London. Just for a little while.'

'London?' Helen echoed, a look of panic replacing the doubt. 'I've never been.'

'It's lovely,' Dot cooed, crossing her fingers as she thought of the grimy streets, bombed-out buildings and rubble littering what was left of the pavements. 'Or at least the parts Hitler ain't bombed are.'

'Could you take me to Liberty's to look at the wool?' Helen asked, the idea clearly taking root in her mind.

''Course,' Dot said. 'And I'll take you for a posh tea up at Lyons Corner House, and we'll go to the pictures afterwards.'

'Really?'

'Really,' Dot promised. 'I'll take you to Regent's Park. And we can go up Trafalgar Square, and to see Big Ben too.'

Helen thought for a moment, her mind clearly full of new places.

'So what do you think?' Dot asked gently.

'How long would I stay?' Helen asked, that look of doubt returning to her eyes.

'As long as you want,' Dot promised.

'I had better ask Connie,' Helen said finally. 'And I should talk to the Sunday school teachers too. And I don't know if I have enough clean clothes.'

'All that can be sorted out,' Dot said firmly. 'I'll talk to Connie and the Sunday school teachers with you if you like.'

'Would you?' Helen asked, her voice full of hope now.

'Yes. Now, we will leave on Sunday afternoon. Can you be ready by then?'

Helen nodded.

'Good,' Dot said with a smile. 'I shall come over early on Saturday morning and together we can talk to everyone.'

Helen nodded again and Dot checked her watch. To her amazement she saw it was half past five. Quite where the time had gone she wasn't sure. Getting to her feet, she slipped her cardigan on and watched as Helen did the same.

'Are you going to take those tongue sandwiches home with you?' Dot asked, looking at the leftovers still stood on the plate.

Helen shrugged. 'I'm not hungry.'

Dot said nothing. Instead she reached into her handbag, pulled out a clean handkerchief and wrapped them deftly inside the thin fabric, then put them into Helen's cardigan pocket. 'You eat them later.'

'All right,' Helen agreed.

With that Dot settled the bill and together the two walked outside into the warm August air.

'So I'll see you on Saturday,' Dot said. 'Eight o'clock be all right?'

'Yes.'

Dot smiled. 'Good.'

She was about to walk away when Helen launched herself towards her and wrapped her arms around her neck. A stab of emotion tugged at Dot's heart as she pulled the girl into her embrace and held her tight.

'Thank you, Dot,' she heard Helen say into her chest. 'Thank you.'

Dot said nothing. Not only did she know that Helen wouldn't be able to hear her but she also knew that what she felt in that moment could never truly be put into words. She held on to Helen even tighter, knowing she never wanted to let her go.

Chapter Thirty-Seven

By the time the rest of the Liberty's contingent arrived at Lady Humm's mansion on Friday night, Dot, Mary and Rose were worn out. All week the trio had put together fabric samples, organised seating charts and timetables, gone through workshop ideas and thought about anything and everything to do with fabrics that would showcase the Liberty prints to the designers. Now, Dot and Mary were fit for bed, as was Rose, who was still exhausted thanks to her ever-growing bump.

Yet, despite the tiredness, Dot felt happier than she could remember since Ivy's death. It had broken her heart to see Helen so grief-stricken but knowing she had the chance to help her gave Dot a renewed sense of purpose. She was sure that taking Helen back to London was for the best and that with a bit of love and affection, not to mention some home-cooked meals, Helen would get back on her feet. Then they could consider what would happen next. Obviously, Dot would love Helen to stay in London, but she knew that she couldn't push the girl. She was like a frightened rabbit and if Dot pressed her too hard she had a feeling Helen would run. For now, Dot was thrilled that she and Helen would have the chance to really get to know one another.

Now, she just had to let Alice know that someone else would be moving into the little box room. But she had a feeling Alice would be as thrilled as she was that Helen was staying. They had always taken in waifs and strays over the years so this would be no different. At least, not as far as Alice was concerned.

The other issue would of course be Edwin. Watching him now amble up the steps and make his way into the house, she had to resist the urge to run to him and welcome him in front of the staff. She had missed him more than she could have anticipated and, seeing him pause and take in the essence of the house, her heart felt as if it was bursting with love. Edwin was her home, her family; he would be as supportive of Helen coming to London as Dot, of that she was sure.

'Hello, stranger,' she said, settling for a peck on the cheek rather than the full-blown embrace she secretly wanted.

'Dotty!' Edwin's face lit up with delight at the sight of her. 'How I've missed you.'

'And I you,' Dot replied, the warmth in her voice unmistakeable. 'We've been busy here.'

'So I can see,' Edwin said, his eyes sweeping across the hallway and drinking in the Liberty fabrics they had artfully draped around the walls.

Dot beamed. 'I think we've done well.'

'I should say you've done brilliantly,' Alice's voice sang from behind.

Dot whirled around and saw her old friend standing in the entrance, holding Arthur balanced on one hip with one hand and her suitcase in the other.

'I'd give you a hug, but I've nowhere to put my arms,' she said wryly.

'And there's me thinking you'd have been straight over to pick up my suitcase,' Alice quipped.

Dot was amazed at how much she had missed the two of them this week. At dinner, while Jenkins served her wine, Dot didn't feel guilty or ashamed that she wasn't up on her feet helping. Instead, she relaxed in the moment and enjoyed the fact that everyone that should be here was here.

The designers had arrived at the same time as the Liberty's group and it was fair to say everyone was getting along well. With the table fully engrossed in conversation, Dot turned to Edwin and asked the one question that had been on her mind since he had arrived.

'Has Brenda been found yet?'

Edwin pursed his lips and shook his head sadly. 'Not a word. We've gone back to Mrs Rogers and Peter has even checked her old room, but there was nothing.'

Dot shook her head in disbelief. How could the girl just disappear like that?

'And the mystery of the intruder?'

Dot was sure she saw Edwin roll his eyes heavenwards before he turned and addressed her. 'I did speak to the police, but they found no sign of a break-in or of anything amiss.'

Dot grimaced. 'Are they quite sure? Did they do a thorough check?'

'They checked everywhere, Dorothy, and I can promise you nothing was discovered. Apart from some empty teacups in your stockroom, I might add. You know you can't eat or drink down there,' Edwin said in a mock teasing tone.

'We don't!' Dot said, feeling a flush of colour creep across her cheeks. 'Well, not often.'

Edwin raised an eyebrow as he returned to his chicken breast. 'I turn a blind eye to many things, Dorothy, including you lot eating in the stockroom, but what I will say is: clear up after yourselves and don't make a habit of it. Honestly, it rather looked as though you had set up for the afternoon down there, there were teacups and bits of bread in the corner.'

'Bread?' Dot asked in surprise. They didn't eat toast or sandwiches down there, at least not unless they were very busy. 'Oh, it must have been from the stock-take. I'll have a word with the girls.'

'Make sure you do,' Edwin replied. 'You know we can't have mice in the building.'

Dot was about to agree when she caught sight of Rose doing her best not to yawn whilst chatting to designer Madame DuPont. Dot knew that Madame DuPont was a close friend of Lady Humm having moved to Britain with her in the thirties and set up home in Buckinghamshire.

'Rose, darlin',' Dot hissed as discreetly as she could after Madame Dupont broke away to talk to Lady Humm. 'Are you all right?'

'Fine.' Rose nodded, doing her best to stifle yet another yawn. 'All this sea air, I think, making me tired.'

'You sure that's all it is?' Dot frowned. 'You look peaky.'

'Thanks for the compliment,' Rose said with a smile.

Dot frowned again. She didn't want to be rude but Rose was looking greyer with every passing day.

Just then Madame DuPont turned back to Rose and smiled, resting a hand over her bump. 'You are very pregnant, yes? When are you due?'

'In about a month,' Rose said. 'Not long now.'

'Oh Rose, I remember just what it was like,' Alice said across the table. 'You feel tired all the time and can barely get up. You're doing wonderfully, but do take a rest when you can.'

'Because heaven knows you won't get one when he or she is here,' Dot said sagely.

At that, the table erupted into laughter, and Dot shook her head. She had never understood why she was often the subject of much hilarity when she was usually only speaking her mind.

'Anyway, Dot, have you shared your news with Edwin yet?' Mary asked as the plates were cleared away.

'Oh yes?' Edwin looked expectantly at Dot. 'What news is this?'

Dot glared at Mary. She had wanted to share this news in private, not at the dinner table in front of all and sundry. 'I've invited Helen to come and stay in London for a little while. She can help us with the wedding plans.'

'How wonderful.' Edwin beamed. 'When will she arrive?'

'Well, I said she could come back with us on Sunday if that suits?' Dot said, thinking she perhaps oughtn't to have been quite so hasty.

Edwin smiled up at Jenkins as he took his plate and then looked back at Dot. 'I think we can find a space for her on the train. Lady Humm isn't coming back with us now, she will be staying here to talk to the designers some more so I think she can have her seat.'

'Of course.' Lady Humm beamed. 'I should be glad to. Is this the girl you went to see yesterday, Mrs Hanson? The young woman who lost her mother recently?'

'Yes, Lady Humm, and that really is very kind of you,' Dot said sincerely. She had become rather fond of the aristocrat in the last few days.

'Well, really,' Mary's mother piped up. 'I think that's very generous of you, Patricia, but you shouldn't go around taking advantage, Dorothy. It's not for you to accept charity from Liberty's for a free ticket for your friend's daughter, no matter how grief-stricken she might be. There's a little thing called self-respect.'

Dot felt her hackles rise, but to her surprise Lady Humm came to her rescue.

'I don't know how many times I have to ask you, Geraldine, but I would appreciate it if you didn't speak to people that way, especially in my home. There is no need for it,' she said firmly, before turning to Dot. 'My dear, I am sure the girl can't be having an easy time. Would you like to bring her here tomorrow? Perhaps give her a tour of the house? Then you can all set off together on Sunday.'

'Oh I don't know about that, Lady Humm. I shouldn't want to put you to any trouble,' Dot said truthfully. It was kind enough of her ladyship to give up her train seat never mind allow Dot to bring in her lost souls.

'It's no trouble at all,' Lady Humm said. 'From what I remember you telling me, she's deaf, is that right?'

'She is, your ladyship,' Dot confirmed. 'But she lip-reads wonderfully as long as you speak slowly.'

Mary's mother shook her head in disgust. 'It's not right for her to be here. Shouldn't she be in an institution where she can be properly cared for? I don't wish to be cruel but surely you can see the whole thing is ridiculous.'

'What exactly is ridiculous?' Dot replied, eyeing Geraldine with a steely gaze. 'The fact I wish to help someone I love get back on their feet, or the fact she has been invited into this grand home?'

'Well, really,' Geraldine said under her breath before turning to her daughter, who was also looking at her with disgust in her eyes. 'You know what I meant.'

'I think we know exactly what you meant, Mother,' Mary replied coldly. 'You are a guest in Lady Humm's home and yet your behaviour is letting you down.'

Geraldine's jaw dropped open in surprise. 'What did you just say to me, Mary?'

Dot glanced at Mary and saw her lift her chin a little more defiantly now. 'I said your behaviour is letting you down. You should know better.'

'I quite agree,' Lady Humm said. 'I have a deaf cousin I am extremely fond of. He led a rather wonderful life in India and yet of course if he had been placed in an institution he would have done no such thing. And now,' she added with a smile as she addressed the table, 'I rather think it's time for pudding.'

As Jenkins brought a rich apple crumble, Dot's eyes met Mary's across the table. As Mary lifted her wine glass towards her in silent appreciation, Dot felt a flash of pride. Mary was rising to the occasion and being her true self. The question, thought Dot as she took a sip from her own wine glass, was would *she* ever be able to discover who she truly was and do the same?

Chapter Thirty-Eight

'Could I not just meet you at the station instead?' Helen said, looking at Dot aghast.

Dot frowned as she poured them both a cup of tea from Ivy's elderly brown teapot. It was as though she had suggested shaving her head or a break in Berlin rather than a night in a stately home.

'Well, you could, but what about your luggage and the like?' Dot said. 'It will be difficult to have to come back for you again on Sunday.'

'I would manage,' Helen said, taking the tea Dot had poured for her. 'Connie would help.'

Sinking back into the hard wooden chair in Helen's kitchen, Dot looked at the girl in dismay. She had woken up bright and early that morning. Together with Mary, who wanted to take in some more of the sea air before the morning's work began, she'd asked Jenkins to give them a lift to Newton Abbot so they could take the train from there. Arriving shortly after ten, Dot had promised to meet Mary to catch the train back later, before heading to Helen's terraced house. Although Helen had looked pleased to see Dot, she had looked less pleased when Dot told her that Lady Humm had invited her to come and stay for the evening.

'I don't understand why you don't want to come to Lady Humm's, darlin',' Dot said with her usual bluntness.

'Everyone would love to meet you. And they've got some proper fancy food on the go.'

Helen did not reply and Dot decided not to press her. She cast a glance around the kitchen and felt quite proud of herself for holding her tongue. When she had walked inside the little terrace, it had been a wonder she hadn't fallen down with the shock of it. The place was filthy and the air very thick and stale. Dust you could write your name in covered every surface and dirty laundry littered the stairway, while Helen's good coat had been left in the middle of the floor. Inside the kitchen, Dot had wondered whether it was safe to sit down. Dirty cups were overflowing in the butler sink, tea had been slopped on the surfaces, the table was covered with plates and food debris, and the windows were so dirty it was impossible to see through them.

It was clear that, despite Connie's help, Helen was not managing. She couldn't leave her here, but quite how she was going to corral the young woman into joining her of her own free will, Dot wasn't sure.

Dot was just thinking about how to phrase that when a knock at the door sounded. 'Shall I get that? Or are you expecting someone?'

Confusion passed across Helen's face and so Dot explained that someone had knocked at the door.

'It might be Connie,' Helen said.

'Well, I'll go and find out,' Dot said, getting to her feet, feeling grateful for the chance to open the door and let in a bit of fresh air. Only, flinging the door open, Dot was surprised to come face-to-face not with Connie but Mary.

'What on earth are you doing here? I said I'd meet you at the station.'

Mary smiled. 'Thought I'd surprise you and help you with Helen's luggage. Can I come in?'

Reluctantly, Dot stepped back and allowed Mary inside. 'I've got to warn you. Helen isn't doing so well.'

'I can see that,' Mary said, looking around her at the filthy, dishevelled home. 'I take it that the house wasn't in this state when Ivy was alive.'

'It most certainly was not,' Dot replied in a firm tone. Her friend had been house-proud and she thought she had drummed that into Helen too.

Mary shrugged. 'Oh well. Perhaps she'll feel more like cleaning up when she's had a bit of time away.'

'That's just it,' Dot replied. 'She's not coming.'

'What do you mean, she's not coming?'

'Well, she's coming to London, but she's not coming to Lady Humm's. She doesn't want to meet everyone.'

'Oh what rot!' Mary said, pushing her way past Dot and into the kitchen.

'Hello, Helen,' Dot heard her say in a loud tone as she scuttled in behind her.

'She's deaf,' Dot hissed. 'You must look at her when you speak to her.'

Mary looked confused for a moment, then, ashen-faced, looked directly at Helen. 'Hello, Helen, I'm Mary,' she tried again. 'I'm Dot's friend.'

'Very nice to meet you,' Helen said slowly.

'The thing is,' Mary said, helping herself to the seat that Dot had vacated, 'we would all very much like it if you could join us later.'

Helen looked away then and fiddled with her hands under the table. 'I would rather not. I just don't feel very comfortable around large groups of people I don't know.'

There was a silence as Mary and Dot exchanged glances. Then, wordlessly, Mary got to her feet, walked around to where Helen was sitting, crouched down and took her hands.

'I know how you feel,' she said, lifting her chin so Helen could clearly make out her lips. 'But trust me, there is a warm welcome waiting for you. I should love to get to know you better.'

'What if people are horrible to me?' Helen said eventually, her voice so full of emotion it broke Dot's heart.

At that Mary gripped Helen's hands and met her gaze. 'I won't let them,' she said fiercely. 'You and I are friends now, and I won't let anyone be horrible to my friends.'

Helen smiled then and gave a slow nod of her head. 'All right then, I'll come.'

That night, after a delicious dinner of mutton stew, which had seemed a lot finer than the usual rations Dot had to contend with thanks to the cream china plates edged in gold leaf, Dot had to confess she felt as though she had been through the mill. There was no doubt about it, Mary had been a huge hit with Helen, and subsequently she had barely left Mary's side. Even at dinner, Lady Humm had taken care to ensure they were seated together and Mary had ignored her mother's repeated attempts to butt in on the conversation between the two of them, and had turned her back on Geraldine so she could address Helen properly.

In fact, everyone – designers and Liberty staff included – had spoken to Helen slowly, moving their lips so she could understand. Madame DuPont, the dress designer who had asked to look at Dot's wedding gown later, had even struck up a conversation with Helen about the joys of crochet, which was something Dot appreciated.

Now, as the guests made their way on to the terrace that overlooked the gardens to enjoy one final presentation from the designers on this balmy August evening, Dot took a seat in between Edwin and Alice and looked on with interest as Madame DuPont held up her wedding dress for everyone to see.

'This is a classic example of a dress kept for best, am I right, Mrs Hanson?' Madame DuPont called across the crowd.

Nervously, Dot stood up and nodded. 'Yes, that dress was my best dress. We didn't wear white for a wedding in those days. I had a pale green pinstriped dress made from a thick cotton. It was made for me by my friend Ivy who was good enough to buy me the fabric from Liberty's and it never wore out.'

'But of course!' Madame DuPont laughed. 'We should expect nothing less. A dress like this is beautiful and a perfect example of a wedding dress in the last war. Although I will say, that the calf-length hemline would have been considered quite shocking at the time.'

The audience laughed as they thought of the hemlines that had respectably risen to knee length.

'The collar is also telling,' Madame DuPont said, pulling at the V-shaped collar with embroidered insert of bright yellow daisies. 'I take it you had a matching hat.'

'I did.' Dot nodded. 'Wore it with pride, too. I saved up for it, because we didn't have much, but I wanted to look good on my day. The whole street came out to send you on your way you see. I knew I didn't want to wear my overalls like some girls did!'

'Overalls?' Geraldine shrieked from her position across the other side of the room. 'Who on earth would wear overalls?'

'Many working-class girls would have done so,' Madame DuPont acknowledged. 'Or their uniform. What kind of war work were you engaged in at that time, Mrs Hanson?'

'I was in the post office, and I didn't fancy wearing me Royal Mail uniform, so Ivy forced me into Liberty's – I'd never been before. She took me into the fabric department as if she had been there a thousand times and immediately found that fabric. She told me it would look perfect on me.'

'She wasn't wrong,' Madame DuPont said admiringly, 'the colour would have suited you perfectly.'

The memories of that day just a few days before Christmas rushed into Dot's mind. Dot remembered how frightened she had been of going inside the store, sure she would be thrown out for not being good enough. But nobody had said a word; in fact the staff had been very gracious and helpful. Dot remembered how Ivy had walked straight to the fabric department, she and Helen trailing behind her, and they had arrived in a room brimming with colour. Dot had wanted to stay forever, to drink in all the beauty before her, but Ivy hadn't been so sentimental. She had marched straight up to the cottons, pulled the lovely pinstripe green from the rack and summoned an assistant. Dot had marvelled at her confidence, but she always felt safe whenever Ivy was around.

Aware that everyone was looking at her, Dot smiled at the group. 'Ivy found the fabric, bought it for me and made it. She was ever such a good seamstress.'

At the mention of Ivy, Dot's eyes strayed to Helen, and she was pleased to see the girl was smiling. 'The dress means ever such a lot,' Dot continued. 'It was made and worn with love.'

'And I have plenty of ideas as to how you could customise it to bring it more up to date for your wedding this time,' Madame DuPont said kindly.

But as the fashion expert talked about shortening the hemline, nipping in the waist and halving the size of the collar, Dot was surprised to find sadness coursing through her. She didn't want to destroy this dress and most of all she didn't want to bring her past into her future.

Leaning across to Edwin, she whispered in his ear. 'I'm very grateful Madame DuPont has taken such an interest in my dress, but I think I might actually like to wear something new for our wedding. Do you mind?'

Edwin looked at her, a mixture of surprise and delight across his face. 'Why would I mind?'

Dot looked embarrassed. 'Because you don't approve of waste.'

'My darling, a wedding dress isn't wasteful.'

'Now, I'm not saying I want anything fancy,' Dot warned, turning her gaze back to the dress that had made her so happy. 'But I think you and I should start our married life afresh, without the past getting in the way. We've done too much looking back; it's time to look to our future.'

Leaning forward to kiss Dot lightly on the lips, Edwin beamed. 'And what a future we've got ahead of us.'

Chapter Thirty-Nine

After making her decision about the wedding dress, Dot felt as if a weight had been lifted from her shoulders. The matriarch hadn't felt quite right about marrying Edwin in the dress Ivy had made for her, knowing that she had wed George in it. Much as she adored the gown, there seemed something a bit unseemly about reusing it.

Looking at it on her lap, she ran her hands across the material. It was a little faded at the hem where she had folded and stored it, but otherwise it was in perfect condition. Turning her gaze towards Helen, who was busy chatting to Mary, she felt a sudden urge. Tapping the girl lightly on the shoulder, causing her to turn around, Dot smiled apologetically. 'I'm sorry to interrupt,' she began.

'Oh nonsense,' Mary replied, 'I was just boring on to Helen about Liberty's and telling her about all the different departments.'

'It wasn't boring,' Helen argued. 'It sounds like heaven.'

Dot cocked her head and considered the statement. She imagined that on some days it could feel like heaven, yet there were other days when the place felt anything but. However, that wasn't what she wanted to talk about; she shook her head free of such negative thoughts.

'Do you remember the day we went into Liberty's and got this fabric?' Dot said, holding up the dress.

Helen ran her fingers across the material. 'I think so. Was there a big Christmas tree in the window?'

Dot smiled. 'There was. You were as excited as I was at the sight of it.'

'It was beautiful.' Helen laughed. 'We didn't have anything like that in Torquay. Rockheys was the closest we got to something a bit fancy.'

'It was a very special day,' Dot said, 'you, me and your mum together. Your mum made this dress for me, for my special day, but I've been wondering if you might like it?'

Helen gazed at her in surprise. 'Your wedding dress?'

'Yes,' Dot said, feeling wrong-footed now. Had this been a mistake? She had just thought that Helen might like something of her mother's to hold on to and there was so much of Ivy in this gown. She remembered the day Ivy had fitted the dress for her. The fun they had had as Ivy pulled her this way and that, stabbing her with pins as they giggled about the future.

'I thought it might be a nice way to remember your mother,' Dot said, 'but don't feel you have to take it.'

'No,' Helen cried, her hands straying to the material. 'I would love it! That is if you're really sure?'

'I'm sure.' Dot nodded, pressing the fabric into her hands. 'This dress belongs to you.'

Helen picked up the dress and held it up to the fading light to examine it. The gold of the daisies seemed to come alive in the sparkle and Dot knew she had made the right decision.

'Thank you,' Helen murmured, her face alive with the largest smile Dot had seen on her face since she had arrived in Devon. 'It's perfect.'

'You're welcome,' Dot whispered back. Then she turned around and sat back next to Edwin and Alice, who had now joined them.

'That was a nice thing to do.' Alice smiled. 'Helen seemed very touched.'

'Yes, well, it just seemed right. I need to look to the future and it seems only proper that Ivy's dress stays with Helen.'

'She might want to wear it herself one day,' Edwin suggested.

'She might want to bring it up to date first.' Alice frowned. 'It's very beautiful, Dot, but there are some improvements to be made. Perhaps we could have a Liberty girls sewing evening again. We could alter that dress for Helen while she's in London and also make Brenda a short-sleeved dress – she must be terribly hot in all those long sleeves she wears.'

'We'll see,' Dot said with a sigh. 'Brenda may never come back and Helen may not want the dress altered. Besides, we're still a seamstress down with Mary no longer working for us.'

'Yes, I rather wanted to talk to you about that,' Mary said, suddenly appearing alongside Alice with Helen.

'Oh?' Edwin looked at her with hope in his eyes.

'The thing is, I was hoping I might be able to have my old job back,' Mary said, looking a little uncertain.

'We would love to have you back!' Edwin cried. 'But are you sure this is what you want?'

Mary nodded. 'I've so missed my old job and I think it's important that Emma sees me as a working woman rather than a lady who simply pays calls all day. That isn't real life and Emma deserves to see how the world really is so she grows up into a well-rounded woman.'

'Hear, hear,' Alice said, clapping her hands together.

'Well, I'm thrilled,' Dot said with a smile. 'What does your mother say?'

At that Mary's face fell. 'I haven't actually told her yet.'

Dot raised an eyebrow. After their conversation she'd seen Mary was making inroads into getting her life back on track but the girl had to be open and honest if she were to have a chance at the happiness she deserved.

'It's not because I don't want to,' Mary said firmly. 'It's just that I wanted to check there was a job waiting for me before I spoke to her.'

At that moment Geraldine sauntered past. 'What's all this about a job?' she remarked, taking a seat next to her daughter.

Mary looked across at her mother and fixed her steely gaze on her in the evening haze. 'I'm glad you're here, Mother, because I've come to a decision. I'm going back to Liberty's.'

Geraldine's mouth dropped open. 'As a shop girl? You simply can't, Mary, I shan't allow it.'

'Excuse me, darlin',' Dot said, getting to her feet, only for Mary to lay a hand on her forearm.

'Thank you, Dot, but I shall deal with this.' Turning back to her mother as Dot sat down and looked on in awe, Mary continued to address Geraldine. 'I'm so very happy that you are back in my life, Mother. I missed you and Daddy terribly while we were ... apart, shall we say, but I think the time has come for me to stand on my own two feet.'

'Stand on your own two feet?' Geraldine gave a little laugh. 'Whatever do you mean?'

'I mean that I like my new life, the one that wasn't given to me but the one I worked for,' Mary continued, her voice unwavering. 'I like being a working woman and setting a good example to my daughter. None of my choices may be your choices but it is my life, Mother, and if we are to have any kind of future or relationship with one another then you and I have to be honest with each other.'

As Mary brought her speech to a close Geraldine stared at her daughter, aghast. 'Are you sure?'

'Very,' Mary confirmed.

There was a pause then as Geraldine looked her daughter up and down. Dot glanced at her; she was eyeing Mary in a way Dot hadn't seen before, as if she were finally taking in the assured young woman her daughter had become. 'Mary, you're right, I don't like your choices but what I do have is complete and utter respect for you. Your father was proud of the way you carved out your own life, and I suppose I am too. I also suppose I'm a little jealous of the life and the relationships you have formed without my help or anyone else's. This isn't my way, Mary, but I respect you for speaking your mind.'

'Thank you, Mother,' Mary whispered.

Geraldine got to her feet. 'I think I'll go back to Cheshire once this little trip is over. My time in London has come to an end and Lady Humm is right, it's time I used my great big Cheshire pile for good use.'

With that Geraldine leaned forward and kissed her daughter on the cheek. 'I love you, Mary. We parted once; let's never do that again.'

And as she sauntered back into the crowd, Mary turned to look at the group, her face filled with shock.

'Did that really happen?' she asked at last. 'Did my mother accept me?'

'She did more than accept you, darlin',' Dot said with a grin. 'She told you she loved you. What did I say? Be true to yourself – and you were.'

'And I couldn't be more delighted to have you back at work,' Edwin said, jumping to his feet to clap Mary on the back. 'You can start back in your old post next week. Welcome home, Mary.'

Chapter Forty

At the sight of a cup of tea being slid discreetly across the cash register, Dot thought her eyes were deceiving her. She had only just that minute been thinking about a steaming cuppa, and somehow, rather miraculously, one had appeared. She couldn't resist sniffing the cup, unsure if it was a joke. As the steam scalded her nostrils, she raised her chin and smiled in real gratitude at Jean who had made her the illegal treat.

'You look like you needed it,' she said now, checking to see if anyone was around.

'You thought right,' Dot said, also taking a peek around the department to check for prying eyes. Seeing the coast was clear, Dot took a long sip of tea and instantly felt restored.

'It's been a long week and it's only Wednesday,' Jean sighed.

'You're telling me,' Dot said, setting the cup underneath the desk and out of sight. It had been three days since she returned from the beano in Devon. 'I've got reports to write since our week away. And that stockroom's a flaming mess.'

Jean made a face. 'I know. We've all been tidying it.'

'The stock's tidy, I'll give you that,' Dot said. 'But what about the litter? I told you not to eat down there. The board'll have my guts for garters.'

'We haven't been!' Jean protested. 'Honestly, nobody can understand it.'

'Well, someone's telling porkies, and I haven't got time for it,' Dot said firmly. 'If I catch anyone down there chewing anything other than their own tongue they'll have me to deal with! Understood?'

Meekly Jean nodded. 'How's Helen?' she asked, hoping a swift change in subject would improve Dot's mood.

At the question a smile swept across her face. 'She seems to be settling in well. I've invited her in later to meet Mrs Carter from yarns. Helen's a keen crocheter and knitter; I thought the two might be able to help each other.'

'Help each other?' Jean frowned.

'Yes, you know, perhaps Helen could suggest some projects for the department. Like we've done our Beauty is Your Duty event and the fashion show in the past.'

'Isn't that a bit much for Helen?' Jean said gently. 'I mean, she's only just got here.'

'Nonsense,' Dot protested. 'She is just what we need.'

'What do we need?' Alice asked, catching the tail end of the conversation as she hauled a box of buttons up from the stockroom.

'Dot's got it into her head that Helen's going to save yarns with some bright ideas,' Jean said.

Alice raised an eyebrow as Dot shot Jean a menacing stare. 'That is not what I said, lady,' Dot replied, before turning to Alice. 'All I said was Helen and Mrs Carter might be able to help one another out. Anyway, later on she's having lunch with Edwin.'

'Mr Button? Why?' Alice asked. 'Come on, Dot, it's all very well you taking in your old pal's daughter, and good on you I say, but you don't usually bring all your waifs and strays into Liberty's. Why are you doing it now?'

'I'm not,' Dot said, feeling uncomfortable. 'I'm just saying that Helen could use a little help and if we can give it then I'm all for that.'

Alice cocked her head to one side, her blonde waves bouncing on one shoulder. 'You sure there's not more to this?'

'Such as?' Dot asked, her eyes never leaving Alice's.

'I don't know,' Alice replied. 'I really don't, but you seem different with this girl Helen. More protective somehow.'

'She's deaf, her mother's just died and Ivy and I meant a lot to each other,' Dot said, feeling exasperated. 'Why wouldn't I, as her mother's oldest friend, want to help?'

'I'm not saying that you shouldn't,' Alice answered, standing up straight and helping herself to a sip of Dot's tea. 'I'm just saying you weren't like this with me when you took me in.'

'You had Joy as well,' Dot said, 'and I rather think I did enough for you, standing up to your father on a regular basis, always making sure you had clean clothes and a meal.'

'And you know how fond I am of you and how grateful I am for everything you did. But look at when you took Mary in. You made sure you gave her a chance, but you didn't go around setting up meetings for her.'

'I didn't know Edwin then,' Dot protested. 'But as I recall I remember encouraging you to give her a chance.'

Frowning for a moment, as if considering Dot's point, Alice nodded. 'Yes, all right. Perhaps I've got this wrong. It just feels like she's different.'

'Well, she's not,' Dot said firmly as she closed the sales ledger with a thud, indicating the conversation was over.

'I think it's nice,' Jean put in, earning herself a smile from Dot. 'I'll never forget how grateful I was when Flo took Bess and me in, and then, when the truth came out, how she stood by us, protected us. For that I will always owe her.'

'You don't owe nobody nothing,' Alice said, patting her hand. 'Speaking of which, I had a letter from Flo this morning.'

'Oh yes, I thought I recognised the writing,' Dot said. 'What does she have to say?'

'I haven't read it yet,' Alice replied. 'I brought it downstairs with me in case of a quiet moment.'

'Well, open it, darlin',' Dot hissed, seeing there was still nobody around.

As instructed, Alice ripped into the notepaper and pulled out a sheaf of paper.

8th August 1943

Dear Alice,

It feels like forever since I last saw you. How are you? How is Arthur? I bet he's huge now! And how is Jack? And of course how is Liberty's? Dot wrote to me a little while ago to tell me she had taken over the department but that you all missed me, but of course not as much as I miss you.

So far we have travelled everywhere – or at least it seems like everywhere. I can't say where specifically of course but I feel as if I have seen the world, and I love it. And yet there's nowhere like home. Max has been wonderful. He has been ensuring we play to packed theatres filled with troops every night and everyone in the company is wonderful. I've become rather good friends with a lady named Milly. She's a singer like me and we quite often do a duet together at the end of the night. She's a seamstress when she's not singing and the two of us have been trying our best to run up some scarves or make something pretty when we have very limited supplies.

All in all, it has been good for me to leave London and explore what I think is my true calling. I could never see it at the time, but singing every night is what I think I was always meant to do, though of course my heart will always belong to Liberty's.

But I have news – we are returning to London for Christmas! We are doing a tour around some of the West End theatres and I cannot wait to see you all. I'm not sure where I will stay – I hope Jean will let me have my old room for a few days otherwise. I know you asked me in your last letter how things are with Henry, and the truth is I don't know. We adore each other, Alice – you know what that's like – but Neil's death still feels so very recent.

Anyway, that's quite enough from me. I have to go and sort through my stage make-up and then work out what I'm singing tonight.

Looking forward to seeing you all soon.

With all my love,

Your friend forever,
Flo xxx

As Alice finished reading, Dot clapped her hands together in delight. 'Flo is coming home! That's wonderful.'

'What a treat that will be for Christmas,' Alice added, her eyes shining with joy. 'To have Flo back is the best present in the world.'

'I'll go and tell Edwin,' Dot exclaimed, unable to keep the smile off her face. 'What with Mary coming back to work tomorrow and now Flo returning to the fold, well, it'll make his day. It's a shame she can't make it back for the wedding but I'll look forward to telling her all about it.'

'Perhaps we can lay on some sort of party for her. You know – to celebrate?' Jean suggested excitedly.

Alice was just about to reply when the sound of a loud crash coming from the stockroom gave them all a start.

'What the hell was that?' Dot said, clutching her chest, her heart racing like a Derby winner.

'I don't know,' Alice replied. 'Could it be a box that's fallen?'

'Sounded like a flaming big box,' Jean muttered. 'Come on, there's only one way to find out.'

Together the three of them made their way down the wooden stairs to the stockroom. At first glance nothing appeared amiss.

Alice frowned. 'That noise definitely came from the stockroom, didn't it?'

''Course it did.' Dot sighed. 'I felt it as well as heard it.'

Continuing around the corner, Dot saw what had smashed. A dressmaker's dummy had fallen to the floor, taking with it several boxes of zips, threads and old guard books all piled on top of one another. It looked like a Liberty mountain rather than stockroom.

'Oh Christ! This will take ages to clean up,' Alice wailed.

'At least we know what happened,' Jean said. 'It won't take long.'

Dot stepped forward to assess the damage when a groaning sound coming from underneath the boxes gave her a start. 'Someone's under there. Quick, help me get all this stuff off.'

Together the three worked quickly, casting aside the mound of supplies in order to reach whoever was trapped under there.

'We're working as fast as we can, hang on a minute!' Alice puffed as she hauled yet another guard book into the corner.

Within seconds the three had cleared the mound and revealed someone lying on the floor, their face a picture of agony. As Dot stared down, taking in the cuts on their face, their thin frame and their matted hair, all she wanted to do was give them a hug. Yet before she did, there was something she had to know.

'Bloody hell, Brenda. However did you end up here?'

Chapter Forty-One

As the three stared down at Brenda, Dot couldn't believe her eyes. How could Brenda be in the stockroom? Gazing at the girl, Dot saw fear in her eyes and she knew better than to start asking the questions she wanted answers to. Instead she extended her hand and helped her to her feet.

'You all right?' she asked, seeing the girl looked a bit wobbly.

Brenda nodded.

'What are you doing down here?' Alice gasped, clearly not wanting to wait as Dot had. 'We've been worried sick.'

'Where have you been?' Jean tried again.

Seeing tears pool in Brenda's eyes, Dot glared at the girls. This was not the time. The questions could come later.

'Would you like something to eat?' she tried.

Brenda shook her head. 'No thank you. How did you find me?'

At that the girls exchanged wry smiles.

'We heard what sounded like the thud of an elephant down here.' Alice's blonde curls shook gently as she laughed. 'We came down to investigate and here you are.'

'I didn't mean to cause any trouble,' Brenda tried again, wiping her eyes with the back of her grimy hand. 'I've tried so hard to be quiet these past few weeks.'

Dot put out a hand against the shelving unit to try and steady herself as she took in what Brenda was saying. 'Are you telling me that you've been here all this time? All these weeks since your landlady threw you out?'

Brenda nodded. She looked defeated.

'I didn't know where else to go so after traipsing the streets that first night I arrived here early for work but I must have looked a right state as Mrs Claremont said there was no way I could serve customers looking as I did. I burst into tears then; the flour being slung at me was the worst thing that could have happened. I told Mrs Claremont everything and she offered to help me. She said I could stay in the stockroom for a bit, get myself together and she would try and find me somewhere to stay in the meantime.'

'But why did you keep saying you were poorly?' Jean asked.

'I felt so embarrassed,' Brenda said, a fresh round of tears forming in her eyes. 'The last thing you saw was me having flour thrown all over myself for being friends with a conscientious objector. Then when Mrs Rogers threw me out, I couldn't help thinking you must all feel like she did. I wasn't sure what to do but I thought the customers would be upset with the way I looked, and with nowhere to get cleaned up or find clean clothes, I just wanted to buy a bit of time really.'

'The customers wouldn't have thought anything, just like we don't,' Alice said with a sigh. 'Trust me, if there's anyone that knows about getting flack for hanging around with the wrong fella, it's me. But you've got nothing to be ashamed of, and neither has Peter. It's those blokes what threw the flour that ought to be ashamed – and that Mrs Rogers. She should have shown you some compassion, not thrown you out on your ear.'

'Quite right,' Dot agreed, 'but what I don't understand is why Beatrice never told us. She knew how worried we all were.'

'She was trying to help me,' Brenda explained. 'I couldn't face any of you knowing where I was and what had happened to me. Better you all thought I was poorly rather than living down here like one of the mice.'

Silence fell over the group as they took in the painful truth of Brenda's statement.

'What did you do during the day?' Alice asked eventually. 'Because you weren't here.'

'No. I left usually before the store opened. Then I'd go to the park, or help out with the WVS.'

'That was where Bess said she saw you, but she thought you were there looking for food,' Jean put in.

'No, I was helping out, but when I saw Bess I scarpered,' Brenda explained. 'I wasn't ready to be found.'

'But why didn't you come to us? Or even Peter?' Dot begged, knowing how worried the conchie had been.

'I was ashamed. I didn't want you to feel as if I was some problem you needed to take care of. I begged Mrs C. not to say anything.'

At that Brenda began to weep in earnest and the girls exchanged worried glances. Crouching down on to the box beside her, Dot wound an arm around Brenda's bony shoulders and let the girl cry, all the while computing what had been happening right under her very nose.

Suddenly so many of the events over the last few weeks began to make sense. The mysterious debris that had appeared in the stockroom; the stack of cups beside Beatrice that Sunday she had called in to pick up two dresses; and of course the door being open when she knew she had locked it. There never had been any intruder; it had all been Brenda.

As Brenda's crying subsided, Dot used her other arm to stroke her hair. 'I take it Beatrice was the one calling in sick for you?'

Brenda nodded, her face buried in her knees.

'I wish she'd told us,' Jean sighed, sinking on to her haunches and holding Brenda's hands. 'We were all so worried and we would have helped you. You're a Liberty girl, Brenda, through and through.'

'She's right,' Alice said, leaning against the shelving. 'We always help each other out; there's never a need to be embarrassed. My word, when I think of what some of us girls have been through together ...'

'And it can't have been much fun living here the last few weeks,' Dot put in. 'Whatever you do next, you can't still live here, you know that now, don't you?'

Brenda lifted her chin, her face red and blotchy from tears, her eyes filled with panic. 'Are you sacking me? I know I shouldn't have rung in sick like that all the time but I just didn't know what else to do. I'm sorry.'

'It must have been very difficult for you,' Jean put in. 'I've been thrown out with nowhere to go before; I know how terrifying it can be.'

Alice gave Brenda a warm smile. 'Of course you're not getting the sack. But you must admit you can't go on the shop floor like that.'

'We just want you sorted, darlin'.' Dot pulled the girl towards her bosom for another cuddle. 'We're not just a shop, we're a family. Now, first things first, let's tell Mr Button you're safe and sound, he's been worried out of his mind.'

'Really?' Brenda looked surprised.

'Really,' Dot confirmed. 'Did Beatrice sort you out somewhere to live?"

'Not yet. She had no room at her place now she's got all those people living with her what have been bombed out, otherwise she'd have taken me in. She's been very kind though, helping me,' Brenda said. 'She's not going to get into trouble, is she?'

Dot thought for a moment. Privately she wanted to rip the woman to pieces for not telling her where Brenda was when she had been so worried. Beatrice could have stopped that worry in a heartbeat but she had chosen not to and Dot wasn't at all sure she could forgive that. But then, perhaps she was worried that Brenda would bolt if she told the truth, that the girl could get into further trouble? It appeared Beatrice had been acting in Brenda's best interests and she couldn't possibly get upset about that.

'No, she won't.' Dot sighed. 'I'll explain everything to Mr Button. Now, the bigger question is: what are we going to do about you? As I said, you can't stay here any longer. It's a miracle you haven't brought rats and mice in down here with all the food you've been eating.' At that Dot looked around her as if a mouse might suddenly appear.

'You're welcome to come and stay with us,' Jean said suddenly.

'That's a kind offer,' Dot said, brightening for a moment and then frowning as she turned to look at Brenda. The girl was in a bad way; she needed more than a roof over her head, she needed someone to take care of her.

'Look, darlin', why don't you stay with me and Alice for a bit. It's a nice idea, Jean, but I think Brenda might need a bit of building up and you've got enough on your plate seeing as you're still down as Bess's carer.'

'We could manage,' Jean insisted.

'I think you've enough to do. Brenda, darlin', you'd be happy with me and Alice, wouldn't you?'

But before Brenda could bring herself to speak, Alice burst out: 'We haven't got the room, Dot! I'm sorry, Brenda, but it's true. Dot, see reason, we've got Helen in the box room as it is.'

'Then I'll go in the parlour,' Dot said obstinately. 'Or we'll put a temporary bed up in my room. We can find the space, darlin'. Come on, Brenda what do you say?'

'I don't want to be a bother,' Brenda said quietly.

'You're not a bother, and sorry, Jean, darlin', you've made a lovely offer but I think it's best Brenda stays with us.'

'Fine,' Alice sighed, knowing there was no point arguing once Dot had made her mind up to take in one of her strays.

'That's settled then,' Dot said, an air of finality to her tone. Turning back to Brenda, she gave her an affectionate smile. 'Come on, let's tell everyone you're safe and well, including Peter.'

'Peter?' Brenda gasped, getting to her feet. 'Why does Peter need to know?'

'Because he's been worried sick,' Alice explained. 'Surely you must know that.'

Brenda shook her head. 'I didn't think he'd care.'

'Well, he does,' Dot said firmly. 'So we'll go up to the office, explain all that's been going on and send Peter a telegram. It's time you got yourself sorted out once and for all, Brenda. You're a Liberty girl: you'll never have to go through things alone again.'

Chapter Forty-Two

The reaction to Brenda's reappearance had been one of jubilation from all. As Dot and Brenda had walked up to the office, word must have already spread, for Edwin surprised Dot and Brenda by throwing open his office door, embracing the girl, and telling her in a very fatherly fashion she must never do anything as silly as disappear again.

Meanwhile the rest of the Liberty's staff had been equally pleased to see Brenda. Henry especially had taken her aside and told her that if she ever felt upset about anything in the future then she should come to him immediately. Their welcome had clearly moved the girl.

Later on at Dot's, once she had enjoyed a bath and pulled on one of Alice's old nightdresses while her other clothes were washed and dried, she had wept proper tears, grateful to all for the love and help she had received. Even Helen had been emotional, and had insisted that Brenda borrow one of her books to, as she put it, keep her company through the night after her ordeal.

The kindness Helen had shown after such a great loss of her own moved Dot herself to tears. That night, before she went to bed, she found herself saying a silent prayer for her old friend, promising her that she would do everything in her power to ensure Helen was safe and happy.

For once Dot slept a dreamless sleep and, when she woke to find Helen standing above her with a cup of tea in one hand, she gave a jolt of surprise.

'What time is it?' she hissed, watching as Helen threw open the blackout curtains to reveal a sunshine-filled Thursday morning.

But of course Helen, who had her back to Dot, didn't answer, meaning the matriarch had to look at the little alarm clock she kept beside her bed to tell her it was almost eight.

Scrambling out of bed, she laid a hand on Helen's shoulder and the girl, who was already washed and dressed, gave her a smile.

'Thanks, darlin',' Dot said, reaching for the cup. 'I don't know how I slept so long. I should have been up hours ago.'

'You've had a busy couple of days,' Helen said, taking a seat on Dot's bed as Dot scrambled to find her clothes.

'I'm more worried about you,' Dot said as she picked up her skirt, careful to look at Helen as she spoke.

Helen looked surprised. 'I'm fine. Everyone at Liberty's has been so kind to me. I'm going in later to help with a craft lesson.'

Now it was Dot's turn to look surprised. Sitting next to Helen, she leaned forward and took the girl's right hand in hers. 'Are you sure this isn't too much for you, darlin'? You've only been here a few days; I don't want you getting overwhelmed.'

Helen shook her head. 'It's fine. I want to do more. In Devon it was the same thing every day, but here I can be myself and nobody seems to mind about me being deaf. People are curious about me, and ask questions, but nobody has pointed the finger or made me feel like I belong in an institution – well, nobody apart from Mary's mother.'

At the mention of Geraldine, Dot felt her blood boil. The woman was unspeakably rude and Dot was glad that Mary was going to be spending less time with her and returning to work at Liberty's that morning. It would do the girl good to get away from the woman's clutches.

But: 'I'm pleased, darlin',' was all Dot said in the end. She wouldn't give the woman the power of ruining the conversation. 'Just as long as you're not taking on too much.'

'I'm not,' Helen said in that slow, firm way she had. 'I'm enjoying myself. Mrs Carter made me feel like I was useful yesterday and not a burden as so many do. We had a normal conversation about yarn and I felt like anyone else for the first time in my life.'

Dot paused for a moment and took the time to look at Helen properly for the first time since she had got here. She had been here four days and already she seemed more confident. Her cheeks had a healthy glow, her skin seemed less grey and there was a light in her reddish-brown eyes Dot hadn't seen before. Not only that but her hair was washed, brushed and tied up in an elegant chignon. Dot felt a rush of pleasure: perhaps London was doing her the power of good after all. There was just one thing she wanted to check, however.

'Do you mind that Brenda's here, darlin'?' Dot asked quietly. 'You don't feel too crowded? That we've too many under one roof?'

A broad smile broke out across Helen's face. 'I don't mind at all. She's lovely. It's like having a little sister here.'

Dot nodded. 'I'm glad you feel that way.'

'It makes me feel part of a big family,' Helen said. 'I miss Mum so much; for so long it was just the two of us after Dad died. A big noisy house like this is a nice change, it's taking my mind off things.'

'You mean grief,' Dot said a little bluntly.

'Yes.' Helen nodded. 'Brenda needs your help, Dot. I saw the state of her arms when she put on that nightdress; she's been through ever such a lot.'

'She tell you what happened?' Dot asked.

'Yes. I think it's nice you've taken her in. Like me, she needs people around her, folk who will help her get on her feet.'

'I'm glad you think so.'

'Alice told me you like to take in all the waifs and strays,' Helen said.

Dot shrugged. 'It's just summat you do – least it is for my generation.'

'Alice was a stray, wasn't she?' Helen asked, a note of caution in her voice.

Dot looked at her in surprise. 'Yes, she was. The one that never left.'

'Is that what you want for me? To stay here in London?'

There was a pause as Dot was about to say of course not. Then she caught herself. Yes, she might want Helen to stay with her forever and a day, but that wasn't up to her. 'I want you to do whatever you want, Helen, darlin', whether that's going back to Devon or staying in London. It's up to you.'

Helen nodded; then she opened her mouth and looked as if she was about to say something else before she promptly closed it again and smiled at her landlady. 'Me and Brenda got talking last night.'

Dot frowned. 'Sounds ominous.'

'It isn't. But we want to show our appreciation for you. We want to cook you tea at the weekend, and we'll invite everyone too. All your friends.'

'Darlin', that's far too much. Neither you nor Brenda have to do that.'

'We know that, but we want to,' Helen said. 'Let us do this for you.'

At the gesture Dot felt a flush of happiness and she found herself nodding in agreement. 'As long as it's not too much work. Do something simple like mock cheese on toast.'

Helen laughed. 'It will be simple, don't worry. But it won't be mock cheese on toast, you deserve better than that.'

With that Helen got to her feet and kissed Dot tenderly on the cheek. 'Thank you – for everything. I mean that. Bringing me here, well, you've brought me back to life and I know Mum would be thrilled.'

Before Dot could reply, Helen drifted out of the door and for no reason whatsoever Dot found herself sobbing uncontrollably. She had never felt such love and she had no idea what she was supposed to do with it.

Chapter Forty-Three

The morning had been so busy that it was lunchtime before Dot had time to welcome Mary properly back to the fold. She had served customer after customer, as well as sorting out invoices, and she had given a speech at the craft session Mrs Carter was running. This gave her an opportunity to see how Helen was doing, and she was pleased to see that her latest charge was getting on famously. Not only were the participants hanging on Helen's every word as she spoke about the yarns Liberty had on offer, but the joy on Helen's face was obvious too.

As Mary walked back from her lunch break, her face the picture of joy, Dot couldn't help rushing up to her and wrapping her arms around her in front of long-standing customer Mrs Patterson.

'I wanted to welcome you properly.' She beamed. 'I'm delighted you're back, darlin'.'

'And I'm thrilled to be back,' Mary said, her emerald eyes flashing with excitement. 'I should never have left.'

Privately Dot agreed, but knew there was no point saying that now. 'You're here now and that's all that matters.'

'It's such a relief. I feel like my old self here,' Mary said, stepping back and picking a piece of lint from her raspberry blouse. 'I left Emma with our daily, Mrs Bird, and I know I ought to have felt guilty, I mean she's older than me and mother put together, but I didn't. I feel as if I'm showing Emma that women can be so much more than wives and mothers.'

'Too true, darlin',' Dot agreed. 'Everyone knows it's women what really run things, but whether menfolk'll feel the same way whenever they come home once this blasted war is over is another matter.'

Mary frowned. 'You don't think we'll be expected to just go back to how things were, do you?'

'Who knows, darlin', but what I can say is you're here, and you're setting a good example to Emma, showing her the value of hard work and the fact everything ain't gifted to you on a plate,' Dot said with a small sigh.

'I think so.' Mary smiled. 'Anyway, I've got some good news for you.'

'Oh?' Dot raised an eyebrow.

'Mr Button called me into his office before I started and made me an offer. He asked if I would be interested in being joint deputy with Alice. He felt that you needed more support in your role as manager, and that together we would be able to do that.'

For what felt like the longest moment Dot stared at Mary in disbelief. She couldn't believe that Edwin had gone over her head and made a decision about her department without discussing it with her first. Not only that, but could it mean Edwin felt Dot wasn't coping in her job? She knew that he had been making decisions without her, trying to ease her burden after the shock of Ivy's death. But he couldn't keep doing it – unless he thought she wasn't fit to be manager. That old familiar doubt about her capabilities resurfaced once more as she gazed beyond Mary's shoulder and out into fabrics.

Mary's face quickly changed from delight to concern. 'This is a shock to you, isn't it? You're not happy, are you? If you think I'm not up to it, Dot, let me say this: I know I've missed a lot, but I'm determined to prove myself to you. I won't let you down, I promise. I want to work my socks off for you and the department and this chance – it means so much to me.'

Dot came to and turned to Mary, shocked she could feel that way. 'Darlin', it's just a surprise, that's all. I have no doubt you will make a fine deputy and yes, it's true I do have a lot on my plate at the moment what with Brenda and Helen staying with me. But I didn't mean to take the wind out of your sails, Mary. You deserve this and I couldn't be happier for you.'

At that Mary's face broke into another wide smile. 'I won't let you down, Dot, I promise.'

'I know you won't, darlin'.'

All afternoon she watched Alice showing Mary what she needed to know as deputy, and realised Mary would be a wonderful asset to the management in the department. It wasn't Mary she was cross with, but herself, and to some degree Edwin. How could they be wed if he couldn't be honest with her and tell her she wasn't up to the task in hand? As she sorted through the print designs for the next round of utility fabrics, a mix of annoyance and insecurity coursed through her veins.

The only reason he had interfered was because they were together. She knew he was doing it with the best of intentions but as far as Dot was concerned he was taking advantage of their personal relationship.

She wanted to wed Edwin with all her heart, but a part of her wondered if he still just thought of her as his little Dotty. Did he see her as a woman in her own right? Could he talk to her as his equal? And if he could, why hadn't he come right out and said that she was no good at her job and she would be better off being demoted? The moment she finished her tea break, she walked swiftly along to his office and rapped on the door.

'Come in,' came the familiar deep tones.

At the command, Dot burst in, but felt wrong-footed as she saw Henry sitting in a chair beside him. As she came to stand before the two men, she felt a little bit tongue-tied. She had already planned what she was going to say, but now with Henry here it felt too personal.

'I can come back later,' she said, making for the door again.

'No, I can go,' Henry said, getting to his feet.

'Really, that's not necessary.' Dot waved her hand up and down for Henry to sit back down. 'It was just a quick word; it'll keep.'

'Honestly, Dorothy, do spit it out if it's Liberty business,' Edwin encouraged her.

Dot thought for a moment. It was Liberty business, and perhaps in a way it was better Henry should hear it. This way at least she wouldn't be tempted to use bad language.

'I just wanted to talk about Mary's new appointment.'

Henry's eyes lit up. 'Yes, that was my idea. I thought it would be a good incentive now she's back with us.'

'You?' Dot said, feeling a new round of doubt sweep across her. Things must be bad if Henry felt she was underperforming in her managerial role. 'Why didn't you discuss it with me? Why did you go to Edwin?'

'Now, now, Dorothy, it's not like that,' Edwin began as he got up from his chair. 'Henry and I were concerned after Brenda reappeared yesterday. We got to talking and both Henry and I felt that you had quite a bit on your plate and that it would be a good opportunity for Mary and a nice set of helping hands for you.'

Dot felt flustered and balled her hands into fists by her sides. 'Because you both think I'm not fit to be manager, is that it?'

'Not at all, Dot,' Henry said, quickly coming to Edwin's defence. 'This was purely because we want to help you. You're so keen to help others; we wanted to do something for you.'

'Precisely,' Edwin said, shooting Henry a grateful smile. 'This way, you'll be able to delegate a bit more. After all, there's a lot to do before the wedding ...'

'The wedding?' Dot echoed feeling wrong-footed. 'All this is about the wedding?'

'Not all of it, no,' Henry said. 'We want to help.'

'But yes, in a sense, Dorothy,' Edwin interjected. 'I mean, you must admit that the wedding is coming up in a matter of weeks and nothing has been arranged.'

'It's only a few sandwiches up the pub and a pint of bitter that wants organising,' Dot fumed.

'Surely you want more than that?' Edwin asked. 'I know we said we'd wed in a tin hut, but surely you want something more on your special day?'

'Why?' Dot shrugged. 'Given we've both been wed before and with a war on, don't you think that it would be a bit vulgar to opt for anything more than that? What do you want? Buckingham Palace? Tea at the Ritz?'

A look of hurt flashed across Edwin's face. 'What's wrong with wanting more than a pub? I know I said we could keep things simple but why can't we have the wedding of our dreams? The one we should have had all those years ago?'

At that Dot stepped forward to take Edwin's hand. As she glanced into his eyes she saw the serious, genuine boy he had always been and it was as if the years had melted away. 'Because we're not those people any more, we're at different places in our lives, and we should be pleased with that. Not everything in life has to be perfect, Edwin, darlin'.'

Edwin shook his head before he turned his gaze towards the window. Dot followed his eyes and found herself looking at the shelled-out buildings of the city and beyond. 'I want to give you everything, Dorothy. I want to give you the life we should have had all those years ago, before we parted,' he said in a small voice.

Dot turned to ask Henry to give them a moment, and saw to her surprise he had already slipped out to give them their privacy. 'We can't go back. We shouldn't even want to go back.'

'I don't want to go back, Dorothy,' Edwin said, turning away from the window to look at her. 'I want to give you the life you deserve.'

As Dot stepped forward to take hold of Edwin's hands, she felt a stab of guilt. He had always been so good and decent. She had never deserved to find a man like him the first time around, her father had always made that abundantly clear, and deep down she knew it too. Was that why she thought that if she were lucky enough to make it up the aisle with Edwin they didn't deserve to have anything more than a few stale sandwiches? But now, seeing the hurt in Edwin's eyes, Dot wanted to reach him.

'Of course you matter, Edwin, darlin', you've always mattered. Since you came back into my life, you are all I want.'

Edwin spoke, his voice full of sorrow. 'I am sorry I agreed to something that involved your department without talking to you. That was wrong. But, Dorothy, there are times I feel so frustrated.'

'You're right, you should have spoken to me,' Dot said. 'I understand why you did what you did but you went about it all wrong.'

Edwin sighed. 'I know that now.'

'You always come first,' Dot insisted. 'You always will. But you have to remember that we can't go back, Edwin. I'm not that little girl anymore.'

Edwin cupped her face in her hands. 'I know that,' he said, dropping a kiss on to her forehead. 'But is it so very wrong to want to make up for all we've lost?'

Chapter Forty-Four

For a Saturday the shop floor was painfully slow. Dot paced back and forth across the immaculate parquet floor and then opened the stained-glass window and gazed out at Kingly Street. If she craned her neck she could see Regent Street and was surprised to find that the street was almost as quiet as they were.

'Where is everyone?' Dot moaned to Alice and Jean, who were busy reorganising the rayons.

Jean put down the micro floral and turned to meet Dot's gaze. 'I imagine that as it's such a nice day everyone has gone out somewhere .'

Just then Dot saw Peter walking across the shop floor in his khaki uniform. He had been an almost constant presence in the store since Brenda had been found.

'What are you doing here? Don't you ever do any work?' she said mock teasingly.

'I'm on driving duties all day,' he admitted. 'My commander has meetings in London and I was tasked with running him about.'

'Convenient,' Dot remarked. 'I take it Brenda's invited you tonight?'

'She has.' Peter nodded. 'But I wondered if I could have a quick word with you. Before tonight, I mean? In private,' he added, glancing at Jean.

'I know when I'm not wanted,' Jean said, giving the army man an eye roll before making her way across to the cash register.

'What is it?' Dot asked once they were alone.

'Is there somewhere else we can go?' he asked. 'I don't really want Brenda to see me.'

Dot too rolled her eyes as she grabbed him by the forearm and all but dragged him to the door that led to the stockroom.

Once they were safely out of sight, Dot turned to him. 'Well?'

'I know you don't like me very much—' he began, only for Dot to hold her hand up.

'What I think doesn't matter. It's what Brenda thinks. But she's a young girl, making her way in the world, and still has a lot to learn. I'm suspicious of you, I won't lie. You're a conchie, and I've never held with 'em. That said, you seem to do right by Brenda, but I just don't want you interfering while she's trying to get settled.'

'And I'm not trying to interfere.' He sighed, a worried look forming across his features. 'But I've been thinking. All that time she went missing, well, I missed her and I was so worried about her.'

''Course you were, you wouldn't have been in your right mind if you hadn't,' Dot exclaimed.

'Do you think she's all right now?' he asked.

'Has she said something? Or done something to make you think she's not all right?' Dot demanded.

Peter shook his head. 'No, she seems fine. She seems more mature somehow now, more together, as if the worst is behind her.'

'I agree,' Dot said. 'She's calmer now. Though she's still got a long way to go. But I hope she knows she can at least be honest with us and I hope that she knows her job at Liberty's will keep her on a steady path.'

Peter nodded, absent-mindedly running his fingers across his cap. 'Has she said anything about finding somewhere else to live?'

'We haven't crossed that bridge yet,' Dot said in a kindly tone. 'Don't worry, she won't be on the streets again.'

'I know that,' Peter said. 'It's just, well, the thing of it is, I want to look after her.'

Dot said nothing; she had a funny feeling in her stomach that he was about to say something she wouldn't like.

'And, well, I've never met anyone like her.'

'You're what? Thirty?' Dot said.

'Yes. I know I'm a bit older than Brenda, but that's why I can take care of her. All that time she was missing made me realise that I never wanted to lose her. I want to marry her, Dot. I wanted to ask you if you would mind if I ask her tonight,' Peter said, his voice full of hope.

'You want to what?' Dot exclaimed, feeling all the blood rush to her head. 'Have you lost your mind? She's far too young for that.'

'She's almost twenty-one,' Peter pointed out. 'I want to do this, Dot.'

Dot felt her mouth fall open. There was something wrong with this, but she hardly knew where to begin.

'I don't know what to tell you,' she said eventually. 'She's too young and you've only been courting five minutes. Why don't you give it a bit of time to get to know each other first?'

Peter shook his head, a look of determination in his eyes. 'I already know her. She's my world, Dot, and I think she feels the same way about me.'

'Why not get the war out the way first, lad?' Dot suggested not unkindly. 'Then if you're still together you can see if you've a future when there aren't bombs dropping left, right and centre.'

He sighed. 'It won't matter, Dot. My feelings won't change and I can't help thinking that if I ask her sooner rather than later then she might feel more secure, more loved.'

Dot sighed and regarded the man standing before her for a moment before she spoke. 'I don't think it matters what I think, does it?' she said eventually. 'You've come here today to tell me what you're doing, not to ask me, so I'll leave it to you.'

Peter nodded, and gave her a rueful smile. 'Thank you. I promise I'll look after her.'

With that he turned and walked out of the door and back across the shop floor.

Chewing the inside of her lip, Dot watched him walk out of the door. She didn't doubt for one second that he loved Brenda. But the department's latest charge was so young; she had a life to live before she went and tied herself to a man. She needed to grow up a bit, find out who she was, discover her place in the world and become more confident with that version of herself. If she went off and made her mistakes, and then decided that Peter was the one for her, perhaps Dot might be able to support their marriage. Happy endings were so very hard to come by, she mused, especially when they were rushed.

Chapter Forty-Five

'So that's the upstairs function room for forty on the eighth of October?' the landlord confirmed, licking the pencil he kept behind his ear to write the booking down.

'That's the one, Charlie.' Dot nodded, reaching into her bag for a purse, ready to put down a deposit.

At the gesture, Charlie slipped his meaty hand over Dot's and shook his head. 'No need for that, Dot my love. You're like family round here. If I can't make sure your wedding reception is the best south of the river I don't know what I can do for you. You just concentrate on looking bright and beautiful, we'll do the rest.'

Dot smiled. 'I always said you were a good lad, Charlie, darlin'. Ta for this – me and Edwin are very grateful.'

'You're welcome.' Charlie beamed. 'It's nice to see you and Edwin married off after all this time.'

Dot smiled at his kindness. Charlie used to run the pub together with his dad when she and Edwin first courted all those years ago. Charlie had always been good to them, tenderly joking with Edwin how Dot was out of his league, saying to let him know when he'd had enough of Dotty as he'd be more than happy to take her off his hands. They used to laugh about it. Edwin said he would never have enough of Dot, and Charlie used to nod and smile and say, 'I wouldn't myself if I were you either, Eddie my son.' Then he'd find them a nice table in the snug and bring them each a drink.

'Yes, I don't think either one of us can quite believe it's happening after all these years,' Dot replied. 'It's all been such a shock, finding each other again.'

'Well, I always thought you two belonged together.' Charlie laughed. 'Unlike your old man. He used to turn up here wondering what on earth Eddie ever saw in you.'

Dot blushed at the memory. 'I remember only too well.'

'He wasn't being unkind, I don't think,' Charlie said, snapping his notebook shut. 'I don't think he could quite believe it himself that he had such a looker for a daughter – someone who was so well loved in the community.'

Dot stared at him feeling puzzled. 'How do you mean?'

'Well, he never had a good word to say about himself, did he?' Charlie continued. 'Always coming in here moaning after a stint in the docks how his luck was down. He never had any money, he had a wife that wouldn't stop nagging him and two girls to look out for. One that seemed too good to be true, and one that was nothing more than a grass.'

'I think he must have meant our Olive,' Dot said with a sigh. 'I was never a grass but she flamin' well was.'

'You don't have to tell me, Dot.' Charlie chuckled. 'I remember how she went to the police when she caught me nicking beer off the brewery and selling it down the Lane to make a few extra guineas.'

Dot shook her head. 'She always was a spoilsport.'

'You don't see much of her now then?' Charlie asked.

'No I don't. I ought to feel sad about it – she's the only sister I've got – but she's trouble. I'm better off without her and I think she probably feels the same way. We're like chalk and cheese, always have been.'

Charlie shrugged. 'Family ain't always who you're related to.'

'True enough. And sometimes the best family is the one you create yourself,' Dot said, taking a sip of the port and lemon Charlie had offered her on the house and trying not to mind that it wasn't a gimlet.

'Like you and Edwin,' Charlie said with a smile.

'Like me and Edwin.' Dot smiled back, before adding, 'And you and your Maisie.'

At the mention of his long-suffering wife, Charlie shook his head. 'I don't think we're quite the same, Dot. But we have been married over forty years so it's no wonder we can't stand the sight of one another. It's a miracle neither one of us has done time for murder!'

Dot threw her head back and cackled with laughter. 'Well, they do say marriage is an institution.'

With that Dot drained the last of the port and lemon Charlie had made for her, pushed her glass back across the bar and checked the time. Seeing it was almost half past seven in the evening, she pulled a face. 'I'd better be off, Brenda and Helen are cooking tea tonight.'

'Those two little waifs you've got staying with you?' he asked.

'The very same,' Dot confirmed. 'They want to thank me with a supper, Gawd 'elp me. Neither one of 'em's proved they can boil water so all I can say is it's a good job I've an iron stomach.'

Charlie reached down behind the bar and pressed a little bottle of port into Dot's hands. 'Just in case the grub's not up to much, you can always enjoy this instead.' He laughed again.

Shaking her head with mock disdain but gratefully taking the bottle, Dot waved the old landlord goodbye and made her way back to Bell Street. No sooner had she opened her front door than she had been set upon by Helen. In a kind but firm manner she had turned Dot around and told her in no uncertain terms to make herself scarce until half past seven, and that when she returned could she knock please.

Muttering crudely under her breath, Dot had stood for a moment outside her house wondering what to do with herself before she had a sudden brainwave. She would use this opportunity to not only have a drink before eating heaven only knew what, but also to show Edwin that she could put him first. The old Elephant and Castle pub might not be the Ritz and it had not only served Mary and David well, but it had also been a pub where she had Edwin had shared many an illicit drink when they were kids. It would do them proud.

Now, as she arrived again outside her home feeling pleased with herself, she caught sight of Alice, Jean, Rose, Bess, Henry and Stan all turning into the street and walking towards her.

'Blimey, I don't know where we're putting all of you,' Dot exclaimed.

Henry grinned. 'I've told Brenda I'll eat standing up if there aren't enough chairs.'

'Ignore her,' Alice said, giving Dot a playful shove as she turned to her. 'We've had more than this at Christmas. I'm just about to call on Doris and collect Arthur so I'll see you inside.'

'Make sure you knock first,' Dot warned. 'We're not allowed in without permission.'

'Now, now,' Alice cautioned. 'You were asked very nicely earlier if you wouldn't mind making yourself scarce down the pub for half an hour while they got on with the tea.'

'At least I can't smell burning,' Rose said, sniffing the air cautiously and rubbing her aching back at the same time.

'And at least I lined my belly with a pint,' Henry said, patting his stomach.

'Perhaps we should have done the same?' Bess pondered, turning to Jean.

'It will be fine,' Jean assured her and everyone else. 'Now, Dot, what are you waiting for?'

With that, Dot knocked loudly on her own front door, resenting every rap. A couple of seconds later, she was greeted by Helen, who swung the door open with a wide grin on her face.

'Welcome, everyone,' she said in her slow way. 'Let me take your coats.'

'We haven't got coats,' Dot grumbled. 'It's bleedin' hot outside.'

At that Helen looked crestfallen and Dot immediately felt a rush of guilt. 'No matter, darlin',' she said, patting the young woman's hand. 'I'm teasing you and I shouldn't. Sorry.'

Helen smiled. 'We're a bit nervous.'

'I'm not surprised,' Jean exclaimed. 'It's hard work catering for a lot of people.'

Before Helen had time to agree, there was another knock at the door. This time Dot answered, and, throwing open the door, was delighted to find Edwin, flanked by Mary, Alice and Arthur.

'Welcome,' she said, ushering them into the crowded hallway.

'We're not late, are we?' Mary asked as she stepped inside. 'The bus was murder. So packed, I got off a stop early and walked.'

'You're perfectly on time.' Brenda beamed as she bustled in from the kitchen wearing Dot's best floral apron, her hands all covered in flour.

'My word, you do look the part.' Edwin smiled, taking in her appearance. 'What are you making?'

'It's a surprise,' Brenda said, turning to Helen. 'Do you want to offer everyone a drink?'

Nodding, Helen led them all into the kitchen, and asked them what they each wanted. With a round of ports ordered for the girls and bitter for the men, everyone felt themselves relaxed.

'Do you need a hand?' Rose asked, taking care to look directly at Helen so she could lip-read as she returned with a tray of drinks.

'Not from you I don't.' She smiled. 'You need to rest.'

Rose made a face. 'I know.'

'Not long now,' Mary called.

'I remember this bit so well,' Alice groaned, returning to the kitchen after putting Arthur to bed. 'You feel as if it's never going to end, then suddenly there's a baby in your arms.'

'It was certainly that way with you.' Edwin chuckled. 'Arthur made quite the entrance into the world.'

Alice shuddered, remembering how she had gone into labour so quickly she had given birth on the shop floor.

'You won't have a birth like that. You'll be at home,' she promised Rose.

'Yes, surely you're not going to keep on working for much longer?' Henry asked. 'Not that we don't want you around of course, but I do worry.'

'We all do,' Dot said pointedly.

Just then there was another knock at the door and Henry got up to answer it.

'I was thinking of stopping at the end of the week, if you don't mind, Mr Button.' Rose sighed. 'I'm exhausted and most of the time at work these days I'm dreaming of being in bed. I've only a month to go before I'm due.'

'Then I think you should most certainly stop,' Edwin agreed.

'Stop what?' Beatrice asked as Henry ushered her into the room.

'Rose has finally agreed to give up work until the baby comes,' Dot explained, finding a seat for their latest guest. 'Friday will be her last day.'

A look of relief passed across Beatrice's face.

'Thank goodness for that,' Alice said with a distant smile as she turned to Mary. 'How's your mother?'

Mary wrinkled her nose as if considering the question. 'Things are ... fine.'

'As good as that, eh?' Dot enquired.

'It's been tough for her to recognise I'm not her little girl any longer.'

'And tough for you too, I imagine, to show her the wonderful adult you have become,' Edwin offered.

'That's it exactly,' Mary said with a small smile. 'Things are very different now since I stood up for myself, but in a way I think they are better. She respects me now in a way she never has before and she's making plans to return to Cheshire.'

'Well, that is good news.' Henry nodded.

'Anyway, this evening isn't about me, it's about you, Dot, and the wonderful work you've done. Look around you: you're responsible for bringing all of us together,' Mary cried.

'Don't talk daft.' Dot sighed, but as she gazed around the little group she did feel a surge of pride, not for herself but for the friends she found herself amongst. Each one of them had done the other a good turn; they had come together no matter what life threw at them. Whilst it was true that she had taken in Alice and Mary when they had been lost souls with nowhere else to go, it was equally true that each and every one of them had been there for the other in times of need.

'Actually,' Dot said as she hoisted her glass aloft, 'I think that this evening is about all of us and the care we show for one another day after day.'

'I'll drink to that!' Edwin beamed, holding his glass aloft. 'Here's to us and a lifetime of wonderful friendship.'

Chapter Forty-Six

Ten minutes after Edwin's toast, Dot found herself seated at her own dinner table. Sandwiched between Jean and Helen, she felt full of bonhomie as she surveyed the spread in front of her. The girls, it was fair to say, had done her proud. Not only had they laid on a Woolton pie with some mashed potatoes and greens from the garden, but they had made the table look lovely. Dot's best white serviettes had been placed artfully on each white china plate, while the silver cutlery that hadn't seen the light of day in years had been polished until you could see your reflection in it.

'All this must have taken you hours, Helen,' Alice gasped, holding a knife up to the light to admire it.

'Not really,' she said with a shy smile. 'Besides, Brenda and I really wanted tonight to be special.'

'Well, it's that all right.' Dot grinned, lifting her plate for Helen to serve her a piece of pie. 'Thank you, girls.'

As everyone echoed their appreciation, the girls served everyone their food and soon the little group fell into an appreciative silence as they savoured the first few delicious bites.

'I thought Peter was coming tonight,' Henry said, breaking the silence with a question that caused Dot to inwardly grimace.

Brenda nodded. 'He said he would try to pop in later once his driving shift is over.'

'He must not want to take his eyes off you after you went missing,' Mary exclaimed. 'I've never seen a man so worried.'

'What, not even Edwin when the books don't tally?' Dot teased, forking a piece of pie into her mouth, keen to change the subject.

'Well, maybe then.' Mary laughed, turning back to Brenda. 'I've been meaning to ask you if you're settling back in all right.'

Putting down her fork, Brenda smiled at the group. 'Everyone's been very kind to me. I feel a little foolish now for causing such a fuss.'

'Nothing to apologise for,' Dot said. 'You were in a difficult place. Mind, it would have helped if those who knew told the rest of us.'

Beatrice shook her head in irritation. 'I've apologised for that, Dot.'

'And you can't keep having a go at her about the same thing,' Edwin said patiently.

Dot rolled her eyes. 'I'm only teasing.'

'And I'm only making a point,' Edwin said gently.

'The important thing is Brenda is back with us,' Alice interrupted, knowing full well how Dot could argue a point for hours. 'And it's wonderful to have Helen here too. You look like you're having a nice time with Mrs Carter in yarns.'

Helen smiled. 'She's lovely, and the yarns are very pretty.'

'Do you think you might like to stay here and work in the yarn department?' Bess asked, before realising her mistake and turning to Edwin in genuine horror. 'Sorry, I've really put my foot in it. I wasn't thinking. There might not even be a job.'

Edwin waved away her distress. 'It's actually something I've been meaning to talk to you about, Helen. We do have a vacancy for a part-time assistant if it's something you would be interested in?'

Helen's jaw dropped in shock. 'Are you serious? There's a post for me at Liberty's?'

'If you would like it, yes.' Edwin nodded, taking care to speak slowly. 'Obviously, I wasn't sure if you wanted to return to Torquay, but Dot tells me you are thriving here.'

Seeing the look of confusion in Helen's eyes, Dot smiled at her reassuringly. 'It doesn't have to be forever, darlin'. You can stay here as long as you like and go home whenever you want.'

'What about Mum's house?' Helen said doubtfully.

'Well, I could write to Connie and ask her to keep an eye on things until you're ready to go back?' Dot suggested.

Helen nodded happily in agreement, before asking: 'If you think she won't mind?'

'I'm sure she won't,' Dot assured her.

'Well, it rather looks as if we have a new Liberty recruit this evening,' Edwin said with a proud smile on his face.

'You'll love it,' Mary promised her.

As the group welcomed Helen to the fold, there was another knock at the door.

'Ooh, that will be Peter,' Brenda said, jumping to her feet and rushing away.

Watching her go, Dot couldn't help feel a stab of annoyance. She had hoped that Peter would stay away after their conversation earlier but clearly he hadn't heeded the message. Doing her best to smile at him as he walked into the room, Dot couldn't miss the jubilation on Brenda's face.

'Why don't you sit here?' she said, pulling out the stool she kept in the corner of the kitchen and making a space for him at the table. 'There's plenty of pie left, if you'd like a slice.'

'If that's all right?' Peter looked at her slightly pleadingly.

Nodding her assent, Dot reached across the table, cut a slice and placed it in front of him while Brenda fussed around getting him a drink.

Catching Edwin's eyes boring into her, Dot tried to calm down. She had told nobody about the conversation with Peter earlier and she hoped to God he wasn't going to bring it up now.

Watching Brenda now, the way she lit up in Peter's presence, she knew without a shadow of a doubt that the girl would say yes if he asked her to marry him. And while she didn't doubt how much he loved her, Dot wanted nothing more than for the girl to find her own feet. Brenda was just beginning to develop her own wings; the last thing Dot wanted was for her to have them clipped.

'Now everyone's here, I've got good news,' Dot said as she sat back down and addressed the group. 'I've booked the reception.'

Keeping a careful eye on Edwin, she was delighted to see him raise a smile. 'Where did you book?'

'The Elephant.' She smiled, her eyes meeting his. 'I know it ain't fancy, but we don't need fancy, Edwin, darlin', we just need to be together and that place holds a lot of memories for us. I saw old Charlie and I have a feeling he'll lay on a good do.'

Edwin laughed and squeezed Dot's hand affectionately. 'You're right, Dorothy my dear, as always you are right: the Elephant will be very fitting, especially as all I really want is to be your husband.'

Dot smiled. 'And all I want is to be your wife.'

'Well, I think it's ruddy marvellous,' Mary cried, holding her glass aloft. 'It certainly did David and me proud.'

'And it will do us proud as well,' Dot said as Edwin kissed her cheek.

Turning to look at him, she could see the love in his eyes and Dot found herself wishing this was something she had done weeks ago. As much as she loved playing mother to all her lost souls, she knew Edwin had to come first.

'So are we all invited?' Henry asked, ruffling Stan's hair.

'Of course,' Edwin cried. 'The more the merrier.'

'And what about your dress?' Mary asked. 'Have you decided what you're going to do now you've given your old wedding dress away?'

'I thought I would make something.' Dot smiled again. 'Assuming you'll all help me of course? I've saved up some ration coupons and thought I would use a bit of utility print.'

'What about a cake?' Jean asked.

'And bridesmaids?' Mary asked, immediately thinking of Emma.

'And page boys?' Henry teased, planting a kiss on Stan's forehead.

Dot exchanged a weary look with Edwin before she turned back to the group. 'All those are things that haven't been decided yet.'

'Oh come on, you have to have a bridesmaid at the very least,' Mary insisted. 'Think how bally gorgeous Emma will be.'

'She won't be able to walk down the aisle,' Alice scoffed.

'She will still be the very epicentre of the wedding,' Mary said with an air of haughtiness.

'Well, even if Emma is bridesmaid, she won't be the main one,' Helen interrupted.

'Why not?' Mary demanded.

'Because that will be me,' Helen said simply as she took a final bite of pie and pushed her plate aside.

'Why would it be you? Because your mother was Dot's best friend?' Alice asked looking directly at Helen.

Helen shook her head and dabbed her mouth with the serviette. 'No, because Dot is my birth mother so surely it's only right I'm her bridesmaid.'

Chapter Forty-Seven

After Helen's unexpected declaration there was an agonised silence for what seemed like hours. Dot felt she couldn't breathe.

She held Helen's gaze. For a moment she wondered if there had been any malice in the words she had just uttered but that didn't seem to be the case. Helen looked bemused, slightly upset and worried that everyone had stopped speaking.

As for Dot, she was struggling to cope with the idea that Helen knew Dot's closely guarded secret. Her mind strayed to the letter Ivy had left when she died. The letter Dot had still not been able to face opening, and which she now wished she had. Something told her that within that note there would be an explanation. Not for the first time in her life, Dot wished Ivy could be by her side now.

The silence continued to hang heavily in the air; the drip of the kitchen tap, the only sound filling the room. Dot knew she had to say something, that all eyes were on her, but she couldn't find the words. She felt very grateful when Edwin laid a hand on her forearm and gave it a gentle squeeze before he addressed Helen.

'I think there's been some sort of mistake, Helen,' he said in a kindly tone. 'Ivy was your mother.'

'I know,' Helen said matter-of-factly. 'Ivy raised me, but Dot gave birth to me. She's my real mum.'

Lifting her gaze from her lap, Dot could see everyone was looking at her in shock. Catching sight of Alice's face she caught the bewilderment in her eyes, while Rose's mouth was hanging open in shock. Briefly turning to Edwin, she gave him a brief smile but she could see the hurt and confusion in his face. She wanted to talk to him, to say something that would make everything better, but in that moment she knew it was Helen she had to face.

'Helen, darlin', where did you hear that?' she asked gently.

'Mum told me years ago,' she explained. 'She said it was better if I knew the truth from a young age, that way there would never be any surprises. She never told me who my father was though. She said that would have to come from you when you were ready.'

Dot pinched the bridge of her nose and breathed heavily. There were so many questions she knew she needed to answer. Naturally, she had known that this day would come. But there had also been a part of her that had hoped it could be avoided. Because how could she possibly explain everything?

'I take it Mum didn't tell you that she'd told me?' Helen said, interrupting Dot's thoughts.

Shaking her head, Dot did her best to smile at the girl. 'I had no idea you knew, darlin'. If I had, well, I don't know, maybe things would have been different.'

'So it's true?' Alice gasped. 'Helen is your daughter?'

Dot nodded. 'It's true.'

'And you've never said a word,' Mary breathed. 'You've kept it to yourself all these years? Why?'

Dot laughed. 'Why do you think? You of all people know, Mary, darlin', the shame in having a baby out of wedlock – no matter the circumstances. I had to keep it a secret and, thanks to Ivy, I've been able to – up until now.'

Pausing for a moment, she gazed back down at her lap and tried to gather her thoughts. She had carried this secret with her for so long, now that it was out in the open she knew she had to handle it properly. She didn't want to hurt Helen, although she could well imagine that if Ivy had told her the truth then she would have made sure it was done in a responsible way that left Helen in no doubt as to how much Ivy adored her and how difficult it had been for Dot to give up her child.

But there were others to think about too, such as her family, her friends – and George's family of course, as they had never known the truth. But perhaps most important in this moment was dear Edwin. He had no idea and understandably it would rock him.

Dot knew even without looking at him that his eyes would be full of hurt, and she knew too that he would view this as a great betrayal. Whilst her heart went out to Helen, Dot had a feeling that the girl could cope for a few moments while she addressed the bigger issue: her fiancé.

Getting to her feet, she turned to Edwin and felt almost winded as she saw the heady mixture of hurt and fury in his eyes.

'Can we talk, darlin'?' she said, her tone grave as she extended her hand.

But to her surprise he shook his head. 'No, Dorothy, we can't talk. In fact,' he said, getting to his feet and checking the time, 'I should go.'

'Edwin, please don't go, not like this.'

Ignoring Dot, he addressed the group still sitting at the table with a smile. 'My apologies, everyone, but I'm sure you can appreciate this has come as something of a shock to me. So do forgive me for not continuing to dine with you all, but I think it's best I leave.'

As everyone murmured their goodbyes, Edwin walked out into the hallway with Dot following close behind.

'Edwin, darlin', please,' she begged. 'Please stay and talk about this.'

But Edwin continued to ignore her, focusing on slipping on his overcoat and doing up the buttons.

A very real fear gripped Dot's heart as she reached for his hand. Edwin looked as if he had been stung. Lifting her hand from his jacket as though it were something he had stepped in and was having to deposit in the nearest bin, he stared at her with such coldness in his eyes that Dot wasn't sure she recognised him.

'At this moment in time, Dorothy, there is absolutely nothing you can say to me that I want to hear.'

'But, Edwin, please—' Dot began, only for Edwin to hold up a hand and silence her.

He bent down so his face was level with hers and she could feel his breath on her cheek. 'Let me make something very clear. You are a liar, Dorothy. You have lied to me for over thirty years about something so important, so significant and so fundamentally life-altering I currently have no idea who you are, or whether I can trust you again. Whatever you have to tell me, whatever you want to say, will not be something I want to hear.'

With that he leaned back, turned on his heel and made his way to the door.

'There is something else,' Dot called, hearing the panic in her voice. 'There is one thing you should know before you go. Helen's not just my daughter, she's yours too. You're her father, Edwin.'

Edwin paused mid-stride, his hand extended towards the door as he drank in the enormity of Dot's words. For a brief second Dot felt a flash of hope. Edwin was a man of honour, responsibility and duty. She was sure that he would talk to her now. But to her surprise he simply adjusted his hat, opened the door and walked through it, taking care to shut the door quietly on his way out.

As Dot heard his footsteps recede along the street a cold fear gripped her heart as surely as it had all those years ago when she'd first discovered she was expecting. Life as she knew it was over.

Chapter Forty-Eight

It had been almost a week since Helen's outburst at the little Bell Street terrace and to say life had turned on its head had been an understatement. That morning as she washed and dressed for work Dot hoped, not for the first time, that she would see Edwin. Since discovering the truth about Helen's parentage he hadn't been at Liberty's at all, citing meetings or business trips with other Liberty agents. He was obviously avoiding her, Dot knew that, but this morning she was hoping that the two of them would get the chance to talk.

Over the past few days Dot had pressed Henry for information but he had coloured and stumbled over his words when he repeated Edwin's whereabouts. It had been embarrassing for him and Dot, so much so that she had stopped asking, wanting to put them both out of their misery.

Naturally she had been to Edwin's Bermondsey home to try and speak to him but he was either never in or studiously ignoring her when she knocked on the door. Dot felt hurt and frustrated. She knew she hadn't dealt with it well, that she had mishandled the situation, but she had been a sixteen-year-old girl at the time. She'd had the resentment of her family to deal with, not to mention the social stigma of bearing a child out of wedlock. As if that wasn't enough she had also had to think about that child's future and how she could give her the very best start possible.

Closing her eyes, the image of that fateful day when she had given birth encased in Ivy's love and support came flooding back. So often over the years she had done her best to shove the memory from her mind, choosing to block it out and pretend it never happened. But she had never forgotten Helen; she had never stopped loving her. And now she owed Helen, her friends and of course Edwin an explanation about a time in her life she had managed to keep secret for so long.

Over the past week Dot had managed to keep her friends and colleagues at arm's length. She couldn't cope with the idea of telling them the truth, no matter how often they asked. And so she had made herself busy with work, volunteering to do four nights of fire-watch duty so she wouldn't have to go home and face Alice or answer Helen's questions.

She knew the girls would be supportive, and that she couldn't put Helen off much longer. It wasn't fair to anyone, but Dot also knew that by talking she would have to revisit some very painful memories that she had done her best to hide from herself and her friends for years.

Standing up and peering through the window on to her little garden below, Dot had to admit that she could see how stupid she had been to bury her head in the sand like this. Would she really have married Edwin without telling him they had a daughter together? Or would she have told him after they were married, thinking that it would be easier and kinder? Dot felt yet another tear roll down her cheek and she brushed it away. She had done nothing but weep since the news had come out and that was yet another thing she was furious with herself over. Tears weren't Dot's style.

As she took a deep breath to try and steady herself, her eyes strayed to her bedside cabinet and fell on the letter that Ivy had written to her before she died. For a letter she had never had a desire to read following Ivy's death, it had since proved irresistible. Consequently, she had read it relentlessly since Saturday night, each time finding fresh comfort in the words on the page.

Now, she snatched it up from the unit and began to read once more

15th March 1940

My dearest Dot,

I have written many versions of this letter over the last few years. But with war hanging heavily over all our heads I wanted to give you a more up-to-date version. I don't think it will come as any surprise to you that I have told Helen the truth about who you really are. I actually told her when she was ten. I felt it was important she knew where she came from and that she knew the truth about her parentage. Secrets destroy you and I knew if I didn't tell Helen the truth, there was a very real chance I would damage our relationship.

Helen had already begun to ask questions about her father and her grandparents as she got older. Of course, with the death of my own family I could have told her anything. But life is difficult enough for Helen. I didn't want to make it any more so and so I told her the truth. I explained that you had given birth to her, as a very special present to me, because I wanted a baby and couldn't have one. Then I told her that you were too young to take care of her and that's why she, Helen, was so special, because she was loved by not just one woman but two.

Helen liked the idea of having two very special women in her life. However, I told her that despite the love you and

I have for her, it was best not to talk about it to either one of us in future. Society doesn't like difference, I explained – Helen had already seen for herself first-hand how true that statement was – and we never spoke about the matter again.

She has grown up knowing that you and I love her so very much, Dot. I know that when I adopted Helen you and I never really discussed what to do or say if Helen asked. I think there was too much emotion back then for us to consider everything, and so I have acted, as I always have, in Helen's best interests. Certainly she seems unaffected by the knowledge you are her birth mother, but if you are reading this letter, Dot, it's because the unthinkable has happened and I am no longer with you both. I wanted you to hear an explanation from me, Dot, and I also wanted to urge the two of you to find a new relationship. I very much hope that future will include Edwin too now that you have found one another again.

You have always been so strong for everyone. For me, when my husband died, for all your waifs and strays, and now I urge you to be strong for yourself. Coming to terms with the fact that Helen has known all along that you are her birth mother will be a challenge for you but one I know you are very capable of rising to. This is your chance, Dot, for the family you always dreamed of.

I urge you to be strong and to find the happiness you truly deserve.

With all my love as ever,
Your friend Ivy

As Dot read and reread the note once more she clutched the letter to her heart, holding it as if it were Ivy herself she was embracing. Her old friend was right, of course.

Although this revelation had come as a surprise to Dot, this was a chance for her to finally have the family she thought she never would. Now, as she had over thirty years ago, the time had come for her to dig deep into her soul and find the courage to make everything right.

Chapter Forty-Nine

With her head held high Dot made her way to the fabric department as she did every morning, ignoring the way her colleagues gawped and stared. She knew that most of them were aware of what had happened at the weekend and that most of them were more concerned about how she was rather than keen to spread gossip, but that didn't mean Dot was going to make it easy for them. She might be shedding tears in private but she certainly wasn't going to give anyone the satisfaction of seeing in public that she'd come apart at the seams.

'So then,' she said brightly to Jean who was perched over the cash desk and studying the guard books with intent, 'are we all ready for Princess Valentina this morning?'

Jean lifted her head and smiled at the mention of the store's favourite royal customer. 'I think so. Everything's dusted, sorted and where it should be.'

'And we've got all the silk we've got left out on display for Valentina to look at?' Dot asked making her way to the display case to see what was in there.

'We didn't have very much,' Jean said with a hint of apology. 'We took quite a bit of it down to Devon for the beano with those designers.'

Dot frowned. Missing stock wasn't what she needed to hear about at that moment. 'Well, make a note of what you think is missing and we'll look at it later. Where's Brenda?'

'Just seeing if there's any more silk we can bring up.'

'And Alice and Mary?' She looked around the department but saw only Rose walking gingerly across the parquet towards them.

'They are just in with Henry, going through final arrangements for the princess's arrival. As deputies he thought it better to let them deal with the heavy lifting, so to speak,' Jean explained.

Dot raised an eyebrow as Rose approached. 'So Henry doesn't think I'm capable of running the floor now?'

Startled, Rose looked visibly shocked. 'I don't think so, Dot. I think he just thought you've got a lot on your plate at the moment.'

Dot said nothing. She knew he was right, but even so, she didn't want any special treatment. 'And is Edwin here?' she asked.

Rose's cheeks flamed with embarrassment. 'No, he's not, Dot. He's got a meeting with the Board of Trade.'

'I bet he has,' Dot snapped, the weight of the weekend lying heavy on her shoulders. Letting out a large sigh, she turned her gaze towards the knitting department and saw Helen deep in conversation with Mrs Carter. Despite her resentment at the fact Edwin was still missing, she managed to find some joy in her heart that Helen was settling in well amongst the chaos.

'I hope it won't do her any harm now the world knows she's my daughter,' Dot murmured.

'Don't be so silly,' Brenda exclaimed in a stern tone, emerging from the stockroom. 'Helen is clearly thrilled to be your daughter, and why on earth would it do her any harm?'

Dot shrugged as she shot Brenda a weary smile. The conversation was already taking a turn she didn't like. 'I don't know. I mean, the social stigma of it all. You know, being born out of wedlock.'

'What, and taken care of by a woman who loved her?' Rose scoffed as she rubbed her belly tenderly. 'If my child is surrounded by half as much love as Helen has been I would be thrilled.'

'And besides,' Jean said firmly, standing up straight and folding her arms against her navy rayon blouse, 'Liberty's is hardly one to worry about social norms. Let's face it, the whole place is built on bucking the trend.'

Dot felt her shoulders relax at Jean's statement. Perhaps there was a chance this would be all right after all.

'Whatever are you all gossiping about?' Mary asked as she and Alice joined them on the floor.

'Never you mind,' Dot replied sharply as she looked at the two of them. 'You look like the cats that got the cream. What have you been doing?'

Alice and Mary exchanged conspiratorial glances. 'Well, apparently this isn't just any old visit.'

'It never is,' Dot replied impatiently. 'Valentina always has some purpose.'

'Well, today's purpose is a wedding dress!' Alice exclaimed triumphantly. 'She's getting married.'

Dot's hands flew to her chest and her mouth dropped open in delight. Their wonderful friend was getting married. 'Oh my days! That's lovely,' she cried. 'When? Where?'

'We don't know the details.' Mary smiled. 'No doubt Valentina will tell us all when she gets here, but isn't it wonderful?'

Happiness flooded through Dot. It certainly was wonderful. 'Well, girls, we have our work cut out. Brenda, go and check the stockroom for any more fabric we can show the princess. Mary and Alice, get out all the patterns that we think Valentina will like; Jean, ensure that chair over there is clean, and Rose, for goodness' sake, will you please sit down! You look grey. In fact I don't know why you're still here, you're supposed to finish today.'

Rose looked guilty. 'I heard about Valentina's visit and after all that fuss at the weekend I thought it best to keep working and help everyone out.'

Hearing this, Dot was all set to admonish the girl, but there was so much to do there wasn't time. Instead she issued a serious glare in her direction and encouraged the girls to get back to work.

An hour later Valentina floated down the stairs. With her trademark dark hair piled high on her head, matching jacket and skirt – in Liberty print, of course – not to mention her wide smile, Dot felt herself relax. Valentina had an energy about her that made people flock to her and now Dot couldn't wait to spend some time with the princess and get swept up in her fairy-tale romance.

'Your highness,' she said, curtseying as the princess arrived on the floor.

'Oh, my dear Mrs Hanson, do get up!' She laughed. 'We've known one another long enough to dispense with formalities.'

Dot gave her a wry smile. 'I suppose we have. You know everyone, I think. Brenda perhaps is a new one for you.'

'A p-p-p-pleasure, your h-h-highness,' Brenda stammered, her cheeks pink from embarrassment.

Valentina leaned forward and squeezed her shoulder, clearly wanting to ease some of her concerns before she moved on to Helen.

'This is Helen,' Dot explained. 'She works in knitting and is my daughter.'

'Your daughter? Valentina replied, lifting an eyebrow. 'You're a dark horse, Dorothy Hanson.'

'It's a long story.' Dot turned to Helen with pride in her eyes.

'Well, she's a credit to you.' Valentina shook hands with Helen. 'It's a pleasure to meet you.'

'And a pleasure to meet you too,' Helen said with a curtsey.

Valentina smiled, and then surprised the group by raising her hands and making a series of gestures. Helen smiled in her turn, and replied, using similar motions.

'How do you know sign language?' Mary gasped, unable to keep the awe out of her voice.

'My uncle was deaf,' Valentina replied with a smile. 'I adored him and as a girl learned to communicate with him that way. It was wonderful, almost as if we had our own private language.'

Dot gazed at them both in wonder. She had often thought about learning sign language but Ivy had always told her that Helen was a brilliant lip-reader and although she and Helen had learned to sign when Helen was small, Ivy had said it wasn't necessary for everyone else to do the same. Now, seeing her own flesh and blood communicate with such confidence made Dot think again.

'So, shall we see these precious fabrics of yours?' Valentina said, her eyes straying to the silks that had been laid out carefully in the mahogany display case.

'Not until you tell us all about your intended,' Dot said cheekily.

At that the girls laughed and Valentina slipped them a conspiratorial smile. 'All right. He's Georgian like me and we grew up together. We have always been friends and last month he asked me to marry him after many years of friendship and I said yes. How wonderful life can be when you marry your best friend, yes?'

All the girls murmured in agreement as Brenda spoke, 'But how did you know, your highness?'

'Well,' Valentina replied slowly, her brow drawn into a tight line as she considered the question. 'I knew that my life was always better with Yuri in it. And that he made me a better person. That we complement each other. Why, my dear? Is there some reason you want to know the answer to this question?'

Brenda coloured at the question, and Dot felt a flash of concern. Surely Peter hadn't asked her already?

'Well, my sweetheart has asked me. But I'm worried I'm too young and that we are too different.'

'He's asked you?' Dot screeched. 'I told him not to!'

'Dot!' Alice gasped. 'Why? Peter clearly loves the bones of Brenda. It's not for you to meddle.'

'And he's clearly not to be trusted,' Dot snapped, shaking her head so violently that a lock of hair fell from the chignon at the nape of her neck.

'Why?' Valentina asked gently. 'It is not like you to get so upset, Dorothy.'

'He's a bloody conchie! And whilst it's true he might love the bones of you, Brenda, it's too much, you're too young.'

'But I love him,' Brenda said pleadingly. 'I've thought about marrying Peter a lot, especially when I was living here in the stockroom—'

'You were living in the stockroom?' Valentina asked, her eyes as wide as saucers.

'It's a story for another time, your highness,' Rose put in.

'I see,' Valentina replied, clearly not seeing at all. 'But listen to me, Brenda my dear. If you love him, if you don't see a future with anyone else, then why not? Yuri asked me when I was your age and I said no. I too thought I was too young, that I didn't know what I was doing, but I *did* know. Trust your heart and trust your love, Brenda. If you want to marry him then you should, regardless of age, or circumstance,' she said, firing a warning glance at Dot.

'Well, I think it's all wrong,' Dot replied. 'Brenda needs to think about this. She might meet someone more suitable. Who knows what's in her future? This isn't the right path for you, Brenda.'

There was a silence then as Dot's words washed over the group, each one looking from one to the other in amazement.

'Dorothy, my dear,' Valentina said eventually. 'I have the strangest feeling that it is not Brenda's sweetheart you are angry with. I think that there is something on your mind, and, given you are amongst friends, I think it only right you share your heartache with us here and now and see if there is something that can be done.'

'I ... I'm fine,' Dot replied, suddenly feeling very weary.

'I think we all know the last thing you are is fine Dot,' Mary said in a kindly tone. 'Come on, I think the time has come to tell us all what happened all those years ago, don't you?'

'I would like to hear the truth about where I came from,' Helen said in a small tone.

Dot looked at her daughter and felt a flash of concern. Of course she should know the story of her birth – she had earned that right. And glancing around at the very concerned faces of her friends she knew that they too deserved the truth.

Perhaps after all this while it was time to finally share the secret she had been carrying for so many years.

Chapter Fifty

With all eyes on her, Dot felt strangely nervous as she sat in the stockroom perched on an upturned box. She had thought she was ready to tell her story, but now, as her friends looked at her expectantly, Dot felt hesitant.

But as her gaze reached Helen and she saw the pleading in her eyes, Dot realised this wasn't just her story, this was the story of her daughter too. She owed it to her to be honest.

'I'm not sure where to begin,' she admitted, her voice low.

'Wherever you like,' Alice said soothingly, 'we'll piece it together.'

Dot nodded. 'I suppose the best place is the beginning, like any good story, which means going back to when me and Edwin met.'

'Yes, how old were you when you started courting?' Rose asked.

'I was fifteen, he was seventeen.' Dot smiled at the memory. 'We first laid eyes on one another at a dance up the church hall. I knew who he was, Edwin gave me butterflies and I was always too shy to talk to him. Then I saw him a couple of days later down the Lane. He was helping shovel the muck from the sheep and horses they used to keep down there. Bit of extra money for his cobbler's apprenticeship.'

'Sheep and horses?' Alice echoed in disbelief.

'Mr B was working as a cobbler's apprentice?' Mary gasped.

Dot laughed. 'You don't know the half. Anyway, he had a lump of, you know, animal muck,' Dot continued carefully, fully aware of the princess sat nearby, 'all down his trousers, and I told him he'd better get it off if he didn't want to get in trouble with his mother. He looked horrified, of course – his old mother was legendary down the Elephant for being a right old cow and Edwin had been trying to earn a bit extra at weekends without his mother knowing, otherwise she'd have taken the lot, you see.'

'So what did you do?' Mary asked.

'I offered to nip home and get him a pair of me old man's when he'd finished work. My dad never cared about anything like that, and he thought it was funny that old Maisie Button's boy was covered in the proverbial.'

Jean smiled. 'Edwin was grateful?'

'He was over the moon. He got home to his mother and she didn't notice a thing.'

'His secret's still safe then?' Rose pointed out.

Dot nodded. 'My dad told him he could keep the trousers to change into when he'd finished so she'd be none the wiser and he was ever so touched. 'Course that meant he owed me, so he asked me to go out with him. I'd always had a soft spot for him – he was a looker back then, with those lovely copper eyes of his. He knew that, of course, had his pick of the girls.'

'Mr Button?' Mary shrieked.

'Yes, he wasn't always old and grey, you know,' Dot scolded. 'Anyway, he asked me if I wanted to go to another dance, but I said I'd rather go for a stroll up Regent's Park, it was January but he didn't seem to mind. He looked chuffed to bits I'd suggested somewhere different, and he picked me up the next Sunday with a picnic basket all packed if you please, full of ham sandwiches, ginger beer and even a Victoria sponge that his mum had made. We ate it in the freezing cold on a park bench then warmed up with a cuppa in the Lyons Corner House.'

'Blimey, that's so romantic!' Brenda marvelled.

'It was,' Dot agreed. 'Even when I was freezing me bits off. It gave him an excuse to lean in close and wrap an arm around me you see.' Dot smiled at the memory before continuing. 'My sister Olive was jealous as hell Edwin wanted to court me. She was a year younger and had always been sweet on Edwin. When he came to pick me up, her face was green with envy – I shall never forget. 'Course, I didn't think much of it at the time. Edwin wasn't interested in her; she was just a kid.'

'So then what?' Helen pressed.

'Well, then we fell in love and became besotted with one another, you know like kids do?'

At that there was a general nodding of heads as each of the girls – even Valentina, Dot was surprised to note – recognised how they had felt over their first loves.

'We hardly spent a day apart and had all these great plans,' Dot continued, a faraway look in her eyes now as she took herself back all those years. 'We were going to get married and move out of London one day and have a family. Lots and lots of children. Edwin wanted a farm! We were so sure things were meant to be. But then we must have been together about a year when his parents decided to move to Kent. His dad had been offered a new job out there as a tanner and it was too good to turn down, and that meant the whole family had to go.'

'And so that was it?' Alice said sadly.

'Well, yes,' Dot replied. 'Though Edwin tried to find a way to stay in London. I even asked my parents if he could live with us.' She laughed at the memory. Her father's eyes had bulged out of his head. 'He said trousers were one thing, but letting a lad sleep in the same house as us when he had a perfectly good family of his own was another. 'Course Edwin had a full-time job at Bourne and Hollingsworth then – working in offices, fancy like, you know. Anyway Edwin refused to go, said he could pay his own way.'

'So what happened?' Jean asked, captivated by the story.

'It turned out a couple of months later that the real reason for them moving wasn't his father's new job, but the fact his mum was so poorly. She had TB and Edwin's dad thought the sea air would do her the world of good. When Edwin found out why they were really moving, it changed everything and he stopped fighting. He knew his mum more than likely wasn't going to survive, we both did, but Edwin wanted to make the most of his time with her and I understood that.'

'So he left?' Alice asked.

Dot nodded. 'I remember the night he came to tell me as if it happened just this morning. It had been pouring with rain, and he had just finished work. My parents had gone to the pictures with Olive, so I knew we could talk without interruption. I could tell by the look on his face it was bad news and so I pulled him into the parlour where I sat him down and the truth came tumbling out about his mother. I asked him if he was sure, and he gave just one brief nod of his head.

'"Dad's living in denial, he thinks moving to Whitstable will change everything,"' he told me.

'There was this horrible silence then, where neither one of us knew what to say to the other. I think I was imagining how life would be without Edwin in it; it was as if the reality of him going finally hit home. I'd never got on with Dad or Olive, not really; Mum was the only saving grace, but she was strict. I'd looked forward to moving out, getting wed to Edwin as soon as I could, of being with the one person who understood me, and loved me just for who I was; he was my home – I couldn't let him go. So that's when I found myself offering to come with him. For a moment I thought he would say yes, but then …

'"You can't, Dotty," he said, his face stricken. "I would love nothing more, but it's not fair on you or Mum, not when she's so sick."

'I'd expected nothing less, of course, but knowing this was the end, well, it felt so brutal. We sat in silence again, each one trying to think of something to make this awful moment easier, but there was nothing. In the end it was Edwin who spoke first.

'"I can't help feeling as if I'm losing everyone I love," he admitted, tears pooling in his eyes. "I don't want to be without either one of you. I can't stand it, Dotty."'

'Oh, poor Mr B.,' Alice breathed, clutching her hands to her chest.

'What did you do then?' Mary asked, hands balled into fists in anticipation.

Dot smiled. 'Well, I leapt to my feet, crouched down so I was in front of him, then covered his face with kisses. I wanted to take away all his pain.'

'And then what?' Alice demanded.

Looking at her lap for a moment, Dot was silent for a moment before she looked back up at her friends' expectant faces. 'And then we showed each other how much we loved one another. I ain't giving you more than that. Some things are personal,' she said sharply.

Indeed, as Dot said the words aloud, she remembered precisely how the events had unfolded. As she'd kissed his cheeks, his temples, his eyes and finally his lips, Edwin had pulled back for just a moment, held her hands and her gaze.

'I love you, Dotty, and I want you. I will always want you,' he had whispered tenderly. 'I have always wanted you from the moment we met. I want to give you the world.'

Dot remembered how she had nodded. 'And I want to give you everything I have,' she had said, and she'd meant it too.

After that there had been no more words, no more talking about how they would still be with one another, how this wasn't the end and how the future would wait for them. Instead they lost themselves in the moment, living just for each other.

Later there hadn't been time to lie in each other's arms as Dot had wanted. Instead, they had dressed quickly, and then Edwin had walked towards the door. Before he'd left, he had turned to Dot and clasped her hand.

'I shall never ever forget this, Dotty. You and me, we're meant to be, you must know that.'

And Dot had nodded happily, knowing that Edwin would never leave her or desert her. That what they had done was right, when they didn't know when they would see each other again.

'So when did you discover you were expecting?' Valentina asked, wanting to move the story on.

Dot sighed. 'About three months later. Me monthlies had stopped and well, I went to the doctor's, paid me sixpence and was told what I already knew.'

'Oh, Dot, you must have been terrified,' Alice exclaimed.

'I was,' Dot remembered. 'But in a way I thought it was perfect: me and Edwin, with our own little baby, that wonderful little person we had made through our love.'

She looked at Helen then. 'And you were made with love, darlin', never, ever doubt that.'

'But your parents didn't want you to keep the baby?' Helen asked, her voice shaking slightly as she asked the question.

'They didn't.' Dot sighed. 'I wasn't going to tell them, not until I'd sorted things myself. I thought I might be able to hide it, then perhaps ask one of the local women to take the baby in, pass it off as one of theirs, and I'd see it when I could. I hated the idea of not being involved in its upbringing. I was working in the café near the Tabernacle church then, and I became ever such good friends with one of the women there and she had a huge family. But when I asked her, she said she was sorry but no. I was devastated, went home weeping and Olive caught me. She was ever so sympathetic so I told her everything. Unfortunately, Mother and Father came home earlier than I was expecting and heard what I said. Now Olive has always sworn blind it was an accident but I'm not sure, she's always been a crafty little cow. I'm sure she knew their plans had changed and they'd be back early so they'd hear whatever it was that had upset me and I'd get in trouble.'

'If she did do that, that's terrible,' Alice exclaimed.

Dot shrugged. 'That's our Olive. Always looking to get one over on someone, but that's a story for another day. It's fair to say Mother and Father weren't best pleased with the news, though they weren't as bad as they could have been. In a funny way they were supportive, but firm about what had to happen. It was arranged that I would go to an unwed mother's home in Devon. It all happened so quickly, a few days after my parents found out I was on the train and stayed there until I gave birth.'

'And that's where you met Mum?' Helen asked, tears in her eyes as she asked the question.

'That's right.' Dot nodded. 'Funnily enough, we'd bumped into each other on the beach a couple of summers before, when I'd been on a family holiday. We'd got talking about her dog of all things and she remembered me when our paths crossed again after I arrived at the home. She was a godsend as well as a bloody good nurse. I'd caught her having a cheeky fag a few days after I'd arrived. I asked if I could pinch one and she laughed, and said yes. We rekindled our friendship very quickly.'

'And how did you get on to the subject of her adopting Helen?' Valentina asked.

'Well, not that day,' Dot admitted. 'But within a few weeks, and after I said how I wanted to find a mother who would let me be involved in my baby's life. Ivy offered to take her in and raise her as her own – as she and Kenneth couldn't have kids of their own.'

'But you never told Mr B.?' Mary asked.

Dot shook her head. 'No. My parents had drummed it into me that Edwin wouldn't be interested in me after that. That a lad like him with Maisie Button's airs and graces would never want me, the mess I was. I believed them. I couldn't face any more hurt or rejection, so I kept it to myself. Dad said it was for the best, that I could have a clean start when I got back to London. And, besides, I didn't want to muddy the waters for Ivy and Kenneth. The decision to give Helen away had been made.'

'And so you were able to see Helen as she grew?' Valentina confirmed.

Dot nodded happily as she turned to gaze at her daughter once more. 'Yes. Though I always made it clear that Ivy was her mother, not me. But I was honoured that this gave me what I wanted – the chance to be a part of Helen's life. It was more than I could ever have hoped for.

'I didn't want to crowd them, though, so I didn't visit often. I wanted them to get on with their lives as mother and daughter. Just knowing I was welcome and I was wanted was enough for me.'

Helen got to her feet and wrapped an arm around Dot's shoulders. 'And you were more than I could have ever hoped for – you and Edwin. Thank you for telling me where I come from and for giving me a loving home – not just with Ivy, but with you too.'

Chapter Fifty-One

That night, as Dot returned home from work, all she wanted was to bury her head in a port and lemon and weep for the way things had turned out. Reliving out loud a day that she hadn't thought about in many years had been exhausting.

It had been good for her, though, Dot knew that. She had always assumed that talking about the past would be painful and awkward. In fact, she wished she had done so years earlier, because she felt as if something inside her had shifted.

Now, she knew she had to get Edwin to listen to her. She had no idea what the future held, or how she would manage what came next, but she would get through whatever lay ahead as long as she had her wonderful friends around her.

Turning into Bell Street, the gentle wind rustling her hair, reminding her that autumn wasn't far away, she stopped dead in her tracks. Up ahead was Alice, sitting on their front step with Arthur on her lap.

Dot rushed down the road to her side. 'Whatever's happened?'

At the sound of her voice Alice looked up, her face red raw from crying. 'Luke's dead!'

'What?' Dot exclaimed, sitting down next to Alice on the step. 'What are you talking about?'

Alice didn't answer for a moment, and it was then Dot saw the note clutched in Alice's other hand, with Arthur trying to chew the edges. The writing was large and loopy, and not in a hand she recognised.

'Who's the letter from?' she asked gently, wrapping an arm around Alice's trembling shoulders.

'Hélène,' Alice said through relentless tears. 'When I picked Arthur up from Doris an hour ago she said this letter had been delivered to her instead of me by mistake. I ripped it open on my way home without thinking. Only instead ...' Alice said, faltering over her words, 'it was from Hélène, telling me that Luke had been killed in Rome a couple of weeks ago. She thought I ought to know.'

Dot held Alice close. It had been a hell of a time for the girl. Not only had her husband Luke gone missing in action; when he resurfaced it turned out he had been living with another woman, a Resistance fighter named Hélène, for months instead. Alice knew she was better off without Luke. But he was Arthur's father, and Dot guessed that this was what left her most upset.

'Let me read that letter,' Dot said, gently tugging the scrunched paper out of Alice's hand.

Straightening it as best she could, Dot saw it was short and she wasn't sure if that was intended as a blessing on Helene's part or not.

18th August 1943

Dear Alice,

I am sure I am the last person you want to hear from, but I am writing to tell you that Luke has been killed. As you know he returned to me last summer but of course work has been hard for him to come by given the circumstances. Recently we were able to smuggle him out of the country thanks to one of our agents. He found work on the Italian railways and lodgings with my cousin in the San Lorenzo area of Rome.

You may have read how the Americans bombed Rome repeatedly quite recently. Well, during the latest raid they dropped bombs on San Lorenzo and yes Alice, this was how my cousin and my Luke come to be no more. I am so very sorry to tell you that Luke was one of five hundred civilian fatalities. I am sure you are as heartbroken as I am to learn of the news but I felt it best that you and your son know. We held a memorial service for him here yesterday – he was so loved.

Forgive me for being brief. But I cannot stop the tears from falling.

With regret,
Hélène Alminon

As Dot put the note down, she glanced across at Alice and saw she was as white as her good china.

'You can still cry, you know, darlin',' she said softly. 'He was your husband and he's Arthur's father. It's natural to want to cry.'

Alice lifted her head and looked at Dot. 'I know. But the truth is I just feel numb. I said goodbye to Luke a long time ago, and this'– she jabbed at the letter that lay in Dot's lap – 'this doesn't really mean anything. I did my grieving before and I think what I'm really feeling now is guilt.'

'Guilt!' Dot exclaimed. 'Whatever do you have to feel guilty about?'

'That I feel nothing,' Alice replied, planting a kiss on the top of Arthur's head. 'I feel sad for Arthur, and I hope Luke didn't suffer when he was killed. But the truth is that Jack is more of a father now to Arthur than Luke ever was. He takes more interest, showers him with love when he sees him and the two have developed a bond Luke was never interested in nurturing.'

Dot thought for a moment before she spoke. 'I think that's natural, darlin'. I don't think Luke has earned your tears. He had a place in your heart and your life many years ago but he destroyed it. He's not a good man, but Jack is.'

Alice smiled and leaned her head against Dot's shoulder. 'You always know the right thing to say.'

'I suppose this means you're now free to marry Jack,' Dot said carefully, 'if that's what you want, of course.'

Alice laughed; Arthur lay perfectly content and still between them. 'How well you know me. Isn't it terrible that was the first thing I thought of when I read this letter?'

'Not terrible at all, darlin',' Dot said firmly. 'You've moved on with your life. This letter Hélène sent has just drawn a line under it all. It means you're free.'

Lifting her head from Dot's shoulder, Alice took the note and stared at it with both hands. 'I suppose it does mean that.'

'It's the most decent thing either one of them has done for you and Arthur.' Dot sniffed. 'It's time for you to start your new life, Alice, without the past holding you back. And whether that's marrying Jack and moving to America one day, or staying here in London, it's all up to you now. There's nothing standing in your way. You've got a future now, and once this war is over, what you and Arthur do, it's all up to you.'

There was a silence then as the truth of Dot's statement fell across them both. Wordlessly, Alice's hand found Dot's and, as she laced her fingers through the matriarch's and gave them a gentle squeeze, Dot knew what she was telling her with this gesture. That the truth had set them both free. It was now time for them to find the courage to discover exactly what the future held.

Chapter Fifty-Two

The weight of her own situation lay heavily on Dot after Alice's news about Luke had come out. Dot hadn't liked to leave the girl on her own while things were still raw, and so she, Brenda and Helen had stuck to Alice like glue in case the reality of what had happened suddenly hit. Although Edwin had now returned to work, he had barely put in an appearance on the shop floor and for many days Dot had been unable to face the prospect of going up to his office to have it out with him once and for all. That morning, however, Dot felt drained after another night of interrupted sleep. This had gone on long enough and the not knowing was unbearable. If Edwin couldn't forgive her and no longer wanted her to be his wife, she would survive. After all, she had survived without him for over thirty years; she could do it again. But this misery, this limbo, could not go on.

And so, at just after half past ten, when the shop floor was quiet, she nodded to Mary and explained she was just popping up to the offices. Taking the stairs one at a time Dot felt as if she were arriving for an appointment with her executioner rather than to see the man she had agreed to marry. But she rapped lightly on his door, refusing to be deterred.

'Come in,' Edwin's voice called, loud and clear.

Taking a deep breath, Dot pushed the door open and stepped hesitantly inside. As Edwin glanced up, his expression changed from one of expectant welcome to one of cold loathing.

'What is it?'

Dot shut the door and took a step forward. She knew he wasn't going to make this easy for her. 'I think we should talk.'

'We are at work, Dorothy.'

'And you won't talk to me at any other time,' Dot reasoned. 'This doesn't have to get nasty, but for our sakes as well as that of the staff here, not to mention Helen, we should try and sort things out. Nobody else deserves to get caught up in this.'

Edwin leaned back in his chair, his jaw set. 'All right then, let's talk.' He gestured to the hard chair opposite his.

Realising this was likely to be as good as it was ever going to get, Dot took the chair that was offered.

'The first thing I should like to say is that I'm sorry,' Dot said, her tone filled with urgency. 'I should never have kept Helen from you for so long.'

'Were you ever going to tell me?'

Dot opened her mouth to say yes but promptly closed it again. Lies weren't the way out of this, that she knew. It was time for honesty.

'I'm not sure,' she admitted. 'I wasn't sure what good it would do.'

'What good it would do?' Edwin hissed, leaning forward now, his face furious. 'I have a daughter that I knew nothing about! You kept her from me!'

'I kept her from myself as well,' Dot said bitterly. 'I did what I thought was best. I was just a girl at the time. My parents had found out what had happened and banished me to a mother-and-baby home in Devon.'

'But you could have told me,' Edwin insisted. 'I was young too. I went off to Kent thinking that you and I had a future together. That we could be married once we were old enough, but then your letters stopped coming. I was beside myself, Dorothy, and I had no idea why you'd broken things off with me.'

Dot shook her head, the pain of those days coming back with such force it threatened to wind her. 'I know. I wanted to tell you, truly I did. But my parents were so angry with me – I had to do what they told me, I was too young to do anything else.'

There was a silence then as the two locked eyes with one another, each filled with remorse over the past.

'Your letters stopped just a few months after I left for Kent,' Edwin said at last. 'Was that when you found out?'

Dot nodded her head miserably. 'Yes. After we had said goodbye that day, I didn't think nothing of it. And then, well, the unthinkable happened and I was so bereft. I wanted our baby, your baby, Edwin, but you had gone, and I knew Mother and Father would never have stood for me bringing a bastard back into the house. You know what they were like.'

Edwin nodded, steepling his fingers together. 'I remember only too well. Did they say "I told you so" an awful lot?'

Dot nodded miserably. 'They did. I tried arguing with them and told them you would want to know. But Mum and Dad just shook their heads. They said you would be glad to see the back of me, that you wouldn't want anything to do with me, and I believed them. I thought it was best for everyone if I kept my mouth shut and went along with what they thought best.'

'You could have come to me!' Edwin exclaimed. 'I would have helped you. Surely you knew I would have done anything for you?'

'I wanted to believe it, but my head was so muddled.'

Edwin thought over what she said and nodded slowly. 'It must have been awful for you, going through that alone.'

'It was. I felt very lost, and I made the mistake of confiding in our Olive.'

Edwin snorted. 'You'd have been better off confiding in Judas Iscariot.'

'You're not wrong.' Dot gave a rueful smile. 'She caught me at a low point in tears one day on the back step. I made the mistake of telling her everything but my parents overheard and I'm sure Olive was delighted. Couldn't resist the temptation of getting one over on me.'

'All done under the guise of concern, no doubt,' Edwin said with a small smile. 'She always was a poisonous little viper, your sister.'

'And not a lot's changed since,' Dot admitted. 'Anyway, Olive's neither here nor there. The fact is, my parents shipped me off to Devon to an unwed mothers' home and that's where I met Ivy again. She was one of the nurses there.'

Edwin's mouth dropped open in realisation. 'That's how the two of you became friends?'

'Yes.' Dot smiled. 'We became close very quickly and, to cut a long story short, we hatched a plan. She'd not been married that long, and she knew she and her husband couldn't have children themselves so she offered to adopt my baby.'

'Wouldn't it have been better for her to have been adopted by a stranger?' Edwin asked. 'It must have been painful over the years to see her raised by someone else.'

Dot shook her head. 'It was the best decision I could have made. When I arrived at the home, I was determined to find a way to keep my child. But as time wore on that became impossible. Ivy was different. She recognised that people made mistakes and she understood how much I loved you and how much I loved our baby. She knew I wanted a family of my own and because that was something she wanted too we quickly bonded.'

'It must have been heart-breaking handing Helen over though,' Edwin said softly.

'It was. She looked just like you, Edwin – her eyes and the shape of her nose. You'd have loved her,' Dot said, her eyes shining with tears at the memory of holding Helen just moments after she had been born. She had held her so close, and promised to give her the world, then she had given her to Ivy.

'I couldn't tell you, Edwin. It would have broken my heart,' Dot said through tears. 'At night when I was in the home I would dream of a different life, one where you, me and our baby could be together, and then I would wake up and the reality of it all would hit me and it would be like a fresh round of pain all over again. To tell you would mean to invite even more agony into my heart. I just did what I thought was right. And I still believe, even after all this, it *was* right. Helen had a very happy home life, she had a loving mother and despite all the disadvantages life has thrown at her she's thrived, Edwin, darlin'.'

Edwin nodded. 'I agree. She's a wonderful young woman and a credit to Ivy. But whilst I understand why you couldn't tell me at the time, I don't understand why you couldn't tell me when you and I found one another again after all these years.'

Picking at her fingernails, Dot shook her head. 'I just couldn't, Edwin. I couldn't – no, I didn't *want* to bring up the past, I suppose. I thought about it, of course I did. The whole thing gave me nightmares. But I just didn't want us to do this – pick apart the past – and I suppose I worried you would think less of me for doing what I did.'

'For giving away our child, you mean?' Edwin asked bluntly.

'Yes.'

'Dorothy, I would have understood. I would have been as shocked as I am now, but what hurt me the most is the way you've gone about all of this.'

'I understand.'

'I don't think you do.' Edwin sighed. 'You have lived a lie. You have agreed to marry me, to share your life with me, but at no point did you tell me the truth about the real reason behind the parting of our ways when we were teenagers. And by your own admission you have admitted you weren't sure if you were ever going to tell me. Not only that but you have allowed me to get to know my daughter without knowing who she really was.'

'But isn't that a good thing?' Dot cried. 'You've got to know her properly, to see her as a woman in her own right.'

Edwin took off his glasses, rubbed his hands with his face and sighed. 'Dorothy, the very fact you are trying to see the good in what you have done and the decisions you have made shows me that you are not ready to accept the hurt you have caused to me, and to Helen.'

'I know that, Edwin, I do, and I'm trying to make up for all that now. Helen and I have talked; she can see how things were for me and how I've tried over the years to make up for it.'

'I know that, Dorothy, and I can see now why she was so important to you all these years and why you have always wanted to keep her in your life. However, what you fail to realise is the hurt you have caused. The fact that you could keep something like this from me, something so serious, shows me I don't know you at all – and I certainly can't trust you.'

'Edwin please—' Dot began, only for Edwin to shake his head.

'No, Dorothy, I'm sorry. Whilst I shall never regret our time together, it has become abundantly clear that I don't know you at all. I hope you can understand when I say this, but I cannot possibly marry you. Not anymore. It's time for you and me to part ways.'

Dot said nothing. Instead she just stared at Edwin, her heart banging against her chest and feelings of nausea threatening to take over as she tried to take in the shock of his words. She had of course known it was coming; it was possibly why she had been secretly pleased she hadn't been able to find Edwin to talk to for a few days. That way she could kid herself there was a chance they could work things out. But not now.

She felt tears prick the back of her eyes, but she refused to cry in front of him. Instead she glanced down and looked at the diamond on her left hand. Without saying a word, she removed it deftly from her ring finger and placed it on Edwin's desk.

There was nothing that tied them together now.

Chapter Fifty-Three

The late summer sunshine had disappeared behind the clouds and the sudden chill in the air was a stark reminder autumn was well and truly on its way. As Dot finished totting up the sales orders for the week she gazed outside and saw the skies begin to darken. In the nine days since she and Edwin had broken off their relationship there was evidence everywhere that life was changing, she thought, watching Rose pant across the floor towards her.

'How many times have I told you that if you must come into work then you have to stay sitting down in your office upstairs,' Dot grumbled as she crossed the floor towards the heavily pregnant Rose and guided her into a seat near gifts.

'It's good for me to move,' Rose protested weakly. 'Besides, I need to give you the weekly sales report for all the departments.'

Dot snatched the figures from Rose's outstretched hand and frowned. Usually Edwin had been the one to hand her the figures before they went home for the night, but he clearly couldn't face being near her.

'I offered to bring them down,' Rose said hurriedly, anticipating what Dot was thinking. 'Mr B. did say he needed to come down to gifts anyway, but I told him I could do with the exercise.'

'And he believed you?' Dot said scornfully. 'I don't even know what you're doing here. Edwin should have insisted on you staying at home. You were supposed to have given up work two weeks ago and yet you're still flamin' well here!'

'It's boring at home! And besides, all dad does is fuss round me like a mother hen. No thank you.' Rose smiled. 'Besides, it's only for another couple of weeks.'

'Yes, and then you'll have no sleep, bags as black as coal under your eyes and a constant headache from a screaming baby that never shuts up!' Alice chuckled as she said goodbye to the last of the department's customers.

'Stop!' Rose laughed. 'I can't wait for all of it.'

'Be bally careful what you wish for,' Mary said warningly, joining the little group by the stairs. 'Emma is teething and, my word, she's making a fuss over it. Mummy's threatening to call my old nanny and get her to deal with it.'

'You're not going to get a nanny!' Alice gasped in shock. 'What would David say?'

'David, like me, enjoys his sleep and after the interrupted nights I have recently been subjected to I rather think he would agree. Anyway, Mummy has finally decided to go back to Cheshire the week after next and I am wondering how we are going to manage.'

'So she's finally going,' Rose said. 'I wasn't sure if she had changed her mind.'

'I think we were both rather enjoying our new relationship,' Mary said. 'Still, it's time for her to go and for me to move back into David's. The Mayfair house has been requisitioned by the war office, for what I don't know, but I think it's for the best. I was planning on getting everyone around for a small supper to say goodbye and wish her well.'

Dot raised an eyebrow. 'I think I'll pass.'

'Don't be silly,' Mary admonished. 'Everyone else is coming.'

Just then came the sound of footsteps tramping down the stairs. Glancing up, Dot came face-to-face with Edwin, who was now peering down at the group in surprise. Standing stock-still on the stairs, he looked so wrong-footed Dot almost felt sorry for him.

'Edwin,' she said pleasantly. 'How are you?'

He stared at her, all the while grimly clutching the paperwork he was carrying in his other hand, as if it might somehow protect him from the uncomfortable situation he and Dot found themselves in.

'Yes, very well,' he said, shuffling from foot to foot. 'I, er, I've just realised I've brought the wrong papers down with me. Do excuse me.'

With that he turned on his heel and practically ran up the stairs towards the sanctuary of his office.

'Well, that wasn't awkward at all,' Alice said sarcastically.

Dot sighed. 'I don't know what to do. He's been like this ever since he called time on things between us.'

'That can't be easy for you,' Mary said, her tone full of sympathy.

Lifting her gaze heavenwards, Dot tried to fight the daily round of tears that never seemed to be far away. 'It's very far from easy. I miss him so much; there just aren't words for me to express how sorry I am at what has happened. I have handled everything so very, very badly.'

'But Mr B. adores you, Dot,' Mary encouraged, wrapping an arm through Dot's, the material of her silk blouse catching her cheek. 'He'll come around, I'm sure. He just needs time.'

'I'm not so sure,' Dot said sorrowfully. 'He is so hurt.'

'And hurt passes,' Alice said knowledgeably.

'Not this kind.' Dot sighed. 'It's finished – I have to accept that. I just have to decide what lies ahead for me now.'

'What do you mean?' Rose asked.

'Well, I suppose I have to decide whether or not I should carry on working here,' Dot said cautiously.

'Don't be silly,' Rose exclaimed. 'You're the manager and you're a Liberty girl through and through. You can't possibly leave.'

'But things are so dreadful between us, darlin',' Dot said sorrowfully. 'I don't see how I can possibly continue. It's not fair on everyone. I can easily pack up and do something else. Besides, everyone knows I've been a terrible manager. This is a blessing for everyone.'

'What rot!' Mary cried, shaking her head in protest. 'You need to believe in your abilities more. Look at the way you corral us all together day after day.'

Dot smiled kindly at her, sure Mary was merely trying to give her a much needed boost.

'She's right,' Alice agreed. 'I think you just have to give this time, Dot. It will get better but the man is hurt, and so are you. In a few weeks I'm sure things will be much easier.'

Dot kept smiling, but her expression now was rueful. The truth was she wasn't sure she could cope with seeing Edwin every day. The pain of being without him was too much to bear. She had of course done her best to keep her distance, just as he had, but the fact was Edwin was permanently on her mind whenever she was at work and she found it impossible to focus on anything but him. Being apart was pure torture and Dot didn't think she could stand it any longer. For her own sake as much as for anyone else's, she needed to leave and start again.

'The only good thing to come out of all of this,' Dot said wistfully, 'is that Helen and Edwin are getting to know one another.'

'Yes, I thought I saw them going for a stroll in Soho Square the other day,' Rose mused. 'Has Helen said much?'

'Not to me.' Dot frowned. 'Perhaps she's aware things are strained between us and doesn't want to upset me further.'

'And does it upset you that they are spending time together?' Alice asked bluntly.

Dot's face broke into a broad smile. 'No, that's the very last thing it does. I'm thrilled to see the two of them getting to know one another. In different circumstances this was all I ever could have dreamed of. I wanted Helen to have everything: a loving mother and father and a happy home life and she had almost all of it, apart from the father. Now she's lost her mother but gained a father, and I can see the joy in Helen's eyes when she comes back from a visit with him.'

'She looks like that when she sees you too,' Rose said softly. 'It's clear how much she loves you.'

'And I love her. Everything I have ever done was for Helen, but the one thing I can't give her is the family she deserves.'

Alice raised an eyebrow. 'Helen is a grown woman, Dot. It's for her to make her own way in the world.'

'But she's faced so much,' Dot protested. 'She needs my protection.'

'She needs your love,' Mary offered. 'Nothing more. You need to put yourself first for once.'

'I agree.' Alice nodded. 'You spend too much time worrying about all the waifs and strays you take in. What about what you want?'

'Well, I want what everyone wants,' Dot began. 'For the war to be over, to live a peaceful happy life.'

'No, Dot.' Mary shook her head. 'What do *you* want?'

Dot was about to give the same answer when she stopped for a moment. The fact was she didn't know what she wanted. She hadn't known this morning, or yesterday, and she certainly didn't know now.

She was just about to say as much when the sound of footsteps overhead broke her train of thought. Edwin was on his way back down the stairs, his hands full of paperwork as usual. As he stopped halfway down the stairs and caught Dot's gaze, she offered him a small smile which he ignored. Instead he gave her a cold hard stare, which made Dot's heart break all over again. Without uttering a word he turned on his heel and went back to his office. In that moment Dot knew precisely what she wanted.

'I want Edwin,' she said in a small voice. 'For us to be together again just as we're supposed to be.'

With that, she broke into a round of tears and allowed the girls to wrap their arms around her. Whilst Dot was grateful for their comfort, no amount of words of love could give her the one thing she wanted. And being near the man she loved most in the world, while he wouldn't even look her in the eye, was too much for her injured heart to stand. The only answer was for her to say goodbye to Edwin, to the wedding of her dreams and leave her beloved Liberty's behind once and for all.

Chapter Fifty-Four

Almost a fortnight later, with trembling hands and heavy heart, Dot pushed the creamy envelope across the wooden desk and sat back in the chair. Edwin said nothing, merely looking from the envelope to Dot and then back again.

'Is this what I think it is?' he barked.

'That depends on what you think it is,' Dot replied sagely.

This had been a hard enough decision for her to make. Now the deed was done all she really wanted was to press the note into Edwin's hands and leave with her head held high.

Since talking to the girls she had gone back and forth over her decision to resign. But that morning she had woken to dark skies, sleeting rain and Dot had felt as if it was a sign telling her to do what had to be done before it became any more difficult.

Alice, with her hawk-like eyes, had seen the letter on the table as Dot had been getting ready for work. She had known straightaway what it was and had tried to talk Dot out of her decision but Dot couldn't be persuaded. It was time to get on with the next phase of her life, whatever that might be.

Now, as Edwin snatched up the envelope before him, he hesitated a moment. 'Is this really what you want?

Dot looked at him, startled. Of all the questions she had anticipated, that wasn't one of them.

'I'm not sure that want comes into it,' she admitted with slight hesitation. 'It's more about what's best for me now.'

'Would you have done this if we hadn't …' Edwin paused then as he traced his name across the envelope with his fingers. '… if we hadn't parted ways?'

Dot rolled her eyes. Even though her heart was breaking there were times when Edwin's lack of sense drove her up the wall. 'Of course I wouldn't.' She sighed. 'But what's done is done. I'll leave in a month as per my contract.'

'Before the Christmas rush,' Edwin stated.

Dot shrugged. 'There would never have been a good time.'

Edwin nodded and a look of something that felt like affection passed between them.

'What will you do?'

'I'm not sure,' Dot replied. 'First of all I might pop down to Ivy's and sort out the house so it's all ready for whatever Helen wants to do next.'

Edwin looked at her in surprise. 'But Helen lives with you now. She has a job here and is getting along famously.'

Dot nodded. 'She is. But that doesn't mean she will always want to stay here. Devon is her home; I imagine all this is an adventure for her but she'll want to return west eventually.'

Edwin smiled. 'I've become very fond of her in a short space of time.'

'I think the feeling is mutual,' Dot admitted. 'It's been good for you both. I'm pleased something valuable has come out of all this mess.'

There was another silence then, both aware of the weight of the conversation that had passed between them. There was so much Dot wanted to say, so much she wanted Edwin to know – how sorry she was for the way things had turned out, for example. And, most of all, she wanted him to know that she loved him. That the real reason she was leaving Liberty's was because she couldn't bear to spend another day in his company knowing that they would never be together again. Leaving was the only way she could survive.

'Well, I had better be off,' she said as brightly as she could imagine. 'A busy day on the floor today, and of course it's Mary's mother's leaving dinner this evening so we all need to be off on time.'

Edwin raised an eyebrow. 'Ah yes, the inimitable Mrs Holmes-Fotherington. How will you manage without her?'

Dot laughed, grateful at least they were able to share some intimacies. 'I think we'll rub along just fine and I have a feeling Mary will thrive.'

At the mention of Mary a smile passed across Edwin's face. 'Yes, I think it will be the making of her. Knowing she's patched things up with her family and that she can live her own life as Mary Partridge. Good luck to her, I say.'

'And I echo that,' Dot said softly as she got to her feet knowing the meeting was over.

Edwin stood to shake Dot's hand. 'I'll make sure all your paperwork is up to date so you can leave promptly.'

'I appreciate that, Mr Button, sir,' Dot replied as she encased her hand in his and briefly shook it.

Turning to go, she walked quickly to the door and rushed through it, shutting it firmly on her way out. Once she had reached the other side, she stood for a moment and tried to compose herself. But it was no good. The tears wouldn't stop falling, her heart was broken.

Chapter Fifty-Five

At half past seven that night, Dot had barely had a chance to ring the bell of the smart West London house she was standing in front of before the door was flung open by a beaming Mary.

'Come in! You're the last to arrive and Mother's desperate to start her goodbye speech,' Mary hissed, pulling Dot out from under the autumn skies and into the warmth of the hall.

Dot briefly looked around – the grandeur of the house never failed to take her breath away. She wondered for a moment what it would be like to live amongst such riches. But the sounds of Mary's mother shrieking at her daily, Mrs Bird, told Dot wealth most certainly wasn't the way to find happiness.

At the noise Mary made a face. 'She's been on edge about this dinner all day. Poor Mrs Bird, I don't know how she puts up with it.'

'She won't have to for much longer, surely?' Dot offered. 'What with your mother going home and you going back to David's flat, you won't need poor Mrs Bird.'

Mary grinned, her face lighting up with happiness. 'True and I think Mrs Bird might quite like to put her feet up. It's been a pleasure getting to know Mummy again, on more equal terms, but honestly, Dot, it will be nice to feel that I'm standing on my own two feet once more.'

'Something you do very well,' Dot said admiringly as she followed Mary down the hallway into the dining room, which she hadn't been in before. Mary's mother was holding court in the corner, with everyone gathered around her including Alice, Jean and Bess on one side, and Beatrice Claremont sitting down on the other with a glass of what looked suspiciously like champagne in her hand.

'Where's Helen?' Mary asked.

'She's feeling a bit peaky,' Dot admitted. 'She was off colour at Liberty's this afternoon so I said best she stays in and has a rest.'

'Oh, what a shame,' Mary sympathised before her face changed to an expression of concern. 'And you? How are you?'

'Me?' Dot asked, looking blank. 'There's nothing wrong with me.'

'I meant after handing in your notice,' Mary said gently. 'That was quite a decision.'

'Not really,' Dot said, not wanting to dwell on how she really felt about her choice to leave. 'I did what had to be done. I couldn't stay any longer, not after everything.'

Mary sighed. 'Do you really think there's no hope for you and Mr B? I mean, none whatsoever?'

'No,' Dot said with an air of finality. And as she said the words aloud she knew with complete certainty that she was right. There was a chance that the two of them could remain on good terms for Helen's sake but, really, there was no chance of them rekindling their love. That ship had very definitely sailed.

Dot was about to find her seat as the crowd drew back, but before she could do so, a figure sitting in a chair beside the fireplace caught her eye.

'Whatever is Rose doing here?' she hissed to Mary. 'She should be at home. The baby's due any minute.'

Mary sighed. 'She wanted to come and got so upset when I kept refusing her so I relented. I told her to take a taxi but she refused and got the bus, the silly goose.'

'Mary, she looks terrible,' Dot said, looking at Rose aghast. With her pale, almost translucent grey skin, bags as dark as the blackout under her eyes, not to mention her shallow breathing, Dot was concerned.

'I know,' Mary agreed. 'She's been like that since she got here, but she said she didn't want to miss this evening and she wanted to say goodbye to Mother.'

'But why? And why does your mother want girls of our ilk here at all?' Dot asked, her tone dripping sarcasm as she remembered how Geraldine had first described Mary's friends.

'I think she's sorry for how she treated you,' Mary said. 'I think that she's had to face some cold, hard truths in recent weeks, and though it might kill her to actually say she's sorry I think that the reason she wanted you here tonight is to try and make amends.'

'And I suppose it's the end of a long road for you,' Dot remarked. 'You've come a long way since you arrived in London all that time ago. Confident, calm, not in any way afraid or angry with your mother. You're a wonder, Mary Partridge.'

Mary blushed at the compliment. 'I couldn't have done it without you, Dot, without all of the girls.'

'And so, if you would all like to take your seats, the first course will be served,' Geraldine called across the room, interrupting the moment between Mary and Dot.

Flashing Mary an understanding smile, Dot moved to help Rose to her feet, and was delighted to see an older chap helping Rose instead.

'That's Dr Perkins,' Mary whispered, 'an old friend of Mother's. Given the way Rose looks tonight it might not be a bad idea for her to sit next to him.'

'Good idea,' Dot agreed as she watched Mary rush to the table to swap the name cards around.

Finding her own seat in between Alice and Brenda, Dot smiled warmly at the two and took a sip of water from the glass in front of her.

'This is a bit fancy, isn't it?' Brenda said, her eyes full of nervousness.

'Ah, it's still just cutlery and food,' Dot said sagely, giving her lodger a smile. 'Nothing you haven't seen before. And as for her ladyship over there' – she jerked her head in the direction of Mary's mother – 'remember she eats, sleeps and goes to the loo just like you do, so don't take any nonsense off her like last time.'

'All right.' Brenda nodded, giving Dot a small smile.

The sound of a knife chiming against the side of a water glass echoed across the room and Mary's mother got to her feet. As the group looked up at her expectantly she beamed down on them – as if she were Mother Superior, Dot thought, feeling irritated.

'Before we begin,' Geraldine began, 'I would like to say a few words. As you know, Mary has very kindly organised this goodbye dinner for me. That explains why you see so many faces from Liberty's here this evening, as she has invited her colleagues to join us.'

At that everyone bowed and nodded their heads at the girls, and Dot couldn't help feeling aggrieved, as if they were some sort of museum exhibit.

'I have enjoyed being back in London, although of course it has been extremely difficult without my husband to lean on. I have missed him more than I could ever have thought possible, but thanks to my loving daughter Mary and my delightful adopted granddaughter Emma, I have begun to feel more like myself again, and it is for these reasons that I'm now ready to return to Cheshire. But before I go, I should just like to apologise,' she said, taking a deep breath and gazing straight at Dot. 'It's fair to say that I haven't behaved as I know I should have done with certain parties and I have perhaps been a little rude on occasion. For that I'm sorry.'

There was a polite round of applause at that, and Mary's mother continued to beam beatifically at the group. She was just about to speak again, when the sound of a loud bang against the floor made her jump. Dot took her gaze away from Geraldine and glanced over to the direction of the noise and saw to her horror that Rose had fallen to the floor.

'Rose, darlin'!' she cried, getting to her feet and rushing to her side.

As Dot reached her friend, she placed a hand on Rose's head. She was so hot to the touch droplets of sweat had formed on her brow and was clearly in agony, judging by the way she was writhing around on the floor.

'What is it?' Dot asked urgently.

'I don't know,' Rose gasped. 'It hurts; everything hurts.'

With that Dot looked down and saw a pool of clear liquid seeping out from beneath her body. 'Rose, sweetheart, I think your waters have broken,' she whispered.

Geraldine turned in alarm to Mary. 'You said that you didn't think she was due for a few days yet. What do we do now?'

'Help her!' Mary cried. 'Honestly, Mother, there are times when I wonder about you.'

'Ladies, please,' Dot hissed. 'Help me get Rose somewhere comfortable. And as for you,' she said, looking at Dr Perkins, 'can't you do something?'

'I'm a cardiologist,' he protested, looking panicked. 'I specialise in hearts. I haven't delivered a baby in over a decade.'

'Well, you're up on most of us here,' Dot said angrily. 'Now help her, for crying out loud.'

With that Dr Perkins got on the floor and started to tend to Rose. 'How long have you been having contractions?' he asked.

'A while,' Rose panted, her face screwed up with pain. 'I thought it was just tummy ache. I've been having so many of them all the way throughout my pregnancy.'

Dr Perkins shook his head as he looked at his watch and timed Rose's pains. 'Your contractions seem to be just two minutes apart. This baby's coming now.'

'Now?' Mary's mother exclaimed. 'She can't have the baby here.'

'This baby's coming now,' Dr Perkins repeated firmly. 'Everyone out.'

'That's right,' Dot said. 'Everyone should go.'

Dr Perkins took off his glasses and glared at Dot. 'That means you too.'

'But I can't leave her,' Dot cried, looking down at Rose, her hand still encased in her's. 'She needs me.'

'And I need to concentrate and deliver this baby,' Dr Perkins said firmly. 'Now, if you wouldn't mind passing me my bag before you join everyone else outside then I would be most grateful.'

Dot looked back down at Rose, who by now looked as if she was being tortured. She was screaming out in pain and it broke Dot's heart to see her like this.

'She needs me.'

'And she needs me more,' Dr Perkins said in a tone that brooked no argument. 'This young lady and I shall manage far better without an audience. Now go.'

Sensing the doctor wasn't going to change his mind, Dot squeezed Rose's hand and dropped a kiss on to her forehead. 'I'll be right outside, darlin'. I'm going nowhere.'

Chapter Fifty-Six

The next couple of hours felt like the longest of Dot's life as she sat outside the room waiting for news. With every scream that emerged from the dining room, she exchanged looks of anguish and concern with Alice, Mary, Jean and even Beatrice Claremont who were all desperate for Dr Perkins to give them some good news.

'It sounds horrendous,' Beatrice said with a wince at the sound of Rose crying out once more in torture.

'It *is* horrendous,' Alice replied as Dot nodded her head in agreement. Whilst Helen had been a wonderful gift, the memory of giving birth, what little she could remember of it anyway, had been terrible. She had never known a pain like it, and she thanked God for Ivy, who as a skilled nurse had known just how to try and ease her suffering, unlike the cardiologist who was in with Rose. Dot gritted her teeth as Rose cried out again; perhaps she and Alice ought to have tried to deliver the baby; at the very least they'd given birth themselves so knew a little of what to expect.

'She's going to be fine,' Mary said, as if reading Dot's mind. 'It always sounds worse than it is. I remember the fuss Alice made.'

'Fuss!' Alice exclaimed. 'Fuss! Don't you dare, Mary Partridge, don't you dare.'

Dot was just about to remonstrate with the pair when she cocked her head against the door. This time the sound wasn't that of Rose screaming in agony. Instead it was the welcome noise of a baby crying, having successfully made its entrance into the world.

'The baby's here,' Dot cried, her eyes shining with joy.

'When can we see him or her?' Alice begged.

'I'll go in and ask,' Dot said.

But as she put a hand on the door, Mary turned to her. 'Don't you think we ought to wait for Dr Perkins to come out and talk to us?'

'Nonsense,' Dot snapped. 'We've been out here long enough without him telling us a word. Rose would have wanted one of us in there with her now, enough's enough. The baby's out now. I'll go and see what's happening; you stay here.'

And without waiting any further, Dot rapped lightly on the door and then pushed it straight open.

Shutting the door behind her, Dot was all ready to offer congratulations, but the scene before her left her wide-eyed with shock. Rather than finding a desperately exhausted but happy new mother lying contentedly on the sofa while the doctor checked her over, what she found instead could only be described as something straight out of *Frankenstein*.

Rose was indeed lying on the sofa, but rather than looking happy at the fact she had just given birth to a bonny baby, she appeared barely conscious. Her baby had been placed on her chest, but Rose's head was turned away from the mite. Instead the girl looked as if she was struggling to keep the baby in place. Her breathing was laboured, her red hair slicked with sweat, but it was the blood that terrified Dot the most. It was everywhere. Her clothes were covered in it, as was the doctor, who seemed to be frantically checking Rose's pulse.

As she stalked over to Dr Perkins, fear gripped Dot's heart. 'What's happened?'

The doctor turned to her, his face grave. 'Rose has lost a lot of blood. It could be down to the fact that this baby is large – over ten pounds I would say by looking at him.'

'It's a boy?' Dot asked.

The doctor nodded. 'Healthy-looking too, unlike his mother.'

'Can't you do something?' Dot begged.

'I'm trying,' he replied. 'Perhaps you could talk to Rose and distract her while I perform the procedures.'

Making her way to Rose's head, Dot crouched down so she was at eye level with her friend and began stroking her cheek just as Rose opened her eyes.

'Congratulations, darlin', you've a very healthy little nipper there.'

Rose's face broke out into a small smile, though Dot could see the effort it cost her. 'I know. He'll be called Daniel. Me and Tommy decided if we ever had a boy we'd call him Daniel, after his granddad.'

Dot patted her hand, noticing how cool it was. 'That's a lovely name, darlin'. He'll grow up to be a fine young man with a name like that. Daniel Harper.'

'That's if I live to see him grow up,' Rose croaked, her gaze never leaving Dot's.

'Don't you talk daft, Rose Harper,' Dot scolded. 'You've just lost a bit of blood, that's all, but Dr Perkins is going to sort you right out.'

Rose turned her head to look down at her son. Slowly, she lifted her hand and stroked the downy hair that covered his head. It was such a tender moment, it caused a lump to form in Dot's throat.

'I think we both know it's my time, Dot,' Rose whispered, a tear sliding down her face. Her glasses were gone, Dot noticed, and she looked beautifully innocent without them.

'You're going nowhere,' Dot said firmly. 'You're just feeling a bit weak because you've had a baby. It's perfectly normal.'

As Rose tried to open her mouth to reply, Dot could see the energy slipping away from her, as fast as the blood seeping from her body. Dot glared at Dr Perkins. He was raising Rose's legs high above her heart in an effort to stem the bleeding, but his efforts appeared to be in vain. Rose's eyes were fluttering open and shut and she looked as if she was struggling to remain conscious.

'Rose, darlin'!' Dot cried. 'Rose, you stay with me now, do you hear me? Open your eyes, your Daniel needs you.'

At that last statement, Rose's eyes flickered open. 'Look after him for me, Dot,' she rasped. 'Do what I can't and look after him. Love him, like you do all your other waifs and strays.'

Dot was about to protest when she caught sight of the doctor shaking his head. In that moment she realised that Rose really was going to die. That strange sense of knowing the life force was about to drain from her friend's body made Dot want to break down and weep at the cruelness of the world. This wasn't fair; it wasn't right. How could they live without Rose? Dear, sweet, innocent Rose who only ever saw the good in people and who had taught them all so much about the power of forgiveness and the beauty of tolerance. But as she turned back to face her dear friend, Dot knew that this moment wasn't about her, it was about being strong for Rose, and for the new life she had brought into the world.

Her tears and grief would come later. For now, she had to think about Rose and helping make her journey from this world into the next a peaceful one. Reaching for her hand, Dot could see Rose's breath was coming in sharp wheezes now, each one more difficult and tortured than the last. It wouldn't be long now. Dot had to say what she knew mattered most.

'We will all love him,' Dot whispered fiercely. 'That lad will know more love than any other child in this world, I can promise you that.'

At that Rose nodded softly. She managed to open her eyes and gaze briefly at Dot. 'You've always had so much love to give, Dot … It breaks my heart you had to give your baby away and love her from afar.'

With that Rose closed her eyes again and fear curled its grip around Dot's heart. Planting a kiss on Rose's cheek she whispered, 'but I did find my family, darlin'. You girls have all been my family, not by blood, but where it counts: in my heart. Your Daniel will be as much a part of my family as you are, and I will love him more than enough for both of us.'

With that Dot watched helplessly as her friend gave out one deep breath, and then there was no more.

'Goodbye, my darlin',' Dot whispered, kissing her tenderly on the cheek once more, the tears she had kept at bay now streaming down her cheeks like rivers. 'Rest now. Leave your boy to us Liberty girls. We've got him now.'

Chapter Fifty-Seven

Two weeks after Rose's death, Dot found herself staring blankly again in the hallway mirror still unable to believe she had lost another friend. Ever since that awful night Dot hadn't stopped going over the events in her mind. Was there something she could have done? Could she have encouraged Rose to keep off her feet more? Would she have made Edwin insist Rose stay at home if they hadn't ended their relationship? In those difficult days Dot found she was continually blaming herself and Dr Perkins.

After Rose's death the doctor had been beside himself, claiming he had come to the house in Mayfair to eat dinner, not to deliver a baby. He hadn't had the right equipment; he'd had no oxygen to help. Dot wanted to blame him for how everything had unfolded – all the girls did – but one look at baby Daniel's sweet, forgiving face and she knew there was no point. Rose wouldn't have wanted them to be torn up with remorse, but the trouble was they were all racked with guilt. As Dot turned to watch Alice now, it wasn't lost on her the way she crept down the stairs in her best black dress, her son clutched to her bosom. Dot gave her a tender smile. She had carried Arthur like that for the past fortnight, unable to bear the idea of letting him out of her sight. Dot understood. After all, Rose's death had been so shocking; the idea of a mother dying just moments after she held her son in her arms was breathtakingly cruel.

But Daniel, who was now being cared for by Rose's father, Malcolm, would know how much he was loved, and how brave, special, kind and true his mother was. On that Dot was adamant. In fact, it was something all the Liberty girls felt strongly about. They had spent many hours discussing Dot's promise to Rose, and how they were going to keep Rose's memory alive. All of them were determined Daniel would never fall short on love, and that through them he would know his mother. Of course Tommy would want to do that too, of that Dot was sure; at least he would when he had recovered a little. Naturally, he had been devastated by the news. Malcolm had sent him a telegram immediately to let him know, and his reply had been brief. It had simply said, 'Heartbroken.'

Dot could well imagine that was how he felt. She hadn't been much older than him when her George had died and she could remember every detail of the moment she received that dreaded telegram. She had never felt a pain like it and she knew for Tommy it would be as if his world had ended. With a baby to care for and a war to fight, he wouldn't be able to grieve the way he deserved, and he wouldn't even be able to return for his wife's funeral. Instead he would have to say goodbye to her privately, and Dot could only hope he had a friend to help him during the dark, difficult days ahead.

'Shall I nip to the pub and check they've got everything in order?' Helen asked, appearing at the hall doorway and breaking Dot's train of thought.

Dot smiled. Helen had been a tower of strength to her and the rest of the girls since Rose's passing. 'If you don't mind, darlin', that would be very much appreciated, thank you.'

Helen nodded and reached for her coat before her eyes met Dot's in the mirror. 'Today would have been your wedding day, wouldn't it?'

The pain of the words sliced through Dot as sharply as any knife. It was not lost on her that today should have been the happiest of her life, whereas now it was one of the saddest. She hadn't expected anyone else to remember that today was the day she and Edwin were supposed to be married, yet here was Helen, in her sweet, kind way, showing that she was always thinking of others.

'It was darlin', yes,' Dot said softly. 'But Charlie was very good about it. Said we could still have the function room for Rose's wake.'

'It's a nice tribute in a way,' Helen said slowly, her gaze never leaving Dot's. 'That room was booked with love in mind and we will carry that love through Rose's funeral.'

This was such a beautiful sentiment that it caused Dot's eyes to fill with tears. Turning around to face Helen, she threw her arms around her and breathed in her daughter's familiar scent. Motherhood had not been kind to either her or Rose, but at least Dot had been able to see her child grow up – and what a child she had become, full of love and kindness. Even though Dot had lost the love of her life, Helen was the greatest gift that she had ever been blessed with. To regret anything surrounding her birth would be to deny that.

As they pulled apart, Helen smiled at Dot, took her thumb and carefully wiped the tear from under her eye. Then she kissed her tenderly on the cheek.

'I'll see you at the church,' she said. 'Where we'll do Rose proud.'

At the funeral, Dot and the rest of the Liberty girls did just that. Facing the altar, with Rose's coffin at the front, the girls stood as straight as stair rods as they sang their hearts out, determined to honour their friend and the life that had been cruelly cut short.

As Dot sang the closing verse of 'Jerusalem' at the top of her lungs, her mind was full of Rose. She smiled as she remembered how brave Rose had been when she had first lost much of her sight. Many would have faltered at the hurdles placed in front of them but not Rose. She had vowed to carry on, running first-aid evenings, helping others understand that being partially sighted didn't mean life was over. Her positive, happy nature would be missed, not just by her but by customers and staff at Liberty's alike. As Dot looked around now at the church, packed to the rafters with people, including Princess Valentina, who had all gathered to pay their respects, she felt moved. She could only hope that there would be half as much love in the room when her time came to pass.

As the hymn ended her eyes strayed across the aisle towards Malcolm. He looked terrible, Dot thought, as she watched him do his best to hold back tears and juggle a fractious baby Daniel in his arms. Dot could see the pain etched across his face and in that moment she felt as if she too had been sliced in half – feeling every inch of his torment as keenly as if it were own.

Malcolm was on a difficult and unyielding path. Not only was his wife still away with the women's army while war raged on, but he was now having to raise his grandson all by himself, as well as deal with the sudden loss of his daughter and his own injuries received during the last war. It was a lot and Dot knew it would fall to the Liberty girls to make sure he didn't go under. They had all rallied round since Rose's death, bringing him food, helping bathe and care for Daniel, but Malcolm was so lost in pain he was insistent that he try to do most of it himself, saying that he owed it to Rose.

As if to further reinforce the point, when the hymn ended, Daniel decided now was the time to burst into his own song, and produced such a cacophony of cries that the vicar leading the service was forced to stop for a moment. Dot and Alice exchanged glances as Malcolm struggled to get him to quieten down. In a flash, Alice deposited a sleeping Arthur into Dot's arms and raced across the aisle to help Rose's father. Within moments she had expertly scooped Daniel into her arms, and was rushing him outside so the service could continue.

'I wonder if anyone's taught him how to feed a baby?' Mary whispered in hushed tones as the vicar continued.

Dot raised an eyebrow. 'When I popped in last week he said he was managing. That he'd got a bottle down the mite's mouth.'

'Well he's clearly not managing is he?' Mary hissed as Arthur stirred in Dot's arms. 'Look at the poor man, he's clueless and naturally bereft.'

'We're all bereft,' Dot said in a loud murmur. 'But Daniel will give Malcolm comfort while he grieves for Rose.'

'Not if he can't cope,' Mary replied. 'Look at him now.'

Dot followed Mary's gaze and saw that Malcolm was struggling to get up for the next hymn, and was leaning heavily on Edwin for support. Much as it pained her to admit it, she knew Mary was right, Malcolm wasn't coping. Before Rose had lost much of her sight, he had leaned heavily on his daughter for support and afterwards Mary had moved in and helped to care for him and Rose.

'Poor man, we must find another way to help him.' Dot sighed as the organist struck up the opening chords to 'Abide with Me'.

As they trooped out of the church and into the graveyard for the interment, Dot felt exhausted. She didn't think she had ever shed as many tears as she had in the past fortnight for her precious friend. With the cool October wind whispering around her neck, Dot couldn't tear her eyes from the coffin as it was lowered into the ground. She found herself wondering how on earth they would cope without Rose's love that shone as naturally from her as the scent from the flower that was her namesake.

Then a burly undertaker offered a clod of earth to Malcolm to throw on to the coffin, but he shook his head. With some difficulty he bent down and Dot saw him pick up a pale pink rose. Leaning on Edwin once more for support, he dropped the flower on to the coffin. 'A rose for my Rose,' he said aloud, his voice shaking with emotion.

Chapter Fifty-Eight

Afterwards, at Rose's wake, the mood in the pub was sombre. There had been funerals Dot had gone to that had been uplifting, celebrating a life well lived, but there was no joy in this funeral, Dot thought as she took a large gulp of port and lemon to try and numb the pain.

'You all right?' Brenda asked as she took a seat in the snug beside her.

Dot did her best to smile at the girl, who had looked very respectable in her knee-length black dress and worn but polished court shoes.

'Fine, darlin',' Dot said softly. 'Just taking it all in.'

'I see Mr Button's been doing the rounds, chatting to everyone and making sure they're all right,' Brenda said, gesturing to their store manager.

Dot followed her gaze and saw Edwin politely asking everyone if they were well or if he could get them another drink.

'He's always very good at doing the right thing,' Dot said with a hint of bitterness to her voice.

Just then she felt the heat of Brenda's palm on top of her forearm. 'His heart's breaking just like yours.'

'What makes you say that?' Dot asked, turning to look at Brenda in surprise.

'You can tell,' she said softly, 'The sadness at the corners of his mouth, the lines under his eyes. But it's more the way he can't take his eyes off you whenever you're about. He's always watching you, keeping an eye on you.'

Dot smiled. 'When did you get so wise? You're a changed person since you've come back to work. You seem much more sure of yourself.'

'I think it was knowing that I'm a survivor,' Brenda said carefully. 'I mean, I never knew my father, my mother died when I was fourteen, I was beaten by a countess. I moved to a new town, found love and was thrown out of my lodgings for it, leaving me to fend for myself.'

'When you put it like that it does sound as though you've been through a lifetime's worth of trouble,' Dot said, regarding the girl thoughtfully.

Brenda met her gaze. 'Sleeping in the stockroom as I did and now living with you has given me a lot of time to think about things. I'm a grown adult now, not a victim who has things happen to them. It's down to me to say how I feel about something, not to be afraid because of what others might think. I've survived what you kindly called a lifetime of troubles, Dot, and, thanks to the friends I've made along the way and the strength and confidence they've given me, I know I'll survive anything that comes along in the future.'

Dot looked at her, feeling flabbergasted. The girl was right, of course, she was strong and she was capable of doing anything she put her mind to. But it was the strength of self-belief that stunned Dot and she couldn't help admiring the new Brenda that sat beside her. She was just about to say as much when Mary and Alice with Emma and Arthur in their arms came to sit beside them.

'It's a lovely spread, Dot,' Alice marvelled. 'You've done 'em all proud.'

'Yes, it was kind of you to pay for it,' Mary said.

Shrugging her shoulders, Dot took another slug of her drink. 'I'd already booked the reception. Made sense for me to take a little of the burden from Malcolm's shoulders.'

With that the girls turned to see Rose's father coming towards them, a crying Daniel in his arms.

'Oh, bless him,' Dot tutted, holding her hands out for a cuddle.

'He knows something's not right,' Malcolm said as he handed him over to Dot.

'You're doing fine, but looking after babies isn't easy,' Alice admitted.

'It bally well isn't,' Mary agreed. 'And the washing pile is horrendous.'

'You'll get there,' Alice promised. 'Daniel knows you love him.'

'But this is woman's work, mothering,' Malcolm cried in frustration. 'It should be for me, his granddad, to show him how to fish in the River Lea when he's old enough, take him for his first pint with his dad, not change his nappies. I want to do this for Rose, but it's so difficult.'

At that Mary leaned over and squeezed his shoulder. 'How would it be if you and Daniel came to stay with me and Emma for a while? We could help you out and we've plenty of space in the flat.'

Malcolm reached out a hand and stroked Daniel's cheek, who by now was lying peacefully in Dot's arms. 'It's very kind of you, love, but we don't want to be a burden.'

Mary smiled. 'You would be very welcome. Or I can perhaps come over a bit more? Show you how to put Daniel down – that sort of thing.'

'You would really do that?' Malcolm looked as if a load had been lifted.

'Of course she would,' Alice shrugged. 'We all would.'

'I really don't know what to say,' Malcolm said, looking very much as if he might cry. 'I shouldn't have tried to do this alone. You have all been so kind to me. Rose was so lucky to count you as her friends.'

'It's us that were lucky, darlin',' Dot said, gently handing a now-sleeping Daniel back to his grandfather. 'We were the ones who were fortunate enough to count Rose as our friend, and in turn, looking after her child, helping to keep him safe, letting him know he's loved as he grows up, seems a small thing compared to the happiness Rose gave to us every single day.'

At that Malcolm couldn't hold back any longer and the tears he had managed to keep at bay throughout the funeral began to spill down his cheeks.

'I'm sorry,' he said, getting up as quickly as he could with a baby in his arms and scurrying away from the girls.

'Should we go after him?' Alice asked, looking uneasy.

Dot shook her head and sipped the last of her port and lemon. 'Let him go. He needs to grieve; that pain needs to come out one way or another.'

Alice nodded and turned her attentions back to her own son, who like Emma was now happily sleeping in his own pram. A silence fell across the group as they each took in Dot's wisdom. Yes, the funeral was over, but now the grieving really began as they each contemplated a life without the kindest person they knew by their side.

'Well, this is no good,' Jean said, breaking the quiet. 'Rose wouldn't want us sitting about all maudlin like this. She would have chivvied us along and encouraged us to find some joy.'

Dot raised her glass in agreement. 'You're right, Jean. She hated misery. If she was here now she'd be telling us off.'

'Bit hard to feel anything but miserable though, isn't it,' Alice pointed out, 'when you've lost someone close.'

'It is.' Mary nodded. 'And I don't think any one of us will forget the pain losing Rose has caused us, but perhaps we need to look ahead. I for example had some good news this morning.'

'Oh?' Jean asked.

'David sent me a telegram. He will be home for Christmas!' she said triumphantly.

Dot felt a flash of pleasure. 'Oh, that is good news, darlin'.'

'You must be over the moon.' Brenda beamed. 'He'll get to know his new daughter.'

Mary made a face. 'Well, niece and daughter, but let's not get into all that. The point is he's coming home and we should celebrate these triumphs in life when we can.'

'Too right,' Alice said. 'I'm delighted for you Mary.'

'I've got a bit of news as well,' Brenda said, a small smile playing on her lips. 'I told Peter at the weekend that I would marry him.'

There was a chorus of gasps at the news as each of the girls pulled Brenda towards them for a hug and a kiss.

'You're a dark horse,' Alice exclaimed.

'Fancy keeping that all to yourself,' Mary gasped theatrically. 'I could never have done it.'

'Huge congratulations, Brenda,' Jean said shyly. 'It's wonderful news.'

'Thank you,' Brenda said, looking bashful. 'He's asked me twice now. The first time I said no, but now, well, he makes me happy, and it strikes me if there's one thing that we can all learn from Rose's death it's that we should seize any chance of happiness we find.'

'Too true,' Mary agreed as she turned to Dot. 'You're very quiet.'

Dot got to her feet and raised a glass. 'The truth is I couldn't be more thrilled for you, Brenda. Your Peter's a very lucky man and I wish you a lifetime of happiness together.'

With that the girls clinked their glasses and as they took a sip Brenda met Dot's gaze. 'Thank you,' she mouthed, while Dot lifted her glass in celebration towards her.

It didn't matter what Dot thought about Peter: Brenda was old enough to know her own mind and make her own mistakes. And Peter, despite being a conchie, was a decent-enough lad. Dot in fact felt proud because she knew that no matter what happened in the future Brenda was more than capable of standing up for herself and dealing with whatever obstacles came her way.

'Well, it seems happiness is all around if you want to find it,' Jean offered as she glanced towards the other end of the pub, keen to change the subject.

'Would you look at that?' Alice gasped, following Jean's gaze.

As Dot turned to see what had got the girls in a spin, she gave a sudden start: she saw Edwin and Helen, their arms wrapped around each other in what was clearly an affectionate father–daughter embrace.

In that moment she felt something like joy dart through her chest and realised this was just how things were meant to be. 'You know what, Brenda darlin',' she said suddenly, feeling a flash of understanding, 'you go and find your contentment with your Peter. Truth is none of us knows how long we've got in this world and when that chance for happiness could be gone.'

With that Dot stood up to leave. Smiling at the girls, she weaved her way through the smoke-filled room, nodded her thanks at Charlie and made her way outside. She had endured enough for one day. She had said goodbye to her friend and had put on a brave face in front of Edwin. It was time to go home now and be alone. She wanted to give in to the heartbreak that had threatened to be her undoing all day.

Leaning against the pub doors Dot took a deep breath and looked up at the sky. The sunshine from earlier had been replaced with a gloomy grey sky and the black clouds appeared unforgiving and full of threat. Dot tried not to mind. If she was honest the weather suited her mood. Pulling the collar of her good wool coat up close around her neck she set off for home as the rain began to fall. Bell Street wasn't far, and if she was quick she wouldn't get too wet.

Only as she turned the corner was she aware of footsteps pounding behind her. Spinning round, she was surprised to see Edwin walking briskly towards her, shoulders hunched as he did his best to avoid the rainfall.

'What are you doing here?'

'I wanted to see you,' he said. 'Before you left.'

'Why?' Dot asked, feeling wrong-footed. Although they had been civil to one another for Rose and Malcolm's sake, she had taken care to ensure they were never alone together. Dot wasn't sure she could trust herself not to beg him to listen to her once more.

'I wanted to say how very sorry I am at the way things have turned out, Dorothy,' Edwin said. As he spoke, the rain began to fall heavily. 'Getting to know Helen has become my greatest joy. To find that I have a daughter after all this time, well, it's a dream come true. I never expected to have a family of my own.'

Dot didn't know what to say. She felt exactly the same in a way, but she was too mindful of Ivy to want to lay any kind of motherly claim to Helen. Ivy was Helen's mother and always would be. However, Helen and Edwin had clearly established an emotional bond and Dot would never destroy that.

'But that's not all I came to say,' Edwin continued, clearly aware that Dot was lost for words. 'What I really wanted to say was thank you.'

'Thank you?' Dot looked at him in surprise. 'What are you thanking me for?'

'For all the love you have given me over the years,' Edwin said. 'I shall always be grateful for that. And I want you to know, Dorothy, that I shall always love you, and that you will always have a special place in my heart.'

Looking into his copper-brown eyes, Dot was taken back to a time more than thirty years ago when she and Edwin had been childhood sweethearts, when he had first told her that he loved her. At the time she had thought that meant they would be together forever, bound by love. What Dot had only realised now, so many years later, was that love sometimes wasn't enough.

'You're never going to be able to forgive me, are you?' she blurted.

For a moment Edwin paused, looking at the ground, before meeting Dot's gaze once more. 'No, Dorothy. I can't. I want to. Believe me I do. A future without you in it is unthinkable. The joy of finding you again has been a wonder after the pain of losing you all those years ago. But too much has happened between us and I can't move past the lies. Helen is a gift, but to think I could have known her so much earlier, loved her all her life ... well, it breaks my heart. I just came here to say that I love you and I am so glad that you and I have a daughter together and that I want to wish you well, whatever you decide to do next.'

With that he turned and walked away and Dot stood in the pouring rain having never felt emptier.

Chapter Fifty-Nine

'I still don't see why you're leaving,' Alice cried for the umpteenth time.

As Dot turned away from her half-empty wardrobe she saw her friend and lodger sitting on the edge of the bed looking forlornly at Dot's open suitcase. She contemplated Alice. In that moment she reminded Dot of the scrap of a child she had taken in all those years ago.

'You know why, darlin',' she said kindly, sitting down next to her and taking her hand. 'I need a break, and I need to get Helen settled.'

'I can't believe she's going too,' Alice said miserably. 'I'm going to miss you both.'

'It's not forever.' Dot chuckled. 'A couple of weeks, a month at most.'

'But you'll be back for Christmas?' Alice begged. 'David's coming back, and Jack is hoping to get some leave too.'

''Course I will.' Dot sighed. 'And Helen might even be persuaded. But I have to get on with this next phase of my life, and whatever that may be I need time to think it through.'

'You've got the WVS,' Alice objected. 'And you could easily get a job somewhere else. Mr B. said he'd write you a decent letter of recommendation, and Henry said he'd be more than happy to put in a word anywhere you liked.'

Dot snorted with contempt. 'That's good of them. Truth is I just need a bit of a break from London and now that I know Helen wants to go back home too, it gives me a chance to get things sorted for both of us at the same time.'

'I understand,' Alice said, getting to her feet, although the look of sadness did not leave her face. 'I'll just miss you, that's all. Everything feels awfully quiet. What with Rose gone, Flo and Jack away, and now you and Helen off, it feels like everyone is leaving.'

Reaching out to hold Alice, Dot rubbed her back as if she were a new-born baby. 'I know, darlin', but trust me, this isn't forever. Aren't you off for pastures new yourself?'

Alice pulled away and smiled. 'I don't know. Jack says we should get married now, and I should come and live in Bristol with him, get a job at Jolly's in Bath and we could all live happily ever after.'

'And don't you think you could?' Dot demanded.

'I don't know.' Alice sighed. 'London is my home; it's all I've ever known.'

Dot said nothing; instead she looked through the window and out into the grey murky city skies. London was all she had ever known too. She'd thought she would live and die in the city. These days, however, Dot felt less sure. It had been several weeks now since her last day at Liberty's and what with Rose's death and the end of her courtship with Edwin, Dot had to confess the capital felt more like a prison than her hometown. On every corner there was a memory: the Lyons Corner House where they had all enjoyed happier times as the Liberty's team, the Lane where she and Rose had sourced fabric at weekends, and Hampstead Heath, where she and Edwin had often enjoyed a Sunday stroll.

There were too many painful memories for her here. Her heart-to-heart with Brenda had made her see that she needed to take a leaf out of the younger girl's book. She too needed to start believing in herself and her own capabilities. It was time for Dot to push away the nagging doubts her parents had plagued her with all these years; it was time now for her to rely on herself. To do that, she needed to get away. When she had asked Helen the other night if she was happy in London she had been surprised to see the girl frown.

'I have had a wonderful time,' she had said carefully, 'but I wouldn't want to stay here forever. This isn't real life.'

'Would you like to go back to Torquay then?' Dot had asked.

Helen had put down her crochet and thought for a moment. 'I think I would.'

And so, the following day, arrangements had been made for Helen to leave her post at Liberty's so she and Dot could return to Devon.

'Besides, there's Malcolm and baby Daniel to think about,' Alice pointed out, breaking Dot's train of thought.

'Mary's looking after them, and I spoke to Malcolm yesterday. I invited him and Daniel down for a holiday anytime they like.' Dot replied. She had done her best to think of everyone.

Alice nodded. 'Looks like you've thought of everything. How are you getting to the station?' she asked.

'Tube, darlin'.' Dot smiled. 'I don't think Edwin will be giving me a lift anywhere any time soon.'

'Are you sure there's really no hope?' Alice began, only for Dot to shut her down.

'None at all. We have to go our separate ways now; we have to carve our own paths. I need time to do that and to work out what's next.'

'And you will definitely be back by Christmas?'

Dot sighed in exasperation. 'Why do you keep on about Christmas? I've said I'll be back.'

Alice rolled her eyes theatrically. 'I want to make sure you're back for Brenda's wedding!'

Sinking back on to the bed, Dot smiled. How could she have forgotten? 'Yes, of course I'll be back for that. Helen will too no doubt.'

'I hope so, she's bridesmaid!'

At that Dot raised her eyebrows in surprise. 'Is she? She never said.'

'Brenda only just asked last night while you were at the pictures. I'm sure she would've mentioned it to you.'

'Well, anyway,' Dot said, getting to her feet, 'I had better be going. Helen and I need to leave for our train in a few minutes.'

Alice said nothing, but instinctively leapt to her feet and threw her arms around Dot. 'Don't stay away too long,' she begged. 'You might not feel as if you have much here for you, but me and Arthur need you. We always will.'

Surprised by this sudden outpouring of emotion, Dot said nothing and instead just held the woman she considered to be both daughter and friend. 'I'm always here for you, darlin', no matter how far away I go.'

With that Dot pulled away, kissed Alice's tear-streaked cheek and slammed her suitcase shut. Making her way down the stairs she saw Helen in the kitchen, sitting in her best hat and coat, waiting patiently.

'Come on then,' Dot said. 'Let's get you home.'

Helen stood up smiled. 'Can you manage that suitcase by yourself?'

Dot chuckled. 'Cheek! I'm not that old yet. Yes, I can manage. Now let's get going – we don't want to miss the train.'

Opening the door, she was surprised to come face-to-face with Brenda, who looked startled.

'Oh Dot! I ran all the way from the station, I was worried I would miss you.'

'Well, you nearly did,' Dot grumbled. 'Me and Helen are just leaving.'

'I won't keep you long. Mary told me to run here; she said if anyone asked she would say I was at the Counting House.'

'What is it you want? Is there a problem with Emma? Do you need me to talk to Doris?'

Since Alice had taken over as fabric manager Doris had kindly agreed to take care of both Emma and Arthur when Alice and Mary were working. Dot filled in when she could but now she was off to Devon for a while, Doris was stepping into the breach full-time.

Brenda shook her head. 'No, it's nothing like that. I wanted to talk to you last night but you weren't here and then you were in bed when I got back.'

'Oh?'

'I've got something to ask you.'

'Well, get on with it then!' Dot said in exasperation. 'I've got a train to catch.'

'I know. Well, the thing is, I wasn't sure whether to ask you,' Brenda babbled, 'but the truth is, you've been so good to me, Dot, so kind, and, well, I've come to think of you as a bit like a mother to me, and well, I wonder if you would consider being a bridesmaid when I get married, like?'

Dot's jaw dropped open in shock as she looked at the woman in front of her. Brenda had changed so much from the timid young girl who first arrived on her doorstep, blossoming into a confident and capable young woman. It was wonderful to see her find such happiness. 'I would be honoured, darlin', she said, her voice trembling with emotion. 'I'll do you proud on your very special day, I can promise you that.'

With that Brenda's face broke into a delighted smile and Dot found herself returning the gesture. Perhaps there was more to come back to London for than she had first imagined. But it still wouldn't be enough to stop her leaving for now.

Chapter Sixty

It had been three weeks since Helen and Dot had returned to Torquay and they had each settled into a steady rhythm living in Ivy's home, which Dot realised was actually now Helen's. Helen had returned to her job at the factory, and Dot had found work in the local chemist's where she nattered with the customers as if she were a local.

Helen had a new-found confidence since her stay in London, Dot was pleased to note. And now, as they sat in the tiny café overlooking the sea at Babbacombe Downs, Dot smiled at the view. It did her heart good to come here.

'You look like you could be a local,' Helen remarked over the pot of tea that stood on the table between them.

Dot turned to face her. 'You know I love it here. Always have. It feels like a second home.'

Helen reached out and clamped her small cold hand over Dot's warm gloved one. 'Even though you came here to have me and give me away?'

'Even in spite of that,' Dot admitted. 'It was different for me than it was for a lot of the other girls. I knew you were going to a good home. I knew I would still see you, be involved in your life.'

Helen nodded, satisfied with Dot's answer. 'But you must miss London?'

Staring back out to sea and the emptiness beyond, Dot thought for a moment. She had been in Devon three weeks now and she had been surprised at how quickly she had settled in. There were days she barely gave London a second thought, though of course Edwin was never far from her mind. Despite doing her best to forget him, she only had to look at a pot of Brylcreem to recall the smell of his hair. But these gentle reminders of the past were becoming easier to live with now. She felt settled and rested somehow, and the nightmares that had plagued her sleep for the best part of thirty years had disappeared. Now as she cast her gaze towards the sun peeping through the clouds she wondered if London had always been the problem. Or had the fact that her secrets were now out in the open set her mind free once and for all?

'No, I don't, darlin',' Dot replied honestly.

'But what about the people?' Helen pressed.

'Well, of course I miss the people, but they all have their own lives. Alice will be moving away soon to be with Jack, whether it's to Bristol in a few weeks or to America if the war ever ends. Rose has gone, Mary and David have their own lives, as do Jean, Bess and Flo of course. Brenda is getting wed and Malcolm will be busy with Daniel.'

'And what about Edwin?' Helen asked, pouring them both a cup of tea and pushing one across the table towards Dot.

'He has his own life too,' Dot replied a little too sharply before catching herself. 'But no matter what happens between him and me, he will always want to be in your life, darlin'.'

Helen nodded. 'We write to one another regularly.'

Dot said nothing. She had guessed as much, spotting the familiar slope of Edwin's hand from the letters that arrived every few days in the post. But although Edwin was in Helen's present, he was no longer in Dot's, and he had made it very clear on the day of Rose's funeral that he would never change his mind. Dot had no idea if she would stay in Devon forever, or whether Helen would want her to, but for the moment it suited her well and that was all she could really hope for. Whether she would feel any differently when she returned next month for Christmas she wasn't sure, but Dot was a big believer in taking things a day at a time.

'You look like you've settled back in well here yourself, darlin',' Dot said, turning the conversation to Helen.

Helen nodded. 'It was good for me to get away. Gave me a chance to sort myself out.'

'And do you think that you have?' Dot asked.

'I do. I feel as if I can stand on my own two feet a bit more now,' Helen admitted.

'Your mother and I knew you had it in you.' Dot smiled. 'You just needed time, and of course without your mum around, it's been harder for you ...' Her voice trailed off. She was aware of how much they both still missed her.

'I still look around for her, and expect to see her there beside me,' Helen said with a hint of wistfulness to her voice.

'She would be very proud of you, Helen,' Dot said. 'You were all she and Kenneth ever wanted.'

'But what about you?' Helen asked.

Dot looked taken aback by the question. 'Helen, darlin', you are everything I could ever have wanted and more. I never expected to have this relationship with you either. It's been a blessing.'

'But I cost you your relationship with Edwin,' Helen said in a small voice. 'If it weren't for me then the two of you might still be together.'

'Don't you ever say that,' Dot said fiercely. 'It was all down to me. I should have been honest with him from the start. This has nothing to do with you.'

Helen said nothing at that point and merely smiled as she checked the time. 'Hadn't you better be getting back to work?'

Dot looked at her watch and groaned. 'That time already? Yes, I'd better be off or Mr Myers will have me guts for garters. He's already suspicious of London folk.'

Helen giggled. 'You don't help yourself by stuffing supplies in your pockets when you're restocking the shelves.'

'Well, where would the fun be if I did it properly? Anyway my hands are always full. Saves me two trips. He's all right, old Myers, I quite enjoy pulling his leg. I half thought about inviting him over for supper tonight,' Dot said.

Helen's jaw dropped open in shock. 'You can't. Poor Connie, you can't saddle her with him.'

'No, but it might make for an interesting little dinner party.' Dot laughed.

As Helen chuckled, Dot mentally ran through the list of things she had to prepare for that night, having just made a simple vegetable stew with that week's rations. Connie next door had offered to give them some of her own but Dot and Helen wouldn't hear of it. They had become quite good friends since Dot had moved back into Ivy's house, with Connie taking an interest in both of the women and often popping round to check they were all right. Dot had been grateful for the friendship and wanted to say thank you with a meal. She didn't have much, and she knew Connie, who had been living alone for years, wouldn't expect much either, but Dot did still want to make her a pudding.

In London Dot was used to nipping down the Lane and eking out her supplies with some black-market goodies. Here in Devon, however, she knew no one who could help her out with such a request and so Dot had a feeling it might be baked apples for dessert, and resolved to pass by the fruit and veg shop after she finished work.

Taking a sip of her scalding hot tea, she caught sight of a woman of about her own age across from them in the café gawping quite openly at Helen. Her heart sank. Since Helen's return the town had been full of welcome and it had made Dot's heart sing with joy. She should have known it would only be a matter of time before tongues started wagging at Helen's disability again.

Glancing across the table, Dot could tell that Helen had seen. Her jaw was clenched and her brow knitted with fury.

'Ignore her,' Dot said firmly.

But to her surprise, Helen paid no attention to Dot and instead got to her feet. She walked deliberately towards the woman who was still staring and plastered on a smile.

'Excuse me,' Helen said in that slow, careful way she had. 'I noticed you looking over, and I wondered if everything was all right?'

The woman looked taken aback to be asked and then, as if bolstering her courage, she jabbed her finger at the girl. 'You're different. What's wrong with you?'

Dot sprang to her feet, ready to defend Helen, but to her surprise Helen seemed to have the situation under control.

'I'm deaf,' she said slowly, her voice even. 'That means I can't hear you but I can lip-read so my voice is a bit funny.'

'Oh.' The woman looked wrong-footed. 'Well, it's not right you walking about the streets like this. You should be in an institution or summat.'

'Why?' Helen asked calmly.

'Well, you're not normal,' the woman protested. 'You're different.'

'And are you?' Helen quizzed. 'Normal, I mean. Would you say you're normal?'

'I'm more normal than you.'

'Well, I would say you're very rude,' Helen said. 'Staring at me like that for a start.'

As the woman opened and closed her mouth like a goldfish, Dot couldn't help laugh. Walking over to join Helen, she linked arms with the girl and grinned.

'Everything all right?'

'This woman', the older lady said, 'has just been very rude to me.'

'In the same way that you were rude to her?' Dot enquired.

The woman said nothing, seemingly lost for words, still opening and closing her mouth like a goldfish.

'So perhaps next time you'll have a think before you stare and point, then open your big gob,' Dot said in a polite tone.

Helen nodded. 'I've been glad to help you, madam, now have a good day.'

With that Helen turned on her heel and together with Dot walked out of the tea room. As Dot stood back to let her out of the door she felt a flash of pride. Helen had blossomed from a timid nervous creature into a woman with her own mind who could stand up for herself.

Chapter Sixty-One

By the time Dot got home from work that night, her feet were killing her and she was exhausted from going through medicines all afternoon. As she walked through the door and saw Helen and Connie sitting at the kitchen table with a port and lemon in hand, Dot smiled in relief. This was just what she needed, gimlets she noticed with some regret had been a bit harder to come by in St Marychurch.

'I hope you've got one of those ready for me?' she asked, slipping out of her raincoat and kicking off her heavily repaired court shoes.

Helen immediately pushed a glass across the scrubbed pine table towards her while Connie took the top off the half-empty bottle and filled Dot's glass to the brim.

'Has it been one of those days?' Connie asked as she surveyed Dot.

'Every day is one of those days.' Dot laughed, sinking into the chair nearest the range. 'And I have a confession to make. I'm ever so sorry, Connie darlin', but I haven't had time to get in any pudding. I was going to do baked apples but the veggie shop was shut on my way home.'

'Don't you worry.' Connie grinned. 'I had a bit of time this afternoon so I made almond tarts.'

As Connie pulled a tea towel off a tray beside her the sweet smell of almond filled the air and Dot thought she had died and gone to heaven. There was something about that scent which felt like luxury and Dot was half tempted to suggest they forget the stew she had made and just eat the tarts.

'They look and smell beautiful,' she said admiringly, resisting the urge to dive in and eat. 'Shall I serve up supper if you've all been waiting for me?'

'No rush, Dot.' Connie smiled, her earthy brown fringe falling into her light green eyes. 'Take the weight off. Me and Helen here were just gossiping.'

'About anything interesting?'

'About what I'll wear as bridesmaid,' Helen said with a look of pride on her face. 'I still can't believe Brenda has asked me.'

'Why wouldn't she?' Dot countered. 'You and her have become very close.'

Helen smiled happily. 'Yes. She wrote to me this morning and told me to wear anything I wanted.'

'She said the same to me,' Dot mused.

Connie clapped her hands together. 'How exciting. We could go pop into town and see if we can find any utility fabric. Have you got any coupons left?'

Dot smiled. 'I think after Liberty's that'd be like taking coals to Newcastle. Thanks, Connie, but I've a feeling we can make do with what we've got. I've some stuff upstairs I brought with us from Liberty's.'

'And I thought I would knit flower buttonholes for us all. Mrs Carter was ever so good about letting me take a few bits from Liberty's before I left so I've got a nice assortment of pinks.'

'What wonderful idea.' Dot grinned. 'Brenda will love that, darlin', the personal touch.'

'Sounds like you ladies have it all sorted!' Connie marvelled.

'Well, I don't now about all, but we're certainly getting there,' Dot added. 'It's a funny do, and a bit rushed, but who are we to argue? Life is short. Make the most of it all while you can.'

Connie nodded. 'You're not wrong, Dorothy, but you seem to be getting on well here in Devon. Do you think you'll come back after Christmas or will you stay in London?'

Dot blanched at the question. She hadn't given it much thought. She had blindly hoped the answer would come to her when she was least expecting it.

'In truth I don't know. I like it here,' she said carefully.

'But there's a whole other world for you in London,' Helen said knowingly.

'That's right.' Dot sighed. 'Whether or not it's a world I want to go back to I'm not sure.'

Connie smiled. 'Well, these things usually come out in the wash.'

Dot lifted her glass and nodded her head in agreement. 'Too true, Connie darlin'.' Taking another slug of her drink, she got to her feet. 'I'll sort out that stew otherwise we won't eat until midnight.'

'You sure?' Helen asked, about to stand up and help.

'I'm very sure. You stay here and entertain Connie,' Dot said, just as there was a loud rap at the door. 'On second thoughts, could you answer the door, darlin'? Someone's just knocked.'

Helen frowned as she got up from the table. 'You didn't ask Mr Myers did you?'

Dot laughed. 'No, I never. Might be one of the ladies from church though, asking if you're helping out with Sunday school again tomorrow.'

With that she made her way into the kitchen and began to prepare the dinner. Thankfully the lion's share was done. Dot was getting the plates when she became aware of the sound of a man's voice in the hallway. She couldn't make out who it was or what he was saying, but his tone sounded firm and insistent while Helen's, in reply, sounded unsure and Connie, who had now apparently become involved, seemed cross.

Wiping her hands on a teacloth, she rushed into the passageway to see what was going on. Only as she reached the doorway, her mouth fell open, because there, standing on the step looking very much as if he wanted the ground to swallow him whole as he did battle with Helen and Connie for entry, was Edwin.

As she approached, he lifted his gaze and his face lit up at the sight of her.

'Hello, Dorothy,' he said nervously. 'I wondered perhaps if we could talk?'

Chapter Sixty-Two

Dot wasn't sure how long she stared at Edwin as he stood on the doorstep. A barrage of conflicting emotions flooded through her – elation at seeing him and anger at him for invading the one place she always thought of as a safe haven.

'What do you want, Edwin?' she asked crossly. She wasn't going to make this easy for him. 'We're about to eat.'

'We can easily set an extra place,' Helen said hurriedly.

Dot glared at her. 'No, we cannot.'

'I'm fine, really,' Edwin said, holding out a hand to wave away Helen's offer. 'What I have to say won't take long and then I can leave you to your evening.'

Dot said nothing, but she was aware that both Helen and Connie's eyes were boring into her. She was equally aware that Edwin, whilst a polite and genteel man, was not likely to give up on something having made his mind up. If he had travelled all this way just to talk to her, chances were he wasn't going anywhere before he had done so.

'Come through to the parlour,' Dot said eventually, gesturing to the little front room. Turning to Helen and Connie, she smiled in apology. 'You girls go back through to the kitchen and have another port. I won't be long. And Helen, just keep an eye on that stew on the range, I won't be long.'

Making her way into the parlour, she was aware of Edwin's presence close behind her. Shutting the door firmly after him, she snapped on the light and offered him a seat in the brown velvet easy chair by the window.

'So what do you want?'

Edwin still seemed nervous. 'Dorothy, I am very sorry about barging in on your evening.'

'Expected me to be sat here in this house pining for you with only Helen for company, did you?' Dot spat. She hadn't meant to sound so angry, but really the point had been made and without him around every day she was beginning to heal. The sight of him now was threatening to undo all the progress she had made in recent weeks.

'No, of course not,' Edwin replied. 'I just, well, I didn't want to intrude.'

Dot let out a breath she hadn't realised she had been holding. 'You won't be here long enough for it to have an impact. Now, can we get on with it?'

If Edwin was upset or surprised by Dot's reaction he didn't show it. Instead he moved forward in his chair so he was on the edge of it and looked at Dot intently. 'I have come here to say that I am sorry. I made a terrible mistake ending things between us. My only excuse is that I was in a deep state of shock. The revelation that you were pregnant after our one intimate evening was enough of a thunderbolt, never mind the fact I have had a daughter all this time. But I handled the whole thing very, very badly, Dorothy, and I am truly sorry.'

Dot said nothing for a moment and instead regarded the man sitting opposite her. She had spent weeks in the aftermath of Helen's revelation praying for Edwin to say these very words, to put an end to her torment, but now he had done so she was surprised to find she felt strangely numb.

'What's brought all this on?' she asked eventually. Her barriers were up now, and while she was stunned to see him here she couldn't, wouldn't, soften. Her heart was only just starting to mend; to show him any sort of kindness could have untold impact upon it. She couldn't open herself up to that kind of hurt again.

'Rose,' Edwin said simply. 'I haven't been able to get that girl's death out of my mind. She was an innocent, a kind-hearted soul taken from us too soon. And after you left I couldn't stop thinking about what Rose would do and what Rose would think.'

'And what conclusion did you reach?'

Edwin smiled. 'I realised she would never have been stupid enough to let you go. She would have understood why you did what you did; she would have apologised for not being around at what was a difficult time. She would have known that this was the time to put past mistakes right.' He got out of his chair and walked towards her.

'Is that it?' Dot said, shrinking back as she watched him crouch down by her side.

'No, of course not,' he said, a look of anguish crossing his face. 'Dorothy, I know I have made a terrible mistake. The truth is I cannot live without you. You are on my mind every moment of every day. I miss your smile, the way you call everyone "darlin'", the way you're never shy about barking orders. I miss your kindness. I miss everything about you. I have been an utter fool, Dorothy, to ever have let you go, and now I wonder if you will consider taking me back. Please – I love you and I simply don't want to live another minute without you.'

There was silence as Dot took in what Edwin had just said. He was asking for another chance. In that moment there was a very large part of her that wanted to wrap her arms around him and never let him go. But there had been too much pain, and Dot wasn't sure she could take the chance that one day Edwin might change his mind and hurt her all over again.

'No, Edwin,' she said eventually, hating herself as she said it. 'You were right when you said it's over between us. Too much has happened. We can't go back.'

'But what if we could change things? Life is too short, Dotty, surely you can see that? We were so lucky to have found one another for a second time. We may never get that chance again, to find real love, the love you and I have shared,' Edwin begged.

'I can see that,' she said, her eyes brimming with tears now. 'But you broke my heart. I know I didn't handle things well. I know I should have told you about Helen. But you have no idea what it was like for me to learn I was expecting when I had said goodbye to you, so young. I had to cope without you and deal with the shame my family heaped on me. Is it any wonder I worried about telling you when you walked back into my life? I know I made mistakes but the fact that you wouldn't give me a chance to explain those mistakes is not something I'm sure I can get over. What if we were to marry? What if I forgave you and made another mistake in the future? Would you cut me out of your life then too?'

'I would never do that again Dorothy. Please, you have to see that I do understand,' Edwin said imploringly.

Dot shook her head bitterly. 'No, I don't think you do. You have no idea what it was like being sent away like a dirty little secret and to have to give my beautiful baby girl away. While you were right to have felt the way you did, what really hurt me is you wouldn't listen to me or let me explain things.'

Edwin hung his head now. 'And I am so very sorry.'

'But sorry might not be enough,' Dot said softly. 'And although I am very grateful you have come here and apologised to me, I don't know if it's enough for me to come back to you. My heart is aching without you, Edwin, and nothing would make me happier than to say yes, that I'll be with you forever. But I keep thinking of what my old mum used to say – that you were too good for me – and I can't help wondering if maybe she was right. Maybe you and I were never meant to be and the truth is I just don't think I can risk this sort of hurt again, not at my age, not now.'

'Please, Dorothy,' Edwin begged, his own eyes filling with tears as he clasped Dot's hands. 'Please don't let your parents' stupidity get in the way of our happiness, not after all these years. We could have such a wonderful life together. I will never let you down again, I promise I won't. We can get married, we can be together for the rest of our lives and be happy. What do you say? Please, Dot, please.'

Dot was about to open her mouth and say no once more but as she looked into his eyes she felt a small corner of her heart begin to melt. It had taken courage for Edwin to come all the way down here. Her mind strayed to Rose too. What would she do in this situation? She knew Edwin was sure she would forgive, but Rose was also a tough sort when pushed. Wrestling her hands free from Edwin's grasp, Dot got to her feet and turned away from him. She needed time to think. This was a decision she couldn't get wrong, not when her future happiness depended on it.

Chapter Sixty-Three

As Dot sank back into the old hard kitchen chair and surveyed the garden outside, she thought of how strange it was to be back in London and her little home in Bell Street once again. She had returned four days ago and was still struggling to get used to the fact the blue sea and great swathes of countryside had been replaced by soot, grime and shelled-out buildings.

Her friends were certainly helping her as she settled back into life in the city. And now, as she looked at Alice, Brenda, Mary and Jean, heads bent low as they worked on Brenda's beautiful white wedding gown, she felt a sense of peace descend upon her. It helped too that Flo had returned from faraway shores the night before last and was staying in the little box room that had been Helen's. Although Jean and Bess had of course insisted on Flo staying in her old room in her own house, Flo hadn't liked to impose and she knew that her old friend had the space. Unlike Dot, Helen hadn't felt a burning desire to return to the capital, and although she thought it right and proper that Dot came back to deal with her 'unfinished business', as she put it, she was staying put in Devon for the time being as she wanted to celebrate her birthday by the sea as she always had with her mother.

Watching Flo now taking charge of the intricate embroidery on Brenda's veil, Dot smiled. It was almost possible to believe nothing had changed since Flo had left all those months ago, but of course so much had. Although they were all doing a very good job of pretending that everything was normal, Rose's absence was very much felt at this kitchen table. Dot's fingers strayed to the place where Edwin's engagement ring used to sit. She had found twiddling his grandmother's old ring a comfort when she felt lost and alone. Without it she still felt something was amiss, something she wasn't too good at hiding, judging by the way Alice was looking at her now.

'You all right?' she asked in a kindly tone.

Dot let out a sigh. 'I'm fine. You don't need to keep asking.'

'I'm just checking,' Alice said.

'And as I said, I'm fine. Why wouldn't I be, with all you girls around me, and Flo back from Gawd knows where?'

At the sound of her name, Flo looked up and smiled. 'And it's lovely to be back. I've missed this.'

'We've missed you,' Mary exclaimed. 'Wish you were back at Liberty's though, the new fabric manager's a right old cow.'

The group erupted into laughter as Alice glared at Mary. 'As your manager I can make your job as deputy a lot, lot worse, you know.'

Mary nudged her playfully in the ribs. 'Don't I know it! Doesn't this take you back to the sewing evenings we used to hold?'

'Oh, in the pleating room?' Alice said, smiling at the memory. 'We'd put the world to rights in there.'

'Why did you stop?' Brenda asked.

Mary, Flo, Dot and Alice looked at each other and paused.

'I think other things just got in the way,' Alice said at last.

'Like a certain American soldier?' Flo teased.

Alice blushed. 'Not just that.'

'You buggering off to ENSA didn't help,' Dot said, winking at Alice as she drained her tea.

Flo laughed. 'You haven't changed a bit, Dorothy Hanson.'

'Well, you have.' Mary laughed. 'Look how long your hair is now, Flo. And you've lost weight.'

'We're on the go so much.' Flo sighed. 'And performing most nights can really take it out of you.'

'Is that why you're back for six weeks?' Jean asked.

'Yes, that is a long break,' Dot mused.

Flo put down her needle and thread and looked at the girls. 'No, our tour had come to a natural end so I would be here for that long anyway. When we start up again I've asked Max if I can tour Britain instead and he's promised to think about it.'

'Any particular reason?' Dot asked.

Colour crept up Flo's cheeks. 'Well, it's tiring travelling all the time. And I suppose if I'm honest I want to see if there's anything here for me that makes it worth staying in England for.'

'Like a certain deputy store manager?' Mary teased.

'Henry and I have been writing to each other a lot, yes,' Flo admitted.

'Have you seen him since you came back?' Brenda asked, her mouth full of pins.

Flo nodded. 'He was waiting for me at the station when I got back, and it was very special. That's all I'm saying. I'm looking forward to being his guest at your wedding, Brenda.'

'Of course,' Brenda exclaimed. 'You were always invited, you're a Liberty girl.'

Smiling, Flo surveyed the table. 'We all are and all always will be.'

'Here's to that,' Mary said, lifting her cup of tea aloft.

As the girls did the same, Flo turned back to Brenda.

'So are you all ready for your wedding?'

'I think so. Just the dress to sew and that's it,' she confirmed. 'Neither of us has family so it's just friends attending.'

'Friends are family,' Dot said, clasping her hand over Brenda's and giving it a reassuring squeeze.

Brenda smiled. 'And I'm grateful for everyone here.'

'Where will you live after you're married?' Mary asked.

'She'll live here, of course!' Dot exclaimed. 'At least, Brenda, until you and Peter can sort yourselves out with some accommodation. I'm assuming he hasn't got property tucked up his sleeve?'

Brenda laughed. 'No, he's as poor as a church mouse. We'll find somewhere when the war is over, but yes, if I could stay here until then I would be very happy to.'

''Course, darlin',' Dot said, patting Brenda's hand again. 'Call it a wedding present.'

'And what about you?' Flo asked, cocking her head to one side and looking at the matriarch. 'Are you staying here?'

Dot shuffled uncomfortably in her chair. 'What, in London you mean?'

'You know perfectly well what we mean, Dot,' Mary said, putting down her needle. 'We've done the pleasantries, we've chatted about the weather, we've told Flo all our news, and we've even shared the fact you've got a secret daughter nobody knew about ...'

'Which I think is wonderful, by the way,' Flo said hurriedly. 'I can't wait to meet her.'

'But all that aside,' Mary continued, determined not to be put off, 'it doesn't tell us what you intend to do now you're here. Are you coming back to Liberty's? Do you want your old manager's job back?'

'Oh Gawd no!' Dot exclaimed. 'No, Alice, darlin', that post's all yours. You're a far better manager than I ever was and I'm happy about that. I know my skills lie in dealing with people not paperwork.'

'So if you don't want your job back, why are you here?' Mary pressed.

'Yes, and what about your job at the chemist in Devon? What's happened to that?'

'It's still there for me if I want it,' she mumbled. 'I've got some savings so thought I'd have a bit of time off and come back early for Brenda's wedding.'

'Which isn't for over two weeks,' Brenda pointed out. 'There's a difference between early and premature.'

Dot put her teacup back on its saucer and took a deep breath. She knew she owed the girls an explanation, but so far she'd been putting it off, unsure of their reaction.

'Edwin came to see me last month,' she admitted.

'What?' Alice gasped. 'In Devon?'

Dot nodded her head in confirmation. 'He came to say he was sorry and that he wanted us to try again.'

'And are you? Is that why you're back?' Mary demanded.

Dot rubbed the place where her engagement ring once rested. 'I don't know. I told him no at the time, but the truth is my heart is breaking without him.'

'So you've come back to say yes?' Brenda asked, her eyes alight with excitement at the thought of their reunion.

'It's not that simple, darlin',' Dot said kindly. 'I came back here because I thought I might be able to think about things a bit easier in home surroundings.'

'And are you any closer to a decision?' Alice asked.

Dot let out a wail of anguish. 'No. I keep going backwards and forwards. One minute I think I can't live without him, that life is too short and I should go to him and say let's get married. But then I remember all the hurt and all the things my parents used to say ...'

'What things?' Mary asked, a puzzled look on her face.

Sighing, Dot felt a pang of regret. She had only ever confided in Ivy and Edwin about the daft comments her parents used to make.

'My parents were a bit old-fashioned,' she said carefully. 'They were very keen on us knowing our place in society; we were working class and proud. My mum and dad didn't trust anyone that wasn't like them, and they brought me and Olive up to think the same: that we shouldn't get ideas above our station.'

'You're not serious,' Jean gasped.

Dot laughed at the incredulity on Jean's face. 'I'm very serious. Mum used to say I was useless so when I was a kid I had no confidence at all. It took Ivy and Edwin to finally convince me that I was worth something.'

'But why?' Flo asked. 'Didn't they love you?'

'Oh, they adored me and Olive,' Dot explained. 'It wasn't about love. I think it was about fear. They were terrified of anything or anyone they didn't understand coming into our lives, so I think they saw it as protection, that they were, in their own funny way, trying to protect me and Olive from heartbreak.'

'How silly,' Mary breathed.

'It was really,' Dot admitted. 'I remember how Mum used to take me up to Liberty's every Christmas to look in the windows but she'd never take me inside.'

'Why not?' Jean asked.

'Because she thought we weren't good enough, that they'd look down on us, so far better to say no to them before they could say it to us. The first time I went into Liberty's was with Ivy when she came to visit me when Helen was a nipper.'

'Really?' Mary marvelled. 'You must have loved it.'

Dot cast her mind back and smiled at the memory. 'I wouldn't quite say that. I was terrified but Ivy made me go in. She told me to ignore what my parents said for once, but I still thought we were going to get chucked out. Even when Ivy bought me that lovely material for my wedding dress.'

Mary sighed. 'Oh Dot, that's so sad.' Mary sighed.

Dot shrugged before continuing. 'We had a very special day out, and it was the first time I thought that perhaps my parents were wrong and I could carve a life out for myself where I wasn't stupid or useless. The fact that I had fallen pregnant out of wedlock had only reinforced their belief I was hopeless and I spent years trying to make up for what I'd done to them so I toed the line. I forgot all about Edwin, who they liked but never trusted because they thought he was a cut above. George, however, well, he lived down the Lane and my old dad thought he was a wonder, which of course he was. But when George died, I still couldn't shift the feeling that I didn't deserve to be happy. I suppose that's why I've stayed on my own all this time, doing my best to take care of everyone in the community that needed help, trying to prove in some way that I've got some worth.'

There was a silence then as the girls took in Dot's story.

'You surely can't believe you're useless now,' Mary breathed. 'Not after everything you've done for all of us, never mind everyone else around here.'

Dot sighed. 'No, but those old feelings of not being good enough are hard to shift.'

'What did Ivy think about your parents?' Alice asked suddenly.

'She thought they were lovely people but they talked out of their backsides.' Dot laughed. 'She was always good at building me up, telling me I deserved to be happy, and she was also very good at working out what I really wanted, which is why she dragged me into Liberty's that day because even though I was scared stiff it was probably one of the happiest days of my life. That dress she made me was a reminder of the fact I'd faced my fear. I think that's why I wanted Helen to have it, so she could absorb a bit of her mother's confidence too.'

'What do you think Ivy would say if she was here?' Jean asked gently.

'She would ask me why I was messing about.' Dot laughed again, bringing an image of her old friend to mind. 'She'd no doubt tell me to shift myself, stop making excuses and go and grab hold of what I wanted in life before it was too late.'

Another silence fell across the table as the girls considered how for Ivy and indeed Rose it was too late, that their chance of finding happiness had gone forever.

'Well then,' Brenda said, fixing her gaze on Dot. 'Can I suggest that you follow your friend's advice and that you get yourself round to Edwin's to tell him how you feel?'

Panic coursed through Dot. 'What if he's changed his mind?'

'If he's changed his mind, then your mum and dad were right, you two aren't meant to be,' Alice said simply.

'But you've helped each and every one of us at this table, and I think it's time to find your feet and go and see for yourself,' Flo said with an air of finality.

Looking at the girls' faces, Dot felt a sense of certainty she had never experienced before. These girls, these friends of hers, had all developed their own confidence by facing their fears, not backing away from them. It was time for Dot to do the same.

Chapter Sixty-Four

She had promised herself that she wouldn't cry, but now as she stood in the church on this very special Christmas Day surrounded by her friends, Dot didn't think she had ever known happiness like it. Everyone from the community was there: Doris from down the road, Charlie from the pub and even old Mr Mantle from the fabric stall on the Lane. It seemed as though all of the staff from Liberty's was filling the wooden pews of the little Elephant and Castle church too.

Everything looked wonderful. Whilst there was of course no tree, wreaths of holly and ivy hung from the stone pillars. Elsewhere candles had been laid out for Advent and the soft light they emitted gave the church a wonderful golden glow.

Malcolm was there with his wife, Nellie, whom Dot had never met before. She looked much older than Rose had said she was but then, Dot reasoned, suffering the death of your own child would do that to you. She had been granted compassionate leave from the army and was putting in a request to leave permanently so she could take care of Daniel full time. Dot thought it was for the best. Nellie was holding baby Daniel as if he were made of gold, and Dot didn't blame her. She resolved, after the wedding was over, to talk to her about how they were going to make sure Rose's memory stayed alive for Daniel's sake. Things might have changed with Nellie returning to care for her grandchild but Dot's promise to Rose hadn't: she and the rest of the girls would always be there for that boy in one form or another.

Next to them were Alice and Jack, who had returned briefly from his posting, hands wrapped around one another as they listened to the vicar's sermon about love while Arthur lay sleeping in his pram beside them. Then there was Mary, David and Emma. David had only managed to get home late on Christmas Eve and so this was the first time Dot had seen him in months. She was pleased to note that he looked well, and couldn't take his eyes off his wife or baby Emma who was cradled snugly in his arms. Bess and Jean were next to him and then there was her darling Flo seated next to Henry with Stan nestled between them.

Last on the pew was Helen, who looked radiant. Dot flashed her a smile and was delighted when Helen gave her an excited grin in return. She seemed happy Dot thought, and she looked lovely in Dot's old wedding dress. In fact, Dot thought, as she looked at her properly for a second, she wasn't sure if it didn't suit her more than it had Dot.

Lastly of course was the bride, Brenda. Standing at the altar, she looked breathtaking in her white dress which the Liberty girls had all come together to make. Dot was surprised she had chosen to wear a design with sleeves that came to her elbow, assuming she would want to cover her scars as she usually did. But when Dot had asked Brenda about them, she had smiled and said she wasn't covering anything up any more. She was who she was, finally comfortable in her own skin.

As for Dot herself, she had chosen to wear a simple tweed suit. It was as old as the hills, but during the last week when the girls had gathered to make the final adjustments to Brenda's dress they had suggested updating Dot's suit by taking up the hem, Helen had knitted her a very special raspberry-coloured rose corsage in the same shade as the blouse that she had made for herself for the occasion. It had been perfect, and a wonderful way to commemorate Rose and keep her memory alive.

The vicar paused before he asked Peter the question: 'And do you, Peter Marshall, take Brenda Higginson to be your lawful wedded wife?'

Peter paused for a moment, the joy on his face evident for the entire congregation to see. 'I do,' he said loudly.

'And now, do you, Brenda Higginson, take Peter Marshall to be your lawful wedded husband?' boomed the vicar.

'I do,' Brenda whispered, her eyes never leaving Peter's as the vicar carried on with the ceremony.

Dot felt a flash of happiness for the girl. Marriage was a tough path, but ultimately a worthwhile one and Dot knew this marriage between Peter and Brenda would be the making of her young friend. Peter certainly seemed as if he were in clover.

'And now, do you, Edwin Button, take Dorothy Hanson to be your lawful wedded wife?' boomed the vicar once more.

At those words Dot's eyes turned to Edwin and she saw the love shining in his. She knew that this was the man she was always supposed to have spent her life with.

'I do,' Edwin whispered, his voice thick with emotion.

As the vicar continued through the rest of the vows Dot's eyes never left Edwin's. He was her soulmate and in that moment she knew the decision to return to London and marry the man she knew to be the love of her life was the right one. Their past, all the problems they had endured, would only make them stronger, of that she was sure.

'I now pronounce you man and wife,' the vicar finished.

At that, there was a huge roar from the congregation and Dot turned to exchange a happy smile with Brenda. A double wedding would never have been something she would have thought of, but the moment she had agreed to marry Edwin, Brenda had tentatively made the suggestion. Once the words were out of Brenda's mouth Dot had realised that sharing their special day would make the whole occasion even more perfect. After all, you could never have too much love on Christmas Day.

In the end it hadn't taken long for Dot to decide to marry Edwin. After he had turned up in Devon to apologise all those weeks ago, Dot had sent him away as she'd felt so upset and confused. Once he had gone, she had talked everything over at length with Connie and Helen and, after a night of tossing and turning, had woken the next morning full of indecision. It had been Helen who had suggested she return to London a bit earlier than planned to help Brenda with her wedding arrangements and that way she could see how she felt.

And so, after confessing all to the Liberty girls when she returned, with their encouragement, Dot had gone to Edwin's Bermondsey home that evening. As the rain poured down she had banged on the door for all she was worth.

He had flung open the door looking baffled by the sight of her standing on his doorstep.

'Are you going to invite me in?' she'd said at last. 'Or have I got to be wet through before you realise it's tipping down out here?'

Wordlessly he'd held the door open for her and ushered her inside. Once he had closed the door behind them, he had pulled her into his arms and they had kissed as they had all those years ago when they were discovering those feelings of passion for the first time.

When they'd finally parted Edwin had held her gaze, as though worried that if he looked away he might wake up from this dream.

'Does this mean ...?' he'd asked, barely able to get the words out. 'Does this mean that you've come back to me?'

'It does,' Dot had whispered. 'Edwin, I never want to be apart from you again.'

'Nor I you,' he had declared. 'Life just isn't the same without you in it. Forgive me.'

'Let's forgive each other,' Dot had replied.

'I can think of nothing I would like more,' he'd said softly.

And so they had agreed to marry as soon as possible. Dot would have waited for a date after Brenda's – she didn't want to steal the girl's thunder, after all. But Brenda had pointed out that as she and Peter had no family of their own, it would be wonderful to feel as though they were marrying amongst her Liberty's family.

Now, as Dot linked her arm through her new husband's to pose for photographs outside the church, she couldn't stop smiling.

'Thank you,' Edwin said, turning to his wife and kissing her tenderly on the cheek.

'For what?' Dot asked in surprise.

'For making me the happiest man alive.'

Chapter Sixty-Five

An hour later and the celebrations were continuing at the Elephant and Castle pub. Once again Charlie had done them proud and today, rather than letting them hold the party in the function room where they had held Rose's funeral, he had given them the run of the pub as his Christmas gift to them.

It was a wonderful gesture and as Dot, with Edwin, walked into the snug that had been decorated with a small Christmas tree in the corner, complete with glass baubles and red ribbon, she felt an overwhelming sense of elation. All of her nearest and dearest were there, with ready smiles and glasses full to the brim, ready to share in today's joy.

Christmas Day was a funny date to hold a wedding, Dot mused as the crowd chorused with cheers, but what a wonderful day it was too. Many couples in recent years had chosen to marry on this day as they knew they would have the day off work, and family and friends would most likely be able to celebrate with them. But Dot felt it was a perfect way to come together on this very special day with those she would never usually see, which made this joint wedding even more special.

Hearing Brenda gasp in delight, Dot glanced towards her fellow bride to see what had caught her attention. On the other side of the snug, Charlie had pushed together three tables groaning under the weight of so much food that Dot couldn't believe it was still wartime. Not only was there a large joint of pork in the centre, topped with crackling and surrounded by roast potatoes, but there was also a rather large Christmas pudding to the side, the likes of which Dot hadn't seen in years. She couldn't bear to think what Charlie must have done to get his hands on such a spread.

To the right stood a framed copy of a mocked-up edition of the *Liberty Lamp*. Peering closer, Dot could see the words 'Special edition' splashed across the front. Underneath were photographs of her and Edwin and Brenda and Peter, with 'Reunited' written below in large letters. Dot felt a surge of elation as she had never seen her name and face in print before.

'Beatrice mocked the cover up with Peter.' Alice grinned as she sidled up to Dot, Arthur gurgling contentedly in her arms. 'Isn't it lovely?'

'It's wonderful,' Dot breathed, struggling to keep her emotions under control. 'And so is this spread.'

'Everyone gave up their rations to pull it together,' Alice said softly. 'They wanted you to have a special day.'

At that Dot gave in to the tears. 'I've never felt as much love before as I do in this room today.'

'I must admit I haven't myself,' Edwin exclaimed. 'The kindness and generosity of people is astounding.'

'Congratulations,' Malcolm said, kissing Dot tenderly on the cheek as he and Nellie came to join them, with Daniel asleep in her arms.

'Yes, it's nice to celebrate a happy occasion,' Nellie chimed in.

Dot smiled sympathetically, before holding out her hands for a cuddle from Daniel. 'Thank you both for coming, and for bringing this little one,' she said softly, before planting a kiss on Daniel's forehead. 'I know it can't have been easy.'

'It's not,' Nellie said. Her brown hair was filled with grey flecks that Dot guessed had appeared within the last few weeks. 'But we know how much you meant to Rose – all of you – and we wanted to be here in her place.'

'It's very good of you,' Edwin said gently.

'And it's very good of you to do so much for us, and for Daniel,' Nellie replied, her eyes filling with tears.

'Yes, that cot filled with baby clothes and toys was a wonderful gesture,' Malcolm said, his voice trembling with emotion.

'It's not all from us,' Dot said, 'the Liberty girls chipped in too.'

'We will always be here for Daniel, for all of you,' Mary vowed.

'And we're ever so grateful,' Nellie said, doing her best to plaster on a smile as she took Daniel back into her arms. 'Now, let's stop all these tears. Whatever would Rose say!'

'She would say that she was worried about all the water coming out of your eyes, Dot,' Mary teased, 'it's so unlike you. If you're not careful people will mistake you for a soft touch.'

'Get off with you,' Dot scolded, playfully nudging her in the ribs as David arrived with Emma asleep in his arms.

'Congratulations, Mrs Button,' he said, bending forward to kiss her cheek. 'I couldn't be more thrilled.'

'I'll second that,' another voice chorused.

'Bess!' Dot cried, hugging the girl warmly. 'You're looking well.'

As she stood back to admire the girl Dot could see it was true. Bess looked positively radiant dressed in a tailored man's navy suit and floral scarf. Jean, standing next to her, also looked beautiful in a Liberty's dress Dot knew she had made herself.

'She's doing more than looking well, she's thriving,' Jean informed them. 'The factory want her there full-time!'

'Well, that's wonderful!' Dot exclaimed.

'It is, but it means moving back to Hayes.' Bess sighed. 'And that means moving out of Flo's and back into lodgings.'

'That doesn't matter,' Jean insisted. 'It's good you feel up to full-time work again.'

'I know,' Bess agreed, 'it will just be hard being apart again.'

There was a murmur of agreement then. Everyone could understand how Bess would have felt at the opportunity to serve her country to the fullest of her abilities once more, but be apart from Jean.

Dot was about to try and offer some words of comfort when she saw Brenda and Peter walking towards them.

'If it isn't the new Mr and Mrs Marshall,' Dot exclaimed, pulling the young girl in for an embrace.

'And the new Mr and Mrs Button!' Brenda smiled back as Dot released her. 'I shall never forget all you have done for me.'

'Neither of us will,' Peter said, offering Dot his hand to shake. 'You've shown us both huge generosity.'

'She's famous for that,' came a voice.

'Flo!' Mary beamed, wrapping her arms around the former fabric manager and pulling her in for a hug. 'I still can't get over the fact you're here.'

'And likely to be here a bit longer.' Flo smiled as Henry pressed a drink into her hand.

'What do you mean?' Alice asked, joining the party with a glass of wine in one hand and Jack's palm in the other.

'Max popped round this morning in typical dramatic fashion,' Flo said, rolling her eyes at her boss's theatrics. 'He said they need people here for a while and so I can definitely stay in the country for a little bit.'

Dot clapped her hands together in delight. 'That's wonderful news, darlin',' she said, looking at Henry and spotting him smiling coyly. 'Though I've a feeling there's more to you wanting to stay than you being tired of travelling.'

Flo blushed and Henry leapt to her defence. 'Now, now, Dot, so what if there is something between me and Flo here? I should have thought that today of all days you'd be glad of a little romance in the air.'

''Course I am.' Dot chuckled. 'Especially if it means I'm going to see more of you, Flo.'

'Well, that all depends on where you're thinking of living,' Flo said, arching an eyebrow. 'Yesterday you were talking about going back to Devon.'

'They're going nowhere,' Helen said, having just returned from wishing Brenda and Peter well. 'They're staying in London.'

'Well, we haven't made our minds up yet, darlin' ...' Dot said, looking anxiously at Edwin. 'I'm not sure I'm going back to Liberty's in any case.'

Edwin nodded. 'And I'm wondering about taking early retirement, if truth be told.'

At that, the group around him looked shocked.

'You can't be serious, sir,' Henry gasped.

'Yes, steady on,' David cautioned. 'We need you at Liberty's to keep the girls in line. What would we do without you?'

Edwin laughed. 'I rather think the girls do a better job than I do at keeping everything in order. I am, as they call it, surplus to requirements.'

'Hardly,' Mary scoffed.

'Absolutely,' Alice agreed.

'He's going nowhere,' Dot said, echoing Helen's sentiments and rolling her eyes at her husband with affection.

'He's fussing. He thinks now we're wed we need to make some changes.'

'Changes, sir?' Jack asked, raising an eyebrow.

'Well, I just thought it might be the thing to do now Dot and I have found one another again. I want to make the most of the time we have together.'

'I'm not sure spending all your time together is the way to do that,' cautioned Mary. 'If you spend every day with Dot she'll drive you up the wall.'

'Exactly,' Edwin said, turning to his bride and smiling lovingly at her. 'And I can't wait to let her try.'

Dot kissed Edwin on the cheek and squeezed his hand. 'I think there's been enough shock and change of late. What we want is for things to stay the same.'

'Agreed,' Helen said. 'I'm just getting to know my mother and my father: I would rather like it if things could just be for a while.'

Edwin coughed as he looked fondly at his daughter. 'Well, with regard to that, we wondered if you would like to come back to London. Have your old job back.'

'Really?' Helen asked. 'What about my home and my job in the factory?'

'I'm sure we could sort something out if you wanted to come back and live here,' Edwin said.

Helen thought for a moment. 'Would you like me to?'

Dot and Edwin exchanged a knowing look. Dot could tell without even asking what her husband felt. Like her, she knew that he couldn't believe they had all been given this second chance to find a family, and also like her Edwin would want to make the most of every precious second.

''Course, darlin', but we don't want to pressure you. It's up to you wherever you feel most comfortable.'

'Then yes, I think I would rather like to come back and live here, if you don't mind,' Helen said. 'I spent all my life living with Mum in Devon and it felt like home. Now she's not there it doesn't feel the same any more. I reckon home is more about people. Does that make sense?'

'It does,' Edwin said quietly.

'And we'd be thrilled if you'd come here and live with us,' Dot added, her eyes brimming with tears. 'For as long as you want.'

'Good.' Helen smiled as she looked between Dot, Edwin and the rest of the Liberty girls. 'Because I think here, amongst you all, I haven't just found a home, I've found brothers and sisters as well as a mother and a father.'

With that Dot felt the arms of her husband and daughter around her and gave in to the tears of joy that had been threatening to come all day. Because while she was surrounded by love on this very special day, it was impossible to forget the friends who couldn't be with them, whom she would always remember in her heart. Dear sweet Rose, who had taught her the value of forgiveness and the simple joy in seeing the positive in life where you could. And then of course there was Ivy.

At the thought of her old friend Dot felt her resolve weaken. Ivy had never been far from her thoughts all day, and she had felt her by her side today just as she had been as Dot's matron of honour when she'd wed George. It still seemed unthinkable to Dot that Ivy, who had been her rock and her confidante for so long, wasn't here. But she would have been thrilled to see Helen and Edwin forging a new relationship together, and to see Dot and Helen getting to know one another in a more honest way too. Most of all, her friend would have been delighted that Dot had finally discovered the inner confidence that Ivy had always been so sure Dot possessed, buried deep within her. Closing her eyes, Dot said a silent thank you to her friend for helping her become the person she was today.

And now, as she opened her eyes and looked at the faces that surrounded her, the family and friends she was proud to hold dear, she couldn't help feeling that all the torture, misery and shame was truly behind her. The happiness that she felt now was all-encompassing. It was almost too much for one person to hold on to and she vowed to share it with the friends that she had made, and the family she felt blessed to have found.

ALSO AVAILABLE IN ARROW

September, 1941: Mary arrives in war-torn London nursing a broken heart and a painful secret.

When she is offered her dream post as an assistant in the fabric department at Liberty store, she knows this is the fresh start she needs. Amid the store's vibrant prints and sumptuous interiors, Mary finds a new family who can help her to heal.

But not everyone will give Mary such a warm welcome, and the trauma of her past will soon catch up with her.

As Mary and the Liberty Girls endure the heartache and uncertainty of war, it will take a steady heart to keep the magic of Christmas alive.

ORDER YOUR COPY NOW

Available in paperback and e-book

arrow books